OBARION

Justine Sparks

To my husband Ryan, who would not let me give up on this book, despite how often I wanted to.

And to my sweet sister Isabella, whose love for this story and its characters helped me believe how deeply my little world could connect with other people too.

CONTENTS

PART I:

THE VEDAS

CHAPTER ONE

When Atlas opened his eyes, he found himself lying on a thin cot. The ceiling was cracked, grey, and unfamiliar.

He glanced around the room, and spotted a urinal in the corner, and a small table about three feet to his right. A tall, blurred shape in dark clothes stood silhouetted against the doorway.

Atlas slowly sat up, and the lumpy cot shifted beneath his body. The guard faced away from him, and if Atlas moved quietly enough, the man might not even have time to fend off his attack.

He dangled his legs off of the cot, pushing himself to his feet silently.

Atlas lunged towards the table and clenched its sturdy wooden legs, preparing to swing it as hard as he could at the back of the guard's head—

But the table, it turned out, was bolted to the wall. Its joints gave a great groan as Atlas pulled, and he cursed.

The guard turned, his eyebrows shooting up in surprise.

"You're awake!" he exclaimed.

The moron had not even reached for his gun. Atlas suppressed a smirk. He shifted his feet and swung his fist as hard as he could. The guard's nose broke with a hollow thud, and he stumbled backwards, letting out a cry of pain. The skin on Atlas' knuckles split, but he ignored it, shoving past the guard and into the hall, looking in either direction down the long, brightly lit corridor.

"We've got a runner!" called the guard, his voice muffled beneath the hand that clenched his bleeding nose.

Atlas made a split-second decision and bolted to the right, his feet carrying him faster, he was sure, than he had ever run in his entire life. Up ahead, another guard emerged from behind a door, ten feet away from him. He skidded to a stop, fear coursing through his body, for this guard had not hesitated to reach for his gun.

Except, it was not a gun at all. Atlas stared at the strange black object for a second too long and then, quite suddenly, a *pop* split the air. Two metal probes rocketed towards him and buried themselves into the skin of his chest. All at once every muscle in his body cramped, and Atlas fell to the ground, his legs spasming violently. To his horror, urine trickled down the inside of his pant leg.

His cheeks burned as he stared up at the guard— a portly old man, to add insult to injury—who chuckled heartily.

"Never been tased before, I take it?" he asked in a deep voice, his pale, wrinkled face flushed red from his laughter. He glanced down at Atlas' legs, still twitching and spasming. "Don't worry, that happens sometimes. It'll wear off any second now."

Indeed, even as the guard spoke, the pain began to recede. Atlas clambered to his feet with as much dignity as he could muster.

"Not gonna run again, are you?" the guard asked.

Atlas eyed the strange device in his hand then looked past him, to where two more guards waited at the end of the corridor. He shook his head.

The old man chuckled again. "Good, good. We'll get your cut cleaned up, then take you to see Moonstone..." He glanced over his shoulder at the other guards, lowering his voice as he added, "And how's about a change of pants, too?"

Atlas nodded tersely, the color in his cheeks spreading to his neck. The old man turned and strode down the hall, and after a moment of hesitation, Atlas followed. As the two other guards fell into step with them, the racing of his heart started to settle, though his skin still crawled with apprehension.

His mind churned as he followed the old man through the winding corridors. How many hours had passed since he'd been captured—and where were Coral and Bettoni? Had they been captured too, or was he on his own? And where *was* he?

Once Atlas had changed, he was taken up a flight of stairs to a large chamber with dozens of windows and two long rows of metal-framed beds. It must have been nearing sunset, for orange light flooded into the hall, casting a golden glow over the glossy hardwood floor. He glanced down at his watch—scuffed, from the tussle between his squad and the Vedas' back at the Pass, he presumed—and saw that it was indeed a little after six in the evening.

The old man strode over to a plump woman in a dark tunic, and conversed with her in whispers. The two other guards stationed themselves stiffly near the doorway, their eyes fixed on Atlas. He stood still for a few moments, trying to formulate a plan, but he quickly grew impatient, and after casting a wary glance at the pair by the door, he edged towards the window to try to get a better look outside. The taller of the pair arched a suspicious brow, but neither moved to stop him, so he sidled up, until his face was nearly pressed against the glass, and peered outside. His heart stuttered in the cavity of his chest.

The view beyond the pane was unrecognizable. In the distance were vast blue mountains peaked with snow and miles and miles of dense pines, taller than he'd ever seen. Just below the window was a lawn of thick green grass—a shade of green so vibrant that he hadn't realized it existed outside of the pages of books— which stretched to the edge of the woods, its thick trees casting the forest floor beneath into blackness.

The ground must have been at least twenty feet below the window, and metal beams jutted out from the side of the building indiscriminately. It would make for an impossible jump, but if he could find a way to break the glass and climb down—

"The windows are unbreakable."

He turned. A girl with umber skin, wild, waist-length curly hair, and strange, brightly colored clothing blinked back at him. She held a water pitcher, and was refilling the glass next to the bed nearest him, but when their gazes met, she gave him a knowing look. Atlas raised his eyebrows, and she set the water pitcher down.

"Watch," she instructed.

Before he could respond, she grasped the metal end of the bedpost and began to unscrew the top. Atlas had half a mind to turn away—he didn't much care for taking orders from someone whose pants looked like scraps of fabric all sewn together in strange patterns—

but his curiosity won out.

She walked five paces away, turned, and hurled the post-top as hard as she could at the window. He watched with fascination as the metal impacted the glass—or what he had presumed to be glass—and promptly bounced off, falling to the floor. The window did not look as though it had even been scratched.

Atlas schooled his features into an expression of boredom, shrugged, and turned away from the strange girl to walk back towards his guard.

He allowed the plump woman—Dr. Finny, he learned, was her name—to patch up his knuckle. Her voice was warm and she spoke far more kindly than one of the Vedas had any business speaking to an Obarion, so Atlas spent the time amusing himself by coming up with different ways he could kill her with the scalpel tucked into her apron.

Once Dr. Finny finished, the old guard reappeared at his side.

"Moonstone is expecting you in the meeting hall," the guard informed him. Atlas said nothing, but followed him out of the infirmary, down two flights of stairs this time, and into another long corridor. The walls were blank, almost sterile in their vacancy, and the polished tile made his boots clink with every step. Down here the light was dimmer, the air heavier, as though they were underground.

They came to the last door at the very end of the corridor. It was made of a dense metal, and Atlas was certain that it was soundproof.

When they entered, a tall, stern-looking woman with chestnut-brown skin and short black hair stood peering at a chalkboard that had writing covering every inch of its surface. She wore the Vedas' uniform—dark blue, with five bronze stars across the front that demarcated her rank. Atlas recognized her immediately from the various newspaper clippings he had seen around General Talikoth's office: their enemy clan's central commander, the Vedas' General, Moonstone.

A group of Vedas sat around the long table that took up most of the room. Their mumbling quieted as soon as Atlas entered with his guards, and he straightened unconsciously. This was the sort of presence General Talikoth carried when he entered a room—people noticed his presence, they listened when he spoke.

"Thank you, Bowduck," Moonstone said, and the old guard beside Atlas nodded. Bowduck and his companion fell back, posting themselves on either side of the door.

Atlas' eyes fastened on the chalkboard beside Moonstone. He tried to make out some of the words, but the script was small and untidy. He was so focused it took him a moment to register that Moonstone was speaking to him.

"Please, have a seat."

He blinked, but did not move from where he stood.

Moonstone followed his gaze and smiled a little, tapping the chalkboard with her finger.

"I am afraid you will not find any useful information to carry back to the Obarion there, Atlas. We are mainly just concerned with mining enough coal for the winter."

Still, Atlas said nothing, but continued to stare at Moonstone coldly. She stared back at him with distinguishable curiosity. Her eyes were dark, deep-set, and shrewd.

"You look just like your father," she said finally.

Atlas' back straightened pridefully, despite the fact that he'd heard this acknowledgement most of his life. They had the same pale complexion, the same ash brown hair, the same long nose and heavy brow. His only similarity to his mother were his eyes, though Atlas did not know for sure, since he had been so young when the Vedas killed her.

Whispers broke out among those who were seated, and one of them, a pallid-skinned, balding man with a feeble frame, shot Atlas a fearful glance as he addressed Moonstone in a stammer.

"So, it's—it's true, General? This really is the son of Talikoth?"

Moonstone had not taken her eyes off of Atlas. "It is true."

The whispers grew louder, like a horde of angry bees.

"We have to kill him!" one of them cried, louder than the rest.

"He'll reveal our base! We'll be dead by morning!"

A rotund bearded man who sat at the opposite end of the table gave Atlas a harsh glare, and rumbled, "You know the crimes Talikoth has committed, General. It is only justice."

Atlas rolled his eyes, tapping his foot impatiently against the tile. His gaze flickered around the room. One door, no windows—yes, he was almost certain they were underground—but the ceiling was the old-fashioned kind with the pop-out panels. It was possible he could crawl through one and navigate the ducts until he found an escape route...

"You know our laws, Council," Moonstone said, holding up a hand to silence the hubbub. "We do not, under any circumstances, kill children."

Atlas bristled. He wasn't as muscular as Maddex or Jemahl, but he hardly thought he looked like a *child*.

The council members seemed to agree.

"That boy is at least eighteen, or close enough to it!" the bearded man said gruffly.

"Surely—surely an *exception* could be made, General," the weedy man added, throwing Atlas another terrified glance. Atlas gave the man a smirk, and the man shrank a little lower into his seat.

Their back-and-forth squabbling, as it were, was growing rather dull. Atlas straightened up in his seat and cleared his throat, a surge of satisfaction pulsing through him when the Council instantaneously silenced, and each of their heads turned towards him.

"I hate to sign my own death warrant, General," Atlas drawled. "But the lumberjack is right. I'll be eighteen in less than two weeks." He gave her a charming smile, the sort of smile he'd seen General Talikoth employ when he appealed to the other Officers to sway them in his favor, and held his arms out at his sides. "Wouldn't you prefer to take your opportunity now, while I'm defenseless?" He nodded towards the scrawny balding man. "Perhaps this valiant fellow ought to do the honors?"

"General, I'd really rather not—" the man began squeakily.

"Quiet, Augusto," Moonstone commanded. She gave Atlas a hard frown before turning to look at each of the members of the Council. "We do not compromise on our values. That is what makes us different from them.

That is what makes us Vedas."

Atlas nearly snorted at that. He knew enough about the Vedas to know that they had about as much of a moral compass as a wild animal.

"We have two options," Moonstone continued. "We let him go or we keep him here." The bearded man started to protest, but she held up a hand to silence him. "He was unconscious upon arrival and we can ensure that he would be unconscious upon departure, should we choose to let him go. He has seen nothing here that would make us any more vulnerable to the Obarion than we already are." She looked around at all of them once more, her tone speculative as she pondered aloud, "If we kept him here...there is a potential that he would prove to be useful."

Atlas couldn't be bothered to school his features this time, and he stared at her with unabashed disbelief. White hot anger flared to life in his chest, his blood pounding in his ears, and though he could no longer keep up any pretense of amiability, he managed to keep his tone neutral as he quietly said, "I'd sooner kill you while you slept."

Something like disappointment crossed Moonstone's face, but before she could reply, the bearded man grunted, "See? Just like his father."

"What would you expect, growing up in such a clan?" a bony blonde woman said with a snort.

"Enough," Moonstone said sharply. "This could be an ideal opportunity that may not be afforded to us again. Between Atlas' arrival and the assistance of the Ren, this may be just the chance we were looking for. We shall reconvene on the matter in a week's time. For the present, the Obarion will be kept under guard, with no opportunity for escape or attack. Agreed?"

There were grumbles of assent throughout the room, but Atlas hardly paid them any mind. His ears perked at the mention of the Ren. He had only ever heard tales of the nomadic peoples that roamed up and down the coast of the Westland, foraging for food and garnering resources, as neither Vedas nor Obarion. They took no side and refused to take part in the conflict. General Talikoth called them spineless cowards, more concerned with looking out for their own backs than a cause larger than themselves, but if the Vedas were getting assistance from the Ren, General Talikoth needed to know. The Ren did not have weapons or military training, but they understood the land better than either clan, and their knowledge could give the Vedas an advantage.

Atlas' mind was racing as he followed the guards out of the meeting room. If the Vedas and the Ren *were* working together, and Atlas didn't find a way to escape, General Talikoth might not find out about it until it was too late.

His thoughts were still occupied even as he was deposited back into the room he had fled. Bowduck closed the door this time, but Atlas could hear the old man's voice on the other side, an assurance that he'd not ventured far.

Atlas sighed. Until he could formulate a plan to escape, this would be his life, for the foreseeable future. Not even able to take a piss without someone breathing down his neck.

Atlas laid down on his thin, lumpy cot, his hands folded behind his head as he peered up at the ceiling.

A glance at his watch told him that it was nearly

nine o'clock. So much had changed in the span of just a few hours—though in reality, he had no idea how much time had actually passed. Had it been days since he was captured, or weeks? Judging by the landscape he had seen from the infirmary window, they had to be clear on the other side of the Pass, hundreds of miles from the Santa Monica Mountains, where Obarion headquarters were nestled. Atlas had never been any further north than the southernmost border of the Pass —just east of the shores of what the old maps called Pyramid Lake—but he knew that the channel stretched several hundreds of miles. Had the Vedas kept him unconscious all of this time, in order to preserve the confidentiality of their base? Would General Talikoth have been notified of his disappearance yet? Presuming the rest of his squad got away, it still would take them a few days to reach Headquarters.

There was a knock on the door. It swung open, and to his surprise, Moonstone stepped inside, her hands occupied with a steaming tray laden with food.

"I figured I would bring this, since you missed dinner," she said quietly, closing the door. He sat up, watching, unblinking, as she moved across the room and set the tray on his table. His stomach groaned as though responding to her words, and his cheeks flushed when she gave him a knowing smile.

Atlas' mind flashed with a sudden image of his unconscious form being force-fed mush through tubes like some kind of invalid as they carted him north, and a fresh surge of anger swelled in the pit of his stomach.

"Do you eat meat?" Moonstone asked.

He arched a brow, momentarily distracted from his anger. The Great Famine had come and gone by the time Atlas was born, but he knew that choosiness was not an attribute of those who wished to survive. "Some of the Ren do not," Moonstone explained, shrugging. "We have had to speak to the kitchen staff to accommodate them."

Atlas leaned over and picked up a piece of chicken, eyeing it warily.

"If we wanted to kill you, we could do it much more affordably," Moonstone added with a wry smile. "Poison is hard to come by, you know."

Atlas' lips twitched, but he hid it by biting into the chicken. He had to suppress a moan as the savory flavor hit his taste buds, and he took his time chewing the tender tissue. He couldn't remember the last time he had eaten chicken. General Talikoth had relocated part of the food budget to the weaponry division over the past year, so most of the meals in the dining hall consisted of rice and beans.

"How long have you been entertaining the Ren?" he asked. His tone was calculatedly disinterested as he placed the scoured chicken bone back onto the plate and spooned a heaping load of potatoes into his mouth.

Moonstone leaned against the wall across from him, and Atlas observed her from his peripherals. She was tall, for a woman, and, despite quite certainly being at least ten or fifteen years older than General Talikoth, she looked strong. Still, if he caught her at the right moment...

Atlas quickly cleared his mind of those thoughts. This game would be a practice of patience.

"Just a few weeks now," Moonstone answered. "There are only two of them here. They were traveling along the shore just north of the Pass and had been discovered by a couple of Obarion soldiers. We only managed to help them escape by setting off a few explosives down shore. The Obarion fled, but one of the Ren was injured, and they were separated from the other half of their tribe, so we have been accomodating them since."

Atlas nodded. It would take much longer than a few weeks for the Vedas to convince any of the Ren to aid their cause, no matter how much the Vedas were feeding them.

But...what had Obarion soldiers been doing north of the Pass? He didn't get the opportunity to deliberate on it further.

"I do not know what your father has told you about us," Moonstone began, and something in her tone made his head snap up. She gazed at him cautiously, an urgency in her voice. "All the Vedas have ever striven for has been the safety and security of the people at large. I hope very much that you will help us to assure that, Atlas."

He gazed at her with a blank expression. Atlas was no stranger to manipulations and political ploys —General Talikoth had allowed him to sit in on clan negotiations since he was twelve, after all—but he had never been the one to whom a party appealed. He had never had to make a choice that would mean the difference of life and death for the people he led. That had always come down to General Talikoth.

But now Atlas felt the weight of his position like a sack of rocks slung across his shoulders. It was not, perhaps, the first time that he recognized exactly what it meant to be the son of the celebrated Obarion General, the man who had led the conquest through the

Southwest, who had decimated every clan within the span of one thousand miles, but it never felt quite as tangible as it did now.

And Atlas realized, quite suddenly, that there was only one choice. Only one option that would make General Talikoth proud. Only one choice that would avenge his mother in the way that she deserved.

He set down his spoon, meeting Moonstone's eyes unflinchingly, and gave her a solemn nod. When Atlas spoke, his voice was measured. "I know very little of the Vedas, but assuring safety and security for the people is the Obarion way. I hope very much that I will be able to assist, General."

CHAPTER TWO

On Saturday morning a new guard came to lead Atlas to the breakfast hall at eight o'clock sharp. He was a young man with russet-brown skin, perhaps a year or two older than Atlas. His hair was cropped close, like many of the soldiers back at the Obarion headquarters, and he wore an easy grin. His dark eyes looked strangely familiar.

"So you're the Obarion, huh?" the new guard remarked as he slung a quarterstaff over his shoulder. "How you likin' the cold?"

"Haven't been outside yet," Atlas mumbled, his voice gravelly as he rubbed the sleep out of his eyes.

The young guard made a sharp turn down a new corridor, and Atlas quickly followed. He tried cataloguing the layout of the Vedas' base as they walked, but his groggy brain did not seem to want to comply.

"Maybe they'll let you come out to the training yard with us after breakfast." The young guard's mouth curled up in a challenging grin as he gave Atlas a sideways glance. "You do any sparring, Obarion?" It was strange, how the guard spoke to him casually, as though Atlas were a friend, rather than a member of his enemy clan.

Atlas shrugged, trying very hard to repress a smug smirk. "A bit."

He decided not to mention the fact that in all of

his years training, he had only lost one fight. He wasn't the strongest soldier in his training squad, but he was fast, and understood how to use his limbs better than anyone else in his year at Academy.

"I'm Whitsom," the guard offered, turning another corner and pulling open a set of heavy double doors.

The delicious scent of bacon wafted over them, and Atlas' mouth watered.

"You're Atlas, right?" the guard continued. Atlas nodded and followed Whitsom to a long table near the back of the massive dining hall. There were no windows, which meant they were probably somewhere in the center of the building. The ceiling was high, and the fluorescent glow emanating from the suspended light fixtures was so glaring that he grimaced.

He went to sit down, but stopped short when Whitsom leaned against the table, casually gripping his quarterstaff.

"You go on," Whitsom said. "I'm not *technically* supposed to eat with you."

Atlas nodded, plopping down onto the bench and immediately reaching for a platter of sausage. Whitsom gazed down at the steaming sausage forlornly.

"Cryin' shame," he muttered. "Foolish of me to skip breakfast." Whitsom shot a furtive glance over his shoulder at a copper-skinned man with a buzz cut. He wore the same uniform as Moonstone, with a single star near the lapel of his jacket, and Atlas presumed he must have been Whitsom's superior.

"Oh, what'll it hurt?" Whitsom said. Quick as a whistle, he snatched a couple pieces of meat off of the platter, finishing them in two large bites. He caught

Atlas' eye and shrugged. "Never been much good at following the rules."

Atlas filed that away for later.

"Shouldn't you be used to them by now?" Atlas asked off-handed.

"Oh, I didn't grow up in all this," Whitsom said. "Only been here three weeks now."

Atlas held in a snort, partially amused and partially insulted. How little respect they must have had for him, to assign this newbie guard to be his babysitter.

He must not have done a good job in schooling his expression though, because Whitsom gave him an amused glance.

"Don't look so offended, Obarion. They only stuck me here because I took out two of their best fighters."

Whitsom didn't speak with arrogance, but matter-of-fact. He glanced over his shoulder once more and snatched another sausage from the platter, adding, around his mouthful, "They didn't much appreciate my talents back home."

Atlas turned and studied the young guard more closely. "Where's back home, then?"

Whitsom had apparently grown bored of eating and was now sharpening the pointed end of his quarterstaff with a knife. "Oh, you know, wherever the wind carried us."

Something clicked in Atlas' brain then. "You're with the Ren."

Whitsom sniggered. "You're the third or fourth person I've heard call us that. What's it mean anyway?"

Atlas stabbed at a baked potato as he considered how to answer. Whitsom could very well be a useful ally, given how easily he let information slip. Atlas didn't want to offend him so soon in their acquaintanceship.

"It's short for 'renegades'," Atlas said finally. "The Ren aren't exactly held in high esteem among the Obarion." He took a bite and chewed it thoughtfully, before adding in a neutral tone, "General Talikoth has always maintained that there is no greater dishonor than to run from a fight."

A strange look passed over Whitsom's face. He seemed to battle with himself for several moments, before he leaned forward and quietly said, "I've always believed that if you can't stand up and fight for what you believe in—if you aren't willing to die for anything —then there's no sense in trying to hang on for another day. Might as well let the wolves take you."

Atlas regarded the Ren boy with approval, though he hastily shoved it down, taking another bite of his potatoes. There was no use making any friends here, especially given the fact that part of his escape plan was to kill as many of the Vedas as he could on his way out.

The actually escaping element was still blurry, but that was another matter.

"The General said that there are more of you here?" Atlas asked.

Whitsom shrugged. "It's just me and my little sis. She helps out in the infirmary."

Atlas nodded, pushing his empty plate away, and Whitsom sprang up, slinging his quarterstaff back over his shoulder.

"Moonstone wanted you to sit in on the morning meeting," he told Atlas, waving to a few guards as they passed. "After that we can head to the training yard."

Atlas nodded, following him silently through the maze of corridors, until they came to one that looked familiar, and indeed, moments later they arrived in front of the heavy metal door from the previous night.

"Good morning, Atlas. Whitsom," Moonstone greeted as they entered and took up a few chairs near the end of the table. Only a couple of people had arrived: a tall, shrewd-looking man with long black hair, and the bearded man from the evening before. He glared at Atlas with unmasked disdain, though no one else at the table seemed to notice.

The room slowly filled with men and women, filing in sporadically, until every seat was taken. A few, who Atlas recognized from the last meeting, threw him wary glances, while the newcomers gazed at him with curiosity.

As the chatter died down, Moonstone turned to face them, and launched into a thorough run-down of the last week's activity. Atlas tried to focus, but his attention waned. It was all just particulars: how much food had been foraged for the week, how much of a coal surplus they had achieved, progress in water conservation efforts. He had to stop himself from rolling his eyes. It was no wonder General Talikoth's military trounced Moonstone's. These buffoons were only trying to *survive*.

Survival had been integral, of course, for the Obarion clan—in the beginning, anyway. But this had been before General Talikoth had assumed power— before he had encouraged their people to travel west, where the resources were plentiful, before he had opened his people's eyes to opportunities beyond mere survival.

The council members suddenly got to their feet, their chairs scraping against the floor, startling Atlas from his thoughts. Moonstone had apparently adjourned the meeting. She had not tried to get any information about the Obarion, nor indeed, had she even spoken to him. Was she simply biding her time?

Whitsom hung back after everyone else had left, so Atlas, who didn't know where else he could go, did too. Perhaps he could give his guard the slip later to begin to find a way off of the Vedas' base, but it would be rather conspicuous now, with Moonstone and the rest of the council members mulling about.

"General, I just wanted to ask you—"

"No sign of them yet, Whitsom," Moonstone cut in, gathering a stack of papers into a neat pile and tucking them methodically beneath her arm. "I have sent another group out to the eastern lake, but it may take time."

Whitsom's face fell, but he nodded, starting towards the door. Moonstone, however, stopped him.

"Whitsom? I am grateful that you have been so eager to help in our efforts since your arrival here, and we are doing our best to find your friends, but..." She hesitated, frowning. "Perhaps you could talk to your sister. She is... less eager to assist."

Whitsom gave Moonstone a dubious look. "General, I love her to death, but my sister has a will of iron. I can talk to her all day long, but I promise you, she won't budge until Maggi and Rasta are found."

The General gave him a piercing look, before exhaling heavily and turning away from them. "Very well. You are dismissed."

It wasn't until they were back in the narrow

corridor that Atlas glanced at Whitsom. His dark brows were furrowed.

"Are Maggi and Rasta more of the Ren?" Atlas asked.

Whitsom nodded. "We were all one big tribe, initially, but then Gai and I lost our parents, Maggi and Rasta lost each of theirs, and we were on our own. They're a bit younger than us, so we try to look out for them, but when we hit the land mines, we got separated."

Atlas tried to imagine two kids traversing the Westland on their own, in landmine territory. They were probably dead.

They had climbed three flights of stairs and emerged into a wide corridor that Atlas did not recognize.

"What does Moonstone want from your sister?" Atlas asked.

Whitsom pushed open a door and Atlas blinked as they stepped out into bright, blinding sunshine. Despite the dazzling light, the air was frigid. They exited onto what looked like a massive rooftop deck. A chain-link fence ran the perimeter, perhaps twenty feet in height and topped with barbed wire.

It reminded Atlas of the training gym back at headquarters—granted, the equipment here was a little more worn, and the soldiers sparring on the mats spread across the deck did not look quite as fit as the ones Atlas trained with.

Whitsom led him to a corner of the deck where a set of about thirty lockers stood. He opened one, withdrawing a pair of boxing gloves and tossing them to Atlas.

"Gai is a little geek," the Ren boy told him, opening the locker below and withdrawing a second set of gloves. "I'm borrowing your gear, Kendo!" Whitsom shouted across the yard.

Atlas turned. A brawny blond boy working with a speed bag glanced over at the sound of his name.

"Like hell you are, you smelly deserter!" Kendo shouted back with a good-natured grin.

Whitsom shook his head, smiling as he velcroed his gloves. "Anyway, I think she figured out a way to store solar energy and convert it to gas or something."

Atlas stared at him for a moment, waiting for him to crack a smile. When he didn't, Atlas drew his brows together in befuddlement.

"How—"

Whitsom held up his hands in front of his chest. "Don't ask me a single question, I don't have a clue. I told you, she's a geek. It was something she was working on with Dad before he...before...before we ended up on our own."

Atlas knelt down, pretending to tie his shoelace as Whitsom's face contorted into a grimace of pain.

As the two of them made their way across the training yard to find a spot to spar, Atlas' mind raced. If what Whitsom had shared was true, the Vedas had an invaluable resource on their hands.

Whitsom squared up across from him, his grin playful.

"Alright, Obarion. Any fancy rules you Southerners go by that I should know about?"

Atlas shrugged, flexing and unflexing his fingers inside the gloves. "No junk shots."

They began to circle each other, and Atlas'

eyes tracked Whitsom's movements carefully. Atlas' first few jabs were calculating, and Whitsom easily danced around him, his movements fluid, like water circumventing stone.

The frustration of the last twenty-four hours melted away as Atlas threw punch after punch, until every last one of his thoughts seemed to vanish and all he could feel was his burning lungs and the steady ache of lactic acid building in his muscles.

Whitsom blocked the majority of his shots, and Atlas' steadily growing admiration for the Ren boy was only tampered by the confusion it caused.

How was it that a deserter, with no formal training, could have learned to fight as well as a good number of the soldiers that Atlas had gone through Academy with? Renegades only ever ran from the fight, but this one fought like he had a hunger for it.

Whitsom threw a particularly quick punch and stumbled off balance. Without thinking, Atlas lashed out with an uppercut, his gloved fist making contact with Whitsom's nose, and he stumbled backwards, a stream of blood pouring from his nostrils.

Atlas immediately lowered his gloves. "Sorry, man. Shouldn't have come in so hot."

Whitsom waved him off. His grin looked decidedly menacing with blood dripping into his teeth. "You're good. Where'd you learn to spar like that?" He led Atlas back over towards the lockers, seemingly unfazed by the blood dripping onto his shirt.

Atlas shrugged, tossing his gloves into the locker. "Lots of practice, I guess."

The truth was, General Talikoth had started training him from the time he was six, after an incident in which one of the other boys his age had shoved him down and knocked out one of his teeth.

You don't lose fights, boy, General Talikoth told him. *I'm not going to have some loser for a son.*

"You probably should get that looked at, make sure it's not broken," Atlas said, more to change the subject than anything else.

So the two of them made their way to the infirmary. They were halfway down the first flight of stairs when Whitsom said, "Can I ask you something?"

Atlas immediately tensed, but forced himself to nod.

"Why do you call him Talikoth?"

Whatever Atlas had been expecting, it was not that.

Whitsom peered at him with raised eyebrows. "Back in the dining hall this morning," he clarified, "You called him 'General Talikoth', but...isn't he your pops?"

Atlas frowned, and he faced forward again, watching his feet rise and fall against the shiny tile squares beneath his boots. Talikoth had always been around officers, or other soldiers, and he had demanded that, in company, Atlas would always call him by his proper title. It was only when they were alone that Atlas was allowed to call him 'Dad', and they were alone so rarely it had begun to feel odd. He wasn't sure when it had happened, but eventually, he'd stopped calling him 'Dad' altogether.

"He's sort of a father-figure for our entire clan," Atlas said finally, his tone measured and blank. "His title just feels more fitting."

Whitsom still looked at him strangely, but said nothing, pulling open the infirmary doors. Dr. Finny was leaning over a small boy who could not have been older than twelve, her hands carefully wrapping a bandage around his arm. She glanced up, and the moment her eyes fell on Whitsom, they narrowed.

"No, no, *no* more causing trouble in here, young man—" Dr. Finny began, clicking her tongue. Despite her admonition, her tone was affectionate

Whitsom pointed to his face, where the blood had dried around his upper lip and along his chin. "Honest, Doc, I'm actually injured this time!"

"Bah!" Dr. Finny exclaimed, hiding a smile. She glanced across the room, saying, "Dear, will you get your delinquent brother out of here before he sets the place on fire?"

Atlas turned, and was a little surprised to see the wild-haired girl whom he'd encountered the night before climbing down from where she had been perched on the window sill, sliding her book into a bag that looked like it might have been made of leaves, all woven together.

Whitsom grinned dopily at her as she approached, and the puzzle pieces all slid into place. Her skin was darker than Whitsom's, but she wore the same easy grin.

"Who punched you in the face?" she asked, jerking her head towards the bed nearest them. Whitsom sat down on the edge of it, and Atlas hovered nearby, shuffling his weight awkwardly between his feet.

Whitsom gestured excitedly towards Atlas. "This dude! He can spar, Gai."

She gave Atlas an appraising once-over, smirking as she turned to dig through a bag of what he assumed were medical supplies.

"Don't get too attached to your new sparring partner, Whit. When I met him yesterday, he was trying to find a way to jump out of the infirmary window."

Atlas' cheeks flushed. "I wasn't—"

"Atlas is Obarion, Gai," Whitsom interrupted, giving her a meaningful look.

Her brows knitted together.

"And you're supposed to be *guarding* him. Not getting all chummy." Her frown deepened as she threw a suspicious glance towards Atlas. "We're not here for anything except help finding Rasta and Maggi. Once we find them—"

"The Vedas will find them," Whitsom interjected. "In the meantime, no harm making friends so I can *really* learn how to fight—"

"Oh great gooseberries, Whit, you *aren't* fighting!" his sister hissed, swatting him on the shoulder with a pack of sanitizing wipes. "Stop trying to play the hero —"

Atlas got the feeling that this was an argument that had come up a number of times. "And why shouldn't I?" Whitsom returned fiercely. "Dad would want—"

"Dad would want us *safe*." The gentleness with which his sister wiped away the blood coating Whitsom's face contrasted jarringly with the harshness of her tone. "Which is exactly how I'm trying to keep us."

Whitsom looked like he was going to argue, but Atlas was growing rather irritated with their squabbling.

"Where would your friends have gone, do you think?" he asked the two of them.

The siblings looked at one another.

"I think we can trust him, Gai," Whitsom said earnestly.

His sister gave him an incredulous look. "Whit, you've known him for, what, three hours?"

Atlas couldn't help but agree, though he wasn't going to say it out loud.

Whitsom gave her a wide, infectious grin, and her lips twitched. "I've got good instincts. You know I do."

She looked between the two of them for several moments, her gaze calculating, before she sighed. "I'm ninety-nine percent sure they would have headed for the mountains."

"That's your territory, then?" Atlas asked nonchalantly. When they began their full-fledged siege north, General Talikoth, he knew, would want to scout out the last of the Ren, and drag the cowards from hiding.

Whitsom's sister tossed her wild hair over her shoulder.

"Our *territory* is wherever we can survive, Obarion. We don't claim land that doesn't belong to us." She nudged Whitsom, and once he rose to his feet, she moved to straighten the sheets that had been beneath him. "And your nose isn't broken by the way, so you can get out of here before Finny fleeces you."

Whitsom hesitated, running a hand over his short hair. "Moonstone asked me to talk to you—"

His sister whirled to face him, her gaze so ferocious that Whitsom, who was visibly much larger and stronger than her, flinched.

"*Don't.* I'm no accomplice. All these people want is war and death."

"Gai, you *promised*," Whitsom groused, frowning at her. "Besides, Moonstone only wants the information so she can keep her people alive—"

"*Moonstone* wants the information so that she can create more *weapons*," his sister snapped scathingly. "Don't be a sheep, Whit. The coal is almost gone, they all know it. They need a new fire-power source."

Whitsom started to reply, but his sister had already stomped away. He let out a disparaging noise, stalking out of the infirmary, and Atlas quickly followed after him.

"As you can see, my sister totally buys into the whole *pacifist* nonsense," Whitsom muttered.

Atlas understood immediately what he meant. Whitsom had been a refreshing surprise, but if the rest of the Ren were like his sister—Gai, he had called her— then General Talikoth had been right about them. They were nothing more than spineless opportunists who pursued their own self-interest over the good of the people.

Atlas' mind toiled as Whitsom led him through the winding corridors. He did not even pay attention to where they were going.

Was Whitsom's sister correct in her assertion that the coal was almost gone? Did General Talikoth know? This information could completely shift his plans. If the petroleum *and* coal ran out, where would that leave his clan?

I think she figured out a way to store solar energy and convert it to gas or something.

He had some recon to do. If what he'd learned about the Ren girl was true, and she really did know how to store and convert solar energy, Atlas needed to find out—then he could make his escape.

He smirked a little as he imagined the look on General Talikoth's face. He might even promote Atlas to Lieutenant General and remove that old fool Crowley from office once and for all.

His back straightened at the thought of it. Surely he would be the youngest Lieutenant General in his clan's history—perhaps even in all of time.

Whitsom stopped walking and turned to give him an apologetic look. They had stopped back in front of the door to Atlas' room.

"I've got to go do rounds, so I'm supposed to leave you in here," Whitsom told him remorsefully. "It's probably pretty boring. Cratz and Vins will be guarding your door. I'll come get you for lunch."

Atlas glanced sideways at him, a little bewildered. Even if Whitsom hadn't told him he'd not grown up as a soldier-in-training, Atlas probably would have figured it out quickly enough. The Ren boy was far too pleasant to his supposed prisoner.

Though admittedly, Atlas didn't *feel* much like a prisoner. Sure, he had a constant nanny, but he had been given food, been allowed to spar, had even sat in on a council meeting. It certainly wasn't how General Talikoth treated their prisoners back at Headquarters.

As Atlas lay back on his cot, staring, once again, up at the cracked, sloping ceiling, he could not help but feel a presiding sense of optimism. His position now, perhaps, was bleak, but very soon, he could get the information he needed, execute his escape, and return to his clan. Things would only be looking up from there.

He thought back to what Whitsom had said that morning in the dining hall, about believing in something worth dying for. Atlas had never really contemplated death; it had always felt far-off, like something that happened to other people. But as he thought of the devastation he had seen, the desecrated forests and dried up lakes in the South, the decades of war and famine and hardships that he'd only ever had to read about, Atlas determined that, yes, he would be willing to die for something like peace.

Peace the Obarion way, of course. For anything else would look nothing like peace at all.

CHAPTER THREE

T he next week passed in monotony. Whitsom had not been assigned to Atlas since that first day, and his latest guards were not nearly so pleasant. Sunday brought him a pale, taciturn fellow who spoke very little English, and mostly communicated in grunts and scowls. Monday ushered in a colossal brunette woman with a face that greatly resembled the pictures of warthogs he had seen in the wildlife books Delurah had shown him as a child.

On Tuesday, someone—Atlas was almost certain it had been Whitsom—slid a deck of cards beneath the crack in his door. He had been entertaining himself with a few games Delurah taught him, but he quickly grew bored.

The grumpy fellow was back on Wednesday, and on Thursday, the old man who had witnessed Atlas urinating on himself that very first night—Bowduck— came strolling into his room, looking far too smug to be allowed.

He had started to memorize the guards' routines: they would take him to breakfast at exactly 8 o' clock, and then head down to the (completely useless) morning meetings. At the start, Atlas had spent this time amusing himself by seeing how many offensive strikes he could recall to memory, or, if he was feeling particularly ornery, trying to make eye contact with Augusto, which tended to frighten the enfeebled weakling right out of the room.

But by the third meeting he found himself listening to their drivel, though more out of befuddlement than anything. He had concluded that it would be quite unforgivable should he return to General Talikoth with *nothing* to report—nothing but the whispered rumors of the Vedas' allegiance with the Ren.

The matter of fact, though, was that even with his undivided attention, the meetings didn't provide Atlas with anything worth relaying to General Talikoth. His initial conclusion had not been far off—the Vedas didn't appear to have any plans of expanding beyond their corner in the North. Though if they did, those conversations could have been happening when he wasn't around. Perhaps Moonstone was only trying to persuade him that her clan was not a threat, so that the Obarion might be caught unawares?

None of his guards had been so generous as Whitsom as to allow him anywhere near the training yard—"Too many weapons!" Sunday's guard had grunted in his thick accent—so after the meeting he typically was deposited into his room until lunch, though Thursday morning he convinced Bowduck to allow him a stroll outside, provided, of course, that the old man (and two younger guards, who looked far better equipped to out-sprint him, should he try to make a dash for it) came with him.

The Vedas base, he surmised, must be very far north, if the cool weather and dense woodland were anything to go by. Moonstone had provided him with a week's worth of thick, wool-lined sweaters for his stay, and he was grateful for it. Though it was only the last month of autumn, it could not have been warmer than fifty degrees. Even in the times that he had traveled with the other soldiers all the way to the Pass, he'd never felt anything quite so frigid.

The North was enviable in its beauty. The desert had its own sort of charm, but in the South, the land was sparsely populated with stumpy flora, often dull green and barbed. The only real woodland was the jungle of trees that enveloped Headquarters, though none nearly so tall as these in the North.

In contrast, the forests here were dense and stretched on further than his eyes could see, sloping up tall mountains topped with snow. Nestled in a valley, tucked between two peaks, he could see a lake, its glassy black surface reflecting the clear sky.

This, he was sure, was part of why General Talikoth so passionately despised the Vedas. Here they sat, comfortable, on riches of plentiful lumber and water, while the Obarion struggled in the drought-ridden South, their resources diminishing more rapidly every day.

"We try very hard to use the foliage and branches so that we can avoid exhausting the woodland," Bowduck told him, as they strolled beside the forest's edge. Atlas ran his hands along the bark of the cambering pines. The sharp, thin pine needles that jutted from the low-hanging branches gathered in brown deadened mounds that crunched beneath the soles of his boots. "And we try to re-plant what we must take."

Atlas doubted this was true. The greenery that used to run all along the Fringe down south had been mostly destroyed. Further inland, where tall maple trees once stood was now a barren wasteland, from which people and creatures alike had fled. General Talikoth told him that when he led the Obarion into the Westland, when Atlas had been only a baby, the Vedas had already caused irreparable damage. Why would they be so considerate now?

After lunch he returned to his room, where he was left until dinner. There Atlas had counted and memorized exactly how many cinder blocks made up the walls of his little prison (three hundred and thirty-nine) and determined the precise dimensions of his cell using only his feet as measurement tools. When those activities bored him, he stared into the cold gray of the concrete ceiling for what felt like hours on end.

Moonstone had continued to all-but-ignore him during the morning meetings, and she hadn't tried to obtain any information from him. Atlas hadn't attempted an escape, and the week of evaluation that Moonstone had coaxed the Council into granting him was almost up; he was certain that, if she called on him that Saturday, it would be to send him back to the South —or worse, if the lumberjack got his way.

He could not afford to be killed—not before General Talikoth had been informed of the Ren's assistance to the Vedas. And even if they decided to send him back south, it would be the same way they brought him north—unconscious and incapacitated. He'd have no chance of perusing the surrounding area, of charting a path back to Headquarters and reporting to General Talikoth exactly where the Vedas were hiding.

No, Atlas would not allow Moonstone, or any of the Vedas, to decide the terms of how he left the base, and this was the boost of courage that he needed to carry out his plans for giving his guards the slip that Friday.

He had gone over his scheme several times: after lunch, when he was returned to his room, his guard-of-the-day usually took their opportunity to get some food, while another guard watched his door. If the stand-in guard was particularly hungry, which, it seemed, they usually were, they would leave a few minutes before his guard-of-the-day had returned. Atlas knew because he had been watching their shadows moving beneath the crack under the door and heard their muffled voices. There was almost always a three-minute gap between when one of the shadows vanished and the next appeared. This was when he would make his move.

That morning, his fingers twitched with a jittery sort of anticipation as the warthog-faced woman led him into the dining hall. Instead of heading to his usual table towards the back, Atlas scanned the crowd, his eyes jumping between clusters of people until he found what he was looking for. Barely repressing a smirk, he strode towards a table near the middle of the hall, his guard following.

Atlas slipped into a seat beside a tan brunette girl with her hair pulled up in an elaborate bun. When she turned to look at him, he flashed her a smile and she blushed, fumbling with the biscuit that she had been buttering.

Atlas loaded up his own plate hastily. His guard hovered near him, but not so near that he felt nervous. Her small, watery blue eyes flickered over the hall disinterestedly, though her hand rested just a few inches from the taser on her belt.

Atlas glanced down the table, spotting the plate of biscuits in front of the brunette girl, who was turned away from him, deep in conversation with her companion. He reached across her, moving with precision.

"Oh, I'm sorry," Atlas said, for he had jostled her a bit. "Just trying to grab a biscuit, didn't want to interrupt you." He slid the plate of biscuits toward himself with his other hand, barely repressing a snigger as she, predictably, turned bright pink and giggled.

"Oh, it's no problem!" she gushed, turning back to her friend as they both started to titter, throwing him rather conspicuous glances every few moments.

Atlas smirked as he took a bite of his biscuit, sliding the bobby pin he had snagged from the idiotic girl's hair into his pocket. A glance in his peripherals told him that his guard had not noticed a thing.

The morning dragged on so slowly that Atlas briefly wondered if whatever gods of old his ancestors had worshipped were taunting him. As Moonstone droned on during the morning meeting, he found his attention wandering even more readily than usual.

He would have a very limited amount of time during this afternoon's excursion. There was a chance one of his guards might notice he had disappeared, but he doubted it; they only ever came into his room to take him to meals, and outside of Moonstone, his assigned guards, and the council members, who he rarely saw outside of meeting hours, no one else around the base would be familiar enough with him to recognize him on sight.

Atlas followed his guard back to his room without complaint, sinking down onto his cot and staring blankly at the ceiling. His excitement had begun to dwindle, to be replaced, in part, by some nervousness. He was taking a huge risk, but the greater risk lie in doing nothing.

At lunch, he tried very hard to force down his beef stew. He knew if he didn't eat anything it would look suspicious, but each mouthful felt dry against his tongue.

When Atlas was taken back to his room, he did not even bother lying down. He sat very still, his back against the cold masonry wall, watching the shadows move on the other side of his door. He heard the murmur of conversation, punctuated by loud peals of laughter, and he barely breathed for fear of missing something.

Finally, *finally*, after it felt like he had been sitting stiffly for hours, the shadow underneath the door crack shifted forward.

"Quiet?" asked a gruff voice.

"As usual," came the warthog woman's snort. "Always looks so damn condescending though. I'll be glad to be rid of this one."

"Moonstone is wasting her time," the gruff voice agreed, before adding, "Enjoy your lunch, Bonamay."

Her clunky footsteps grew fainter, and the second shadow took its place stationed outside of the door.

Atlas let out a slow breath, rising to his feet and withdrawing the bobby pin from the pocket of his pants. He quickly turned to his cot, pulling back the covers, shoving the pillow beneath them, and clumping the blanket together at random intervals until it crudely resembled the shape of a body. It was by no means a work of art, and certainly wouldn't convince anyone who took more than a quick glance, but it would do.

He moved across the room and stood behind the door, waiting. He stood so close that he could hear every movement that the guard on the other side made —every time the guard shifted his stance, every cough, every heavy, tired sigh.

Atlas' legs had started to ache when he saw it. The guard's shadow began to move away from the door, his footsteps echoing loudly in the hallway. Atlas glanced down at his watch: *1:57.* Right on time.

He waited until he could not hear even the faintest whisper of footsteps, before he hastily knelt in front of the door, placing a steadying hand on the cold metal and slipping the bobby pin into the lock, jiggling it about until he found the first binding driver pin. He pressed the bobby pin further into the lock, until he found the next key pin that was binding. Atlas continued to work, hardly breathing, his brow furrowed in concentration, until each of the driver pins were set. Atlas held his breath, pressing the bobby pin in nearly as far as it could go. He was almost positive this was the last driver pin to set—

The lock turned, and he straightened up, pushing the door open and glancing in either direction. The hall was completely deserted, and Atlas had to resist the urge to fist pump in the air. He flipped off the light in his room—the makeshift doppelgänger in his cot would be more convincing that way—and closed his door with a quiet *snap.*

A giddy sort of euphoria swelled up inside of him, for it had been *so long* since he had been free to just go wherever he pleased, to do whatever he wanted without someone peering over his shoulder.

On a whim, Atlas went left, relaxing his posture. He needed to act natural, as though he had as much of a right to be strolling around the base uninhibited as anyone else.

He turned left again and found himself at the central stairwell. His first test came more quickly than he had been prepared for. As he approached the stairs, a pair of guards came down the steep steps. But they did not even look in his direction, and Atlas grinned widely, taking the steps two at a time as he merrily made his way down to the next floor.

He wanted to detail as much of the base as he possibly could, but it was difficult. The building had many levels of winding corridors, and most of the hallways were sterile, white, and identical, with very few windows and virtually no landmarks or indicators to guide him.

Still, his memory was very good, and he was able to get a rough idea of the layout: four levels, including the basement floor where the morning meetings took place. The training yard, he discovered, was accessed via the fourth floor. His room, along with the dining hall, was on the second, and the infirmary on the third.

Atlas came to a large pair of massive oak doors and frowned. This was the way out onto the grounds. Bowduck had led him through these doors just yesterday. Atlas glanced over his shoulder. Only a couple of people milled around, none paying him any attention.

He pulled the heavy wooden door open and winced as a blast of cold air accosted him.

Despite the cold, the sun shone brightly, and the

sky was cloudless. A wave of ease overcame Atlas as he breathed in the pleasant pine scent of the trees that stretched in every direction.

The muscles in his arms and legs pulsed with adrenaline, and the urge to run, as fast as he possibly could, had his body twitching with anticipation. But Atlas wasn't stupid. Perhaps two hundred feet from where he stood, coils of barbed wire glinted under the glare of the sun—a fence towered in the distance. If the Vedas had even a shred of self-preservation—if they were anything like the Obarion—it was electrified.

Atlas eyed the edge of the forest. The thick canopy of leaves blocked out most of the sunshine, and from where he stood, the forest floor looked nearly black. Could that be his escape route, when the time came?

Was that time now?

Hesitation cooled the adrenaline surging beneath his skin, though he couldn't pin down why. He should be making a run for it—now, before any of his guards found him.

The fence could run straight through the forest. It could encircle the base—there was really no telling whether or not the forest would be his path to freedom.

Still, he should try.

He edged towards the forest perimeter, but as he moved across the long stretch of lawn, a familiar figure caught his eye.

Whitsom's sister sat with her legs folded beneath her, not five yards away. She wore a flowy white shirt, a long red skirt, and, perhaps most strangely, had donned a crown of flowers atop her unruly curls. A gold chain adorned with a bright blue gemstone pendant hung around her neck. A notebook sat in her lap, and she scrawled across it furiously, her dark brows knitted together.

Atlas started to turn away, worrying that she might report him to Moonstone if she saw him, but she muttered, "It's rude to stare, Obarion."

He stopped in his tracks, fumbling to come up with an excuse, but before he could say anything she continued, her eyes still on her notes. "Is this a sanctioned stroll?"

"Of course," Atlas lied quickly.

Whitsom's sister looked up at him, arching an eyebrow.

"Excellent. Moonstone was just looking for you. I'll tell her you—" Her hickory brown eyes zeroed in on something behind him. "Oh, perfect, she's actually right there—"

Instinctively, he whirled around, cursing internally and already preparing for another round of tasing—

But the only thing behind him was a cluster of trees, and a group of three or four guards ambling across the grounds some twenty feet away, talking animatedly.

Atlas' eyes narrowed as he turned back around. The Ren girl grinned up at him cheekily. She had exceptionally white teeth, like eggshells.

"Unsanctioned, then, I take it. If your suspicious reaction is anything to go by." She winked, turning back to her notes. "Don't worry, Obarion. Your secret's safe with me."

Atlas tilted his head as he observed her.

I think she figured out a way to store solar energy and convert it to gas or something.

This peculiar Ren girl knew something that could help him. Knew something that could help *all* of them, if Whitsom was telling the truth. Something that she wasn't willing to share with Moonstone out of the goodness of her heart. But if there was one thing Atlas had learned from General Talikoth, it was that everyone had a price, and he was ninety percent sure he already knew hers.

"My name is Atlas, actually," he said finally. "May I sit?"

Her eyes flashed with surprise, and Atlas had to fight down a satisfied smirk at having caught her off guard. This odd girl seemed to constantly shake his composure, and it made him uneasy.

She nodded slowly, though her expression remained suspicious. Atlas sat beside her, resting his arms across his knees as he tried to glimpse what she was writing.

"Gaiomere," she said suddenly, and his eyes shot to her face. Her brow was still furrowed, but her gaze had returned to her notes. "My name. It's Gaiomere. My brother calls me Gai, but you don't. Got it?"

Atlas stared at her, amusement and irritation warring in his mind. It was the second time in a week she had given him orders.

"What are you working on?" he asked, for he was sure if he said anything else, he might reveal his vexation and ruin his chance of getting information from her.

Gaiomere brushed a stray curl from her face, frowning down at her notes. "Nothing you'd care about, unless you have a vested interest in the thermo-chemical cycle."

His intrigue spiked at that. He didn't, as she had correctly deduced, have any interest in the thermo-chemical cycle—whatever that meant—but if her experimentation was practical, rather than theoretical, he knew that General Talikoth most certainly would.

"Oh, actually, loads of interest," he said, feigning enthusiasm. She arched a brow, giving him a sideways glance, before turning back to her notes. He studied her profile for a moment, his mind whirling, before he decided the best mode of operation here was at least partial honesty.

"Whitsom said that you'd found a way to convert solar energy to gas," Atlas divulged slowly, picking absently at the grass tickling the palms of his hands.

Gaiomere let out a breathless laugh. "Great garbanzos, did he promise you his first-born, too?"

Atlas snorted. It would be difficult to deny that he liked Whitsom, but the Ren boy was a little too trustful for his own good.

"Perhaps it's just that he and I have similar motives."

Her head whipped towards him, as though he'd said something offensive, and the look she gave him was penetrating.

"My brother likes the *idea* of war," she said quietly. "Growing up with a tribe of pacifists didn't suit him. But his motives aren't the same as yours. Not really."

Once again, her keen ability to dissect his intentions threw him off balance. He looked away, carefully schooling his features as his eyes roved over the grounds.

"I'm not an idiot," Gaiomere pressed on. "I can see that you don't want to be here any more than I do. What do you want with me?"

A vein in his temple twitched. Atlas briefly lamented the fact that Gaiomere couldn't be like the idiotic girl in the dining hall from whom he had stolen the bobby pin—so easily swayed by a charming smile. But then, he supposed, if she were, she probably wouldn't know how to convert solar energy.

"If I go back to the Obarion headquarters with no information of value, the General will be...displeased."

A crease appeared between her brows. "I'm not going to be an accessory—"

"*Unless* your terms are met first," he snapped, annoyance seeping into his tone at last. The hypocrisy of the Renegades' attitude was glaring: to practice pacifism, turning a blind eye to death and destruction on every side of them. And in Gaiomere's case, withholding information that could *end* the war, sparing countless lives—all for her own selfish ends.

Gaiomere stood, her cheeks darkening with color and eyes narrowing to slits. Atlas got to his feet too, so that she was no longer looking down on him.

"I'm just trying to keep my family alive," she hissed. She tucked her notebook under her arm and made to stride off, but then stopped in her tracks, turning back. "And don't act so sanctimonious, Obarion. All of you clansmen act *so* high-and-mighty and treat us 'Renegades' like we're cowardly criminals. But you aren't any better."

Atlas raised his eyebrows, sliding his hands into his pockets and trying very hard to maintain an expression of nonchalance, though inside he fumed.

"Oh? Care to elaborate?"

"*We* do whatever we have to, to protect our tribes.

And however much you pretend to be motivated by *'the good of the people,'*" the sarcasm dripped from her voice here, "you're just looking out for yourself too." She deepened her voice, reciting, "*'If I go back to the Obarion headquarters with no information, the General will be displeased.'*"

If he wasn't so angry, he might have found her imitation of him amusing.

"Act like you're better than us all you want, but you're exactly the same," Gaiomere continued. "Some of us are just more honest with ourselves."

With that, she stomped off, her wild curls bobbing behind her. Atlas watched her for a few moments, before flopping back down into the grass with an irritated huff.

Well that had gone just about as poorly as it possibly could have. Though, the afternoon had not been a complete waste. He had learned one thing from the catastrophic conversation with the Ren girl: she did know *something* of merit, though he hadn't yet learned what that something was.

He stood up once more and glanced over his shoulder. None of the soldiers lingering on the lawn were paying any attention. He could make a break for it, and he doubted any of them would even glance in his direction.

The hesitation swelled up in his stomach once more, heavy like a boulder.

But Atlas scowled, forcing the feeling down determinedly, his feet carrying him towards the treeline. Once he got the information back to General Talikoth, and the Obarion laid siege on the North, Talikoth would extract the information from the Ren girl himself.

His steps, though, had slowed to little more than a shuffle, and he stared at the canopy of trees fifty feet away with a growing uncertainty.

"Ah, Atlas, there you are," came Moonstone's voice from behind him.

He stopped dead in his tracks, his face going blank as he contemplated how best to mitigate this situation. Atlas turned to face her, his hands clenched at his sides. She had an unfamiliar guard at her side, black haired and brawny, and his hands were already clenching a taser. He gave Atlas a menacing scowl.

"Off on a ramble?" Moonstone asked, her lips quirking upwards as she stopped in front of him.

"Not sure where my guard wandered off to, she was behind me just a moment ago," Atlas said smoothly, looking around him in mock confusion.

Moonstone arched a black brow.

"The same guard still standing outside of your room oblivious to the fact that you are not in it?" Atlas' face betrayed him with spasm, and Moonstone sighed. "We are not so primitive as you might think, Atlas. We do have *cameras*, you know."

His cheeks flushed, but before he could say anything in his defense, Moonstone jerked her head towards the tall oak doors behind her. "Come with me, please."

Atlas glanced towards the forest once more. His hands and feet twitched, as though his body was already preparing him to make a dash for it.

But the guard was watching him carefully, his fingers flexing around the taser's trigger. Moonstone's eyes were affixed on him too.

After a few moments, he nodded and followed her silently inside, mentally berating himself all the way. He'd had his chance, and he had *failed.*

He hoped that grouchy bearded man got his way— he hoped that the Vedas elected to kill him. Surely that would be better than returning to Headquarters with nothing to show.

Perhaps he could tell General Talikoth that they had held him imprisoned and blindfolded for a week straight, and *that* was why he returned with such measly information. Talikoth, though, had a disturbingly good radar for dishonesty. The last time Atlas had attempted to lie, he had been twelve, and the sting of leather against his back had been a sufficient reminder, even throughout the five years since, not to attempt it again. Not when it came to General Talikoth, anyway.

Atlas zeroed in on the back of Moonstone's head. If he *was* going to be killed, he would at least take her down with him. If he managed to kill the Vedas' general, he was sure any of his other failures would be forgiven.

Moonstone led him not to the meeting room, but into a smaller room a few doors down the hall from it, with a wooden desk and a tall chair behind it. She sat down, and gestured to the seat across from her, for Atlas to do the same.

If he were to guess, she'd brought him to her office. It held few personal effects, save for a picture frame on the desk that he could not quite get a glimpse of, and a stack of books that sat on a chair in the corner of the room. A black, oval shaped object beeped noisily, vibrating against the wood of her desk, before she switched it off.

Newspaper clippings covered the walls, maps marked in all sorts of formations, with certain locations crossed out, and others circled in bright red ink.

From one of the clippings, General Talikoth's face glared back at Atlas. His brows were drawn together above deep carob eyes, so dark that they looked almost black, and his mouth curled into a sneer. Atlas looked away quickly and sat down.

Moonstone flicked through a file folder on top of her desk, her dark, shrewd eyes examining its contents exhaustively.

"I was going to pull you aside tomorrow, but your actions today necessitated intervention." She set the file folder down, looking up at Atlas with a piercing steel gaze. "So, what did you learn this week?"

Atlas stared at her blankly for several moments, his mind stalling. "Sorry—what?"

"What did you learn this week?" she repeated patiently. "In your time at our base—I am sure it has been quite a different experience for you."

The absurdity of her statement might have induced laughter if Atlas wasn't being so careful to control his expressions.

"Uh—yeah, I suppose you could say that." He wasn't sure where Moonstone was going with her line of questioning. Was she merely toying with him before she called in her soldiers to blast a hole through his skull?

Moonstone leaned back in her chair, watching Atlas carefully.

It would be easy to strike now, with her so relaxed. He could snatch the picture frame off of her desk, bring the corner down against her temple—

"I would like to know what you have learned about us, in your time here," Moonstone said.

She had to be a sadist, Atlas decided. That was the only explanation for why she toyed with him before she fed him to the wolves.

"I'm not going to play whatever little game you're playing," Atlas said finally, his voice cold. "If you're going to kill me, be done with it already."

Moonstone sighed again, the sort of noise an exhausted parent might give their child after a long day, and Atlas' blood boiled.

"I told you, Atlas, we do not kill children—"

"I'm *not* a child—"

"And what is more, I *could* not, even if I wanted to. I owe it to your mother."

Atlas froze, his breath catching in his throat. Moonstone's face remained calm, disinterested almost, but her eyes studied him intently.

"What did you say?" he said finally, his voice deathly quiet.

"I said that I owe it to your mother. I knew her, and I made a promise a long time ago that I still believe I am bound to."

Atlas straightened. He wanted to ask a thousand questions, but his brain seemed to have ceased coordination with his mouth. How had Moonstone known his mother? Had it been *she*, personally, who had killed her? Why would she feel bound to honor a promise made to an Obarion? Could Atlas even trust anything she was saying, or was it just more lies to manipulate him?

As though sensing his indecision, Moonstone

leaned forward.

"I want to show you something, Atlas. Something I think you will appreciate. But first I need you to tell me: what have you learned here? Think. I know you are a clever boy."

A part of Atlas, primitive and feral, wanted to attack her. Wanted to shove all of her condescension down her throat, until she couldn't draw breath. He was tired of being a pawn in enemy territory, and would rather be dead than risk being used.

But another part of Atlas ached to understand. The part of him that General Talikoth had always so adamantly opposed.

Talikoth hadn't liked questions, and Atlas quickly learned to shove them deep into the recesses of his mind. Now, though, they came tumbling forth unwittingly, as he sat stiffly across from Moonstone, feeling far more vulnerable than he had in a long time. He wanted to squash this feeling like an insect beneath his shoe.

Atlas leaned his head back, peering at the ceiling as he thought.

"Your military fleet is relatively small," he said finally, his voice careful, measured. "It sounds as though your main coal mines are directly north and southwest of you, and your coal production is almost entirely funneled into electricity output."

She nodded for Atlas to continue, so he did.

"Your agriculture unit is struggling because of the chemical leaching into the soil. That's why you've had to send foragers further north to look for new resources—you're running out here."

Moonstone smiled a little. "And, in conclusion?"

Atlas' brow furrowed, his lips pulling down at the corners, and before he could help himself, he burst out, "Your only focus seems to be making it through the winter. You deploy troops to the Southern Pass, but only enough to defend a disorganized strike—you'd be doomed if our actual front line were able to penetrate. You don't seem to be concerned about counterstrikes, and your base guards don't even carry *guns*, just those weird taser things."

Atlas scowled, shaking his head.

"You'd lose. You *will* lose. You're not trying to win a war. You're just trying to keep your constituents alive."

The last sentence slipped out of Atlas's mouth before he realized it, and the moment the words left his lips, he wanted to take them back. Moonstone gazed at him with a strangely satisfied look, her fingers drumming against her desk as her eyes bored into him.

Safety and security for the people is the Obarion way.

Moonstone rifled through her desk for something. When she straightened, she grasped a small photograph, which she held out to him. Atlas' brows furrowed as he looked between her impassive face and the photo. He hesitated, then reached out and took it.

Moonstone had to have been over a decade younger in this photo. The wrinkles around her eyes and mouth were absent, and she smiled in an unbothered sort of way that made her face appear less severe. But Atlas' eyes were drawn to the woman standing beside Moonstone.

She stood a good half foot shorter than her companion, and her arm was wrapped around Moonstone's back. She grinned at the camera, her stormy grey eyes bright. A small boy clutched her leg.

He could not have been older than two or three, with ash brown hair, pale skin, and round cheeks.

A lump formed in Atlas' throat that he could not seem to force down. There was a strange burning in his nose, and his eyes prickled.

"What is this?" he managed hoarsely, ripping his eyes away from the photograph to glare at Moonstone. "What is—what are you—what, you think this is *funny*?"

Anger coursed through Atlas so intensely that he trembled, and the commiseration in Moonstone's expression did not help.

"I do not think anything is funny, Atlas," Moonstone said softly. "I just wanted you to know the truth. And I want you to understand that there are things at play here bigger than what your father might have told you."

Atlas stood abruptly, breathing harshly through his nose.

"Don't you—don't you dare—don't say a *thing* about General Talikoth," he seethed. He ran an agitated hand through his hair, shoving his chair so hard that it toppled over as he paced in front of Moonstone's desk.

"I want out," Atlas spat. "I want to go back to the Obarion base—I'm certainly not going to help you."

Moonstone watched him pace, her expression so calm that Atlas wanted to tear it off of her face.

"Of course, we cannot force you," Moonstone allowed. "The Council reconvenes tomorrow, and we will make our decision from there. If it becomes clear that you will be more of a danger to our people here, then of course, we will let you go."

She had hardly finished speaking before Atlas

threw open the door, stalking down the hallway so quickly that several startled passersby sprang out of his way. He paid them no mind.

He had no idea where he was going, just that if he didn't keep walking, he was going to punch something. His lungs burned, and his fingers shook. Atlas realized belatedly that he still had the photograph clutched in his hand, and the thought made him angry all over again. He flung open the door to the stairwell and pounded up the steps.

No guards followed him—Moonstone hadn't bothered to send any after him, it seemed—but it didn't matter. All that mattered was getting as far away from that presumptuous, egotistical, sadistic fiend of a woman as he possibly could.

Atlas rounded a corner and ran into someone. He stumbled backwards, blinking.

"Been a bit—" Whitsom began, but his jovial grin melted as he peered more closely at Atlas. Atlas tried to move around him, but Whitsom put a hand on his shoulder. "What's up?"

"Nothing," Atlas snapped. "Just need to blow off some steam." He yanked his shoulder out of Whitsom's grasp and strode away. He was *sick* of this horrible place. Sick of Moonstone toying with him like some kind of plaything, sick of Whitsom pretending they were *friends*. Sick of Gaiomere and her stupid astuteness He just wanted to go back home—

"Wanna spar?"

Whitsom's voice broke through his angry thoughts, and Atlas' feet stopped of their own accord. He half turned. Whitsom still stood in the spot where they had collided. The Ren boy almost looked annoyed, and Atlas felt a flicker of guilt for being so rude.

He needed to get back to the Obarion base, to relay to General Talikoth everything that he had learned. There he would be back with his squad. He could spar with Coral and Bettoni, and crash in his *own* bed, or spend an entire Sunday in the library. Things could go back to *normal*.

But Atlas wanted to know how one converted solar energy to gas, especially if the coal really *was* almost gone. He wanted to find out what was north of the North. To play a part in ending this war. A part that might require abandoning normalcy.

He glanced down at his hand, where Moonstone's photograph was still crumbled in his fist.

What he *really* wanted was to understand why his mother was standing beside the Vedas General as though they were old friends, with a two-year-old Atlas clinging to her leg, and Talikoth nowhere in sight.

Whitsom still waited for him, and after a moment of hesitation, Atlas nodded, following him up the stairwell and towards the training yard.

Atlas wanted freedom, but more than freedom, he wanted the truth.

CHAPTER FOUR

"**H**e's *already* snuck out. We *know* he's trouble. What more proof do we need?"

Atlas massaged his temples and sank a little deeper into his chair. It was only a few minutes after nine in the morning and he already had a headache blooming. The heavy-set bearded man—whom Atlas learned was named Vailhelm—had spent the last fifteen minutes railing on him, appealing vehemently to the Council that he should be executed.

"I'm not sure if you've ever been stuck in a six by eight room for a week, but it gets old," Atlas said in a bored voice.

"Atlas, be quiet," Moonstone snapped from the front of the room. "Vailhelm, thank you, you have made your case."

"He won't give us information—he said himself he'd rather kill us," pointed out the blonde woman. "Without information, he's only a liability."

"That is true, Jaina, but perhaps a fresh perspective is more valuable than information," Moonstone mused.

"What motivation would he have to give us any assistance?" Augusto piped up.

Moonstone turned her gaze on Atlas, arching an eyebrow, and he sighed, tilting back in his chair and propping his feet up on the table. The sallow-faced man made an indignant noise.

"Don't we all want the same thing?" Atlas drawled. "An end to the Long War and prosperity for all of the people?"

"War can't end if the Obarion keep waging it, boy," Vailhelm grunted.

Atlas smirked a little, his eyes on the ceiling as he retorted, "Can't stop waging war until you stop giving us a reason to."

The angry horde of bees returned. He sniggered under his breath. It really was too easy to get them going.

"He's *heartless,* General, just like his father—"

"The violence won't end, General Moonstone. Not with people like them—"

"Let's get rid of him now, General, while we've still got the chance—"

Moonstone's eyes were affixed on Atlas.

"You really are not helping your case," she pointed out. Atlas rolled his eyes, the front two legs of his chair coming back to the ground as the angry horde momentarily quieted. Moonstone continued, "You want to be here. If you did not, you would have left yesterday. You would found a way to escape on your own terms, rather than letting us dictate when and how you would leave."

The rest of the Council was silent now, their gazes darting between Atlas and their General. Atlas' eyes narrowed and his lips thinned as he glowered at her. He didn't want to admit that she was right; he had spent the rest of yesterday afternoon, and all into the night going back and forth, his mind weighing every option, all of the pros and cons, but he kept coming back to the same conclusion: he could not leave without knowing the truth.

"I want to be here," he said finally. "I won't give you information about the Obarion base or General Talikoth's plans, but..." His jaw flexed, and he forced the words out before he lost his nerve. "But I will help in whatever way I can to prevent any more destruction. For the good of the people."

There. That didn't sound too disingenuous.

Moonstone examined him, and after a moment, she nodded slowly, her gaze flickering around the circle of council members.

"I propose a settlement. Atlas may stay here, assuming that he is granting the assistance promised. He will be able to move about the base freely, provided that he *does* have a guard with him at all times. Agreed?"

Jaina and a few of the other council members nodded, but Augusto and Vailhelm still looked apprehensive. The former began, "General, this poses a h-huge risk to our people—"

"I trust the competence and capability of our guards," Moonstone said firmly.

Vailhelm looked at him scathingly, and Atlas couldn't help but wonder if there was a particular motive for the man's sentiments. Augusto seemed afraid of him, sure, but this man—this man seemed to genuinely despise him. Him, personally, rather than just the clan he hailed from.

"General," Vailhelm started gruffly. "If he...makes us regret our generosity...if he attacks one of the guards, kills one of them, if he betrays us in any way... we kill him."

Moonstone frowned, her eyes flickering to Atlas for half a second before remarking, "I agree to those terms."

And just like that, the meeting adjourned, and the council members began to file out. Moonstone was deep in conversation with the man with the long black hair. Atlas tried to catch her eye, but by the time he was able to nudge his way through the crowd of people, she had disappeared down the long corridor.

He let out a sharp, frustrated exhale, his eyes absently roving over toward his guard. Today's was the taciturn man with the accent, and when Atlas looked at him, the guard arched a heavy brow, silently awaiting direction.

Atlas' irritation evaporated, replaced by a whimsical elation. He could go *wherever* he wanted. He could explore the grounds, or wander the forest to determine if it would be a viable escape route. He could even spend hours in the training yard, and *no one* could stop him.

Unable to repress his grin, he sauntered towards the stairwell, throwing the door open and vaulting up the steps. His guard's footsteps pounded in his wake, but Atlas ignored him. Not even having a tag-along could ruin his mood today.

When he exited onto the rooftop deck, the air was warmer than usual, and the sun was bright. Across the training yard, Whitsom, already sporting his headgear and gloves, was sparring speedily with the blond boy that Atlas recognized from his first day.

When Whitsom spotted him, he let out a low whistle, shaking his head.

"So, you live to see another day," he called. Whitsom clapped the blond boy next to him on the back, adding, "This is Kendo. Kendo, this is Atlas."

Kendo was nearly as tall as Atlas, and twice as muscular.

"Must be nice, having Moonstone in your back pocket," he said, pulling off his gloves to shake Atlas' hand. His words were playful, but his eyes were quite serious, and Atlas did not miss his suspicious once-over.

"Play nice, Kendo," Whitsom said, jostling the taller boy. "Atlas is alright."

The blond rolled his eyes, snatching his gloves up and stalking away, but not before he muttered, "Yeah, you say that about *everyone*."

"Don't mind him," Whitsom said immediately, tossing Atlas a pair of gloves as the two of them moved towards the sparring circle. "His brother died at Obarion hands. He's a little testy when it comes to you Southerners."

Atlas shrugged, pulling on his gloves and securing his head piece. He had expected, upon arriving, to be treated with nothing but contempt from *all* of the Vedas—which had not been the case. The occasional opprobrium from a guard or a council member was the least of his worries.

Sparring with Whitsom was more gratifying than any other fighting he had done in his life. Being a part of the same training squad for almost four years meant that they were all used to the others' fighting styles. Maddex was big, but he moved slowly, and predictably. Coral was short and remarkably strong, but relied too much on brute strength. Bettoni was lean and fast, but once Atlas got his arms around him, he was easy to out-muscle.

But Whitsom didn't fight like anyone else Atlas had ever met. He was strong and sturdy, and he sparred like it were a dance. His feet moved so quickly that even though Atlas was taller, Whitsom could dart beneath the span of his arms and deliver a strike before Atlas was able to stop him. Whitsom wasn't practiced, though. All his movements came from sheer instinct. He had never trained under experts like Atlas had, and didn't have any knowledge of fighting styles, or offensive and defensive maneuvers. And Atlas made sure to capitalize on that.

They had gone three rounds—Atlas had just sent Whitsom careening back into the fence, and the boy collapsed into a fit of laughter, as though they were playing some *game*—when an unfamiliar voice said, "Mind if I cut in?"

Whitsom made a face, and it was his expression that made Atlas turn, curious as to who would induce such a reaction from the boy seemingly determined to approve of everyone he met.

A young man with red hair stood just outside of the sparring circle, peering at Atlas from behind thick glasses. He was short—nearly an entire foot shorter than Atlas—fairly stout, and wore an expression that suggested he would be offended if Atlas refused.

"It's not often I see anyone beat Whitsom," he added, grinning hopefully.

Whitsom scrambled to his feet and came to stand beside Atlas.

"He's not from here. They teach them different in the South, I suppose."

The ginger arched an eyebrow.

"An Obarion, then?" He scrutinized Atlas for a moment, before adding casually to Whitsom. "I knew he wasn't with the Ren. He fights calculated—not like you, you've got no real technique."

Whitsom scowled, and Atlas arched an eyebrow. Belatedly, the redhead must have realized he said something wrong, because he flushed, hastily appending, "You're an excellent fighter, though. I just meant, in terms of formal training—you know, fighting methodology and all, you're—uh—not super great—"

"Jacoby, this is Atlas," Whitsom cut in, giving Atlas a look that made it very difficult for him to repress a laugh. "Atlas, Jacoby. Jacoby works down in the basement—with the *rest* of the engineers." Whitsom's tone was pointed.

Jacoby either ignored the jibe or was not keen enough to pick it up.

"So, what do you say, Atlas?"

Atlas gave Whitsom a sideways glance. "Um— maybe some other time. I'm a bit tired now—"

"Hey, Gai!" Whitsom called suddenly, a tad too cheerful. His sister had come wandering into the training yard, looking very out of place between all of the sweaty, shirtless men in her yellow blouse and ruffled skirt. She had braided a massive sunflower into her hair.

"Hello, sweet brother of mine," she said, beaming. Her eyes flickered to Atlas for a split second, and narrowed, just a fraction of an inch, before they returned to her brother. Atlas smirked.

Whitsom raised his eyebrows, though his grin was playful. "What do you want?"

Gaiomere stepped a bit closer, lowering her voice as she said, "I need access to the mainframe."

Whitsom burst out laughing, his hands coming

to his knees as he doubled over. Atlas peered at her inquisitively.

"Why do you need access to the mainframe?" he asked, raising his voice to be heard over Whitsom's chortling.

"Multiple reasons, *none* of which require your input," she snapped frostily.

"Nice to see you, too," Atlas muttered, though Gaiomere must have heard him, for the corners of her lips lifted marginally.

"Gai, you *do* realize they've only let me be a guard short-term, right?" Whitsom asked when he'd finally resurfaced from his bout of laughter. "I don't even have a taser—you think they'd give me access to the *mainframe*?"

Gaiomere frowned, drumming her fingers against her notebook as she thought.

"I—I have access to the mainframe."

Atlas started. He had completely forgotten that Jacoby was still standing there, and if Gaiomere's face was anything to go by, she hadn't noticed him at all.

She hastily scrambled to cover her tracks, mumbling, "Oh—um—I don't—"

"As long as you aren't up to anything nefarious, I'd be happy to help," Jacoby offered, his hands ruffling his hair nervously as he gazed at Gaiomere with rather conspicuous interest. Atlas rolled his eyes.

"Well, okay," Gaiomere said slowly, looking between Whitsom and the red-haired boy uncertainly. "Lead the way."

Jacoby eagerly started back towards the fourth-floor access, and Gaiomere started to follow, but stopped when she saw Whitsom and Atlas still rooted to the spot.

"Oh no, big brother, you are *not* getting out of this one!" she said in a fierce whisper, grasping Whitsom's wrist and giving him a sharp tug.

"Oh come on, Gai, don't make me tag along. This guy's a chowderhead—"

"Then it'd be awfully unkind of you to leave me alone with him, wouldn't it?" Gaiomere retorted, yanking him after her.

Whitsom grumbled under his breath, but allowed her to drag him across the training yard. Atlas watched them go, going back and forth in his mind. He hadn't technically been invited along on their little sojourn— but he was terribly curious what Whitsom's sister was up to.

In the end, his curiosity won out. Atlas glanced over at his guard, who leaned against the wall, watching another pair sparring with a bored look on his face. The guard probably thought Atlas wouldn't dare try anything with so many other soldiers mulling around.

Slipping seamlessly into a throng of people, Atlas made his way towards the door, catching up with the trio and falling into step with Whitsom.

"I will need to know what you're using the mainframe for though," Jacoby said, his tone apologetic as he threw Gaiomere a guilty glance.

"I need to see the Vedas' maps of the North," she said. "I'm scouting potential hot spots for rhodium." Jacoby looked a little suspicious, and she quickly added, "It's a project for Moonstone." Gaiomere glanced over at the bespectacled boy, her cheeks lifting as she gave him a captivating smile. "I'm actually surprised you haven't heard about it—I've heard your name around—

I've heard you're one of the best minds the Vedas' have at their disposal."

Jacoby cheeks heated under her praise, and he straightened, his chest puffing infinitesimally.

Atlas arched a brow, studying the back of the Ren girl's head. Oh, she was good. Just the right amount of flattery to halt the boy's questions, without any unnecessary sycophantism. It certainly wasn't something he would have expected from someone who braided flowers into their hair.

Jacoby led them all the way down to the basement, but rather than heading to the end of the corridor like Atlas was used to, towards the meeting room, they turned in the opposite direction.

Jacoby stopped in front of a heavy metal door, pressing the pad of his thumb against the scanner beside the door. The scanner beeped and flashed bright green before the lock clicked, and Jacoby pushed the door open.

A handful of panels dimly lit the room, and the plethora of monitor screens lined up across perhaps a dozen identical desks cast an iridescent glow across the stone floor. The back wall was lined with perhaps twenty massive, block structures, each around four feet wide, and a few inches taller than Atlas. They all emitted the same droning, static hum.

"Here's my station," Jacoby bumbled, leading the three of them over to a desk in the corner. Atlas glanced at Gaiomere. Her face was lit up, as though they had arrived in a room covered wall-to-wall with chocolate fountains, rather than a dingy dungeon full of clunky machines. Atlas had only been into the control room back at Headquarters a handful of times, but he understood enough to recognize these machines were ancient—perhaps even from before the First War, or the Great Famine.

Jacoby sank down into his plushy office chair. His fingers flew across the keyboard as he entered a password—too quickly for Atlas to follow—and pulled up a series of maps, layered atop one another. Atlas couldn't make sense of all the lines and arbitrary symbols, but Gaiomere seemed to, for she leaned down beside Jacoby, her eyes wide.

"You are...*awesome*, Jacoby, thank you."

He chuckled, his ears turning pink. "Happy to help, I think it's—"

"Are you familiar with cryptographics?" Gaiomere interrupted, pulling up a chair beside him and pulling his keyboard toward her.

Jacoby blinked. "Of course I am—I helped design ours."

Gaiomere nodded distractedly. She had pulled up a screen with a series of codes blinking across it.

She typed a sequence of digits that looked random, but must have meant something, for Jacoby asked, "How do you—how do you know how to do that?"

"I taught myself," Gaiomere replied impatiently as she pulled up a new screen and began to insert another procession of codes.

"Oh," Jacoby muttered. He suddenly looked rather put out, his back slouching against his seat.

"We used to sneak into abandoned military bases for cover," Whitsom whispered to Atlas. "Gaiomere would override their systems so that we could find the nearest food sources—they had *massive* lists of their supply locations. Sometimes they were outdated, but a lot of times, they led us to dozens and dozens of old harvesting grounds that still had loads of native fruits and nuts."

Atlas looked between the two siblings with a new-found sense of wonder. Were all of the Renegades this resourceful? And if they were, did General Talikoth know?

"So, uh—what exactly are we looking for?" Jacoby asked. Whitsom peered over Gaiomere's shoulder, his dark eyes narrowed.

"Moonstone must keep a database for soldier deployments," Gaiomere said as she continued to type. She brushed back a curl that had escaped her braid, gnawing at her lip as she worked.

"Oh, well of course she does," Jacoby said, leaning back in his chair. "Those are encrypted, though. For security purposes." He sat up suddenly, his eyes narrowing as he glanced between the three of them. "Wait, but I thought you were looking for rhodium hotspots...for your...project?"

"I already found those," Gaiomere muttered, hardly paying the ginger boy any attention.

Jacoby still frowned suspiciously at her, but his attention shifted, for an engineer across the room called, "Hey Cobes, my transmitter's busted. Can I borrow yours?"

Jacoby yanked open a drawer and withdrew a small, oval shaped object with an array of buttons and knobs. As soon as he moved towards the other side of the room, Gaiomere spun around in her chair, grabbed the front of Whitsom's shirt, and yanked him towards her.

"Distract him," she hissed.

"What—Gaiomere!" Whitsom spluttered, trying to extract himself from her vice-like grip. "What am I supposed to do?"

"*Think* of something, Whit!" she snapped, turning back around just as Jacoby reappeared at her side. Whitsom looked between Jacoby and his sister with a helpless expression.

"So, I was just thinking," the redhead began, "Shouldn't Moonstone have given you guys some kind of clearance—"

"Say, Jacoby," Atlas interrupted, striding over to one of the humming machines that lined the back wall. "How do these work exactly? Are these all connected?"

Jacoby's brown eyes lit up behind his thick glasses.

"Yeah, they are!" he exclaimed excitedly. "The mainframe technology is pretty outdated. It's very bulky and clunky compared to a lot of the machines developed just after the First War. But it's still remarkable, given how long ago it was manufactured. Each of these towers communicate with one another—"

He continued to drone on, excitedly moving from tower to tower, his hands gesticulating wildly. Atlas followed him around the room, nodding enthusiastically and interjecting questions at all the right times.

In his peripherals, Gaiomere tapped away at the keyboard with dizzying rapidity. He could barely make out the map she was analyzing. There were clusters of red dots, bunched together so closely they formed a mass. It looked vaguely like a heat map.

Gaiomere stood suddenly, clicking a button, and the screen went black. She inconspicuously slid her notebook under her arm and gave Atlas a curt nod.

"Found all I needed, Jacoby, thanks!" she said brightly. "Your software is really impressive."

He grinned delightedly. "Oh, you think so? Well, not many people have an interest in it—"

"Bad taste, for sure," Gaiomere muttered as the four of them made their way out of the mainframe room and down the corridor. She seemed preoccupied, which forced Atlas and Whitsom to make conversation with Jacoby, who seemed delighted to have found company so interested in talking about computer engineering.

It was not until they reached the dining hall that they managed to shake him. As they sat down and began to pile food atop their plates, the two boys looked expectantly at Gaiomere. She had not even touched the food, but flipped through her notebook with concentration.

"*So*, what was that all about?" Whitsom asked finally, arching a brow as he cut into his chicken.

Gaiomere was jotting something down onto a blank page. "Hmm?"

"Oh, I don't know, care to explain to me why we just *broke into the mainframe* of the people who are feeding and clothing us?"

"We didn't *break* in, we were *invited* in," she amended, sniffing loftily as she closed her notebook and ladled herself a spoonful of beans. "And for the record, the only reason they're still *having* to feed and clothe us is because they haven't fulfilled their end of the deal. I'm remedying that." She froze suddenly, her knife stilling over the potato she'd been cutting into. "And *also,* for the record, they haven't been clothing me." She eyed her brother's dark pants and bomber jacket with disdain.

"You look like such a conformist."

Atlas couldn't help it. He snorted, wryly remarking, "Better than you, flower power."

Whitsom burst out laughing. Gaiomere's eyes narrowed into a glare, but when she looked back down at her plate, Atlas could have sworn her lips twitched.

"Wait, so what do you mean you're remedying it?" Whitsom asked incredulously. "Moonstone already has soldiers out there looking for Maggi and Rasta, doesn't she?"

"Yeah, and they've been out there since the last moon, Whit, and found nothing." She took a bite of her beans, chewing pensively before pointing out, "We know the mountains better than anyone. And I'm almost *sure* that's where they would have gone." She lowered her voice. "The search parties Moonstone sent were all too close to the Vedas base—within twenty miles or less. Maggi and Rasta would have stayed as far from civilization as possible."

Whitsom said nothing, but his expression was torn.

"And what's more," Gaiomere continued, "what would happen, even if the soldiers *had* found Maggi and Rasta?"

Whitsom straightened, his frown deepening.

"They would have run," he said slowly.

"Exactly." Gaiomere's expression was grim. "We have to go after them ourselves."

Her brother let out a harsh breath. "Gai, I don't know. We haven't been here that long, and—hey, who knows, maybe they came across another tribe who are helping them—why are you looking at me like that?"

Gaiomere had dropped her spoon and glared at

Whitsom with so much venom that Atlas was surprised he didn't drop dead on the spot.

"You're *unbelievable*. Completely, utterly, *selfishly* unbelievable!" She pushed her plate away, snatching her notebook back into her arms as she climbed to her feet.

"How 'm bein' selfish?" Whitsom said indistinctly. He had already resumed shoveling food into his mouth.

"You don't even care about them! They could have been captured by Flesh Flayers—they could be—they could be *dead* for all we know, and all you're concerned about is leaving behind your warm food and cushy bed!"

"That's not true!" Whitsom insisted, though it did not help his case that as he spoke, he reached for another serving of chicken.

Gaiomere lunged forward and smacked his hand so hard he let out a yelp.

"*Selfish*," she huffed, holding her notebook against her chest rather like a shield. "Fine. I'll go by myself. Stay here with your plushy bed and three-course meals. Meanwhile Maggi and Rasta are out there starving." She gave him another disgusted look and stormed out of the dining hall.

Atlas stared after her for several moments, before he looked back at Whitsom, who cursed under his breath as he loaded another two servings of chicken onto his plate.

"Um—she's not actually going to go out there, is she?" Atlas asked.

Whitsom snorted, hastily shoveling chicken into his mouth.

"Oh, she'll go alright," he said angrily. "Of course she will." He shook his head, glaring at the door through which his sister had disappeared. "Nah, but she won't go now. She'll sneak out early tomorrow morning, when most everyone's asleep."

Atlas watched Whitsom carefully. "But I mean— by herself?"

Whitsom had made it clear that he had no understanding of solar conversion, nor did he seem particularly gifted with technology the way that Gaiomere was. It wouldn't do for such a rich source of information that Atlas could carry back to General Talikoth to go and get herself killed.

"Course not, I've got to go with her," Whitsom grumbled, stabbing at his chicken aggressively. He continued to mutter under his breath, before he asked Atlas, "I'm not being selfish, am I? I mean, we've only been here a moon cycle, and I've been waiting ages to be a part of something. Something bigger than just running for our lives, you know?" He frowned down at his plate. "Doesn't feel selfish."

Atlas shrugged, training his eyes back on the food in front of him. He had never had to choose between his friends or family and the cause he stood for. He wondered now though—if Coral or Bettoni's lives were on the line, would he sacrifice them in the name of something bigger?

He thought he would—thought he would have the courage to do so. That was the choice General Talikoth would approve of.

But then he thought of Bettoni's little brother, who could not have been older than seven. Could Atlas make such a sacrifice *then*? Whitsom said that the tribe members they were separated from were young, perhaps even too young to fend for themselves.

As he finished the last of his meal, he toiled over

his options. If he stayed at the Vedas base, he could get the information that he wanted out of Moonstone. He'd have the chance to get the truth, once and for all, and finally quell the curiosity that had been eating him alive since he'd first laid eyes on that photograph.

But if he let Whitsom and Gaiomere go...he might never see them again, and the knowledge that Gaiomere possessed would be lost. For all he knew, Moonstone had already coerced her into sharing what she knew— General Talikoth could *already* be at a disadvantage.

If he went with them, he could escape the Vedas base, just as he'd planned. And if he helped Whitsom and Gaiomere find their friends...surely she'd be inclined to share what she knew then.

But in the back of his mind, unwillingness lingered. Could he really get what he needed from Gaiomere, return to Talikoth, and just...forget what he'd seen?

Atlas' fingers flexed on the tabletop, and he shook his head. His own curiosity, his own self-interest, did not matter in the end. He had a duty to his clan, a duty to General Talikoth, that superseded any individual motivations he might possess. Even if he knew it might haunt him for the rest of his life.

"I can come with you," Atlas said, before he could change his mind.

Whitsom's gaze shot up to meet his. "You don't need to—"

"I know I don't need to." He took a bite of potatoes.

"We might be gone awhile," Whitsom pointed out.

Atlas shrugged. "I figured as much."

"There'll be animals."

Atlas snorted. "The horror."

"Wild fires and toxic gases."

"Sounds like a Thursday." Atlas had not, in fact, ever encountered toxic gases on any day of the week, but he didn't think mentioning that now would do him any favors.

Whitsom arched a dark brow. "Some of the other tribes aren't very friendly."

Atlas met his gaze evenly.

"All the more reason for me to come," he reasoned, shrugging. "I'm sure you could use another pair of fists."

Whitsom sighed, leaning back in his seat. For the first time, Atlas could discern suspicion in his eyes. "Okay, for real—why are you helping us?"

Atlas' mind raced as he contemplated what to tell him. Honesty would mean admitting that he didn't care a bit about whether or not their friends were safe. Honesty would mean revealing that Whitom's sister would be no use to General Talikoth dead.

"We're both outsiders here, aren't we?" Atlas said finally, the corner of his mouth lifting into an attempted smile. "We've got to stick together. Besides, what are friends for?"

Atlas knew immediately he had said the magic words, for Whitsom's face relaxed into a wide grin, and he clapped him on the back.

"See, I told Gai from the beginning, I've got good instincts."

Atlas turned back to his food and cut into his chicken, trying very hard to shove down the nagging sense of guilt twisting in his stomach.

CHAPTER FIVE

T owards the end of lunch his guard appeared, red-faced and furious, and Atlas had to put on his most convincing act yet.

"I thought you were right behind me, honest," he insisted, but the guard just shook his head, muttering something in a different language that Atlas would have bet his last bullet was not appropriate for the ears of children.

After lunch, following almost five solid minutes of going back and forth over the matter, Atlas made his way to Moonstone's office. It was not, he convinced himself, a betrayal to his father's agenda. No, but if there was even the slightest chance that he could corner Moonstone before he left and get his information—well, he could have his cake and eat it too, couldn't he?

As it was, Moonstone was not in her office. Nor was she anywhere near the meeting room, or the infirmary, the training yard, or outside on the grounds.

Atlas' frustration was mounting, and it was only after about an hour of wandering around that his sulky guard decided to inform him that Moonstone had gone off base for a project and would not be returning until the evening of the next day.

Atlas retreated to his room dejected. His body felt sluggish as he trudged over to the cot and collapsed atop it.

He had resolved to go after the information that

would be most beneficial to General Talikoth—to his clan—but there had still been a part of him, however small, that had hoped...

His mood remained glum the rest of the afternoon, and he stayed in his bed until Whitsom came and dragged him out to the training yard for a few rounds of sparring just before dinner. In between exchanged blows they went over their plan for the following morning in whispers, and by the time they made their way down to the dining hall, Atlas' melancholy over Moonstone's absence had been replaced by a mixture of nervousness and excitement.

That entire evening, he was antsy. He struggled to fall asleep, and once he did, his slumber was interrupted by strange dreams in which Talikoth stood across a courtyard screaming something. But Atlas couldn't hear over Moonstone and Whitsom standing on either side of him, shouting in his ears.

He was awoken early the next morning, jittery and on-edge, by the sound of voices outside of his door.

"—thought Bowduck was scheduled this morning?"

"Yeah, he came down with a bug last night, so I got asked to cover last minute," came Whitsom's reply. Atlas sprang out of bed, pulling on his sweater and rubbing the sleep out of his eyes.

"It's been quiet, should be no trouble. Have a good shift!"

The departing guard's footsteps fell heavy against the floor, growing farther and farther away, until Atlas could not hear them. Hardly a beat passed before Whitsom threw open the door, his quarterstaff slung over his shoulder.

"Ready?" he asked. Atlas nodded, following him into the corridor and towards the stairwell.

Whitsom led the way down the many winding corridors. Though they looked annoyingly similar, Atlas was starting to remember his way a little better. They'd almost reached the infirmary when Whitsom suddenly stopped, glanced in either direction, and leaned against the wall next to a grey door, not twenty feet from the infirmary entrance.

Bewildered, Atlas followed his lead. On the other side of the wall they leaned against, something shuffled, then came a thud and a muffled curse. No more than thirty seconds passed before the door opened, and Gaiomere emerged.

Atlas blinked. She wore dark pants and the traditional Vedas blue jacket. Her wild hair was carefully pulled back from her face in a tight braid down her back, not a flower in sight. As strange and foreign as her usual Ren garb was, Atlas had grown rather used to it.

Gaiomere blinked up at them for several moments, her brown eyes wide, and Atlas might have laughed at the astonishment on her face if he weren't so tired.

"What are you two—never mind, get in here." Before either of them could speak, she grabbed them both by the elbow and tugged them into her room, closing the door hastily behind her.

Her room looked nothing like Atlas'. She had jars and jars of plants—succulents and cacti and bristling ferns—so many that he wondered where she could have possibly gotten them. Drawings decorated nearly every inch of the wall: a massive waterfall, spilling tumultuously into a lake, dense stretches of forest that looked similar to the wood surrounding the Vedas' base, and a strange, rugged canyon, so deep and vast Atlas was certain it couldn't be real.

"What are you doing?" she snapped, shoving Whitsom forcefully, though he hardly moved an inch.

"Stopping you from getting yourself killed, *dummy*," he retorted, shoving her back. She stumbled a few feet, but caught herself.

"You could have gotten me caught, you idiots!" she said in an angry whisper, glaring at her older brother mutinously.

Whitsom rolled his eyes. "Psh, what, you think we're stupid or something?"

Gaiomere looked between the two of them in such a way that indicated that was exactly what she thought, and Atlas' lips pulled up at the corners.

"*Ugh*, fine," she mumbled. "I don't have time for this. But if you get in my way, I will leave you behind."

Whitsom looked like he wanted to fire back a response, but before he could, Gaiomere dug through the bag slung over her back, withdrawing her familiar notebook. She flipped open to a page on which she'd drawn a map.

Atlas and Whitsom both moved closer and peered down at her notebook. This close, Atlas couldn't help but notice that Gaiomere was tiny—the top of her head only barely reached his shoulder, though he supposed her riotous curls normally added a few inches.

"See these sections of the borders, here and here?" She pointed at each section with the tip of her pencil. "These are the portions of the fence where the electric grid doesn't quite reach—I noticed a perforation of sorts when I was looking at the maps on Jacoby's computer." She traced her pencil along the edge of the map. Atlas spotted where she had marked the entrance doors and recognized the portion of the forest that ran along the front lawns.

Gaiomere continued. "If we cut through the forest *here*, we should be able to sneak off base through one of those access points."

Atlas' inhale caught in his throat, and he had to force himself to breathe normally. That was the sort of information that General Talikoth would find invaluable. If the access points were large enough, it could be the perfect opportunity for a stealth attack.

"They could be guarded," Atlas pointed out, glancing sideways at Gaiomere.

"They could be," she agreed, slipping her hand into her bag and withdrawing something else. "And that's why I nabbed *this*."

She held up a taser, smirking a little, and Whitsom gawked at her, spluttering, "Um, okay, one, where did you get that? And two, now we're *tasing* the people who are feeding and clothing us?"

Gaiomere rolled her eyes, shoving the taser back in her bag.

"I took it from Kendo. He was...distracted." Atlas didn't miss the way her cheeks flushed. "And besides, I'll only tase them if they get in my way." She slung her bag back on her shoulder, her eyes suddenly snapping to Atlas. "Speaking of getting in my way...what are you doing here?"

He shrugged. "I wanted to help."

Gaiomere raised an eyebrow, giving him that same penetrating stare she had given him on the grounds, and he tensed. Lying to Gaiomere would not be nearly so easy as lying to her brother.

"Oh, give him a break, Gai," Whitsom said, knocking his shoulder into hers playfully. "Stop being so suspicious of everyone."

Her brows knitted together. She hitched her bag onto her shoulder a little higher, starting towards the door, and jostling Atlas as she passed, muttering, "Just as soon as he stops giving me a reason to be."

Atlas scowled as he and Whitsom followed Gaiomere out of the door and down the hall.

He fell into step with Whitsom and asked quietly, "Why do you two need to sneak out anyway? You aren't confined here, are you?"

Whitsom glanced at the back of Gaiomere's head, before replying lowly, "Moonstone doesn't want to run the risk of the Obarion discovering their base. We were blindfolded on the way in—figure they probably want to escort us out that way, too."

Atlas said nothing. If Moonstone was so concerned with protecting their base from the Obarion, why would she risk keeping Atlas there? Could her promise that she had allegedly made to his mother really mean that much?

The tug of unwillingness in the back of his mind slowed his steps for a split second. His thoughts flashed to the photograph Moonstone had shown him—all of the questions he had—

Not important, he reminded himself. Not nearly so important as getting information that General Talikoth would kill for.

It was only when they arrived outside large infirmary doors that Atlas realized Gaiomere had led them down the hall, not to the oak doors that exited onto the grounds. "What are we—"

"The entrance will be guarded at this hour," she explained. She pulled the doors open quietly and crept inside, Atlas and Whitsom on her heels. The sun peaked above the mountaintops, bathing the room in an orange glow.

"You said the windows were unbreakable," Atlas said, but Gaiomere immediately shushed him.

"Come here," she whispered. She herded the two of them into a corner, behind one of the tall privacy curtains, and said, "I've already disabled the infirmary cameras—the security footage is just reflecting a looped image to the soldiers in the control room—"

"*How* did you do that?" Whitsom said in a very loud whisper.

Gaiomere gave him a chiding glare, and explained. "I interrupted the feed."

"You interrupted the—"

But Atlas cut him off impatiently. "What's it matter if the cameras are disabled when we can't get out of the windows?"

"Leave that to me," Gaiomere said firmly. "You two wait here—do *not* make a sound. I'll be back in a moment."

She flounced across the hall without another word, and Whitsom and Atlas watched from between the folds of the curtain. Gaiomere stopped in front of a door at the end of the hall—Atlas could only assume it was Dr. Finny's office—and pounded a fist against the wood, crying, in a voice suddenly laden with distress, "Oh, Dr. Finny, please come quick!"

It was just a few moments before the door swung

open. "Gaiomere! What is it, dear?" came Dr. Finny's reply.

"I'm so sorry—I know it's so early, I just—I didn't know what to do—" Gaiomere sounded tearful. "I got up to go to the bathroom, and a couple of soldiers were —well, they were fighting in the hallway, right by the bathrooms, and—and one of them was lying on the ground and I—I wanted to help, but his neck was at such a strange angle, and there was just—there was so much blood—"

"Good heavens, these boys," Finny said, clicking her tongue. She disappeared from the doorway, returning moments later with a robe wrapped around her nightgown, and a bag of medical supplies beneath her arm. "Could you bring the stretcher, dear?"

But Gaiomere was swaying on the spot, as though she were going to pass out. "I can—I can bring it," she said weakly. "I'm sorry, it's just—I've never seen so much blood–"

Finny grasped a chair from next to a nearby bed and thrust it towards Gaiomere. "Have a seat dear, you look woozy. I'll send word to Dr. Winnipeg for help." She bustled out of the room without another word.

"Jeez-o-Pete," Atlas breathed out, as soon as the door closed behind her. He and Whitsom emerged from behind the privacy curtain and strode across the room, into the office, where Gaiomere was already unlatching a window in the corner that looked towards the forest.

"It's disgusting, isn't it?" Whitsom muttered, shaking his head. "Got me in trouble all the time—our ma and pops never believed me 'cause she could just cry on command—"

"I haven't done that since I was like seven!"

Gaiomere retorted, shooting her brother a scowl. She slid open the window and popped off the screen as she continued, "There's a ledge just beneath us. We'll be able to climb down from there."

Atlas slid through first, and his feet found the ledge easily. About ten feet to his left, it overlapped another ledge on the second level, where he could climb down. The platforms were wide, extending about three feet from the side of the building, but their distance from the ground still made his heart race.

Atlas clambered down from the third-floor ledge, stumbling a little. Adrenaline shot through him as he caught himself against the wall.

The morning air nipped at the tip of nose, and the corners of his ears, and within minutes, it felt as though his fingers were going numb.

A wave of relief washed over him when his feet finally hit solid ground. The siblings followed a few minutes behind. Gaiomere was so short that Whitsom had to help her from each level to the next, since her legs couldn't reach the ledges.

Atlas glanced across the grounds. A low mist hung over the dewy grass that would help to obscure their movements, but it also made it next to impossible to spot anyone that might be headed towards them.

"Let's get under tree cover," Gaiomere said the moment her feet hit the grass. The three of them sped across the grounds, not slowing until they reached the edge of the forest. At this hour, the dark woods looked decidedly sinister. The shadows cast on the ground shifted ominously, and the wind made the trees creak and groan with every lurch. Atlas found himself wishing that he had a weapon of his own. The taser was better than nothing, but if Gaiomere had been able to steal a *gun*...

The silence became more and more oppressive the deeper they moved into the forest. The mist slowly lifted as the sun crept higher into the sky, but the light filtering through the treetops was weak, and made it difficult to see more than ten feet in any direction.

The pair of siblings seemed significantly more comfortable moving through the woods than Atlas felt. Whitsom's shoulders were relaxed as he tossed his quarterstaff between his palms, and Gaiomere's gaze was affixed on her hand drawn map, her feet dancing proficiently over rocks and protruding roots. They hardly flinched any time leaves rustled, or branches cracked nearby.

Of course, Atlas had done his fair share of exploring the Westland, but only ever with his squadron, and never without a gun. He was shielded then, protected. Nothing could touch him as he traveled beneath the Obarion flag.

But out here, in the wilderness of the North, with nothing but his own fists and a couple of deserters, he felt helplessly exposed.

After Atlas had jumped at nothing for the fourth or fifth time, Gaiomere said, in a surprisingly gentle tone, "The last of the black bears were killed off generations ago. The only things in these woods are deer, squirrels, and raccoons. Maybe the occasional fox."

He nodded, his cheeks prickling with heat.

On and on they walked, till all three of them were sweating. Several times, Gaiomere held her map up in front of her and corrected their course, leading them deeper into the woods.

They had to have been going for over an hour when she finally muttered, "I think we're almost there." And indeed, not five more minutes passed before Atlas spotted the fence: fifteen feet ahead, twenty feet tall and topped with barbed wire identical to the fence surrounding the training yard.

"Now we've just got to find the perforation point," Gaiomere said quietly.

Atlas and Whitsom stopped on either side of her, peering at the fence. Gaiomere seemed to be searching for the point at which the electrical grid cut out, but Atlas saw another problem.

"Uh—are we going to climb this?"

She was not listening. Her hickory brown eyes had grown wide and bright with excitement, and she eagerly began scanning the ground for something.

"Help me find a big stick," she told them.

Atlas and Whitsom shared a bewildered look, before doing what she said.

"Will this work?" Whitsom asked, offering a branch the length of his arm.

"Perfect." She took it from him and turned, hurling it at the fence. It collided with a clatter, and she let out a little "*Whoop!*"

Gaiomere crossed the clearing and drew a line in the dirt where the branch had fallen, and then picked it up, repeating the same process until she had found the boundaries of where the electrical charge had malfunctioned. She tossed the branch, charred black and smoking, onto the ground beside her.

"And, *voila!*"

She turned back to Whitsom and Atlas, her face lit up with a luminescent smile. The smile promptly slipped off of her face however, upon seeing the two boys' flabbergasted expressions.

"What?" She demanded, frowning.

Atlas raised his eyebrows, looking between she and the fence, and repeated, "Are we going to *climb* this?"

She rolled her eyes. "No, we're going to fly over it."

"Gai, this fence is *massive!*" Whitsom burst out.

She looked up at the fence, awareness dawning on her face as the furrow in her brow deepened.

"I guess it is—yeah, sort of bit—I hadn't really...hmm." She whirled back on the two of them, exclaiming, "Well, *I'm* the one who came up with our escape plan. I don't see you two coming up with any ideas!"

Atlas frowned, his eyes flickering to the barbed wire atop the fence as he approached it. After a moment of thinking, he shrugged his sweater off and slung it over his shoulder. His palms felt clammy and damp, so he wiped them on his pants before grasping the chain-link fence. The long walk had, at least, unthawed his fingers, otherwise he was quite sure this would have been impossible. He stopped just a few moments in and cursed—he couldn't get a good enough grip with his feet. Dropping back to the ground, he knelt to untie his boots.

"Toss these over once I'm on the other side," he told Whitsom, before beginning to climb once more.

It was slow-going, even without his shoes. Only a third of the way up, the muscles in his arms were beginning to burn.

"It would be a shame if one of us tased him right now," Atlas heard Gaiomere mutter, and he let out a breathless laugh.

"You're about halfway now!" Whitsom called.

The fence grew less rigid the higher he climbed, and as Atlas approached the top, it began to sway. His stomach clenched when he glanced over his shoulder at the ground. If he fell now, he would probably break a bone.

Atlas gripped the sturdy metal bar that ran along the top of the fence, holding on with all his strength as his other hand—trembling and clammy—pulled his sweater from across his shoulder and draped it over the barbed wire.

"He's going to fall and die." Gaiomere sounded as though she were determined to be indifferent, but her voice betrayed just a hint of apprehension, and Atlas gritted his teeth, his concentration momentarily breaking.

"Whitsom, if you don't tell your sister to shut up, I'm going to push her off of the top of here when she climbs over." He had no energy to maintain his pretense of amiability dangling one-handed twenty feet above the ground.

To his surprise, Gaiomere laughed a full, genuine laugh, remarking, "There's the real Atlas. I knew it was only a matter of time before he came out."

He grasped the metal bar and lugged himself up, turning sideways and sliding his legs over first. His sweater covered most of the barbed wire, but the metal coils snagged his pants and the outsides of his arms. He gripped the bar as he slowly lowered his legs down, dangling until his feet caught a couple of the chain links.

"Here come your boots!" Whitsom called. He

hurled them over the fence, and they landed with a thud on the other side. Gaiomere started up the fence next.

When he was about ten feet from the ground, he let go, landing with a grunt, and walked over to where his boots had landed. Whitsom had started up after his sister, and his forehead gleamed with sweat as he climbed.

"Hey Gai, does this remind you of climbing that dried up waterfall down South?"

Gaiomere clung to the top bar, her eyes wide with evident fear, but at her brother's words, a peal of laughter slipped from her lips. "This is *nothing* like that, Whitsom!"

She had begun to swing her legs over to the other side of the fence when they heard the sound of heavy footsteps. Whitsom's eyes met Atlas' through the fence, and he swore, climbing faster.

Atlas leapt to his feet, scanning the fence line.

"I heard voices this way!" a man's voice shouted.

Whitsom caught up to his sister and scrambled down past her, and Atlas moved towards the fence.

"Here, come on, jump," he called up to Gaiomere.

She looked down with a mixture of disbelief and terror. "Are you *insane*? I'm not going to—"

The footsteps grew closer, and Atlas snapped impatiently, "I won't let you fall. And anyway, you're fifteen feet above the ground—even if I didn't catch you, you're not going to break your neck."

"I'm not jumping! You think I *trust* you, you selfish, backstabbing, Obarion—"

But the decision was made for her, because at that moment, several guards emerged from the thicket, and her fingers slipped from the chain link. Atlas surged forward, letting out a grunt, the air knocked from his lungs as she slammed into his chest, but he managed to stay on his feet.

Whitsom landed a second later, snatching up he and Gaiomere's shoes.

"Let's go, let's go, let's go!" He grabbed his sister's arm, and the three of them bolted under the cover of the brush. A succession of loud bangs made Atlas' blood run cold as bullets ripped through the foliage.

"Are they *shooting* at us?" Gaiomere panted, a few strides behind Atlas and Whitsom.

"The perimeter guards have guns!" Whitsom shouted back. The three of them sprinted through the forest, leaping over roots and fallen trees, until the shouts and gunfire faded into the distance.

"Think we lost them?" Whitsom asked him as they slowed to a jog. Atlas nodded, stooping as he attempted to recover his breath. Gaiomere withdrew a bottle of water from her bag and passed it to Whitsom first, before she offered it to Atlas.

So much for the Vedas not killing children, Atlas thought, scowling.

"I don't think they recognized who we were, otherwise I don't think they would have shot," Whitsom said, as though he had been reading Atlas' mind. Atlas said nothing, taking a long sip of water.

"I think they still would have," Gaiomere muttered angrily. "You've seen how protective the Vedas are of their base and their information. And the Obarion are the same way. They'll kill whoever they need to in order to keep their secrets."

"It's only to keep their people safe," Atlas snapped before he could stop himself.

Gaiomere shook her head, saying. "It isn't about safety, otherwise there'd be no separate bases and secrets in the first place. The safest thing for the people would be an *end* to the Long War, for the clans to merge and reach a compromise."

Atlas rolled his eyes. "It's not that simple. Don't be naive—"

Her face darkened, and a flare of fury ignited in her eyes. *"Don't* call me naive—"

"That's enough, guys," Whitsom said sharply, looking uncharacteristically aggravated. "Just give it a rest. We've got a long way to go."

Gaiomere nodded in agreement, sitting cross-legged on the forest floor as she pulled out her map. "We've got at least twenty-five miles to get out of range of the area that Moonstone's soldiers have already searched."

"And you're certain they wouldn't be in that area?" Atlas asked, taking another sip of water.

"Positive." She glanced up at Whitsom. "If I know them well as I think I do, I'm certain they would have gone to the Crystal Cave."

Whitsom's face lit up, and he sprang to his feet.

"Of course they would have." He turned to Atlas, explaining, "We found this cave up in the mountains about four moons ago—real secluded, with lots of food and water in the surrounding area."

Atlas frowned. "Why'd you leave?"

The siblings shared a dark look, and Whitsom opened his mouth to answer, but then just shook his head, turning his back on Atlas and Gaiomere. His shoulders were taut, and his hands clenched into fists. Gaiomere leaned forward, and explained in a low voice.

"There used to be five of us. Me, Whit, Maggi, Rasta, and Gwena. She was—" She bit her lip, glancing at her brother, before amending, "She *is* Whit's girl. We were out foraging one day, and the Obarion, they—they took her."

She sighed, closing her notebook with a snap. "That's why we were headed down south. We figured maybe we could help her escape the Obarion base, or that we'd run into her if she'd escaped on the way. We had just hit the landmines when we ran into another group of Obarion, and the Vedas captured us—"

"*Rescued* us," Whitsom interjected. Gaiomere shot an exasperated look at the back of his head, but said nothing, shoving her notebook back into her bag.

Atlas stopped listening. He'd thought his clan never sent units this far north, but this was the second occasion he'd heard of them doing so.

Not, he reminded himself, that he was privy to *all* of the goings-on at Headquarters. General Talikoth had made it clear that the fact that Atlas was his son would give him no special treatment, so Atlas had to earn his title of Squad Captain the same way that anyone else would. And because of this, he also hadn't yet earned a place in the Inner Ring—the branch of the Obarion army reserved for Talikoth's best-trained soldiers—and it was they that received the most critical and classified information when it came to the Obarion troops' operations. If it had been a squadron of Inner Ring soldiers infiltrating the North, Atlas certainly would have been none the wiser.

"If she was taken to Obarion headquarters she would have been sent to work on the Rigs," Atlas said.

Whitsom turned back to face them, his expression

brightening considerably, though Atlas wasn't sure why. Work on the oil rigs was brutal, though he supposed it was a step up from being dead.

Gaiomere did not look as convinced, but she managed a weak smile when her brother glanced at her. "We've got to head northwest," she told them. "We should arrive at the Crystal Cave sometime around nightfall."

The first hour of the trek was uphill, and the foliage grew so thick that the ground beneath them was almost completely obscured at times.

Soon the sun rose high in the sky. The three of them had all shed their jackets and sweaters, and Whitsom had stripped off his shirt, sweat glinting on the skin of his back.

Atlas wondered, an hour and a half into their journey, if Gaiomere had brought any food or water in that backpack of hers. The water was half-empty the last time he had taken a sip, and from what he understood, it would take at least a few days to recover their lost comrades, and that wasn't even accounting for Atlas' journey south.

He was just about to voice his concern when Whitsom suddenly stopped and held up a hand.

"Do you hear that?" he mused.

Atlas glanced at the shorter boy. His eyes were narrowed, and he tilted his nose towards the sky like a dog trying to catch a scent.

Before either Atlas or Gaiomere could respond, Whitsom started moving again, faster now. Gaiomere practically jogged to keep up. Several minutes passed, before they emerged into a clearing. Along its opposite edge ran a small river.

"*Whoop*, that's my big brother!" Gaiomere cheered, leaping onto Whitsom's back and squeezing him around the shoulders. He sniggered, carrying her towards the river. "We called him Whitsom the Wolf back home. Nobody can hunt like him," she added to Atlas, who trailed behind them.

They stumbled over the riverbank rocks, and Gaiomere hopped down from her brother's back, kneeling beside the water to splash her face.

"So if Whitsom hunted, were you the only one that didn't eat meat, then?" Atlas asked her.

Whitsom barked a laugh. "Oh, good grief, don't get her started—"

"*None* of us ate meat, none of us!" Gaiomere burst out, straightening up so quickly that her backpack slipped from her shoulders and landed in the rocks at her feet. "And then the *moment* we get to the Vedas base, Whitsom is eating it for breakfast, lunch, and dinner—"

"I'd been wanting to for years, in my defense," Whitsom protested, flopping onto his back. "It just tastes so *good*—"

"Yeah, I bet the Flesh Flayers say that too," Gaiomere grumbled under her breath, as her fingers deftly undid her braid.

"Hey, that's different—"

"I'm just saying that if I can sustain myself without animals having to *die* for my benefit—"

"They would die either way," Atlas interrupted, catching the water bottle that Whitsom tossed in his direction and giving him a grateful nod. "It's just the life cycle. Would you fault a wolf for killing its prey so its cubs could eat?"

"We aren't *wolves*," Gaiomere snapped. She carded

her fingers carefully through her long curls, piling them high atop her head in a bun. "We have the consciousness to *choose*. A wolf can't contemplate the morality of its choices. A higher capability for intellectual reasoning constitutes an obligation for responsible stewardship."

Atlas sat back on his haunches, his eyes flickering over her face. She was such a strange, contradictory creature. Morally sanctimonious in all her scruples—on paper, anyway. Yet he had seen with his own eyes her refusal to let anything get in the way of her own ends.

"I'm going to take a piss," Whitsom interjected, clambering to his feet and wandering into the foliage. Both of them ignored him.

"We're animals, at the end of the day," Atlas reasoned, sitting up a little straighter. "You wouldn't take a life, if Maggi or Rasta were endangered?"

She blinked, frowning as though she'd never thought about it before.

"I would do whatever I needed to, in order to keep my family safe," she conceded.

He nodded. "Of course you would. That's not a moral issue. That choice doesn't arrive after a deep contemplation on the obligations for responsible stewardship. That's animal instinct."

Gaiomere stared at the ground for several moments, her brow furrowed, before she shook her head, scowling at him and moving to refill the water.

"I'm not like you, you know," she said quietly. "Your people kill for the fun of it. You use people like pawns for your own amusement."

Atlas arched a brow.

"No, of course. How could I be so stupid?" he

posed. "Flirting with one of the engineers to get into the mainframe, or with Kendo to steal his taser isn't using people at all."

She whirled around on him, nearly dropping the water bottle into the river.

"I'm just—"

"Keeping your tribe safe, right," he snapped, tossing a rock from one hand to the other. "Likewise."

She stared at him a second longer, before shaking her head again and turning back to her task. Atlas frowned, looking down at the stone in his hands.

Though he had hated the Vedas for longer than he could keep track of, he had never contemplated what it meant to be hated. To be hated for being Obarion, something that he couldn't control. The injustice of it made his blood boil, made his hands curl into fists. They all assumed the same about him—the Council, Kendo, his guards, and Gaiomere. They all saw him as a bloodthirsty hound who *desired* war and chaos. But for his people war was only means to an end. General Talikoth had made that clear.

"We didn't hunt animals."

Gaiomere's voice broke through his thoughts, and he looked up sharply. Some of the anger had faded from her face, though her brows were still drawn together.

"Herbivorous animals are experts at finding food sources. Gwena made us animal traps, and covered the bottom of the traps in paint. We followed their tracks to wherever they were getting food . Sometimes it was only grass or inedible plants—but sometimes we would find berries, potatoes, onions, dandelion. We lived in harmony with them, because it was mutually beneficial."

Atlas did not miss the pointedness in her tone, but Whitsom came ambling back into the clearing before he could respond.

"Glad to see you two haven't killed each other," Whitsom quipped. Gaiomere rolled her eyes, plunking down at the water's edge and digging through her bag.

"That water—it's safe to drink, is it?" Atlas asked curiously.

In the South, the pollution was so bad that even the strongest iodine solution could not cleanse the water thoroughly enough for drinking.

"That's what *these* are for." She had withdrawn a container of dark pellets, and dropped one into the water bottle, closing it and giving it a shake. "Detoxifiers. They take about fifteen minutes to take effect, but they'll eliminate most chemicals and toxins —the ones found up north anyway."

Atlas arched a brow. "And you made them?"

Gaiomere shrugged, brushing a stray curl from her face. "It was my dad's formula, but I adjusted it to be more powerful."

They rested fifteen more minutes before resuming their journey. Gaiomere double and triple checked their map, and Whitsom managed to forage several handfuls of berries before they went on their way.

Atlas found himself immensely grateful for the cool weather in the North. In the South, the heat would have been sweltering. Judging by where the sun rested in the sky, it was quickly approaching noon.

"Do you think that Moonstone will have noticed we're gone?" Whitsom pondered. He had relieved his sister of the backpack—it was now slung over his shoulders, and he spun his quarterstaff from hand to hand as they walked.

"She'll have certainly noticed he's gone," Gaiomere said, jerking her head in Atlas' direction. "But it doesn't matter, they'll be too far behind us. Moonstone wouldn't bother sending her troops farther than twenty miles for Maggi and Rasta. She won't bother for us, either."

Atlas wondered how true that was. How desperately did Moonstone want the knowledge that the Ren—that Gaiomere—possessed?

What would Talikoth do, were such knowledge at his disposal? Would he make an exception for Gaiomere and Whitsom? Give them a place in the clan rather than banishing them to work on the Rigs like he did with the rest of their kind?

"Is it true y'all got an army of three thousand men?" Whitsom asked suddenly. He leapt atop a log and balanced along it precariously.

Atlas blinked. "Uh, yeah, but I'm not technically supposed to tell you that."

Whitsom swore. "*Three thousand men*. I've never seen that many people in my *life*—"

"It was three times larger when the Obarion started west," Atlas said. "That's what General Talikoth told me anyway. We lost six thousand soldiers on the way. And that's not even including civilian losses—women and children, too."

"How old were you?"

He shrugged. "Maybe one or two. I don't remember any of it, of course."

Morning turned to early afternoon, and on they walked. Whitsom indeed seemed to have a particular proclivity for hunting. He followed a rabbit to scavenge them wild berries and pine nuts, enough to stave off an insistent hunger, but only just. As the afternoon wore on, the water ran lower, and Atlas' feet ached something dreadful.

At some point, Whitsom and Gaiomere had started to argue, but Atlas had been too grouchy to bother listening to what their quarrel was about, until he heard his name.

"What do you think, Atlas?" Whitsom asked, glancing over his shoulder.

Atlas looked between the two of them. "Uh—what was that?"

"There's a lake directly north of us," Gaiomere explained. "Whitsom says we should head up to it, refill and see if we can find some more food. But it'll take us off our route—"

"Only half an hour or so," Whitsom pointed out. "Come on, Gai, I'm *starving*—"

"We can't afford to waste any more time," she argued, but even as she spoke, Atlas could hear the indecision in her voice.

"We'll be no good to your friends if we die of thirst," Atlas reasoned.

Gaiomere nodded slowly. "Okay, fine, but we've got to be quick."

The journey north took them mostly downhill, which would have been a relief, except for the fact that it would make their journey back rather difficult.

In a matter of minutes, Atlas saw it. Nestled between mountains on every side, its waters glinting beneath the afternoon sun, was the lake. It was not the largest lake he had ever seen—its shoreline stretched perhaps five miles northwest—but surrounded by pine trees in each direction, it embodied a serenity that he had never associated with the polluted waters of the South.

"Keep a sharp eye out," Whitsom said quietly. He gripped his quarterstaff tightly, and Gaiomere withdrew the taser from the bag, her jaw tensed.

They moved silently towards the waters' edge. The ground was made of black rock, crumbled and uneven, like it might have been a road before the bombings of the First War.

Gaiomere handed Atlas the water bottle. "I've got to go to the bathroom. Refill this, will you?"

"Don't go too far," Whitsom warned in a low voice, eyeing her retreating form apprehensively.

Atlas knelt to refill the water, the hairs on the back of his neck standing on end.

"More than just deer and squirrels around here?" he asked, feigning nonchalance.

"Maybe cougars," Whitsom said. He stood with a foot atop a large boulder, his dark eyes surveying the area. "They avoid people, if they can help it. No, we're more worried about running into other folks."

Something surfaced in Atlas' memory. "The 'Flesh Flayers' that you and your sister have mentioned?"

Whitsom nodded, looking uneasy.

"Most of the tribes are peaceful, but a few of them..." He wrinkled his nose, and his throat bobbed as he swallowed. "Story goes that right after the First War, rations were lower than they've ever been. A lot of people starved."

Atlas nodded. The Obarion called it the Great Famine.

"Well, some folks were desperate enough to stay

alive by any means necessary. My people call them 'Flesh Flayers'. They hunt down other wanderers, kill them, or sometimes eat them alive."

Atlas stared at Whitsom. His mouth dried, and his stomach turned. "How do they—I mean—how can they possibly..."

Whitsom cleared his throat.

"Dad used to say that you judge the character of a man based on what he'd do in his darkest hour." He shrugged, shifting his weight from one foot to the other. "World's always been made up of all sorts of people. Ma didn't believe people were only good or bad. But—I don't know. When I think about the Flesh Flayers I—" He shook his head, scowling. "There are things I'd never do. Anyway, that was back before the animals began to repopulate, and the plants started growing back. I guess they just got the taste for people, though, 'cuz even once there *were* other things to eat, they never stopped."

Atlas said nothing, but inside he was wondering how a person could be so desperate to stay alive that they could bring themselves to do something so horrendous.

He dug through Gaiomere's bag until he found the detoxifiers, and dropped one into the water, shaking it up, just as he'd seen her do.

Atlas had never starved in his seventeen years of life. He had been hungry, certainly, and gone without food and water, but never long enough to be desperate. Desperation, though, could make people do terrible things.

"Oh, but speaking of things I would do," Whitsom said, leaning towards Atlas and lowering his voice,

"Man, I gotta hunt." Before Atlas could say anything, he clarified, "Like *actually* hunt. I got used to all that meat back at the Vedas' base. I can't take these seeds and nuts —I've been hungry all day."

Atlas felt a wave of relief. His stomach had been grumbling for the last five hours, but he hadn't wanted to be the one to show weakness first.

"Do you know how to?"

Whitsom shrugged. He was already rolling up the legs of his pants and wading into the water.

"Can't be that hard, can it?" He raised the sharpened end of his quarterstaff, giving the taller boy a serious look. "Just watch my six."

Atlas nodded, clambering to his feet, grabbing a rock as he rose. He turned his back to Whitsom, his eyes skirting the edges of the forest, carefully looking for any signs of movement.

Behind him, Whitsom splashed around, grunting forcefully as, Atlas presumed, he plunged his makeshift spear into the water. There was a chance there wouldn't even be fish in the lake—most of the fish in the South had died off or fled to cleaner water.

A bush to his left quivered, and Atlas' hands unconsciously tightened around the rock—but it was only Gaiomere, emerging with leaves tangled in her bun.

"I found some more wild berries, and I *think* these seeds are edible..." She stopped short, her mouth popping open into a small 'o' as her eyes landed on her brother. "What are you doing?" she demanded loudly.

"Holy smokes, Gai, lower your voice!" Whitsom chided. Atlas glanced over his shoulder and saw that he had now waded into the water up to his waist. "Atlas, do not let her near me."

He was confused, at first, by Whitsom's directive—until he saw Gaiomere charging towards him, her eyes ablaze and her expression set with determination.

"We have enough food!" she snarled, making to move around Atlas, but he stepped in front of her, his arms crossed over his chest.

She looked up at him, her eyes narrowing.

"Obarion," she ground out through gritted teeth, "*Move.*"

"I'm afraid I'm under strict orders that cannot be disobeyed on pain of death," Atlas said with a straight face. Behind him, Whitsom laughed, and for a split second, Gaiomere's furious expression faltered. But then she took a deep breath, straightening up and pulling the taser from her pocket.

"Oh, you're going to tase me, are you?" Atlas asked, his lips curling into a smirk. Her eyes narrowed.

"Oh, *oh*, I got a big one!" Whitsom exclaimed excitedly from behind him. His words seemed to send a surge of courage through his sister, for her gaze became steely.

Atlas glanced back and saw a large fish thrashing and flailing on the point of Whitsom's quarterstaff.

He turned to Gaiomere with a second to spare, just as her fingers tightened on the taser's trigger. Atlas snatched it from her hands, his eyebrows shooting up to his hairline.

"You were *actually* going to tase me," he said disbelievingly.

"You shouldn't doubt me next time, Obarion," she mumbled, though her lips had pulled upwards into a reluctant smile. Atlas couldn't help but notice that she was remarkably pretty when she wasn't scowling at him.

Whitsom trudged to the shoreline, his arms wrapped snugly around the ugly, scaly creature, whose body still twitched grotesquely. He gave his sister a toothy grin. "Come on, Gai. We're grown men. You're *tiny*. Maybe you feel full after a few handfuls of berries, but you're killing us out here."

She sighed, plopping down onto a rock and pulling off her shoes.

"Obviously I can't control what you choose to put in your body," she sniffed loftily. "I just hope you've thought thoroughly about the consequences of your actions. It could have had babies for all we know!"

Atlas and Whitsom shared a mischievous grin.

"Can you imagine?" Atlas said quietly.

Whitsom puckered his lips. "Glub glub...please don't eat me...glub glub...I've got to get home to put my three hundred fish eggs to bed—"

Atlas burst out laughing, and Gaiomere tried to give them a chastening look, but the effect was muted by the laugh that bubbled from her lips.

"Really mature, Whit."

Whitsom wrapped the fish in a scrap of fabric he tore from his sweater.

"Don't worry, we'll save some for Maggi and Rasta this evening—*if* they want some!" he added upon seeing Gaiomere's face.

They set back uphill in much higher spirits, and though Atlas' stomach had only been temporarily sated by the berries and seeds Gaiomere gathered, the thought of the fish they would be feasting on in just a few hours was enough to keep him motivated as they ascended the steep mountainside.

CHAPTER SIX

"Y ou've never been to the Devil's Abyss?"

"Um—I don't *think* so. What's it like?"

Whitsom snorted. "Oh, you'd know if you'd been there."

The sun had made its way steadily across the sky, and it now began to slip behind the mountains in the far distance.

The trio scaled the peak that, according to Gaiomere, housed the Crystal Cave where they believed their friends would be hiding. Whitsom had spent the last hour and a half interrogating Atlas about his journeys with the Obarion, and he and Gaiomere seemed perplexed that Atlas had never ventured more than a hundred miles away from Obarion headquarters.

"Never been to Big Wheel?" Whitsom queried.

"Wait, wait..." Atlas frowned, racking distant memories in the recesses of his brain. He vaguely recalled a patrol route he'd run with Bettoni and Coral a year and a half ago, thirty miles south of Headquarters, near what once had been—according to the old maps —a colossal amusement park. "The giant ferris wheel tipped over on its side? Next to the—"

"The Steel Mountain!" Gaiomere exclaimed, nodding excitedly. "The one that's missing all of its tracks—"

"It's called a rollercoaster," Atlas informed her,

eager to finally offer a bit of knowledge that his companions didn't already know. "According to what I've read, anyway. Delurah had a book on them—"

"You call your ma by her first name, too?" Whitsom asked, giving him a strange look. "You Obarions are bizarre, man."

Atlas' cheeks warmed. "Oh, no. Delurah isn't my mother. She was my...caretaker, sort of. Like a nanny, I guess."

His jaw clenched, and his gaze dropped to his feet. He hoped that they would just drop it, but Whitsom still looked at him curiously. "What happened to—"

Gaiomere suddenly stopped, sliding the backpack off of her back and flinging it towards her brother. "I have been carrying this for *two hours*, you unchivalrous leech!"

Whitsom caught the bag with an incredulous look.

"You coulda just *asked nicely*, you nutcase." Nonetheless, he pulled the backpack onto his shoulders.

The two of them continued to bicker, but Atlas did not miss the way that Gaiomere's eyes flickered back to him, very briefly, before she continued up the mountain.

Atlas' brow furrowed as he studied the back of Gaiomere's head. He didn't understand how someone could be so disdainful towards him one moment and cover for him the next.

He shook his head, scowling as he followed behind the two siblings. He had never understood girls. Back at Headquarters, his best friends had all been guys, and even when Bettoni and Coral had begun to notice the opposite sex, and had begun to act strangely around girls their age, Atlas had always felt oddly disinterested. Not that he hadn't noticed pretty girls —just that any time he had the inclination to talk to one of them, Talikoth's disapproving glare would swim unrelentingly in the forefront of his mind.

"They're just a distraction," Talikoth had grunted one day when Atlas, who had been fourteen at the time, mentioned Bettoni had a girlfriend. *"You don't waste your time with distractions, Atlas. You're building a legacy."*

Whitsom stopped walking quite suddenly, his head tilting back.

"Do you smell that?" he asked Gaiomere quietly.

She stopped walking, too, her brows knitting together. "Smoke."

Whitsom nodded, gripping his quarterstaff tighter. "How far are we?"

Gaiomere peered up the cliffside through narrowed eyes. "Maybe a quarter mile. Do you think—"

But she did not get to finish her sentence, for at that moment, a piercing scream cut across the mountainside, so high and clear that Atlas was sure the person who'd emitted such a chilling sound could not have been far.

Gaiomere whirled around, her eyes finding Whitsom, and Atlas saw real fear on her face.

"Maggi," she whispered, and Whitsom nodded. The two took off, and Atlas raced after them, all three scrambling clumsily over the rock that bedecked the last stretch of the peak. He could see the fire ahead of them now, its smoke spiraling towards the sky.

Just as they came to the summit, Whitsom pulled Gaiomere behind a tree, and Atlas quickly ducked into the bushes after them, the brambles scratching at his skin. Through the foliage, he could make out two men, both at least twice his age, with scraggly hair, long nails, and dirt caked on every inch of their skin.

"Flesh Flayers," Gaiomere whispered, her voice trembling. "Where are—"

"There!" Whitsom said quietly. He pointed past the men, where two tiny figures were bound in rope. The smaller of the two was a tan little boy with messy brunette hair and a freckled face. His mouth was gagged with a scrap of fabric, and he laid on his side, his eyes wide and terrified.

The taller child—a girl with onyx black hair, pale skin, and dark, angular eyes—was being dragged by a third man towards where the other two Flesh Flayers stoked the fire. She could not have been older than eleven or twelve, but she writhed with impressive opposition in the third man's grasp.

"Whitsom, we've got to hurry—" Gaiomere started to move out of the thicket, but Whitsom pulled her back, clapping a hand over her mouth.

"Gaiomere, listen very carefully," he ordered in a remarkably calm tone. "Here's what we're going to do. You're going to give the taser to Atlas, and you're going to wait here. Do you understand?"

She ripped his hand away from her mouth and snapped, "If you think for a second I'm just going to *wait here*—"

Whitsom rolled his eyes. "Yeah, kinda figured you'd say that." Whitsom grabbed the bag before Gaiomere could stop him, fished out the taser, and tossed it to Atlas.

"Let's go," Whitsom said. Atlas nodded,

swallowing thickly as the two of them pushed through the foliage. All at once, his stomach turned, and adrenaline spiked through his veins. His fingers twitched over the trigger of the taser.

The three men had their backs turned, so they did not notice the two of them approaching. One of them, blond haired and thickly muscled, knelt over the little girl with some difficulty, as she thrashed so forcefully that he could scarcely keep a hold on her.

"*Argh...stay...still...*you little—" the man said through gritted teeth.

The other two chuckled.

"Aww, what's the matter, Saber? Is the wittle girlie *too strong* for you?"

"*Now,*" Whitsom breathed.

Atlas aimed the taser towards the Flesh Flayer nearest him and pulled the trigger. The probes shot out from the cartridge and pierced through the man's heavy sweater. He let out a cry of pain, crumbling to the ground as his body convulsed and spasmed.

Whitsom rammed the sharp end of his quarterstaff into the second man's back, and he let out a wail of agony. The man spun, unhooking a knife from the loop of his belt. He swung wildly at Whitsom, who dodged him easily, and swung his quarterstaff to slam into the Flesh Flayer's knees, knocking him to the ground.

Atlas darted towards the man he tased, still convulsing on the ground at his feet. He had tangled brown hair, and was rail thin. When the man tried to lunge for him, Atlas easily pressed a boot against his wrist, reaching down and deftly unhooking the knife from around his belt.

"That's ENOUGH!"

Atlas and Whitsom froze. The blond man held the little Ren girl to his chest, his knife pressed against her throat. He leered once he saw that he had their attention, his teeth were blackened and rotting.

"*Now*...you two are going to turn back around and trot down that mountain, or the little girl's blood is on your hands."

The brown-haired man whom Atlas had tased rolled onto his side, groaning in pain as he started to sit up. Whitsom had stilled with his foot on the chest of the second man, the sharp end of his quarterstaff aimed directly at the man's throat, but he lifted his foot, his dark eyes trained on Maggi and the knife at her neck.

"That's it, boys," the blond man crooned. "Now drop your weapons and get out of our—"

There was a sudden flash of movement behind him, and he let out a cry of pain, toppling forward and releasing the little girl as he fell. Gaiomere stood behind him, a rock spattered with blood clutched in her hand. The little boy who had been tied up stood at her side, clutching onto the fabric of her shirt.

The momentary distraction gave the other two men just the chance they needed. They both got to their feet, and Maggi scrambled towards Whitsom, and nestled into the crook of his arm.

"You're gonna regret that, pretty thing," the second man snarled. Blood still dripped from his back where Whitsom had stabbed him, and he looked almost deranged with his stringy black hair falling into his eyes.

Without even thinking, Atlas took half a step towards the Flesh Flayers, saying, "There are about five hundred Obarion troops a mile from here."

Six pairs of eyes landed on him.

"What'd you say, boy?" The brown-haired man turned and looked him up and down. "Why the hell would we listen to you—"

"You certainly don't have to," Atlas interrupted, his face blank as his gaze fixed on the man who had spoken. "They were perhaps a half mile behind us when we came up the mountain, and headed directly this way —but if you'd rather take your chances..."

The two men looked at each other. The first looked uncertain, but a flicker of fear crossed the second man's face.

"He's bluffing," the stringy-haired man said, his eyes narrowing. "'Member, Mack snuck into the Obarion's camp for food once, 'fore he was caught and killed—they don't ever come this far North. 'Sides, these kids ain't Obarion—"

Atlas arched an eyebrow.

"See for yourself," he said coldly. "But fate bends to the will of the Obarion people."

It was a long-shot, Atlas knew, but he could see on their faces that his words landed where they meant to. The first man's eyes widened, and the second man stumbled backwards, as though he had been burned.

"He's not fibbin', Cruce. Let's get out of here. They could be here any minute."

The two of them peeled off, glancing over their shoulders every few moments as though they expected Atlas to chase after them. The anxiety in his chest began to ease, and he let out a heavy breath.

"That was terrifying—" he began, glancing back at the others, but broke off when he saw Gaiomere and

Whitsom both staring at him.

"What?" he asked.

"Um—what was *that*?" Whitsom burst out. He bounced excitedly on the balls of his feet, as though he had just witnessed an invigorating sparring match.

"Wait—what?"

"You just like…made a couple of Flesh Flayers scamper off like overgrown puppies!" Whitsom snickered. Maggi and Rasta both giggled, though their faces were still very pale.

Atlas shrugged, his gaze dropping to the knife he had stolen as he turned it over in his hand.

"It was nothing. I just—well, that was luck, really —"

"I thought you were very brave," Rasta said quietly.

His voice seemed to bring Whitsom and Gaiomere back to their senses. Whitsom's face lit up as he enveloped Maggi in a hug, and Gaiomere pulled Rasta into her arms, squeezing him so tightly that he let out a little, "*Oof.*"

"We thought you two were goners for sure," Whitsom mumbled into Maggi's hair.

The little girl seemed to regain some of her wits, for she rolled her eyes. "You shouldn't have worried. You know I carry the weight of this tribe."

Whitsom smacked her lightly on the back of the head, and Atlas snorted.

Both of the children looked at him. The little boy's eyes were wide as he tugged gently on Gaiomere's arm, asking quietly, "He's a…friend?"

She frowned, glancing sharply at Atlas before muttering, "He helped us find you."

"But he's Obarion," Maggi said, peering at him

curiously. "He doesn't look like what I thought an Obarion would look like."

Whitsom wiped some of the blood off of his quarterstaff as he asked, "What did you expect them to look like, Mags?"

She shrugged, moving across the clearing to collect a small black bag that lay near the Flesh Flayers' fire pit.

"I don't know. Long pointed ears. Fangs. Sharpened talons."

The two siblings burst into laughter, and a reluctant smile tugged at Atlas' lips.

"We don't get the fangs till we come of age," he said dryly.

"Y'all been in the cave all this time?" Whitsom asked.

Maggi shook her head. "We only just made it a few days ago. It took us weeks to travel here from the land mines—we had to move extra slow to make sure we stayed out of sight."

Whitsom nodded, taking Maggi's bag from her and tossing it onto his back.

"Let's get out of here—they might come back once they figure out Atlas was lying. We'll head down the mountain and find a place to camp for the night."

He threw an arm around either of the children, leading them back towards the thicket, and Atlas started to follow them, but stopped short.

Gaiomere stood very still, her eyes intent on the third man who lay prone and unmoving, blood trickling from beneath his matted blond hair at the point where she'd struck him.

"Gaiomere?" Atlas asked quietly. She jumped, her

gaze darting over to him. Her eyes were wide, rather like a frightened baby doe, and her hands were trembling.

"You okay?"

She swallowed, absently wringing her quivering hands in front of her. They had blood on them too.

"I killed him," she said softly.

Atlas looked between she and the fallen Flesh Flayer. "He might just be unconscious."

She shook her head. "I felt for his pulse."

He clenched and unclenched his jaw, and cast a brief glance down the mountain towards her brother. Whitsom would know what to say—he dealt with emotions significantly better than Atlas.

He rubbed absently at the back of his neck. Still, he felt remiss not saying *something*.

"He was going to kill Maggi," Atlas reasoned. "You saved her life."

Gaiomere's brow furrowed, and she hiked her backpack up onto her shoulders, moving away from the Flesh Flayer's corpse.

"I'm glad she isn't dead," she said slowly. "But...but it's not like her life has more value than his..."

Atlas frowned as he fell into step with her. He couldn't tell if she was stating a matter of fact, asking what he thought, or considering the question for herself. Not that it mattered. It wasn't as though he'd ever given much thought to whose lives meant more than others.

"The Flesh Flayers have no qualms about slaying whoever crosses their path," Atlas mused. "In a way, your actions probably saved other lives." She didn't look convinced, so he pressed on, "Have you ever read any of this land's history?"

She gave him a patronizing glance. "We didn't exactly have the luxury of carting around a library of information, Atlas."

"Well, right before the First War, President Krev had accumulated so much power that no one could really stand up to him. He was slaughtering his opponents in droves, and it was estimated that by the end of his life span—according to what I've read—he had killed or ordered the death of around seventeen million people."

"That's horrible."

"It was. I'm sure more would have died, if he hadn't been assassinated before the start of the First War. Imagine how many more people he would have killed under the guise of defending his nation." Gaiomere said nothing, but her brows were drawn together, and he could tell she was listening intently to what he said. "However wrong murder may be on an individual level, that assassin—Masaweli, was what they called him—potentially saved the lives of millions more people."

They had almost caught up to Whitsom and the children, whose laughter drifted back to the pair of them, but Atlas didn't pay them any mind.

Gaiomere gave him a shrewd look, her eyes narrowing imperceptibly.

"And that's the Obarion place in history too, is it?"

Atlas' lips twitched. He had not been so discreet, it seemed, that she had not been able to see through to his authentic intentions.

"War is means to an end. The Obarion want peace. This is just the path we have to take to get there."

Gaiomere shook her head. "Some ends aren't

worth the means, Atlas."

Before he could ask her what she meant, Whitsom called, "'Bout another two miles and we'll park it for the night!" Gaiomere cast him an indiscernible frown, and lengthened her strides to catch up with their companions.

The sun fell rapidly, until it became difficult to see. Gaiomere and Maggi began to collect firewood as they walked, and Atlas hurriedly followed their lead. He didn't particularly like the idea of wandering around an unfamiliar wood after dark, even with his newly-claimed knife secured to his belt.

They stopped in a thick grove of trees, and the Ren moved in to a sort of practiced dance so fluid that Atlas couldn't help but admire it. Rasta and Gaiomere piled leaves and pine needles on the forest floor. Atop the leaves they carefully constructed a pyramid of small twigs and branches, leaning against one another.

"Toss me your knife, will you, Atlas?" Whitsom called. He obliged, and the shorter boy began to carve a notch into one of the logs. He carried it over to their makeshift fire pit , and whittled a spindle from one of the twigs the girls had gathered. Atlas watched in fascination as he rubbed the spindle between his hands rapidly, until the friction gave rise to a small coil of smoke.

Atlas moved across the clearing to where Maggi was working. She unwound a long wire from inside her pack, and strung it between several trees' trunks, encircling their camp site. When she was finished, she tied off the wire and threaded it around a large rock, placing it a few feet away on the ground and piling a stack of additional rocks on top.

"What are you doing?" he asked her quietly.

She glanced up at him. "It's a tripwire. If anyone tries to attack us in the middle of the night, hopefully we'll hear them before they make it closer than ten feet."

Atlas' eyebrows shot up to his hairline. "That's clever."

Maggi shrugged. "Gaiomere taught me."

He nearly rolled his eyes, but refrained. "Of course she did."

Nearly half an hour later they had a real fire going. Atlas and Whitsom dragged over a couple of logs for the five of them to sit on, and when they returned, Maggi passed out handfuls of pine nuts and berries.

"Collected these on our way up north," she explained.

"You have to tell us everything," Gaiomere said, casting Whitsom a disapproving glance as he began to unwrap the fish beside her. "What happened once we were separated?"

"Well, after you told us to take off, we ran all the way to the Claw. We waited a bit and then decided to double back—see if we could find you. When we returned, the Obarion had gone, but so had you two. We waited there about twelve hours, but when you didn't return, I figured we probably shouldn't stay in one spot too long. And then we saw some Vedas troops, and decided we'd better get out of there."

Gaiomere muttered a swear word under her breath. "Those were the troops Moonstone told us she'd sent to look for you. Oh, Whit, I *knew* we should have gone ourselves—"

"*We* couldn't have done anything," Whitsom

interrupted, giving his sister a reprimanding frown as he explained to Maggi and Rasta, "Gaiomere got a side blast from one of the landmines. Her leg was torn up, she couldn't walk at all. That's why we went with the Vedas—they said they could provide her medical care. But then they just sort of...." He trailed off.

"Wouldn't let us leave," Gaiomere finished, leaning forward and stoking the fire. "We had to sneak out to come find you two. But never mind that—how was your journey north?"

"Not bad, for the most part," Maggi said, as she plopped down on the log next to Atlas. "We mostly kept to the trees. Water was the trickiest thing to figure out, since you had the detoxifiers when we got separated. We didn't want to boil it—fire could draw unwanted attention—so we ended up just taking the risk. Rasta got sick twice, but he puked it all up and came out okay."

The little girl hesitated, shifting uncomfortably on the log as she glanced up at Gaiomere. "There's um—there's something else too."

"What is it?"

Maggi looked at her feet, her black hair falling like a curtain around her face.

"Um...we hit the Dead Land on the way up, and we —well, we ran out of food pretty quickly. Our passage took longer than I thought it would. We had—we had gone without food for about four days."

Gaiomere and Whitsom looked at each other, wearing identical expressions of guilt.

"I'm *so* sorry, Mag," Gaiomere said. "We should have left to find you so much sooner—"

"No, it's not that," Maggi said, her ebony eyes round like saucers. "It's just that I—we were starving, so

I—I caught a rabbit—made a trap, you know—and we—we ate it."

She stared at Gaiomere silently, like a criminal awaiting a passage of judgement. Atlas felt a smirk pulling at his lips, and when his eyes met Whitsom's across the fire, he saw that Whitsom, too, was struggling to contain his amusement.

"Oh, Maggi," Gaiomere said softly. "I—I'm so glad you did. I never would have wanted you to starve."

"But—but I'm no better than the Flesh Flayers!" Maggi wailed, suddenly bursting into tears. Atlas briefly considered patting her on the head, but thought better of it.

Gaiomere rushed around the fire, sitting down on Maggi's other side and wrapping an arm around her shoulders.

"Maggi, that's *not* true," she whispered fiercely. "You could've *starved*—there was nothing more you could have done." Gaiomere glared at her brother, who was cooking his fish over the fire, and added, "Besides, look at Whitsom. He's been eating meat for over a month now—you're no worse than him."

"Oh *great*," Maggi mumbled tearfully. "When I'm being measured against Whitsom, that's when I know I'm really losing at life."

Gaiomere and Atlas laughed, and Whitsom chucked a chunk of bark at Maggi's head.

Whitsom made a bed of leaves within the encircled clearing where the kids could sleep, and though Maggi insisted that she was "too old" to need a bedtime song, she snuggled up beside Gaiomere hastily nonetheless.

Atlas idly watched the flames flicker as Gaiomere's

soft voice drifted over to him. The only music he ever heard growing up were the battle drums, and the one time when he was fifteen and Coral got his hands on an instrument he called a banjo.

But Gaiomere's voice was pleasant, soothing even, and he found the tension in his muscles seeping away as he relaxed against the log.

"I can't *believe* you were so nice to her about eating the rabbit, you little brat!" Whitsom whispered once the two of them had made their way back over to the fire. "You tore me to *shreds* when you first found out I'd been eating meat."

"Yeah, because you aren't a twelve-year-old girl, doofus. I figured you could take it." She sank down onto the ground cross-legged and grabbed a handful of nuts. "I feel horrible, honestly. If they had starved, it would have been my fault..."

"Don't be stupid, our family hasn't eaten meat for generations," Whitsom chided gently. He hesitated, and then said, in a notably more subdued tone, "We uh—we headin' back down south tomorrow?"

Gaiomere arched an eyebrow. "Try not to sound so upset about it—"

"No, I—I'm not," Whitsom said quickly. "I just... learned a lot the last couple months—my fighting's gotten loads better—Kendo said so—"

"So you'd rather stay and learn to fight than rescue your girlfriend?" Gaiomere said furiously.

"I'm not *saying* that," Whitsom said, scowling.

"You sure? Cause if it's more convenient for you *I'll* go down south and find Gwena, and you can stay here and play soldier."

Atlas sensed a full-scale blowout on the verge of

inception, so he hastily interrupted. "Do you know how to get to Obarion headquarters?"

"We have an ally tribe on the Fringe," Gaiomere explained. "They're well-acquainted with the Obarion."

Atlas' mind was moving quickly. If he separated from the Ren now, he'd be forced to return to General Talikoth without the information he'd sought. He could give his clan the general location of the Vedas base—but even that felt like scraps compared to everything that Gaiomere knew.

"I can show you where the Rigs are, once we make it through the Pass," Atlas offered.

The siblings looked at him.

"You'd do that?" Whitsom asked, smiling brightly.

"Why?" Gaiomere added suspiciously.

Atlas shrugged. "I don't know the way back to the South," he admitted. The lie came easily, probably because it wasn't actually a lie—it just wasn't his true motivation for staying with them.

"We're *not* traveling all the way to the Fringe with him," Gaiomere said firmly, for her brother looked contemplative. "Whitsom, for all we know he'd turn us over to Talikoth as soon as we got within ten miles of their base—"

"Atlas wouldn't do that!" Whitsom insisted.

"I wouldn't do that," Atlas said simultaneously.

Gaiomere rolled her eyes, blowing a curl from her face. "Look, traveling to the South is dangerous enough. Taking an Obarion with us would just be painting a giant target on our backs—"

"*Or* it would keep up safe," Whitsom said. "Think about it—maybe being with Atlas would be just the cover we need to get in and out safely."

Atlas shifted uncomfortably where he sat. He wasn't sure *that* was necessarily true. He was only a Captain, and didn't have any sway with the higher-ups, regardless of who his father was. His station wouldn't be enough to stop any Obarion soldiers from questioning them, and it certainly wouldn't be enough to get a Renegade released from the Rigs.

Gaiomere was gazing at him with knitted brows, her lips curled into a frown. "Why would you help us?"

Atlas cleared his throat. "Well, I sort of owe you, don't I? You helped me get off of the Vedas base—"

"And you helped us find Maggi and Rasta," Gaiomere retorted. She tilted her head to the side, her brown eyes narrowing. "Looks like we're even."

"But if you guide me back to the South, we won't be," Atlas said quickly. "I'll owe you again—"

"*And*, if you think about it," Whitsom interjected. "If we're weighing importance here—" He held his hands up in front of them as though they were a scale. "Escaping the base of people that weren't even hurting him—helping us save our friends from being cannibalized—I'm pretty sure we still sorta owe him."

This evidently had been the wrong thing to say. Gaiomere blinked, looking slowly over at Atlas, and her eyes flashed, just for a moment, with pure, unadulterated hatred.

"No," she said, her voice trembling as she got to her feet. "I don't owe him anything."

She strode off before either of them could stop her, stepping carefully over the tripwire and disappearing into the dark. Atlas watched her go, anger and confusion and irritation all swelling up inside him simultaneously.

"Don't take it personally," Whitsom said. "I've never told you this, but our dad—he was killed by the Obarion."

Atlas' head jerked towards Whitsom so quickly that his neck cracked. "I—your—your dad? Really?"

Whitsom nodded, the ghost of a smile around his lips. "Didn't want to mention it to you 'cause I didn't want you lookin' at me like *that*."

Atlas quickly schooled his features. "Like what?"

"Like you're guilty," Whitsom said. "'Cause you're not. Guilty, I mean."

Atlas rubbed his palms against the tops of his pants. He *felt* guilty. Guilty and ashamed and dirty, all at once.

"Why don't you hate me?" Atlas demanded. "That's why she does, isn't it?"

Whitsom shrugged. "You wouldn't have been older than—what—eleven, twelve, when it happened? You weren't even fighting yet." He shook his head, stoking the fire. "And for the record, she doesn't hate you. Gaiomere is...younger than me. A little more immature, though she'll never admit it. I think she feels like if she's kind to you, it's dishonoring his memory or something. Which is...sort of insane, actually. 'Cause Dad was the most forgiving person that ever walked the earth."

He laughed, a little wistfully.

"I remember once, when I was ten or so, we found an Obarion soldier—said he'd been left for dead by the Lieutenant General, 'cause his injuries would make their journey too slow or something. Anyway, Dad spent twelve hours patching him up, just talking to him, asking about his life."

Whitsom shook his head again, still smiling. "Gaiomere was like that. She was so...*happy*. And then Dad died, and she kinda just...shut down. She just got really *angry* and started trying to do everything on her own." He gave Atlas a sideways look, insisting, "So, really, it's not personal."

Atlas nodded, glancing up as the girl in question wandered back into the clearing. She did not look in their direction, but laid down beside Maggi, her wild hair covering her face.

"We'll take you south—I'll talk her into it," Whitsom promised. "Get some sleep." He found a spot about ten feet away and sprawled out across the forest floor.

Atlas laid down too, shivering a little as the fire began to die down. He'd forgotten to grab his sweater off the fence as they'd fled the Vedas base, and he was regretting it now.

He stared blankly up at the infinite stars hanging above them. Gaiomere's words kept playing over and over in his mind, and every time he closed his eyes, all he could see was the way she had looked at him. As though he could drop dead and it wouldn't be enough to satisfy her loathing. It was not until many hours had passed that sleep finally claimed him.

CHAPTER SEVEN

A tlas wiped his perspiring brow as he took another sip of water. The sun beat down on their backs oppressively, and the Renegades had all shed their sweaters. He found himself yearning for the cold that had numbed his fingers and toes the night before.

That morning it had taken Whitsom almost an hour to talk Gaiomere into letting Atlas travel with them. Because of their delayed start, they were only a couple hours into the journey and it was already approaching noon.

Gaiomere had set them on a route that would take them back along the lake they'd stopped at on the journey out, before they veered directly south.

Rasta was slung over Whitsom's back, his head drooping tiredly against Whitsom's shoulder as he asked, "Why do we have to go this way?"

"We've got to restock our food and water supply enough to get us to the southbound river," Gaiomere explained patiently, from where she walked beside Whitsom. "It's about forty miles from the lake. Once we make it to the river, we can follow it south for at least a couple of days."

"We should come back up here, after we've found Gwena," Rasta said. "I like it up here."

"There does seem to be a lot more water," Maggi mused aloud. She was leading the group, and Atlas walked behind her. "It'd be nice to be so close to the

Crystal Cave."

"Where did you guys stay before you found the cave?" Atlas asked curiously.

"Further south," Whitsom said. "Not as far as y'all. We usually hang around the northern border of the Pass —closer to the coastline."

"We've been through the Pass, but only a couple of times," Gaiomere added. "We're originally from the East, though."

Atlas looked up, surprised. "East? You were born in the East?"

"Not like the *East*, east." Whitsom amended. "Just like—whatever's east of the Westland."

"Near the Devil's Abyss," Gaiomere told him. She looked pensive for a moment, before she clarified, "Maybe...five hundred miles from Big Wheel and the... rolling coaster?"

Atlas smiled a little, but decided not to correct her. He thought for a moment, recalling the maps he'd perused in the Obarion library. "*Oh*, there. They used to call it the Grand Canyon, from what I've read. You had a drawing of it in your room at the Vedas' base."

Gaiomere glanced sideways at him, and Atlas' cheeks flushed. He hastily scrambled for something to say to mask his embarrassment. "They say it's haunted. Is that why the Renegades call it the Devil's Abyss?"

Whitsom was the one who answered. "Our mother told us the canyon tribes placed offerings in the river once a month...to keep the canyon spirits appeased. She told us back at the start of the First War people pitched themselves off the side of the canyon in droves—they say there are so many restless spirits roaming the bottom that sometimes you can hear them crying out in the middle of the night..."

Gaiomere's head snapped sideways to glare at her brother. "You're a jerk!"

Whitsom's eyes widened innocently, though a mischievous smirk twitched around the corner of his mouth. "What? I didn't think those stories still scared you."

"I'm *not* scared—you're frightening Rasta!"

Rasta lifted his head from Whitsom's shoulder to give Gaiomere a bewildered look. "I'm not frightened—"

"Whatever," Gaiomere mumbled, shoving her brother and striding haughtily ahead until she'd caught up with Maggi.

Atlas was still enthralled with how many different places they had lived, and his mind swam with dozens of questions. "Why did you come west?"

"Dad was something of a chemist, and he was trying to figure out a better way to get people drinkable water," Whitsom answered. "We kept coming across people that were getting sick from the rivers and lakes, so he started experimenting with uh—something to do with salt—"

"Desalination," Gaiomere supplied.

"Yeah, that. Anyway, he needed saltwater to experiment with, and I suppose we *could* have gone any direction and hit the ocean eventually, but west was the closest—so west it was."

Atlas nodded slowly, his thoughts racing. The Ren had traveled west for water, the Obarion had traveled west for other resources. Was there anything left of the East, or had it all been destroyed and abandoned, like the fallen cities that dotted the coastline? Could it really be that there was *no one* else out there, or had they all just gone into hiding, like the Ren?

"I was born in the East," he mentioned off-hand. "Much further east, though. Over a thousand miles from here." He saw Gaiomere's roused curiosity and clarified, "I don't remember it though. I was just a baby."

"Is it a thousand miles to the Warm Ocean?" she asked, her brown eyes bright.

He smiled. "Closer to three thousand miles. No, not that far east. Texas."

Whitsom shot him a bemused glance. "What the *hell* is a Texas?"

"That's what it used to be called," Atlas explained. "Before the First War and everything."

"What if we went back?" Maggi asked suddenly. "Not *that* far east, I mean, but to the Devil's Abyss?"

"I don't think it's so safe anymore. Last winter Raider told me it's Flesh Flayers territory now," Gaiomere said.

"Oh, well if your *boyfriend* said it, it must be true," Whitsom quipped.

Gaiomere turned and threw the water bottle at him. It collided with his chin.

"*Ow!*" he exclaimed, glaring at her as he leaned down and snatched up the bottle off the ground.

"Not my boyfriend," she snapped, whirling around and setting off again.

A wave of an emotion that Atlas couldn't quite pin down swelled in his chest.

"One of your other tribe members?" he asked in an indifferent tone.

Whitsom shrugged, saying "Nah, sort of like an ally tribe—though they're not really a tribe at all—"

"More like a gang of thugs," Maggi piped up,

in a tone that was decidedly reverent, rather than disapproving.

"We help each other out when we cross paths, share food and all that," Whitsom continued. "Last I heard though, Raider's gang was headed north."

"As north as you can go," Gaiomere confirmed. "We're almost to the lake. Keep an eye out." She had passed Maggi and was picking her way down the hillside deftly. The sunlight glinted off her hair, revealing streaks of honey and copper in her untamed curls.

Atlas peered past her. Down the hillside and past a cluster of trees, the lake was still. The sunlight was nearly blinding as it reflected off its surface, and the trees surrounding it swayed, their leaves rippling against the wind that carried through the valley.

"Stop!" Whitsom called suddenly.

Gaiomere, who had moved about twenty feet ahead of them, did not appear to have heard him.

"Stop!" Whitsom repeated. The urgency in his tone gave Atlas pause, and he looked sharply at Whitsom. He'd slid Rasta off his back, and gripped his quarterstaff in both hands. Gaiomere skidded to a halt too, and her brother waved her over.

"What is it?" Maggi asked nervously. She'd unconsciously drifted closer to Atlas.

Whitsom pointed down the sloping hill, towards a patch of trees. The foliage shifted, and several figures moved in and out from behind the evergreen trunks. If Atlas focused, he could hear the echo of their voices. They weren't even trying to avoid detection. Which meant—

"Let's get under cover," Whitsom said. Gaiomere

put an arm around Maggi and Rasta's shoulders, pulling them along, and Atlas took up the rear. His hunger had instantly vanished, and his heart pounded in his chest. The knife between his fingers felt suddenly minuscule, the blade too dull, and the handle slippery in his sweaty grasp.

His eyes stayed affixed on the group moving beneath the canopy of trees. They headed south, already almost past the point at which the five of them were descending from the mountain. If they moved slowly enough, the strangers might not even notice they were there.

He breathed in relief as they finally reached the cover of the trees. The voices had faded, and he relaxed his grip on his knife ever so slightly.

"We'll want to stay quiet," Whitsom said as they approached the water's edge. "We don't want to give them a reason to come back this way, whoever they are."

Maggi took both of the water bottles and knelt beside the water to refill them. Rasta withdrew the last of their pine nuts from Gaiomere's backpack and distributed them among the group.

"Don't think we should forage too far," Whitsom muttered, and Atlas nodded in agreement.

Whitsom waded into the water, most likely looking for another fish, and his sister stood in the middle of the clearing, her arms wrapped around herself protectively, eyes flitting from tree to tree, as though she feared an adversary would spring from the thicket at any moment.

Atlas moved to the edge of the trees, scanning the forest floor until he found a broken-off branch about as long as his arm and passably straight. He sat on a stump and began to work, nimbly whittling away at the tip of the branch with his knife. He cut and carved until it sharpened into a lethal point.

"Here," he said quietly, crossing the clearing and offering the makeshift spear to Gaiomere. She looked between him and the spear for several moments, her eyes narrowing to slits. He arched an eyebrow, adding, "Unless you'd prefer a rock again, that is. It should be sharp enough to fend off an attack."

She tossed the spear between her hands, testing out its weight, before she looked back up at him, smirking mischievously. "Should we test it out?"

He rolled his eyes, wandering back over to the tree line to search for something she could practice with.

"First you try to tase me and now you're going to spear me? If I didn't know any better, I would think you didn't like me very much."

She laughed, ruffling Rasta's hair as he handed her a few berries he had picked from a bush near the edge of the clearing.

Atlas leaned down, his lips still upturned in a smile as he pushed a few slabs of wood aside until he found one that was rotting. He started to lift it, but stopped when Gaiomere gasped.

He whirled around. A hooded figure, face wrapped in a dark scarf, had stepped into the clearing.

It was a man, based on his height and frame. He hadn't seemed to have seen Atlas, standing just within the tree line. Whitsom, who had waded perhaps twenty feet into the water, his back to the shoreline, hadn't noticed anything, and Maggi still knelt at the lake's edge, her face white as she looked between the newcomer and her companions.

Atlas realized what the man was going to do a second before he did it. In four long strides, he bound towards the masked man, blood pounding in his veins. The man opened his mouth to shout, "I FOUND—"

But Atlas slammed into him, knocking him off balance as one arm wrapped around the man's mouth, and the other encased his throat.

"One word, and I break your neck," he said quietly.

The man jerked his head back, slamming it into Atlas' face. Atlas groaned, but kept his arms locked in a vice grip. He kicked the back of the man's knees, causing him to crumble to the ground.

"I'm warning you—" Atlas tightened his grip around the man's throat, grabbing one of his arms and twisting it behind his back. The man let out a hiss of pain, attempting to wriggle his arm from Atlas' grasp.

"I...ah!   I....don't....take orders...from...filthy.....deserters!" the man gasped out. Atlas paused. Something tickled his memory.

"Who are you with?" Atlas demanded, twisting the man's arm farther.

He suddenly stopped struggling, and attempted to turn his head.

"Is that...Atlas?"

The voice's familiarity clicked into place, and Atlas loosened his grip, his arms falling to his sides.

"Bettoni?"

The man sprang to his feet, ripping the scarf from around his head, and Atlas blinked. Bettoni's rugged, copper-skinned face beamed back at him.

"Atlas! It is you!" Bettoni threw his arms around him. "Man, we thought you were dead!"

Atlas let out a breathless laugh, ruffling Bettoni's

elbow-length hair, which was gathered in an elastic at the nape of his neck.

"I thought I was, too," Atlas confessed. Bettoni clapped him on the back, still smiling broadly as he pulled away.

"Man, wait till the others get here. We saw you guys coming down the mountain—they told me to double back to cut you guys off." He shook his head, snorting disbelievingly. "Can't believe it. Cap, back from the dead."

His eyes suddenly wandered over to the four Renegades, who stood clustered in the center of the clearing. Atlas had nearly forgotten they were there. Maggi and Rasta looked relieved, but Gaiomere and Whitsom watched him and Bettoni's interaction with undisguised suspicion.

"Friends of yours?" Bettoni asked. Atlas did not miss the way his hand casually rested at the hilt of his belt, where his axe hung.

"We escaped the Vedas base together," Atlas said quickly. "They were guiding me back south—I didn't know the way, from this far north."

Bettoni nodded slowly, though the frown on his lips was telling.

"Renegades?" he asked Atlas quietly.

But before Atlas could answer, three more figures emerged from the trees. Atlas recognized Jereis—raven-haired, ghostly-pale, and rail thin—who had been in his year at Academy but assigned to a different training squad. Then there was Macky, who was two years older than Atlas, with ebony skin and a build rather like a rhinoceros. Taking up the rear, to Atlas' surprise, was Crowley, his wrinkled chalky face pinched into a scowl and his sooty grey hair lying perfectly coiffed across his head. The old man had been one of General Talikoth's most trusted advisors for as long as anyone could remember—Coral often joked that none of them needed to read any of the records documenting the events of the First War, for they could just ask Crowley.

"Look who I found, guys!" Bettoni exclaimed.

"*Ooh*, Attie the *baddie!*" Macky said, snickering as he pulled Atlas into a headlock and knuckled his hair. Atlas shoved him off, his cheeks flushing. He glanced sideways towards Gaiomere, but thankfully, her gaze was fixed warily on Bettoni, and she had not noticed anything.

Jereis hung back beside Crowley, and when he caught Atlas' eye, gave him a solemn nod.

"These are some of Atlas' comrades," Bettoni offered, jerking his head towards the Renegades. "They helped him escape the Vedas' base and were guiding him down south before we ran into them."

"Couple of turncoats, huh?" Macky said, smirking devilishly at the quartet.

Whitsom hesitated, then stepped forward.

"I'm Whitsom," he offered. His nerves were only distinguishable to Atlas because he had studied the Ren boy's mannerisms so carefully, but none of the others seemed to notice. Macky, Bettoni, and Jereis moved to introduce themselves, but Crowley hovered near the tree line, his lips curled into his archetypal sneer. Atlas crossed the clearing to shake his hand.

"Lieutenant General. I'm surprised to see you so far north."

As usual, the man's steely grey eyes felt as if they stared directly through Atlas, and he shifted uncomfortably.

"Yes, well, this mission was of utmost importance," Crowley drawled. "General Talikoth thought it best that I come along to supervise his...*soldiers*." The last word was uttered with such palpable disdain that Atlas wondered if Crowley believed that his company did not deserve such titles.

"Yeah, the general thought we needed a babysitter," Macky called with a snort. He plopped down on a log and spread his legs out, stretching with a loud yawn. Gaiomere stood barely five feet from him and watched him timidly, clutching her spear so tightly that her hands had lost some of their color.

Bettoni began to unload several pounds of food wrapped in fabric. The scent of fish wafted over to Atlas, and his mouth watered.

"We've got extra, if you guys are hungry," Bettoni said.

Whitsom sprang forward, his apprehension completely forgotten as he sat down beside the Obarion, and after a moment of hesitation, Maggi and Rasta followed him. Gaiomere, though, didn't move, her eyes flitting between the four Obarion soldiers, teeth gnawing at her lip.

Atlas moved closer to her, pretending to reach for a water bottle, and whispered, "Play it cool, Gaiomere."

She took a deep breath, and tentatively approached the group seated in the center of the clearing, talking noisily around mouthfuls of food. She sat beside Whitsom, outstretching a trembling hand for a cob of corn. Her shoulders were tense and drawn. Atlas sat down on her other side, reaching for a slab of fish. He took a bite and chewed slowly, before saying in a low voice, "When you're finished eating, I want you to take Maggi and Rasta and hide. Do you understand?"

She looked at him sharply, but then quickly looked away again, her mouth barely moving as she asked, "You don't trust them?"

His eyes roved outside of the circle, to where Crowley stood, not eating, but gazing out at the lake with an impassive expression.

"I don't trust him," he replied. "He'd order them to capture you and drag you back to the Rigs without batting an eye."

"You're their captain, aren't you?"

"He's the Lieutenant General."

Her mouth snapped shut, eyes widening as she hastily redirected her gaze back to her lap. He could sense that she wanted to argue, but the lull in the others' chatter prevented their conversation from continuing.

"So, what happened when they took you, Attie?" Macky asked, letting out a loud belch as he slid to the ground and reclined against a log.

"Well, I woke up at their base," Atlas began, his mind spinning as he tried to come up with something believable. Crowley's eyes bore into the side of his head. "Moonstone interrogated me on and off for a week or so—tried every tactic: the caring, concerned general looking out for the good of the people—"

Macky let out a bark of laughter, and Bettoni rolled his eyes, muttering, "Give me a break."

"—then when that wasn't working, she got harsher. I met these two a little over a week in, and they helped me escape."

"That easy, was it?" Crowley asked in a low,

resonant voice. His eyes narrowed, as though he were attempting to peruse the contents of Atlas' mind.

"Of course, it required some planning," Atlas lied smoothly. "I've got Gaiomere to thank for all of that."

The girl in question managed a weak smile as their eyes fell on her.

Jereis and Bettoni began to debate which one of them would last longer under torture. Whitsom stood, muttering something about going to the bathroom, and Macky slid into his unoccupied seat. He waved a fish in front of Gaiomere, giving her a crude smirk.

"Gaiomere, right?"

Her nose wrinkled as she instinctively leaned away from the dead fish, three inches from her nose. "Um...yes."

He smiled wryly. "I didn't know Vedas came so pretty."

Atlas groaned, burying his face in his hands, and Bettoni momentarily ceased his squabbling with Jereis to call, "Macky, you are an embarrassment to our entire clan!"

Macky shrugged, waving the fish in Gaiomere's face once more. "Still hungry?"

"Um...no, thank you."

"Oh, c'mon, you gotta be hungry."

She shook her head. "I don't eat animals. Sorry."

The conversation around the circle seemed to cease instantaneously. Bettoni and Jereis both turned to look at her, and Crowley folded his hands behind his back, his mouth curling up into a sinister smirk. Atlas cursed internally, his hand sliding down to clench the handle of his knife.

Macky leaned back, peering at her inquisitively.

"You don't eat animals, huh?" he mused. "That's pretty strange."

"You're Renegades," Jereis said, his voice soft, and strangely calm.

Whitsom had just walked back to the circle, but he stopped short, his hand instinctively curling around his quarterstaff as he looked between the Obarion soldiers uneasily.

"I never said they weren't," Atlas said, careful to keep his voice cool and dispassionate. "Just that they'd helped me escape the Vedas' base. They were being held prisoner, too."

Macky and Bettoni nodded, but Jereis still looked suspicious. Crowley seemed to be thinking along the same lines as the raven-haired boy, for he stepped forward, his hands folded behind his back.

"Terribly kind of a group of Renegades to provide you guidance to the South out of the goodness of their hearts." His eyes roved over the group of them, his sneer growing more and more pronounced. "I'm sure you know how difficult General Talikoth finds it to persuade the Renegades' compliance."

Atlas shrugged. "I suppose I just got lucky in my choice of allies, then."

Crowley's eyes glittered maliciously, but he said nothing, turning away from the group of them to peer at the lake once more. Atlas could still feel Jereis' stare, but he ignored him, turning to Bettoni and asking, "So what are you guys doing this far north? Did General Talikoth send you looking for me?"

Bettoni's grin faltered, and his expression became apologetic. He shuffled his feet the way he always did whenever he was uncomfortable.

"Uh—no. No, he sent us up here on recon." Trying to cover up for the moment of awkwardness, he quickly added, "Scouting the Vedas' base, you know. There's a pass, skirting the edge of the mountains, just out of the reach of the landmines. That's why it's just the four of us. We figured it'd be easier to stay out of sight if we encountered any of the Vedas' troops."

Atlas nodded, muttering a noncommittal, "That's great."

Even to his own ears, his voice sounded unconvincing, but the plummeting feeling in his stomach made it difficult to feign any level of enthusiasm. Bettoni watched him carefully, and before he could stop himself, Atlas asked, "Were there—uh—there weren't any recovery attempts made, were there?" He scratched the back of his head, trying very hard to look like he did not care about the answer, one way or another.

Bettoni looked away, muttering, "Um...not that I know of—but I'm sure there were! You know we don't know half the going-ons behind the scenes—for all I know, General Talikoth could have been out there looking for you himself!" Bettoni was trying to be kind, but his faux assurance only made Atlas feel worse.

He turned his knife over in his palms, a scowl making its way onto his face. He mumbled something incoherent even to his own ears and stood, striding over to the water's edge.

He shouldn't have been surprised, really. General Talikoth never sent out recovery for any *other* soldier missing in action—surely Atlas hadn't expected Talikoth to behave any differently for him. He didn't have any right to feel hurt. Talikoth had always been clear—he was General first, and father second. It was Atlas' own fault for forgetting that.

But try as he did to convince himself he was in the wrong here, Atlas could not push down the fierce surge of anger that burst to life in his chest. Towards General Talikoth, for abandoning him. Towards Bettoni and his squad, for arriving and alerting him of Talikoth's indifference to his supposed death. Towards Moonstone, for dragging him into this mess with all her tall tales of *promises* and loyalty to the dead.

And then quite suddenly, his anger shifted towards his mother. His mother, who he could scarcely remember, but somehow, he just *knew* that if she were still here, he would not be stuck in this situation. He would not be traversing the woods of the North with a band of Renegades. He would not be forced to tell duplicitous tales to Moonstone in one moment to protect his clan, and to his clan in the next, to protect the people he'd come to know as friends. He would not have been abandoned by a father who only cared for him if he was useful. Or perhaps he would have, but it might not have hurt so bad, if only she had been there to provide condolence.

"I gotta take a whiz!" Macky announced loudly. Atlas glanced over his shoulder and vaguely watched the large boy clamber over the log and disappear into the foliage. Jereis and Bettoni were discussing something in whispers, both of their faces tense. At one point, they glanced over at him.

Atlas frowned. Crowley stood stock-still at the edge of the clearing, and Whitsom sat atop the log Macky had abandoned, and casually sharpened the end of his quarterstaff.

"How many of them have guns?"

He nearly jumped when Gaiomere stepped up beside him, her backpack hanging open in her hands as she loaded their water bottles into it. She had piled her hair up into a bun atop her head, and her spear lay on the ground at her feet.

"I thought I told you to go," he said exasperatedly.

She rolled her eyes. "Last time I checked you weren't *my* captain."

Perhaps it was the residual anger in his system, but he suddenly felt the urge to throttle her. "Gaiomere, when are you going to listen to anyone but yourself—"

"Oh, calm down, *Attie*," she said. "My plan is just better. Answer the question, will you?"

He glowered at her for several moments before he finally conceded.

"Just Macky. But Jereis has a bow and Bettoni has a throwing axe—he can hit thirty feet on a good day."

"What about the old guy?"

Atlas shook his head. "Crowley lets others do the fighting for him."

Gaiomere nodded slowly, biting her lip as she glanced over her shoulder. "Don't look now, but Rasta is taking care of problem number one."

Atlas pretended to be looking at Jereis and Bettoni, but from his peripherals, he could see the little boy on his belly behind the log where Whitsom sat, sliding Macky's rifle, which he had left on the ground, towards him.

"He's taking the bullets out—he already got the extras from Macky's bag. And when that pasty guy isn't looking Maggi will cut the string of his bow. Then we'll only have to worry about Ponytail over there."

Atlas looked at her sideways. "This is relying on a lot of 'ifs', Gaiomere."

Rasta came trotting over at that moment, discreetly slipping the discarded bullets into Gaiomere's pocket. She kissed him on the forehead, murmuring, "Thank you, little fox."

"Ey, we should probably get going!" Macky called as he ambled back into the clearing. "We gotta set up camp before nightfall, and we still got a ways to go before we hit the Ridge!"

Bettoni got to his feet to pack away the remnants of the food, but Jereis' eyes were glued to Atlas.

"You escaped the Vedas' base," Jereis said quietly.

Atlas had been taking a sip of water, but he lowered the bottle slowly, his brows lifting. "Sorry?"

"You escaped the Vedas' base," Jereis repeated, his icy blue eyes narrowing. "You know where it is."

Atlas hesitated. He could feel the weight of Whitsom's stare on him. But it didn't matter. He has a duty to his clan.

"Yes," he said finally.

"*Aww* yeah!" Macky shouted, pumping his fist in the air, and Bettoni strode over and clapped his hand on Atlas' shoulder.

"General Talikoth will be pleased," Crowley said greasily.

Jereis' eyes had still not left Atlas. "Well? Lead the way."

Atlas swallowed. Whitsom was glaring at him now, and it was this that made him falter.

"I—shouldn't I return this information directly back to General Talikoth?" he reasoned. "I'm sure he's anxious to hear."

Crowley stepped forward. "As second-in-command I can assure you General Talikoth would not mind a small delay. After all, if something were to happen to you, the information would be lost."

"Fine," Atlas said curtly. "I'll just return Maggi her knife so they can be on their way." He crossed the clearing and pressed the knife into Maggi's hand.

Crowley let out a laugh, so high and eerie that it made the hairs raise on Atlas' arms.

"Oh, dear, Captain—surely you haven't been away from your people so long that you've forgotten our customs?"

He turned slowly to look at Crowley, a knot of dread forming in his chest.

The old man raised a brow. "The Renegades come with us. You know that General Talikoth will want them submitted for questioning."

"Lieutenant—"

"They will be *submitted for questioning*," Crowley spoke over him, a malicious sort of satisfaction flashing across his face. "And when they *prove* to be unhelpful, as they *always* are, they will be sent to the Rigs."

"Lieutenant, I promised them safety in return for guiding me back to the South," Atlas interjected quickly. Macky and Bettoni were looking between the two of them uncertainly, but Jereis was just smirking.

"Now that *we're* here, their guidance is no longer needed," the black-haired boy said smugly. "We've relieved you of your obligation. You should be grateful." Condescension dripped from every syllable he spoke, and Atlas' mind suddenly flooded with understanding. Jereis, who had always scored just half a point lower than Atlas on every exam they'd ever taken, who had come very close to beating him in each training fight, yet never succeeded, who had always been just a *spot* behind Atlas by every measure the soldiers had ever been tested—and Jereis was enjoying every minute of his recompense.

"Our laws are clear, Atlas," Crowley agreed. "No Renegade walks free. No form of treachery goes unpunished—"

"They're just kids, Lieutenant," Bettoni pointed out, looking nervously between Atlas and the Renegades. "That little one can't be older than ten—"

"They are *deserters*," Crowley snarled. "Their age is irrelevant—"

Atlas glanced back at the four of them. Whitsom glared fiercely at Crowley. Rasta clutched Whitsom's shirt, his eyes fastened fearfully on the Obarion soldiers. Gaiomere watched Atlas, her face astonishingly calm. But where was—

"Enough of this!" Crowley bellowed, spit flying from his mouth as he pointed an accusing finger at Atlas. "You will take us to the Vedas' base, and those *filthy* deserters will come with us! Anything less is disregarding a *direct order* and *insubordination!*"

He was breathing heavily by the time he'd finished. He looked deranged, with spit drying on his chin, his eyes glassy.

Macky, Bettoni and Jereis all stood, awaiting orders. Their eyes were on Atlas, and he knew that the moment Crowley gave the order, they would not hesitate to attack. No matter how good of friends they had been, they would turn on him.

As they should. They had a duty to their clan, after all, just the same as he did. He had an obligation to follow the customs of his clan, even if it meant betraying the Ren that he'd come to trust. Even if it meant turning on Whitsom, who had trusted Atlas before he'd ever given him a reason.

All for the sake of his clan. The clan that had written him off the second he'd disappeared.

Behind Jereis, a flash of silver flickered against the light of the sun, and in a split-second, Atlas made his choice.

"Well?" Crowley demanded furiously.

Atlas tilted his head to the side, a smirk playing around the corners of his lips.

"I always hated your guts," he told him honestly. "NOW!"

There was a splice of metal against fiber, and Jereis let out a cry of fury as the string on his bow snapped against his back.

"RUN, MAGS!" Whitsom shouted, pulling Rasta onto his back and taking off after the little girl, who darted quickly into the cover of the trees. Gaiomere sprinted after them, and Atlas ran hot on her heels.

"*KILL THEM! KILL THEM NOW!*" Crowley shrieked manically.

"I don't want to hit the little kids!" Bettoni protested, his axe hanging half-withdrawn from his belt.

Atlas glanced over his shoulder as Macky shoved Bettoni out of the way.

"I'll do it!" He aimed his rifle right at Atlas, shouting, "Slimy traitor!"

He pulled the trigger, but nothing happened. Macky cursed, dropping his rifle to the ground and lunging for his bag—though Atlas knew he'd find no spare bullets there.

Whitsom was already ascending over the first crest in the hillside, and Atlas and Gaiomere were only a few dozen feet behind him. Macky had started after them now, but he was slow—even Whitsom, with Rasta on his back, had no trouble outrunning him.

Atlas grunted as something plowed into him. He hit the ground, and the air was knocked from his lungs. Before he could get his bearings, Jereis was on top of him, his legs pinning down Atlas' hands.

"You have *no idea*," the inky-haired boy ground out, "how *long* I've been waiting for this." He withdrew a knife from his pocket, and fear coursed through Atlas like roaring water. He tried to scramble out from underneath the scrawny boy, but knew from years of sparring together that Jereis was stronger than he looked.

"Perfect Atlas," he crooned, inching the knife towards Atlas' face. "Perfect little General's son. Can't do anything wrong 'cause Daddy's in charge." He smirked. "Daddy will know what a filthy traitor you are when I carve it into your skin."

Jereis dragged the knife across his forehead and Atlas let out a roar of agony. Jereis laughed deliriously, and started to bring the knife down again, when he suddenly keeled backwards, screaming.

Atlas shot up, the flesh of his forehead throbbing. Gaiomere's spear was lodged inside Jereis' shoulder. Atlas stared numbly at his former training mate as he lay on the ground, clawing helplessly at the spear protruding from his skin.

Gaiomere tugged on Atlas' hand.

"Let's *go*," she urged. Atlas nodded, and the two of

them took off once more. Blood dripped into his eyes, and he hastily swiped it away. Macky ran ahead of them—he must have passed them when Jereis overtook Atlas—but even as they watched, Macky slowed, and by the time they were within twenty feet of him, he was jogging.

"Um—is there a reason we're going *towards* him?" Gaiomere asked breathlessly.

"We have to make sure we aren't followed," Atlas told her. "Stay quiet and stay behind me." He sped up without waiting for her response.

Macky's breath came loud and heavy, and he did not seem to hear Atlas approaching until it was too late.

Atlas wrapped an arm around the beefy boy's shoulders, pressing his fingers as hard as he could into the juncture where Macky's jaw met his neck. He tried to throw Atlas off, but Atlas held tight, and in a matter of seconds, Macky's eyes rolled back in his head, and he collapsed to the ground.

Gaiomere caught up, her eyes wide as she looked between Atlas and the fallen Obarion soldier. He started to explain, "I overstimulated his—"

"Carotid artery, yeah, I know," she said. "I've just never seen it done in person. That's—well, that was kind of impressive."

Atlas shrugged, though his cheeks still prickled with heat. He glanced down the mountain. Jereis' bloodied figure still lay beneath the trees where they'd left him.

"Crowley won't come after us," Atlas said, more to himself than to Gaiomere. The two began their unsteady ascent up the mountain again, loose rocks and dirt flying out from under their feet, and he continued,

"I didn't see Bettoni."

Atlas glanced up and saw Whitsom alone atop the mountain, gesturing for them to hurry.

"Where are Maggi and Rasta?" Gaiomere asked.

"He probably sent them down out of harms' way," Atlas assured her, but a movement to his left caught his eye.

Bettoni raced up the mountain, far faster than Atlas and Gaiomere, his lean, agile frame picking easily over the rocky terrain. In fact, he had not seemed to even notice them, for his gaze was trained on Whitsom.

Atlas' eyes widened, and he rushed forward.

"WHITSOM, MOVE!" he bellowed, but it was too late. Bettoni raised his arm and hurled the axe. Whitsom's eyes were on Atlas and Gaiomere, and at the last minute he turned and tried to scramble backwards —

But the axe sank into his thigh with a sickening sound. Atlas' heart pounded against his ribcage as he scrambled across the loose rock and fell at Whitsom's side. Gaiomere was seconds behind him. All of the blood had drained from her face, and she trembled as she knelt beside her brother.

"Whit," she whispered. He whimpered, tears streaming from his eyes as his hands grasped desperately at where the axe pierced him. She gently pulled his hands away. "Shh, shh, no, we can't—you can't take it out, Whit, you can't—"

Footsteps approached, and Atlas sprang to his feet, knife in hand. Bettoni came to a halt, looking between Atlas and Whitsom with a hesitant expression.

"Atlas—"

He held up his knife, taking a step towards

Bettoni. "*Go.*"

Bettoni held his hands up in front of his chest.

"Atlas, come on, man, you can't do this—"

Atlas took another step. "Bettoni, you've done enough damage. *Go.*"

The long-haired boy looked desperately at Atlas, his expression pleading.

"Atlas, this is treason. He'll—he'll kill you for this."

In a couple of steps, Atlas closed the distance between them. Bettoni tried to scramble away, but Atlas grasped the front of his shirt, yanking the shorter boy towards him and pressing the knife to his throat.

"You're going to leave—go back to Crowley, tell him we got away. Understood?"

Tears streamed from Bettoni's eyes, though whether it was from emotion or the pressure of a knife against his throat, Atlas wasn't sure.

"They're worth this to you?"

Atlas didn't answer, and Bettoni shook his head, looking at him as though he'd never quite seen him before.

"He'll kill you for this," he repeated, backing away slowly.

Atlas shrugged, turning back to Whitsom and calling over his shoulder, "I was already dead to him."

Gaiomere was kneeling over Whitsom's lower body now, her shaking hands ripping away the fabric of his pants so that she could see the full impact. Maggi and Rasta appeared on the other side of the hill, their little faces peering out from behind a pile of rocks.

"Oh...oh, *Whitsom!*" Maggi cried, her eyes wide and horrified as she looked between his ashen face and the axe wedged into his thigh. Rasta looked as though he were going to be sick.

Gaiomere leaned back on her heels, letting out a shuddering breath.

"I—I can't—I don't know what to—" She broke off, burying her face in her hands, her shoulders wracking with violent sobs.

Atlas looked between her and Whitsom. The adrenaline from the last twenty minutes was beginning to wear off, and his forehead ached something dreadful. Rasta cried into Maggi's shoulder, and the little girl looked more hopeless than he'd ever seen.

He knelt down beside Gaiomere. "What do you need?"

She lifted her head from her hands, hiccuping as she told him, "It n-needs to be r-removed, but I can't—can't take it out unless I have e-enough material to st-stop the b-blood flow."

"So, we need material?"

She shook her head.

"You d-don't understand. I c-can't do it. There's bound to be tissue damage, p-possible nerve d-damage, it could get in-infected—he n-needs someone who's an —an expert."

Atlas stood up, gazing southeast, across the stretch of forest that extended in front of them. "The Vedas might be willing to help him—but we've got to be at least ten hours from the Vedas' base."

Gaiomere's head popped up once more, and she clambered to her feet, sniffling, and cleared her throat.

"Wait," she mumbled, her voice raw and hoarse. "Maybe... maybe we don't have to go to the Vedas' base."

Maggi looked up sharply, a sliver of hope blooming on her face.

"Are we—" Gaiomere began to ask.

"Close? Yes." Maggi turned, narrowing her eyes as her gaze swiveled over the vast expanse of trees beneath them. "Maybe...an hour? Not great, but better than trying to make it to the Vedas' base," she frowned, adding, "It's west though—"

"It doesn't matter," Gaiomere said immediately. Her sensible, no-nonsense visage had returned.

She knelt beside Whitsom once more, and ripped more fabric away from his pants. She wound the fabric around his thigh, her hands moving with practiced deliberateness. Atlas realized only belatedly that she was making a tourniquet.

Her hands stretched towards the axe, but then she hesitated, her fingers trembling.

"Do you want me to do it?" Atlas asked quietly. She cast him an embarrassed glance, and gave a timid nod.

Atlas dropped to his knees next to her once more, shoving down the nausea rolling in his stomach, and grasped the handle of the axe. He shot Whitsom an apologetic glance before he pried it carefully from the older boy's thigh. Whitsom let out another faint whimper, his body twitching violently.

Gaiomere had ripped off the lower half of both of her pant legs, and she wrapped the fabric around Whitsom's thigh carefully, until the wound was covered.

"Help me lift him," she said to Atlas.

It was slow-going, but they eventually got him to his feet. Whitsom groaned as his weight shifted onto his injured leg. Gaiomere was too short to provide any real support, and he began to crumple back towards the ground, his body practically dead weight as his muscles gave out.

"This isn't going to work," Atlas muttered. "I'll have to carry him."

"Are you insane?" Gaiomere demanded.

"I must be, to put up with your mouth so frequently," he snapped, glaring at her.

Anger flashed across her face, and she opened her mouth—to fire back a retort, most likely—but Maggi elbowed her, and she promptly closed it again, mumbling, "Sorry."

"That's a first," he said dryly. "Help me stand him up again."

Once they got him back into a standing position, she and Maggi braced themselves against his back so he wouldn't fall over, and Atlas stepped his right leg in-between Whitsom's. He draped Whitsom's arm over his shoulder, tucking his head beneath the older boy's armpit and wrapping his arm around Whitsom's knee.

"This is going to hurt like hell," Atlas warned him as he squatted down, lifting Whitsom over his shoulders and shifting until the older boy's weight was equally distributed across his upper back. Whitsom groaned, writhing as his leg was jostled. Atlas had never been the praying sort, but at the moment, he prayed with all of his might that the poor fellow would just pass out and wake up once they had gotten him some proper treatment.

He turned back to Gaiomere, who looked at him with a slackened jaw.

"What?" he demanded, a little breathlessly.

She jumped, the color in her cheeks deepening.

"Nothing," she said very quickly, turning hastily to Maggi. "Lead the way."

Maggi promptly started down the hillside. Rasta reached over and clutched Gaiomere's hand, and Atlas took up the rear, grasping Whitsom's wrist to keep him from slipping.

Each step felt like a hundred. Whitsom's weight on his shoulders grew heavier with every minute that passed. The muscles of his back ached, and Atlas slouched forward under the pressure and the heat of the sun.

About a half an hour into their trek, Gaiomere fell back beside him.

"Do you need a break? We can stop and—"

"I'm good," he ground out.

She frowned, giving him a curt nod and hastening her steps to walk beside Rasta again.

Twenty minutes passed, and the trees around them grew sparser. "You're sure this is the right way?" Gaiomere asked Maggi. "This doesn't look familiar."

Maggi rolled her eyes. "You doubt me? *I*, who made it from the landmines to the Crystal Cave, *without* a map? *I*, who was the sole navigator for our tribe before you and Whitsom decided to go off on your little *vacation—*"

"Oh, I shouldn't have gotten you started," Gaiomere muttered.

"We're almost there," Maggi declared.

"Where are we going?" Atlas managed to grunt. Maggi glanced over her shoulder at him, and then looked at Gaiomere uncertainly.

"He *is* an Obarion, Gai."

Gaiomere shrugged. "We don't have much of a choice. It's not like we can carry Whitsom in. Besides..." She hesitated, before pressing on, "I trust him."

Despite his exhaustion, a strange, warm feeling filled his chest. Maggi muttered something he couldn't hear, and Gaiomere let out a splutter of indignation, pushing the younger girl not too gently. "Shut up," Atlas heard her mumble.

Ahead of them, a cluster of dilapidated buildings dotted the horizon. As they drew nearer, their details came into focus. One building had walls that were crumbling in heaps, the other's windows had been smashed out. Parts of the roofs were caved in here and there, and a strange smell hung in the air.

"Try to hold your breath as much as you can," Gaiomere said quietly. "The gas is poisonous. It won't kill you immediately, but if you inhale it long enough..."

He hastily followed her advice, wondering why on Earth they had come to a place where they could not even breathe properly to get Whitsom treatment.

Gaiomere glanced around nervously, before approaching what must have once been an old storm cellar. She pulled open the heavy metal door and climbed inside. Rasta and Maggi followed. Bewildered, Atlas clambered in after them, stooping so that he wouldn't hit Whitsom's head on the doorway.

"Maggi, close the doors," Gaiomere instructed, hovering near the back wall. The little girl obliged, and they were flushed in total darkness. A beat passed, and then Atlas heard the sound of hollow metal—Gaiomere knocked against the back wall in a pattern.

One, two, silence, one, two, three, silence, one, silence, one, two, three, four, five.

Quite suddenly, the back wall split apart, washing the cellar in light. Behind the wall was a long set of stairs descending deep into the earth. Two men stood at the top, clad in brown uniforms, each of their hands clasping massive machine guns. Atlas momentarily forgot about the weight on his back. Who on earth *were* these people?

"State your name and business," one of the men commanded.

"I'm Gaiomere, this is Maggi, and Rasta—I'm their caretaker. This is my brother Whitsom—we've come to seek medical care for him. Oh, and this is my...other brother. Um...Raider."

Atlas wrinkled his nose. He wasn't sure which was worse—the fact that she had called him her brother, or the fact that she had used her ex-boyfriend's name as a cover-up. It shouldn't have bothered him—it was probably more sensible, that she pretended he was her brother.

The guard looked them over for a moment longer before he nodded, stepping aside and gesturing to a small table on the landing that Atlas hadn't noticed before.

"Weapons go here. You may retrieve them at the end of your visit."

He watched silently as Gaiomere laid Whitsom's quarterstaff on the table, and Maggi set down her knife.

Gaiomere must have noticed his hesitation, for she said, "It's alright. We're safe here."

His curiosity piqued. What *was* this place, that the Renegades felt comfortable enough to leave their weapons at the door, to trust that nobody, not Flesh Flayers nor soldiers alike, could hurt them here?

He followed Gaiomere, Maggi and Rasta down the stairwell, treading carefully, for Whitsom's body slung across his back made it difficult to balance—one misstep and he could send them both toppling down the stairs. They descended deeper underground, so deep that the air grew heavy and moist.

Finally, *finally*, they reached the bottom, and Maggi pulled open a set of double-doors.

A small gasp slipped from Atlas' lips before he could stop it. They emerged into a massive room, larger, he was sure, than the entire Obarion stadium, where Talikoth held his military demonstrations back at Headquarters.

And there were people *everywhere*. Booths, where vendors sold everything from beans and corn to soaps and necklaces. One man near the entrance had a coop of about ten chickens, and he carefully distributed feed, his large straw hat nearly toppling from his head.

People were chatting, laughing—Atlas heard music in the distance, and he could have sworn he caught a glimpse of people *dancing*—

"What is this?" he demanded, whirling around to look at Gaiomere.

She smiled. "This, Atlas, is the Under."

PART II:

THE RENEGADES

CHAPTER EIGHT

A tlas' prayers had evidently been answered, for by the time they arrived in the infirmary, Whitsom had fallen unconscious, and did not even shift as Atlas laid him down on the thin cot.

"Lucky you got him here so fast," remarked the doctor, a thin, middle-aged man with peppered dark hair. He wore the same brown uniform as the entrance guards.

"He'll be okay, won't he?" Maggi asked, peering around the doctor's back.

"He will be," he agreed, giving the little girl a warm smile as he pulled the curtains closed around Whitsom's bed. "The tourniquet was clever—he would have been dead by now without it."

A tall, blonde woman—his nurse, presumably—came over to check Whitsom's vitals, and then directed them through a door just off the infirmary, which served as a guest suite.

"You can stay in here until your friend gets well," she informed them. "You darlings get cleaned up—you look like you've been through the wringer." She pinched Rasta's cheek as she parted, the door shutting with a *snap* behind her.

"We get to stay here as long as we *want*?" Maggi exclaimed as soon as the door had closed. She bound over to one of the beds, leaping atop it and bouncing up and down.

"Woah, let me try!" Rasta exclaimed, running across the room to join her. Gaiomere laughed.

"Only until Whitsom is better, you two," she corrected. Some of the tension that seemed ever-present in her face the last couple of days melted away. She glanced over at Atlas, and her brows flitted up in surprise.

"Holy honeyberries, your head's still bleeding," she remarked. He reached up to feel at his forehead and cringed. A steady stream of blood leaked through his fingers, and the wound stung to touch.

Gaiomere disappeared from the room. Atlas spotted another door and, as he suspected, found a bathroom behind it. He examined his skin in the mirror. Jereis had not, thankfully, managed to slice more than a single vertical line into his flesh. Not that Atlas was vain by any means; only that he wasn't particularly keen on the idea of walking around with the word 'traitor' etched onto his forehead.

Gaiomere appeared in the doorway, holding out a wet cloth.

"It might sting a bit—there's an antiseptic on it."

He nodded, taking it from her and holding it to his forehead. Gaiomere looked for a moment like she was going to leave, but hesitated, off-handedly observing, "That guy uh...that guy didn't like you very much."

Atlas snorted, leaning against the countertop.

"Yeah, you two seem to have that in common." She stuck out her tongue, and he chuckled, continuing, "He was an old school rival, of sorts. Didn't realize he had it out for me so bad, though."

Gaiomere leaned against the doorframe, her brows lifting as she asked him quizzically, "You went to school?"

"Sort of—not—not *really*." He knew what she was thinking. Formal education was something that, by the start of the First War, had been relegated to the elite rich. "Academy, we called it. It's where I learned to fight."

Gaiomere nodded slowly, her finger absently tracing a pattern on the doorframe, before her lips curled into a wry smirk, and remarked, in a teasing tone, "That's where you learned to break people's necks."

Atlas rubbed the back of his neck, annoyed, for he could feel his cheeks prickling with heat— an occurrence that seemed to be happening more frequently as of late, and perhaps most embarrassingly, almost always around Gaiomere.

"I haven't *actually* ever broken anyone's neck," he confessed. "I just—well, it seemed like an appropriate threat to make at the time."

Her smirk broadened into a full-blown grin, and Atlas was struck once more by how pretty she was. It was sort of irritating, how distracting it was.

She turned to leave again, but stopped herself a second time, her teeth catching her lip. "Thank you, Atlas."

His brows drew together. "You don't have to—I mean—there's no need to thank me. We were all looking out for each other."

"But you protected us against your own clan," Gaiomere said reasonably. "I mean—that can't have been easy."

His argument died on the tip of his tongue. It *hadn't* been easy.

She looked like she wanted to say something else. Her fingers picked restlessly at the door frame, where a piece of wood had chipped away.

"What that ponytail guy said—"

Atlas' lips quirked upwards. Gaiomere was strikingly intelligent, which made him certain her "forgetting" the Obarion soldiers' names was less an issue of memory and more an act of defiance. Atlas cleared his throat.

"Bettoni," he reminded her.

"Right, Pony Toni. What he said—about—I mean— about your dad killing you. He wouldn't—he wouldn't *actually...*" She trailed off, shifting uncomfortably.

Atlas looked away, his hand clenching tighter around the cloth pressed to his head. He did not want to be having this conversation with her, in which he simultaneously felt he might be liable to punch the nearest object, or else to collapse into tears. He had not cried since he was seven, and he was not going to start now.

"I'm sure he would," Atlas said finally, his voice carefully controlled, even indifferent. "That is the penalty for treason—"

"But you're his *son*—" Gaiomere's emotions often played out flagrantly on her face, and now was no different. He could easily detect the fear, uncertainty, disbelief even, in her expression, but it was none of these that sent anger surging through Atlas like a solar whip.

"I don't want your pity, Gaiomere," he spat, throwing the cloth down on the counter and turning away from her. He took a deep breath, trying to steady the torrent of emotions coursing through him like a flood. "I don't *need* your pity, so don't—"

"I don't pity you, Atlas," she snapped.

A wave of relief enveloped him. *This*, he could deal with. He could handle her anger, or annoyance. He could stay in control navigating those arenas.

It was only when she looked at him like he was someone to feel sorry for, like he was something *weak* that his chest clenched up as though he were drowning.

"I think it's awful—that's awful that your own dad would do that to you," Gaiomere said. "But I don't pity you. That implies you're some kind of victim or something. And you're not."

Atlas whirled around to face her, intent upon shouting at her, telling her off, anything to get her to stop speaking to him as though it mattered—as though she *cared* about him, as though she hadn't spent a week treating him like a pariah—

But Gaiomere wasn't finished.

"I won't offer you pity, but at least let me apologize," she pressed on.

He blinked, frowning, his mouth hanging open for several seconds—for he had planned on calling her several names that Maggi and Rasta would probably be better off not hearing—before he shut it quickly, staring down at her.

Despite his obvious fury, Gaiomere met his gaze unflinchingly. "It wasn't fair of me to treat you the way that I did just because of the clan you come from. And I'm sorry."

Atlas exhaled, running a hand through his hair. The anger began to ebb away, and he suddenly felt rather foolish.

"It's okay," he said quietly. It was only after the

words had left his mouth that he realized he genuinely meant them.

She smiled brightly, and he found himself returning her smile without a conscious thought.

Rasta trotted into the bathroom, his curious eyes flickering from the toilet, to the sink, and the shower, before darting between Atlas and Gaiomere.

"What are you doing?"

Before either of them could answer, Maggi came darting into the room.

"Rasta, *watch!*" She reached across the countertop and flipped on the faucet.

Rasta looked between she and the water streaming from the faucet with an expression of wonder. "*What?* That is *so cool!* Let me try!"

Atlas arched an eyebrow, and Gaiomere laughed, squeezing out of the bathroom. He followed her, and she explained, "Rasta's has never seen running water before—he was too little last time we came here to remember."

Atlas let out a low whistle, sitting down on the bed. He couldn't imagine what it would be like, to go without the things that he had come to know as necessities. Running water, electricity, heat in the winter.

Though perhaps it was just that his definition of necessity needed refining, for Gaiomere's tribe had been living without those things—as far as he could tell—for generations.

After the four of them got cleaned up, they went to check on Whitsom. The doctor informed them that he had been moved into the operation room and would be undergoing surgery in a little under a half an hour.

"We've got all the strong stuff, he'll be completely out of it," the doctor assured them when he saw Maggi and Rasta's terrified expressions.

"Let's go explore the main hall," Gaiomere suggested. Her proposition fulfilled its purpose, for the two little ones were immediately distracted, and they eagerly followed her out of the infirmary.

"So, what is this, some secret society?" Atlas asked Gaiomere. The two of them trailed behind Maggi and Rasta, who chattered excitedly to one another, pointing out various colorful displays and flitting from table to table in wonder.

Gaiomere nodded. "It's a hub for all of us 'Renegades,' as you call us. It's where we commune." He arched an eyebrow, and she pointed towards one of the nearest vendors. "See all of these merchants? They grow this food above ground, and then bring it down here to barter. We all bring something different, so we're able to help each other, keep each other's tribes sustained. It's like one big family."

Atlas' mind raced. "They grow the food *above* ground? How do they do that—being nomadic, I mean?"

"Not *all* of the tribes are nomadic. There are tribes that live in groups of forty or fifty—big enough to protect themselves if a couple of Flesh Flayers wander into their territory. They stay put, for the most part, and come down here to barter whatever they can't grow or make themselves."

"How did you know about this?"

"We came here once before. Dad knew the lead doctor then—they bounced ideas off each other, sometimes." Gaiomere shook her head, casting Maggi an admiring glance. "Mags was only five or six at the time, but that girl has the best sense of direction I've ever seen. She never forgets a place."

There was something else that bothered Atlas, though. "The guards at the entrance—they had machine guns."

Gaiomere nodded. "They're just to protect us in case any Flesh Flayers wandered in, or if the Vedas or Obarion somehow found the entrance. That's why we have to leave weapons at the door. This is a refuge."

Atlas fell silent. He had not, in reality, been concerned about their safety in the Under. No, what he was more confounded by was the fact that two guards, Renegades, with supposedly no allies on either side of the clan conflict, possessed automatic firearms that looked as new as the weapons back at Headquarters.

Talikoth told him that the Ren didn't *have* guns— or none nearly so lethal as *machine* guns, at the very least. Were they the only ones, or were there more out there, hiding out in the wilderness with heaps of weapons in their possession?

Then again, Talikoth had also told him that each Renegade only looked out for his own skin, and here was a very evident contradiction of that assertion, for there were *hundreds* of them here, a jovial coalition working to help one another.

On one hand, Atlas thought that it was charming. An underground, peaceful insurgency against the orthodox, a refusal to participate in the violence that had devastated humankind above them.

But a voice in the back of his head, a voice that sounded suspiciously like Talikoth, whispered that it was *dangerous*. For if there were hundreds of them here, there was bound to be hundreds more out there. And if they were mobilized—or worse, if they joined the Vedas...

Maggi and Rasta bounded up to them suddenly, their faces bright and eager.

"Gai, they've got cinnamon bread!" Maggi exclaimed.

"Can we get some? *Please?*" Rasta's big hazel eyes were wide like a doe as he gazed up at the two of them.

Gaiomere frowned, patting her pockets. "I haven't started any drawings yet, guys—"

Atlas unclipped his watch from his wrist, offering it to Maggi. "Will they take this?"

Maggi's eyes widened, and her face split into a grin.

"That might get us *three* loaves!" she exclaimed excitedly to Rasta. "Thanks, Atlas!"

"Thanks, Atlas!" the little boy echoed, and the two of them sprinted off into the throng of people.

Gaiomere frowned. "You didn't have to—"

"I know I didn't have to," he interrupted, glancing at her sideways. "I never used it anyway."

In fact, it had been his Grandfather Seikahri's watch, but all Atlas could remember of him was his constant scowl, or how anytime he entered a room he'd order Atlas to "stand up straight!" in his gruff, intimidating snarl, so Atlas didn't feel particularly attached to it.

Atlas had never seen so many unique commodities in his entire life. There were soaps in every color, handmade pendants, knitted scarves and hats, wicker baskets, and, of course, food—so much food that he could not recognize many of the cuisines.

"What are *those?*" he asked Gaiomere, pointing

to a merchant's tray laden with tiny orbs that looked suspiciously like—

"Tuna eyeballs," she confirmed, grimacing and looking hastily away.

Maggi and Rasta returned, handing each of them a slice of cinnamon bread, and Atlas nearly groaned when the flavor hit his taste buds.

They passed an old woman with a dozen magnificent oil paintings hanging on the wall behind her stand and propped up out front. Gaiomere drifted towards the booth, her eyes raking over the paintings enchantedly.

"These are beautiful," she murmured, and the old woman beamed at her. "You don't sell the oil paints, do you?"

The woman tilted her head.

"I could perhaps make a special batch," she replied in a croaky voice.

Gaiomere's face lit up. "Really? That would be *amazing*—what would you take?"

The old woman cackled, leaning forward, and curled a wizened finger around a strand of Gaiomere's frizzy mane. "Just your lovely locks, darling. *Ooh*, I could make such *wonders* out of that hair..."

Atlas' brows shot up to his hairline, and he started to laugh, before he realized that the old woman wasn't kidding.

"Oh, look, Maggi and Rasta need us," he said quickly, pulling Gaiomere away, for it looked as though she actually might be considering the crazy old woman's offer.

They drew nearer to the music's source, and Atlas saw that he had been correct earlier—people were dancing, a group of about twenty or so couples moving across an improvised dance floor.

"Want some more bread?" Maggi asked, holding out another slice to him. She watched the dancers giddily, her feet tapping against the floor. Atlas took a slice, turning to offer another to Gaiomere, but when he looked behind him, she had vanished.

He frowned, peering over the crowds of people, but it was no use—her dark clothing made it quite easy for her to blend into the crowd, and not even her wild hair gave her away.

Atlas sat down between Maggi and Rasta, trying hard to quell the surge of momentary panic he felt. They were safe here, she had assured him, and it wasn't though anyone would try to hurt her in front of all of these people.

"Rasta, let's dance!" Maggi exclaimed suddenly, dragging the little boy to his feet.

"I'll hold your bread," Atlas offered.

Maggi looked at him sternly. "*Don't* eat it all." He snorted and gave her a thumbs up.

He watched the two of them spin around the dance floor, both of their cheeks bright from laughter.

He glanced behind him and felt a ripple of relief as Gaiomere weaved through the crowd towards him. Her Vedas' garb had vanished, replaced by a yellow strapless pleated top and a floral skirt.

"I feel so much better," she sighed as she plopped down beside him, breaking off a piece of bread and popping it into her mouth.

"I thought maybe you'd gone back to sell your hair," he said.

She laughed, shaking her head and confessing,

"I'm too attached to my hair. Even if Whitsom does make fun of it."

"I like it," he blurted.

She glanced sideways at him, her face blotching with color, but he was saved from any embarrassment, for Maggi and Rasta stumbled over, both breathless and giggling.

"I'm *wiped!*" Rasta declared, leaning against the bench heavily.

"I'm not—come dance, Gaiomere!" Maggi piped up, pulling the older girl to her feet. Gaiomere laughed, allowing herself to be tugged onto the dance floor. She spun the younger girl in circles, her curls flying out behind her, her mouth split open in a smile so wide the corners of her eyes creased.

Atlas looked away, swallowing thickly. Rasta sat beside him, munching on cinnamon bread, but his eyes were glued to Atlas. Atlas lifted the corners of his lips, attempting to smile, but the boy just looked at him blankly, his hazel eyes wide as he asked, "Are you Gai-Gai's boyfriend?"

His cheeks prickled with heat, and Atlas glanced quickly at the dance floor, as though somehow, the girl in question could have heard him over all of the ruckus.

"I—no. No, I'm not. Why would you think that?"

Rasta shrugged. "Maggi says you are."

Atlas was stricken by a sudden stroke of inspiration, and scooted closer to Rasta, lowering his voice.

"Hey, speaking of boyfriends," he began, attempting nonchalance. "You know this Raider guy?"

Rasta gave him a nod. "He—uh—is he actually Gaiomere's boyfriend?"

Rasta looked contemplatively at his lap for a moment, before telling him, "I don't *think* so. Maggi just says they flirted a lot. And I didn't know what that word meant, and Maggi said that's when people are all smiley towards each other all the time, but then I was even more confused, 'cause that's how Gai-Gai is with everyone..."

The little boy drifted off into silence, his brows furrowed, as though he were pondering an issue of immense complexity.

Atlas clicked his tongue impatiently, and glanced towards the twelve-year-old, still spinning in circles with Gaiomere on the dance floor. Perhaps *she* would be better to interrogate—

"He's taller than you," Rasta said all of a sudden, and Atlas looked at him sharply, his brows lifting in disbelief.

"He—no way, can't be," Atlas replied, frowning. The only person he'd met that was taller than him—besides Talikoth—was Maddex, and Maddex was sort of a freak of nature.

"He is!" Rasta insisted. "Whitsom said he was....was..." He furrowed his brow, as though struggling to remember. "*Half* a foot taller than him, I think."

Atlas cursed, scowling.

"Gai-Gai says we shouldn't say those words—"

"Yeah, yeah, I know," Atlas grumbled, taking another slice of cinnamon bread and biting into it with considerably more aggression than was called for. His eyes roved over the hall idly and fell on a stand about fifteen feet away, and then flickered over to the half a loaf of cinnamon bread that sat atop their table.

He grinned, nudging Rasta, and asked, "Hey, buddy, wanna help me with something?"

By the time they got back to the bench, the girls had returned to their seats, both out of breath and still laughing.

"There you guys are!" Maggi exclaimed. She was sprawled across Gaiomere's lap, her hair sticking to her forehead and face so red that she resembled a tomato.

Atlas thrust the flower crown he had bartered for towards Gaiomere, smirking a little as her eyes widened, and she looked at him disbelievingly.

"For me?" she asked.

He rolled his eyes. "Well, I'm certainly not going to wear it."

Her cheeks lifted and she grinned from ear to ear, taking the crown from him and placing it delicately on her head.

"Balance has been restored to the world again," she declared. Atlas chuckled, and she continued, "We should go check on Whitsom. He's probably out of surgery."

So the four of them meandered through the crowd once more, dodging running children and a pair of stumbling men who Atlas was fairly certain were pitifully intoxicated.

Whitsom had indeed been returned to the main room of the infirmary. He sat propped up on pillows and his grin was tired, but bright, when he saw them.

"You scared the socks off me, you big dummy," Gaiomere muttered, wrapping her arms around his neck.

"Now maybe you'll be nicer to me," he replied, tugging on her hair fondly. Maggi and Rasta curled up on either side of him, nuzzling into his side.

Whitsom reached around them, holding out a hand to Atlas.

"Thanks, man. Seriously. I'm indebted to you."

Atlas clasped Whitsom's hand, shrugging as he said, "Just get me a pair of my own sparring gloves so I don't have to suffer you and Kendo's stench and we'll call it even." Whitsom laughed.

Maggi and Rasta animatedly recounted their journey to the Under.

"Oh, and we saved you some cinnamon bread!" Rasta declared, withdrawing the parcel from his pocket and passing it to Whitsom. "Gai-Gai said it's your favorite."

"Oh, you're the *best!*" the older boy exclaimed, ruffling Rasta's hair affectionately.

"So, how long before you're ready to go again?" Gaiomere asked.

Whitsom looked uneasily between she and Atlas.

"Um...'bout a moon cycle, give or take."

Atlas could have sworn his heart skipped a beat in his chest. "A *month?*"

Whitsom nodded, grimacing. "Doc said the way that the blade went in, it hit some nerves and muscle fibers—not too deep, but still got me good enough that it'll be awhile before I'm able to travel again."

Atlas nodded slowly, sinking down into the chair beside Whitsom's bed. He rested his elbows on top of his thighs, his mind working quickly.

He did not have a month to spare—not after their run in with the Obarion soldiers. He needed to get back to General Talikoth before they did. *He* had the location of the Vedas' base, while Crowley's crew was still searching for it. Surely this would be enough to sway Talikoth's hand when Crowley and Jereis and the rest of them did eventually come crawling back with all their tales of Atlas' treachery. Even without the solar conversion intelligence from Gaiomere.

He glanced up at Whitsom, his jaw flexing. Whitsom and his tribe would be safe here—they had medical care, and food, and wouldn't need protection under the umbrella of the refuge.

Atlas forcefully shoved down the voice of self-reproach that surfaced in the back of his mind. It did not matter that Whitsom and Gaiomere had saved his life on more than one account—it didn't matter that he'd promised them he'd take them to the Rigs. If he didn't get back to the South before those soldiers did... well, he did not want to even consider what that would mean for him.

He told the Renegades he needed to go to the bathroom and stalked into the guest suite, closing the door behind him.

Atlas let out a heavy exhale, running a hand through his hair as he paced across the room.

He would move quicker on his own. If he left now and traveled through the night, he could reach the coast in a few hours. All he had to do was follow the shoreline south. He could reach Headquarters in a few weeks if he moved quickly. General Talikoth could have a strike against the Vedas' base organized within a month.

Atlas scowled. Talikoth, who had not been concerned with whether or not Atlas was alive.

He shook his head, clearing those thoughts.

It shouldn't matter how Talikoth had responded to his disappearance. He had a duty to his clan that transcended personal grievances.

He had a duty to his clan.

Atlas stopped pacing, a thrill of fear traveling down his spine.

It wouldn't matter. It wouldn't matter if he reached Talikoth before the Obarion soldiers, or months after. No matter how much he tried to explain, Talikoth would see his actions one way, and one way alone: pure, unforgivable, blatant *treason.* He had no excuse.

Atlas let out a slow exhale, trying to tame the swell of panic vibrating in his chest. He couldn't return to the Vedas' base. He'd foregone Moonstone's protection, and subsequently her information, when he snuck off base with the Ren. If he went to Headquarters, he'd be slaughtered there—even *if* he revealed the location of the Vedas' base.

He had nothing. No one. Nowhere safe to go. He was completely on his own—

"Atlas," Gaiomere's voice floated towards him like he was in a dream. He blinked, the features of the room becoming clearer as some of the fuzziness began to subside from his head. He didn't know when she had entered the room, but she stood by the doorway watching him, her expression uneasy. "You alright? You looked like you were having a panic attack."

He nodded slowly, running a hand through his hair as he took several steadying breaths.

"I—yeah. I'm fine." She looked at him with concern, and he felt a flicker of annoyance, his cheeks flushing as he insisted, "Honestly, I'm fine—"

"I used to have panic attacks all the time,"

Gaiomere said quietly. "Right after our mom died."

Some of his embarrassment trickled away, and he nodded, pushing himself to his feet to get a drink of water. He leaned against the wall as he took several large gulps.

Maggi had come into the room after Gaiomere, and the two of them were talking quietly, but every few moments, Gaiomere glanced over at him, as though making sure he hadn't started hyperventilating.

He was not, he supposed, *completely* alone. For now, he was safe, and surrounded by people that seemed, on the surface anyway, to not want him dead.

Which was refreshing, considering the list of people that applied to seemed to be growing shorter and shorter every day.

CHAPTER NINE

Atlas awoke the next morning with a surge of panic. He clawed desperately at the end table beside the bed, searching for his knife, before he remembered that Maggi had left it at the entrance of the Under.

He fell back against the pillow, letting out a breath of relief. They were safe, a mile below ground. Neither the Vedas nor the Obarion had even the faintest idea of where they were.

His muscles ached as he pulled himself up to a seat and peered around the room. Maggi and Rasta were still fast asleep, curled up beneath the blankets of the bed they'd shared with Gaiomere. The bathroom light was on, and the door was cracked open, casting a sliver of light across the dark stone floor. Atlas didn't think he'd ever get used to being underground, and he wasn't sure he wanted to. The absence of daylight made his skin crawl.

He climbed out of bed and padded across the floor. Gaiomere sat perched atop the sink, her notebook in her lap and her bare feet resting atop the toilet seat. Her pencil moved across the paper with precision, her brows furrowed and tongue poking out from between her lips.

Atlas knocked lightly on the door, and she jumped.

"Sorry. Can I—"

"Oh, yeah, course," she said, hastily sliding down

off the countertop. "I needed light and didn't want to wake you guys." She squeezed past him, and Atlas closed the door behind him. When he came back out, Gaiomere was digging through her bag, and withdrew something small from one of the pockets. She scooted around him again, climbing back onto the counter.

"What are you working on?" Atlas asked her from the doorway.

The corners of her lips lifted, just slightly.

"Oh, you'll just make fun of it," she muttered.

Atlas moved closer, leaning against the counter beside her and peering over her shoulder. It was a black and white sketch of a sunflower, its petals blooming magnificently, each detail rich, from the sticky points of the stigma to the texture of the leaves.

"I like flowers," she mumbled, almost defensively, as she dragged a white tube along the paper, smudging the shading across the leaves. "And however stupid you think that is, I trade the drawings for food, and other necessities, so it's entirely practical."

Atlas rubbed the back of his neck, pulling a face as he recalled the "flower power" comment he had made back on the Vedas' base.

"It's really good," he insisted. "All the other ones— on the walls of your room at the Vedas' base—you did all those, too?"

She nodded, letting out a huff of exasperation as she added, "If I had known we'd be coming here I would have brought them—I could have gotten so much food for all of those." Her pencil stilled quite suddenly, though she did not take her eyes off of her paper as she asked, "So, are you leaving this morning then?"

Atlas looked sharply at her. "What—why would I

—"

Gaiomere gave him a patronizing look. "Come on, Atlas. You're going to try to get back to Obarion headquarters before those soldiers do so you can explain yourself—soften Talikoth up by telling him where the Vedas' base is so you don't get in trouble for what you did at the lake."

Atlas shot her a perturbed glance, though her attention had shifted back to her drawing, a smug smile fixed upon her lips, so she didn't seem to notice. "It wouldn't make a difference," he said, reluctant to acknowledge how easily she'd seen through to his motives. "Treason is treason in Talikoth's eyes. Besides, it wouldn't be beneficial."

Gaiomere snorted. "Why? Because you haven't gotten the solar conversion equation out of me yet?"

He blinked, carefully schooling his features. "I'm not sure what you—"

"Ugh, please spare me your innocent act," Gaiomere snapped. "'Whitsom said you'd found a way to convert solar energy to gas.' Remember that conversation?"

Atlas nodded tersely.

She continued, "You're not willing to go back to Talikoth after you committed treason with so little information. I'm betting you think getting those equations out of me would be enough to earn Talikoth's forgiveness. I mean, why else would you have gotten me the flower crown?"

Atlas swallowed, heat surging to his cheeks, though whether it was from embarrassment or anger, he wasn't sure. His voice was cold when he spoke.

"Funny, I could have sworn you said we were past

all of this Obarion mistrust."

"Oh, I don't doubt you because you're Obarion," Gaiomere said. "I doubt you because since I've known you, I've watched you manipulate everyone around you."

Atlas did not even flinch.

"Pot calling the kettle black," he retorted, crossing his arms over his chest.

Gaiomere frowned, the kindling anger in her eyes momentarily replaced by confusion. "What?"

He shook his head. "I—it's—old phrase, doesn't matter. My *point* is...we're the same, you and I."

She looked for a moment as though she wanted to argue, but thought better of it.

"Fine, so what? I get it—we've got to do what we can to keep our tribes safe, but don't—don't treat me like bobby-pin girl."

His mouth popped open and he stared at her, flabbergasted.

"Wait—how can you—how can you *possibly* know about that?" he demanded.

"I saw you," Gaiomere said quickly. "In the dining hall that morning. I watched you steal it from her."

He must have still looked baffled, because she explained, "I saw you come in, and recognized you from —you know, from the infirmary that evening—and I was watching you—"

Atlas' eyebrows shot up, and her cheeks darkened with color.

"Because you were acting suspicious, that's *all!*" she said quickly.

He smirked, but said nothing.

"Anyway, I watched you take it."

Atlas looked down at his socks, chewing on the inside of his cheek. How positively humiliating, to have his exploitative flirting *witnessed*, and especially by a girl that he—

He cut that train of thought off right there, unwilling to address the implications tied to the end of that sentence.

But then something else occurred to him.

"Why didn't you report what you saw?" he asked, looking back up at her.

Gaiomere smiled sheepishly.

"Um...I was sort of curious to see what you'd do, honestly," she admitted.

"I could have done anything," Atlas pointed out. "I could have killed one of the guards—I could have killed your brother—"

Her eyes narrowed, and she gave him that perceptive look that always unsettled him.

"You don't strike me as the type," Gaiomere said softly.

He scowled, glaring at a spot over her shoulder as Talikoth's words echoed in his head. "I'm not weak—"

"Not because you're weak," she interrupted, rolling her eyes. "But because under the facade of big bad General's son, I think you're actually a decent human being."

His scowl wavered, just slightly, but he said nothing.

"Look," Gaiomere said. "I think we can help each other. All I'm asking is that we shoot straight with one another."

Atlas looked away from her, drumming his fingers against the wall behind him. If he were honest with himself, he had not even *thought* of the solar conversion in ages—a fact that was rather irritating, for it meant he had allowed himself to be distracted.

And, if he were *deeply* honest with himself, he was not exactly inclined to obtain information for Talikoth's benefit anymore. Not when the man was likely after his head.

"Fine," he agreed. "We can help each other. And I'll —I'll shoot straight with you."

"Good." Gaiomere gave him an officious nod as she hopped down from the counter and moved past him. She smirked, adding loftily, "I'd hate for you to waste all your barter chips on flower crowns."

Atlas gave her a dubious look. "Is there no possibility in your mind that I just did it because I wanted to?"

She pretended to look thoughtful for a moment.

"Nope," she said, popping the 'p'.

He rolled his eyes, following her back into the main room just as Rasta sat up and asked, "Why are you guys *always* in the bathroom?"

"Just didn't want our talking to wake you, little fox," Gaiomere said, ruffling his hair affectionately.

"*Talking*. Is that what the kids are calling it nowadays?" Maggi droned, as she stretched her arms above her head sleepily.

Atlas' face burned, and he shot the little girl a dirty look, but Gaiomere didn't miss a beat.

"Since you're feeling so *chatty*, Mags, why don't you go butter up those vendors and see if you can snag us some breakfast?"

She thrust several drawings at Maggi—Atlas wondered how long she had been awake, to have finished all of those—and the little girl took them, mock-saluting her and disappearing out the door.

Atlas was the only one who had not washed up the night before, so he showered while Gaiomere and Rasta went to visit Whitsom. Maggi had just returned with food when Atlas emerged from the guest suite and plopped down into a chair next to Whitsom's sick bed.

Maggi passed out fresh slices of cinnamon bread, and it was not until she had handed him his that he did a double-take, his eyes zeroing in on her hair, which looked several inches shorter then it had been when she'd left the room that morning.

She caught his look and shrugged.

"The drawings weren't quite enough for two loaves. I'd been wanting to cut it for a while anyway." She flicked her now neck-length hair back, plopping down into a chair and grinning wickedly at Gaiomere.

"I just wish you would have *asked* me—" Gaiomere said, frowning.

Maggi snorted. "What, for permission? Okay, Mom."

Atlas could not contain his curiosity any longer. "What's the deal with hair?"

"Oh, you can do tons with it," Gaiomere said, ticking off on her fingers as she told him, "You can make clothes, blankets, rope. Growers can weave it into mats to grow their produce on—it protects the plants from bugs and stuff." He wrinkled his nose, and Gaiomere rolled her eyes. "Don't be close-minded, it's not that weird."

Atlas had to disagree. The Renegades were an odd bunch, to be sure.

They ate in silence, and had almost finished both

loaves of cinnamon bread when Gaiomere said, "Okay, so are we just *not* going to talk about the looming Doomsday?"

Whitsom and Rasta both looked at her blankly, and Maggi said, "Come again, now?"

Gaiomere huffed impatiently, flipping open her notebook and setting it on Whitsom's bed, where each of them could see it. She had scrawled another hand-drawn map, with their location circled in bold red.

"The Obarion soldiers are looking for the Vedas' base. We ran into them *here*—" She circled an area near where she had drawn a depiction of the lake. "Which means they aren't actually that far off from the base. At the *longest*—provided they head west, the opposite direction of the base, it would take them approximately two weeks to find it—assuming they didn't go any further north, and assuming they doubled back the same way they came. At the shortest—say they headed in the correct direction immediately after our encounter with them, they could reach the base in—" She glanced around at the group of them, frowning. "Well, they'd be there by now."

"That's not accounting for their journey back south, though," Atlas pointed out. "It will take them weeks to get back to Headquarters and inform Talikoth about the Vedas' location, and then weeks—probably longer, with a full-fledged battalion—to return north. Based on the maps of the Pass that I've seen, anyway."

"Unless they send the message by transmitter," Whitsom said. "Y'all have those right?"

Atlas gave him a perplexed look, and Whitsom quickly clarified, "Radios, communication devices, you know?"

"Oh, yeah, we call them receivers," Atlas said. "But we don't have any that could send a message that far; it's got to be at least—"

"Six hundred miles, yeah," Gaiomere confirmed. She shot a befuddled look at Whitsom, asking, "How do you know about transmitters?"

"All the guards use them around the base. They're pretty unobtrusive, so they're good for on-the-down-low communication."

"Wait a minute, we saw one of those," Gaiomere said to Atlas. "Remember, Jacoby pulled one out of his desk?"

Atlas snapped his fingers, sitting up straighter.

"I saw one on Moonstone's desk, too," he realized aloud.

Gaiomere stood up, her teeth catching her lip as she paced in front of Whitsom's bed.

"*Maybe*," she said slowly. "Maybe we wouldn't have to leave the Under to let Moonstone know what's coming. Maybe we could send her a message—"

"Wait, sorry, *why* are we now trying to warn the people that basically held you and Whitsom captive for a month that they're about to get their butts handed to them?" Maggi asked, cocking a black brow.

"We're warning them because if the Obarion take control of the North, that's bad news for *us*, too," Gaiomere said firmly. "The Vedas have left us alone, for the most part. They only took us in the first place because I was so badly injured." She lowered her gaze, and though Atlas could tell she was trying to put on a brave face for Maggi and Rasta, he did not miss the way her lower lip trembled. "If the Obarion take the North, there won't be anywhere that's safe."

Atlas thought it better not to mention the added benefit that if Moonstone's soldiers intercepted Crowley's squad, news of Atlas' treason might never reach Talikoth's ears. This line of thinking probably wouldn't endear him to the Renegades. Maggi still looked reluctant. "We still could go east —or north, like Raider's gang. Point is, if the Obarion take the North, *we'd* find a way to survive. It's the Vedas that would really be in trouble—and what do we owe them?"

Atlas straightened up in his seat, his heart jumping in his chest as the idea fired across his mind. "We might not owe them anything, but—it could be a mutually-beneficial exchange of information."

They all looked at him. Atlas hesitated, before withdrawing the folded up photograph from his pocket and passing it to Whitsom.

"Whoa, is that Moonstone?" Whitsom exclaimed, letting out a guffaw of incredulous laughter. "Wild."

Gaiomere moved around the bed and sat down on the mattress beside her brother, peering at the photograph.

"That's my mother next to her," Atlas told them, adding, "She was killed by the Vedas before I turned three." From his peripherals, he saw Gaiomere look up at him sharply. "I'm uh—I'm trying to figure out what Moonstone knows. Because here, it—it almost looked as though they were friends. And if Moonstone betrayed her—if she's the one that killed her..." He trailed off, his jaw flexing. "I—well, I just need to know."

The four Renegades stared at him so intently that a sudden bubbling of discomfort erupted in his stomach. Perhaps he had been too honest with them.

Suddenly, his search for answers—and potentially, revenge—seemed childish. His gaze fell to his hands, and he muttered, "I know it seems foolish—and it doesn't really benefit you guys at all—"

"Don't be stupid," Whitsom said immediately. "It's important to you, so it's important to us."

"You couldn't go back to the South not knowing something like that," Gaiomere added. Rasta nodded emphatically.

"Oh heck yeah!" Maggi exclaimed. "Nothing I love more than an old-fashioned quest for ruthless revenge!"

Atlas looked around at the four of them, and felt a pang in his chest so strong that it took him aback.

"Okay, so if we *are* going to warn the Vedas, why don't we just leave Whitsom here to heal and go warn Moonstone ourselves?" Maggi pointed out.

Gaiomere sighed. "I'd thought of that, but I'm afraid that if we go back, Moonstone might not let us leave again."

Atlas self-consciously rubbed the back of his neck, adding, "Not to mention the fact that some of Moonstone's council members *may* have implied that if I broke the rules again they'd have me executed." Maggi snickered.

"Okay, so assuming we *did* try to send this message," Gaiomere began, "Not only would we have to build a transmitter, but we'd have to build a signal booster—"

Whitsom cleared his throat. "Would it...uh...would it be at all helpful if someone in our party were to—oh, I don't know—have a transmitter on their person?"

Gaiomere stared at him blankly for a full five seconds before her face split into a grin. "Whit, you clever rascal, you—"

"What, you've just *had* it this whole time?" Maggi spluttered disbelievingly.

"Well, when I came to grab Atlas from his room the morning we snuck out, I was pretending to be his guard for the day—it would have looked pretty suspicious if I hadn't had my transmitter."

"So, we've just got to build the signal booster—" Atlas started, but he broke off when he saw Gaiomere's face.

"I'm just not sure we'd be able to find anything I'd need to build it," she said distractedly, tucking a curl behind her ear. "Not here, anyway. And I'm sure anything we are able to find, we won't have the means to barter with..."

"We'll figure it out," Atlas said firmly. "Just tell us what you need."

Gaiomere began to jot down a list. Whitsom watched her with a strange expression, his lips pulled up at the corners and his eyes sparkling with mirth.

"What?" she snapped, when she finally noticed his staring.

His smirk broadened. "You wanna fight."

Gaiomere's cheeks darkened, and she opened her mouth to retort, but Whitsom didn't give her a chance.

"What happened to 'I'm no accomplice, Whitsom?'" he crooned. "What happened to 'Don't be a sheep, Whitsom?'" He sat back in his bed, a self-satisfied look on his face. "Face it. You want a fight just as bad as I do."

"That's not true—" Gaiomere exclaimed, flustered.

"It didn't make you angry, how quickly that big fellow would have shot Maggi, or Rasta, if we hadn't taken the bullets from his gun?" Whitsom demanded.

"Of course it did—"

"And you didn't have a problem with the skinny guy using my leg as a chopping block?"

"Whit, don't be—"

But Whitsom wasn't listening. Atlas wasn't sure he'd ever seen him so impassioned as he declaimed, "Every single 'Renegade' here feels the exact same way about their tribe that you do about ours. Every one of us wants to be able to walk free, without having to fear being killed, or captured, or sent away, like Gwena. You think they like having to conduct all their business five thousand feet underground?"

"No, of course not—"

"We'll always have to hide, as long as this war carries on. The only way we're going to be able to be truly free, to be truly safe, is if we rally against a common enemy. All of us."

Atlas sat very stiffly in his chair, his gaze bouncing between the siblings.

In a matter of moments, it had all come spilling out—exactly what Talikoth feared. No matter how much Gaiomere argued with her brother, Whitsom's words were true. It was why Talikoth worked so diligently to hegemonize the Ren—they were a wild card, a population that did not defer to the reigning power. At any moment in time, they could choose to turn against them, and while Talikoth had an army of three thousand, he had long suspected—and now Atlas thought his suspicion may have been warranted—that the Ren, consolidated, would have more.

Whitsom looked at Gaiomere expectantly, but she had turned her back to him, her shoulders taut and hands clenched into fists at her side.

"No," she said, her voice so quiet that Atlas almost didn't hear her. When she turned around, there were unshed tears in her eyes. "No—we send the message to Moonstone—to keep the Obarion out of the North, that's *it*—and then we'll be on our way. No more fighting. No more bloodshed. Nobody else that I love is going to die for this stupid, endless war."

"Gai—" Whitsom started, but Gaiomere interrupted him.

"I've got to go finish this list." She snatched her notebook off of the bed, covertly swiped at a tear that had slipped from the corner of her eye, and disappeared into the guest suite.

Atlas watched her go, his brow furrowed. He had half a mind to go comfort her—but what could he say that wouldn't be a lie?

No one else that you love is going to die. This war will be over soon enough.

All of it felt like perfunctory poppycock.

Maggi and Rasta soon wandered off to dally around the main hall, and Atlas was left alone with Whitsom, who looked sobered after his argument with his sister.

He was silent for several moments, and Atlas was just contemplating leaving him alone to his thoughts, when Whitsom suddenly said, "You're Obarion. Do you think they can be beaten?"

Atlas sat back, his eyes wandering pensively to the ceiling.

"I've never seen soldiers like Talikoth's—in numbers and in skill," Atlas started. Whitsom nodded, grimacing, and he continued, "But...according to what

I've read, anyway…history is littered with stories of wars that shouldn't have been won by the side that claimed victory." He paused, wondering if he should ask the question on the forefront of his mind. "Why is it a matter of the Obarion being beaten? Why not the Vedas?"

Whitsom frowned, leaning back against the pillows propped up behind him. "We all know the stories. The mighty clan who advanced west—annihilating every tribe in their path."

Atlas shook his head quickly. "The only people killed were those that refused to stop fighting. We assimilated the others."

"They ever tell you how many?"

Atlas looked up sharply at the bed-ridden boy. "What?"

Whitsom wore a strangely knowing look that Atlas didn't like. It made him feel as though he were the last one in on a joke.

"They ever tell you how many refused to stop fighting?" he repeated, unwavering.

Atlas opened his mouth, but then closed it again, scowling at the ground.

"No," he admitted after a few moments.

Whitsom shrugged, folding his hands behind his head. "Of course, I don't know much myself. I only know what our folks told us—and the stories we heard from other nomads while we were on the roam. All I know is we heard some pretty scary tales about the Obarion clan."

"What makes the Vedas any better, though?" Atlas demanded defensively. "It's not as though they've never killed anyone."

"I learned a lot during the month we were there. About how the Vedas replant trees, and about how they're working on a mass-purification solution for all of the lakes in the Westland—about their laws—how they never kill children." He shrugged again. "I don't know—I'm sure they've got their own ugly baggage too, but it seems like, if I've got to pick a side, they're who I'm going with."

Atlas looked away from him, glaring at the opposite wall as he asked, "Even if you know it's the losing side?"

"Better to die for something I believe in than survive to build a world that I wouldn't want to see my children grow up in," Whitsom reasoned. He gestured towards Atlas, adding, "I mean, look at you. Those guys were your buddies and they tried to kill you. Do you really want to live in a world where you can't trust anybody to have your back?"

Whitsom's words, though Atlas was sure he had not meant them to be, felt like a punch in the stomach. Atlas let out a heavy exhale, pushing to his feet.

"Bathroom," he ground out, stalking out of the room before the other boy could get another word in. He pulled open the door so forcefully that it banged against the wall behind it, and Gaiomere, who sat on the bed bent over her notebook, jumped.

"Sorry," he muttered, striding past her and into the bathroom. He slammed the door behind him, leaning against the counter as he attempted to get a handle on the mixture of emotions rushing through him, but he couldn't.

Atlas growled, slamming his fist into the wall beside the sink before he could stop himself. The skin on his fingers split, and his knuckles throbbed, but he ignored the pain, sitting down on the edge of the bathtub and burying his face in his hands.

I think we can trust him, Gai.

Could he even trust anything she was saying?

Moonstone seemed inclined to trust him.

I trust him.

I trust him.

I trust him.

His head jerked up, and he ran a shaky hand through his hair, letting out a breath. There were so many things that didn't make any sense—the Vedas' and Renegades' accounts for the Obarion clan were vastly different from what he grew up learning, and it wasn't as though he could go home and have a heart-to-heart with Talikoth.

But one thing he knew for sure was that Talikoth had *never* trusted him.

Atlas had thought, for many years, that it was him. He had been sure that once he got smarter, faster, stronger, better at tactics, Talikoth might have let him in on some things—may have shared some of his plans, asked for input, or even just treated Atlas like an equal.

But Atlas was the best fighter in his year, and he understood more about tactics than Crowley and Caddo combined. He had stopped growing when he was sixteen, so he was as tall as he would ever be—stronger than he'd ever been—and still, *still,* Talikoth did not trust him.

Had Talikoth known, even then, that Atlas could be captured? Had he thought confiding in him would be too much of a risk, that he would not be able to withstand torture and interrogation without spilling a secret or two?

But no, even Crowley, so drunk on his power, did not *really* have Talikoth's trust. Atlas had seen it in the way that Talikoth had withheld bits and pieces of information from him, information that Atlas had seen scrawled across Talikoth's notes when he'd left them at the dinner table. He had heard him verbally eviscerate the old man when he made a mistake, heard him threaten Crowley's job at the slightest blunder.

No, Atlas didn't believe that anyone had Talikoth's trust—not really. All of these years, he had thought that there was something wrong with *him*—but Whitsom, however naive, trusted him immediately. Moonstone believed the best in him, even if it may have been for some hidden agenda. And Gaiomere, who wanted so badly to hate him for the clan he hailed from...even *she* chose to trust him, in the end.

But not Talikoth. Not his training mates, who jumped at the opportunity to kill him. Not even Bettoni, who was as good as a brother to him, who, out of everyone in his squad, he would have said he had trusted with his life.

He wasn't completely sure Gaiomere wouldn't betray him, if it came down to keeping her family safe. But he could confidently say he trusted Whitsom with his life, and that was more than he could say for anyone else on the planet.

Granted, it did not help that the only person he trusted with his life was currently bound to bed and rendered incapacitated, but he would take what he could get.

Gaiomere was just finishing up the list when he came out of the bathroom.

"Sometimes the wallpaper really offends me, too," she remarked off-handedly, and his lips twitched. He instinctively clutched a hand over his bleeding knuckles and walked over beside her, peering down at her list.

Atlas let out a low whistle. "That is a lot of supplies."

She wrinkled her nose, passing him the sheet of paper. "I did warn you."

"And what happens when we inevitably can't get all of this stuff from the Under?" Atlas asked, his eyes scouring over the items, many of which he did not recognize by name.

Gaiomere pouted a little. "Then we have to go above ground."

Maggi and Rasta joined them soon after that, and the four decided to chunk up the list: Atlas would take the first third, Gaiomere would take the last, and Maggi and Rasta would tackle the middle.

"Alright, empty your pockets," Maggi said. "We have to somehow come up with enough material to barter a small village."

Gaiomere began to divvy out some of the detoxifiers from her container, Rasta untied the laces from his shoes, and Maggi stripped the sheets off of the beds.

"What?" she asked innocently, when she caught Gaiomere's disapproving stare. "They're *charity sheets*."

Gaiomere rolled her eyes, deftly unhooking her earrings and tossing them into the pile.

"Ooh, you *know* she's serious—those were a gift from Raider," Maggi said, grinning wickedly.

"Hmm, I wonder how much the *rest* of your hair would get us?" Gaiomere mused, shooting the younger girl a scathing glare.

Maggi shrugged. "I'd look great."

Thirty minutes later, the four of them stood around their pitiful little pile.

Maggi turned to glare at Gaiomere accusingly.

"Where's that fancy necklace you're always wearing?" she demanded. "That sucker could get us loads of stuff—"

"That was my *mother's!*" Gaiomere exclaimed in an affronted tone. "It's not up for grabs." She eyed the little pile ruefully, her fingers absently toying with her hair. "Maybe I should—"

"DO IT!" Maggi shrieked, jumping up and down and clapping her hands excitedly.

"I like your hair," Rasta said quietly.

Maggi leapt on top of the bed. "FEEL THE LIBERATION!"

Gaiomere looked squeamish. "I just—oh—oh, I don't know, Mags—"

"LET THE CURLY CASTLE FALL!"

"I really don't think it's necessary," Atlas said quickly. "Why don't we just see what we can get for all this and go from there?" Gaiomere nodded in agreement, and after a few moments of grumbling, Maggi climbed down off the bed, snatched their barter items off the ground, and dragged Rasta out of the room. Atlas and Gaiomere followed after them.

Bartering, as Atlas expected, came quite naturally to him. It felt like the evenings he'd wanted to stay in the library after hours back at Headquarters. Avanell, the seventy-year-old librarian with a ridiculous monocle, had a weakness for a charming smile and an earnest petition for the pursuit of knowledge.

And Delurah fared no better when he'd wanted third helpings of dinner, or when he'd asked her to cover for him when he, Coral, and Bettoni snuck out late to play bruiseball in the Stadium. Everyone had a price, and Atlas had a proclivity for unearthing them.

He could haggle fairly well, so when he met back up with the others in the infirmary two hours later, he was unsurprised to see that he had gathered the most supplies by a long shot. Maggi looked at him suspiciously, a measly roll of wire clutch in her hand.

"What'd you do, steal all that?"

Atlas smirked. "That's called talent, pipsqueak. Maybe you should get some."

Maggi snorted. "Your only talent is resembling a squirrel's butt—"

Atlas promptly shoved her, and Maggi toppled sideways, flopping onto the bed next to Whitsom's in a heap. It was unfortunate that, at that moment, Gaiomere had chosen to glance up from her notebook. She arched an eyebrow, and Atlas cheeks flushed. "She started it," he mumbled.

"Did not!" came Maggi's muffled reply.

Gaiomere rolled her eyes, turning back to her notebook. "Alright, as expected, we pretty much only managed to gather the basics," she announced, once she had updated her list with the items they'd acquired. "Which means we're going to have to go above ground."

"How are we going to find anything we need above ground?" Atlas asked. He pulled the list towards him. "Semiconductors, capacitors...these all sound like highly-specified components—"

"Highly-specified components that will be found in highly-specified environments." Gaiomere nodded, looking directly at Whitsom. "I've got to go to the Ramshackles."

Whitsom sat up quickly, wincing as his bad leg was jostled abruptly by the movement.

"Absolutely not."

"Whit, I don't have a choice—"

"You are not going to the Ramshackles without me. You're insane—"

"Wait, clue me in," Atlas interjected, frowning. "What are the Ramshackles?"

Gaiomere sighed, carding a hand through her curls as she explained, "They're the remains of the big —" She broke off, snapping her fingers, as though the phrase were escaping her. "You know the big, sprawling concrete scapes. You've got a lot of them in the South."

Atlas smiled a little. "Cities. They were called cities."

"Right, those. Well, a city is where we're most likely to find an old car—and *that's* my best bet getting everything else we need on this list. I saw Dad take one apart once. It should have everything we need—"

"Unless they've all been scrapped for parts already," Whitsom said, his face tense. "In which case, you travel to the Ramshackles and get yourself killed for nothing." Gaiomere started to argue, but he cut her off. "Gai, the *only* reason we were safe last time we went to the Ramshackles was because Raider's gang ran the place. They're gone now, which means there's nothing that stands in the way of you getting your throat ripped out—"

"*I don't have a choice,*" Gaiomere repeated through gritted teeth. "Whitsom, if we don't get this message to Moonstone, there won't be a corner of the North where we can avoid getting our 'throats ripped out.'"

"We can be sly," Maggi pointed out. "There's less of us now, so easier for us to sneak around—"

Gaiomere whirled around, her face shocked and angry.

"Are you out of your *mind*? You're not coming with me—"

"Why not?" Maggi demanded. "I protected Rasta and I for *weeks*, all on my own—"

"That's not an excuse to put yourself into harm's way," Gaiomere scolded. "You're not going."

"You aren't either," Whitsom broke in, glaring at his sister. "It's too dangerous by yourself—"

"I'll go with her," Atlas offered.

Gaiomere's brow furrowed, and her eyes flashed with annoyance. "Just in case you two didn't realize, I am *not* a child, and I don't need a babysitter—"

"Gaiomere, you're sixteen," Whitsom snapped. "You're barely older than Maggi. You go with Atlas, or not at all."

Her mouth snapped shut, and she glared at her brother for several moments, before she let out a harsh breath, snatching up her notebook and springing to her feet. She rounded on Atlas, snapping, "We leave in half an hour. If you aren't ready, you get left behind."

Whitsom turned to him as soon as she'd left, his face more serious than Atlas had ever seen it.

"If anything happens to my baby sister—"

"I know," Atlas said quickly.

Whitsom nodded, flopping back onto his pillows.

"The Ramshackles are rough," he told him. "Most of us avoid them, if we can help it. The ones up here are run by a few different gangs—they trade scraps and kill animals off in hordes to disrupt the food supply for the warring clans."

Atlas blinked, sitting up straighter. "You're kidding."

"Nope. They're excellent trackers. About a decade back they figured out where the Vedas got their food supply—the gangs in the South did the same for the Obarion—and they started killing off as many animals in the area as they could. The clans caught on to what was happening and moved hunting grounds, but the gangs always find them again eventually. They have to keep on moving hunting grounds—it wastes a lot of fuel and resources—"

"Which is their intention, of course," Atlas said wryly. It was brilliant. Incredibly inconvenient, but brilliant nonetheless.

"Raider believed that they could burn the Obarion out. He started in the South—planted a few gangs there, taught them the ropes—and then moved up north to do the same to the Vedas—before his gang moved on, anyway."

"So, what? They don't want *anyone* to win?" Atlas asked, bewildered.

"They just want to teach the clans a lesson, I think," Maggi said quietly. "That you can't bend the world to your will."

Atlas stared blankly at his hands in his lap. More and more of the Ren were proving to be so much more than he expected.

According to Whitsom, the nearest Ramshackle was not far, but to be safe, they bought a days' worth of food with the leftover barter material. Gaiomere traded her sandals for sneakers, and her skirt for some baggy harem pants, and Whitsom gave Atlas permission to take his quarterstaff. The older boy looked uncharacteristically anxious as Atlas and Gaiomere prepared to set off. Just as they were about to leave the infirmary, he pulled his little sister into a tight hug, whispering, "Please, be safe."

"I'll be fine, Whit," she promised.

She glanced over at Maggi, her expression growing stern as she added, "You keep Rasta out of trouble while we're gone—you know Whitsom's in no condition to run around after you."

"Oh, *I* know," Maggi said, grinning mischievously.

Gaiomere glanced over at Atlas; it was only her eyes that betrayed a hint of apprehension. "Ready?" she asked. He nodded, following her out of the infirmary, through the entrance doors, and up the painfully long staircase. They retrieved the knife and Whitsom's quarterstaff from the guards, and pushed open the heavy cellar doors to step into blinding, bright sunlight.

CHAPTER TEN

As he and Gaiomere began their trek, a strange nervousness fluttered in Atlas' stomach, one he grew more and more suspicious was not due to the threat of impending danger. He had never really struggled with how to navigate social interactions. It was easy enough to listen to people ramble on and on—humans, he observed, loved to talk about themselves. But now, Atlas found himself wracking his brain for something. A remark on the scenery? Drab. A question about the Ramshackles? Disingenuous. An incendiary comment about the role of war in human history to spark an invigorating debate? Exhausting.

They passed the dilapidated buildings he had noticed when they first arrived at the Under, but now Atlas caught a glimpse of others in the distance. Some stood tall, some short and squat. Signs of former civilization cropped up, even miles out from the city, but each structure bore the markings of war—scorch marks staining crumbling brick, shattered windows and doors that hung off their hinges.

Atlas cleared his throat. "So...the ex-boyfriend used to run this particular city?"

Gaiomere glanced at him sideways, and he nearly smacked himself on the forehead.

"He *wasn't* my boyfriend, but...yeah. He did. It was safer, then—for us anyway. Nobody sneezed unless

Raider gave them permission."

Atlas snorted. "Sounds like Talikoth."

Gaiomere's brows creased. "You don't like your dad very much, do you?"

He frowned, looking down at the cracked and crumbling concrete beneath their feet. Atlas had never really given much thought to whether or not he *liked* Talikoth.

"He made me strong," he said finally. "Stronger than I would have been if I were raised by someone else."

Gaiomere didn't reply, but Atlas could tell she still thought about it, for the crease in her brows deepened.

He tossed the quarterstaff between his hands, wondering if he would have to use it. If they were lucky, they could slip in and out of the city without the Ramshackle gangs being any wiser. Experience, though, had taught him to prepare for the worst.

The ground sloped upwards steadily, and soon the both of them were breathing heavily. The noon sun beat down on them, and he and Gaiomere passed the water bottle back and forth.

"I haven't been here in almost a year," Gaiomere said. "So, I'm a little worried that whatever gangs run the place now will have eyes on whoever comes in and out."

"We'll be alright," Atlas said firmly. He glanced at her from the corner of his eye. "You know how to use that, right?"

She looked down at the knife in her hand. A beat passed before she answered.

"Yes."

He arched a brow. "Gaiomere, you're lying."

She glared at him for several stubborn moments, before she let out a huff of air, and admitted, "Fine, I'm lying. But I'm sure it's not so hard to figure out—"

"How do you grow up fleeing Flesh Flayers and clansmen without learning how to fight?"

"I *know* how to fight," she insisted.

He shook his head, chuckling as she muttered mutinously under her breath.

"You should learn how to fight," he told her matter-of-fact.

"Whitsom can teach me just fine," she sniffed haughtily.

"I beat Whitsom. Frequently."

"He's probably not trying."

Atlas laughed, and her vexed expression cracked, a smile lifting the corners of her lips.

"It's worth learning, though. You may not always have a rock or a spear handy—and your opponent may not always be distracted."

"*Fine,*" she agreed, blowing a strand of hair from her face.

He hesitated, and then added with a straight face, "If you're practicing with me, we'll probably have to get you a ladder, though." She shot him a quizzical look, and he continued, "You know—for when you practice face shots and stuff."

He laughed again as she let out a shriek of outrage, and easily dodged the fist that came flying towards his shoulder. She *hmphed,* stomping ahead of him, but he lengthened his strides and easily caught up with her, still snickering.

After what felt like a never ending uphill climb, they eventually reached a plateau. Beyond the plateau, the mountain sloped down into a deep valley, in which the city skyline contrasted against the horizon

The buildings were clustered together here, though many of their walls were also caved in and windows broken. Atlas thought he saw a shadow shift in the doorway, and he tightened his grip on the quarterstaff. Gaiomere unconsciously drifted closer to him.

"Are there—are there people in these houses?" he asked, in an attempt at nonchalance.

Her jaw tensed. "They're drifters who want to stay close enough to the city to utilize its resources, but who don't have the man-power to go toe-to-toe with the gangs. They won't hurt us, as long as we don't pose a threat."

They made their way down into the valley, and Atlas got his first good look at the Ramshackle.

A couple of buildings still stood at their full height, but most looked as though their sides had been blown in or their tops sheared clear off. Craters indented the concrete where bombs had fallen over a hundred years ago. Wildlife had long since begun to reconquer the concrete jungle—weeds sprang up from the cracks in the pathway, vines climbed dozens of feet up the tall, steel towers, and he spotted a couple of deer scampering along an alleyway, their hooves clicking against the pavement.

"Stick to the shadows," Gaiomere whispered, and the two of them moved into the shade of a tall building, picking their way over fallen blockades and piles of shattered glass.

"I'm surprised we haven't seen a car yet," Atlas said quietly.

His concept of the city was entirely informed by what he'd read in history books and what he'd seen in the South. There, cars, busses, even trains in some areas, littered the streets, toppled over and deserted.

But here, there were few vehicles, and the cars they did pass were just metal frames, their insides already stripped clean.

Something clattered ahead, and Atlas yanked Gaiomere deeper into the shadows, both of them stilling. He held his breath as he peered out around the corner, his heart pounding in his chest—

But it was only a deer. He let out a relieved sigh, and Gaiomere, who had grasped onto his arm, released her hold, giving him a sheepish smile.

They continued on, and Atlas' heart beat faster with every step they took. The deeper they went into the city, the longer it would take to make a quick escape.

They had been walking for a half an hour when Gaiomere finally spotted one.

"There!" she exclaimed in a whisper. He followed her finger and saw it too: lying on its side, at the foot of a building that was at least fifty feet high, its wheels stolen and windows smashed out of their frames.

"Come on," Atlas muttered, pulling her across the street. They slipped into the gap between the car and the building, and Gaiomere crouched down, attempting to open the hood, but the sidewalk beside the car jutted up sharply, butting against it, so that it couldn't move.

"We'll have to get it off its side," Atlas observed.

She gave him a nervous look. "That's going to make so much noise."

"We don't really have another choice, do we?"

She sighed, nodding, and the two of them placed

themselves on either end of the car, bracing their hands against the rusted metal roof.

"On three," Atlas said. "One. Two. *Three.*"

It took four tries before they were able to move it. Atlas ended up putting his feet against the wall and using his back to push. The car landed right-side up with a resounding *clang,* so loud that both of them froze for several moments.

"I'll keep watch," Atlas said, when he was certain the coast was clear. Gaiomere nodded, opening the hood and propping it up.

Atlas gripped the quarterstaff in both hands, peering down the long, empty street. He couldn't imagine living in a place that was a constant reminder of the First War. Sometimes, patrolling the deserts in the South, or even traversing the forests during his time in the North, he could forget about the wars. Forget about the dwindling oil, and the raids, and the pollution in the water, if only for a moment. Sometimes he could forget that he lived in a world hanging on by a thread. But here, everywhere he looked spoke of how the Westland once teemed with life.

"How's it coming?" he asked Gaiomere.

"Just disconnected the ground cable," came her reply.

He glanced back to see her bent over the hood, diligently prying at a slab of metal.

"Do you uh—do you need any help?" She gave him an amused glance, before turning back to her work, finally wrenching the metal apart and setting the spare piece on the ground beside her.

Gaiomere had pulled her hair up into a bun atop her head, and Atlas noticed a small scar on the juncture of her jaw and neck that he'd never noticed before.

"Will you hand me the screwdriver in my bag?" she asked without looking at him.

He grabbed her bag from where she'd discarded it and dug through until he found the screwdriver. He passed it to her wordlessly, and she started to unscrew a metal piece near the headlight, which supported a mount affixed with a silver, circular die.

"Is that the capacitor?"

"The semiconductor," she corrected, successfully disconnecting the mount and slipping it into her bag. She turned back to the car and moved over to the other side, beginning to unscrew another component.

Atlas realized he had been watching her too long, and hastily turned back to the street, but there was no movement in either direction. Perhaps the gangs had abandoned the area altogether, and all that was left were the drifters?

"I'm going to have to cut this out, the screw is stripped," Gaiomere muttered. "Shouldn't be hard, with the engine gone."

Atlas started to respond, but a sudden noise towards the end of the nearest alleyway made him freeze. He gripped the quarterstaff even tighter, taking half a step towards the backstreet. Should he head them off? Or hope they were moving in a different direction?

"Almost got the resistor," Gaiomere said behind him. "Then it's just the capacitors—"

He heard a *bang* in the direction of the alleyway, louder this time. "Gaiomere..."

"I know, I know," she said uneasily. He glanced back as she withdrew two tubular objects from beneath the hood and shoved them into her bag. She hastily circled around the back of the car, opening the trunk. "I've still got to find the capacitors—"

Four figures rounded the corner of the alleyway, their voices and laughter echoing through the empty street, and Atlas' blood ran cold.

"Gaiomere, get down," he commanded. He realized belatedly that he had not even needed to issue the order, for when he glanced back, her head was buried in the trunk, virtually invisible to the approaching newcomers.

They caught sight of him and veered in his direction, jostling one another. He heard one of them let out a "*Whoop!*" as he withdrew a switchblade from his jacket.

"Lookie, boys, we got a new friend," taunted the boy on the left, who had a long, hooked nose.

As they approached the car, Atlas watched them carefully. None could be much older than he was, and they didn't appear to have any guns, but even so, Atlas was not so foolish to think he could take all four at once.

"What are you doing here?" asked the fellow on the right, with shockingly red hair. "This is occupied territory."

Atlas straightened.

"Just came to collect some supplies." He kept his tone even and measured as he added, "I apologize, I wasn't aware the area was occupied—"

"He *wasn't aware!*" crooned the shortest of the four. They snickered and advanced with relaxed grins. They had every advantage here, and were aware of the fact. They had the numbers, and knew the territory.

The tallest stopped directly in front of Atlas, so near that Atlas could smell his stale breath. "Who else is with you?"

"Nobody," he lied unflinchingly. "I came alone."

The boy smirked. "People don't usually come here alone. If they're smart. Maybe you're not, though."

"It's just me," Atlas insisted. The tall boy's face contorted with anger, and in a split second, he brought his knee up towards Atlas' groin. But Atlas was prepared. He checked the kick with his right leg and pushed his quarterstaff against the boy's chest, forcing him backwards. Atlas swung the quarterstaff as hard as he could, slamming the bottom knot into the boy's head. He groaned, collapsing, and the other three surged forward.

Atlas dodged the short one's punch and landed a blow to the young man's throat, but then his head split in pain as one of the others slammed their fist into the side of his skull. He staggered, managing to stay on his feet even as dots danced in front of his eyes.

He pointed the sharp end of the quarterstaff towards the two that remained on their feet as they closed in on him, but before they could launch another attack, the roar of an engine exploded through the air. The two jumped, their heads swinging towards the sound.

A car came flying around the corner, its tires screeching against the pavement. Atlas gaped, for cars weren't supposed to be able to run anymore—not when Talikoth had all of the fuel.

In the commotion, he glanced towards the vehicle Gaiomere had been working on, but he could not see her anywhere. Perhaps she had clambered into the trunk—

The car squealed to a stop in front of them, and four more young men climbed out. But before

Atlas could even focus on the new arrivals, he heard pounding footsteps, and realized that there were more approaching from either direction down the street. And these newcomers had guns.

The two boys who had been about to attack him pulled their comrades to their feet, and they clustered together against the wall of the building, each of their expressions alarmed.

"I *thought* we told you that you were *not* assigned the role of welcoming committee," drawled the young man who had exited the driver's seat. He looked about Whitsom's height, with pecan-brown skin, tousled black hair and a thick beard. "All new arrivals go through *us*, Benemitch—"

"I—I know!" stammered the short one who had tried to hit Atlas. "I'm sorry—it was just—we didn't recognize this one!"

The young man frowned, turning to look at Atlas. He walked towards him slowly, his eyes shrewdly flickering over Atlas' face.

"No, I don't know this one either. Where are you from, stranger?"

"The South," Atlas told him honestly. "And I'm just passing through. I really didn't know this area was occupied..." From his peripherals, he could see the others circling them. One of them snatched Gaiomere's bag from the ground and was going through it. A huge, pale, hulking giant of a man—he must have been well over seven feet tall—leaned against one of the cars, his muscles bulging threateningly as he crossed his arms over his chest, a morning star gripped in his meaty fist.

"Yeah, see, thing is. I don't believe you," the young man said, sighing in a belabored way. "*Everybody* comes here with the same old excuse. I'm really growing tired of having to kill liars—"

"Wait!"

Atlas cursed, and several of the gang member's heads whipped towards Gaiomere, who scrambled out of the trunk. He wondered if she didn't notice the menacing way the newcomers surrounded them, or the fact that several of them had guns slung over their shoulders, because when she trotted over, she was beaming.

"I thought I recognized that voice!" she said, prancing over and stopping beside Atlas. "Hey, Koda!"

The black-haired young man blinked, recognition dawning on his face. "Gaiomere?"

She gave him a dazzling smile. "The one and only."

He let out a disbelieving laugh, pulling the girl into a headlock. Atlas started forward, until he realized that this new fellow—Koda, she'd said—was only ruffling her hair affectionately. Several of the other young men started forward to greet her, and Atlas stood there silently, immensely grateful to not be dead, but remarkably confused nonetheless.

Gaiomere wound her way through the gang of boys, looking as comfortable as if she were being swarmed by a gaggle of harmless children. Atlas felt a jolt of fear as she approached the hulking man, but before he could stop her, she threw her arms around his lower back—for that was all she could reach—and hugged him tightly.

"I've missed you, Grit!"

The giant man patted her on the head, his scarred and pockmarked face splitting in a wide grin as he grunted, "Missed you too, little one."

"I haven't seen you in *ages!*" Koda exclaimed as she made her way back over to him and Atlas.

"That's what happens when you leave someone for dead," Gaiomere said waspishly. Her voice lacked any real malice, but Atlas saw her eyes flash. He wanted to pull her aside, to ask her what was going on. Was this an ally tribe, like Whitsom had mentioned, who just *happened* to be in the area at the same time? But no, Koda had made it sound like they had some sort of arrangement with the first group of boys who had come across Atlas. Were Koda and Benemitch part of rival gangs? And how did Gaiomere know Koda in the first place?

Koda waved off her snark. "C'mon, Gaiomere. You know we gotta follow the boss's orders." He glanced back towards Atlas, adding, "So who's your friend?"

Before she could answer, Atlas heard a new set of footsteps approaching, heavy boots clunking against the ground. The only reason that he heard it was because, almost in an instant, the chatter and hubbub silenced.

"Maybe my memory is failing me," said a cold voice. "But I was under the impression that I sent you out here to dispose of the new arrivals." Several of the boys towards the outside of the circle stepped aside, clearing the path for a blond young man with piercing blue eyes. He looked like he was at least three or four years older than Atlas, and as he moved closer, Atlas realized that he was a couple of inches taller, too.

And suddenly, everything clicked into place.

"Figured you'd want us to keep these ones alive," Koda said with a grin, leaning over and pinching Gaiomere's cheek. She swatted his hand away, glaring at him, and he laughed.

The tall boy's eyes flickered first over Atlas, and then to Gaiomere. The corner of his mouth pulled up into the faintest smirk.

"Wouldn't be the first time he tried to kill me," Gaiomere muttered.

The smirk broadened. He held his arms out on either side of him.

"Come on, now. Is that how we greet old friends?" He glanced sideways at one of his lackeys, whose rifle was hitched over his back. The boy immediately spun the rifle around, so that the barrel pointed directly at Gaiomere. The other gunmen did the same, and Atlas' heart jumped in his chest, as the blond boy continued, "We could be enemies...but I know you don't like how I treat my enemies."

Atlas glanced at Gaiomere. Her face was tense, and it looked as though she was battling with herself. Finally, she sighed, crossing her arms over her chest and mumbling, "Hi, Raider."

He gestured to his gunmen, and they immediately hitched their guns onto their backs once more.

"Back to the Hideout," Raider said in a carrying voice. The gang dispersed, sprinting off in every direction, bellowing out cries and whoops as they went. Koda moved towards the car, leaning against the door on the passenger side with a bored expression.

Raider turned back to the two of them. He wore a feral grin, and it made Atlas' stomach turn.

"Hey, Mere-Kat."

CHAPTER ELEVEN

A tlas decided, within five minutes, that he *hated* driving in cars. It might have partially been due to the fact that Raider sped recklessly through the narrow, barren streets with his foot unrelentingly pressed on the gas pedal and had a penchant for taking turns at such speeds that the car felt like it would overturn. Twice, they nearly crashed into a building, and once Raider actually plowed over an old, leaning street sign.

Gaiomere leaned forward, her hands coming to the back of Raider's seat as she asked, "I thought you guys were going north?"

"We did," he told her. "Headed north for three moons, but we had to turn back." He glanced over his shoulder at her. "There's nothing up there. Nothing. No food. No water. Everything is dead."

Gaiomere hummed pensively, leaning back in her seat, and Raider glanced at Atlas in the rearview mirror. "You got a name, Peewee?"

Atlas must not have hidden his irritation well, for the older boy's eyes glittered with amusement.

"Atlas," he muttered.

They drove for a few minutes more before the car jerked to a stop, and Raider and Koda hopped out. The two of them started towards a massive structure. It must have been the tallest building left standing in the Ramshackle, stretching at least four hundred feet high. Raider jerked his head for Atlas and Gaiomere to follow.

Gaiomere moved to join them, but Atlas grabbed her arm, pulling her back and saying in a low voice, "Gaiomere...these guys just pointed guns at us."

She rolled her eyes. "Raider likes his jokes. He won't hurt us. Not without reason." She strode off after them, and Atlas hurriedly lengthened his strides to catch up with her.

"We're just supposed to be getting the capacitors and getting out," Atlas reminded her as he fell into step with her. "We don't have time for detours—"

Gaiomere shook her head, shooting a wary glance up at the pair in front of them.

"You don't understand. We don't get those capacitors without them. They ran this city before they left, and from the looks of it, they took the reins right back when they returned." Atlas did not have time to respond, for they had reached the door, and Koda held it open. He gave a flourished bow and waved them inside.

The building was made of grey concrete, and looked as though it had once been a warehouse, but the gang had transformed it into something of a makeshift hideout. There were sloppily crafted benches and stools constructed from scrap wood, a table with a plethora of papers spread out atop its surface, and, at the front of the room, a massive chair that resembled the thrones Atlas had seen in history books. Unsurprisingly, Raider crossed the room and sprawled across it, kicking his legs up on the armrest.

Koda and another boy, black-haired and pallid-skinned, spent fifteen minutes briefing Raider on—from what Atlas could hear—a hunting expedition they had undertaken a few hours before. He wondered if these were the sabotage attempts that Whitsom told him about.

When it appeared that they were finally finished, Raider called, "Alright, what do you want, Mere-kat?"

Atlas glanced up. Raider waved a hand lazily in their direction, and Gaiomere went over. After a second of hesitation, Atlas followed her. He didn't much care for being summoned like some second-class servant, but he saw little room for complaint in their current predicament.

"We need a capacitor," Gaiomere told Raider immediately. "Several, actually."

The blond boy did not even appear to be listening. He'd leaned his head back against the heavy stone of his chair, and his eyes had drifted closed.

"Oh, capacitors, did you say?" he asked in a disinterested tone.

Gaiomere let out an exasperated huff. "*Yes*, Raider, and I—"

"Whatever for?"

She froze, her eyes darting to Atlas. "Um—we're just—we just are working on a—on storing heat for—for the winter, you know—"

Raider let out a bark of laughter, his eyes popping open suddenly. He pulled himself up, resting his elbows against his knees.

"Oh, little Mere-kat. You still haven't learned to lie, sweetheart."

Sweetheart. Atlas scowled, and his hands clenched into fists at his sides.

"We're trying to send a message to her brother," he supplied in an even tone. "We got separated from him. He's got a recei—a transmitter on him."

Raider looked at him slowly, his lip curling. "Is

that so, Peewee?"

Atlas arched a brow, straightening up a little taller as Raider surveyed him. After a moment, the taller boy sighed, breaking his gaze and settling back into his throne.

"I do happen to have several capacitors at my disposal. I *suppose* I could be persuaded to part with them."

Gaiomere's face brightened. "Really?"

"*If*," he continued, and Gaiomere's face fell. "You would be inclined to help with a little project."

Gaiomere frowned. "Raider, your projects often end with a lot of people getting hurt—"

He shrugged. "Only the people that deserve it."

She bit her lip. "We have to be back to Maggi and Rasta by this evening," she said slowly. Raider grinned wolfishly.

"It won't take long," he promised.

She sighed. "Fine. What is it?"

He leaned forward, smirking. "I need you to override some controls."

Gaiomere blinked, staring at him suspiciously. "Is that it?"

"That's it."

She let out a harsh breath. "I—yeah—fine, okay."

Raider clapped his hands together, springing to his feet.

"Let's do it." He started to walk past her to the door, but she stopped him with a hand on his arm, raising her eyebrows expectantly.

"The capacitors," she intoned.

His eyes widened. "Mere-kat, you don't *trust* me?"

Her eyebrows traveled further towards her hairline, and

he sighed. "I'm hurt, truly." He snapped a finger, and two mousy boys appeared at his side. "Three capacitors in the car in sixty seconds." They nodded and disappeared.

Raider and Gaiomere started towards the car, and Atlas began to follow them, but the blond boy turned, holding up a hand and asking, "Need something, Peewee?"

Atlas thought that if he could make it through this trip without punching Raider in the face, he deserved an award.

"She's not going without me," he ground out.

Raider arched a brow, glancing at Gaiomere. "This your babysitter?"

She gave him a caustic look. "He's right, Raider. If you want my help, he comes too."

The blond rolled his eyes, and shot Atlas a disdainful frown. "Whatever."

The two mousy boys were loading the capacitors into the car when they reached it. Atlas slipped into the back seat, and stealthily slid the capacitors into Gaiomere's backpack. He wouldn't put it past Raider to go back on his end of the bargain, and he wasn't taking any chances.

"How long did it take you to figure out the car?" Gaiomere asked Raider once they had gotten moving.

"About five moons," he told her. "Would have taken ages longer without your notes, though."

Atlas had no desire whatsoever to speak to Raider more than absolutely necessary—all he really wanted to do was to sit in the back and sulk in silence—but his curiosity got the better of him.

"How did you do it?" he asked. "Without gasoline, I mean?"

Raider gave him a patronizing look in the mirror. "Cars can run on booze. You didn't know that?"

Atlas hadn't known that, but he didn't feel inclined to say so.

"Normally, running a car on alcohol can damage the engine," Gaiomere said, glancing over her shoulder at Atlas. "But last winter, Koda and I were working on some adjustments redesigning the engine, so that it would be better suited for ethanol, rather than gasoline."

"That's brilliant," Atlas said. "That would—I mean, that could completely revolutionize warfare—"

"Where did you say you were from, Witless?" Raider interrupted.

Gaiomere glared at him. "His *name* is Atlas and he helped Whitsom and I escape the Vedas' base, *and* find Maggi and Rasta—"

"Do you think they'll erect a statue in his honor when the Long War is finally over?" Raider quipped without missing a beat.

His tone was teasing, but something in Gaiomere seemed to snap. She turned to face him, her cheeks coloring indignantly.

"Better than you, you rat! You left us to the Flesh Flayers—"

"What have I told you time and time again, sweetheart?" Raider interrupted, smirking. He looked wholly unbothered by her outburst, and even had the audacity to reach over and tug on one of her curls. "You gotta fend for yourself."

"They almost slit my throat!" Gaiomere protested, slapping his hand away and pointing a finger at the scar adorning the juncture of her jaw.

"But they *didn't*." He shrugged, grinning crookedly at her. "I knew you guys would be alright." She let out a strangled noise of fury, crossing her arms over her chest and turning to look out the window.

"Besides," Raider continued, "you know that you'd have our protection if you and Whitsom joined our tribe." He glanced sideways at her. "You guys are brilliant. Your brain, his brawn. We could use you."

She arched an eyebrow. "All of us, huh?"

Raider clicked his tongue. "Come on, Mere-kat, you know we don't babysit. It isn't *your* fault their parents died—"

"It isn't theirs, either!" Gaiomere cried. "What, you think we'd just *abandon* them—"

Raider lifted a lazy shoulder, droning indifferently, "The Maggot's gotta be almost a teenager by now, hasn't she? They need to learn to fend for themselves."

Gaiomere shook her head, turning away from him again. "You're unbelievable," she muttered.

The two of them fell into silence. Atlas sat back in his seat and smirked smugly, his spirits lifted, if only marginally.

"Where are we going anyway?" Gaiomere asked quietly.

"The north edge of the Pass," Raider replied.

"Did you *not* hear the part where we needed to be home by this evening?" Gaiomere grumbled.

"Oh calm down, Mere-kat," Raider said, rolling his eyes. "We'll be quick, and I'll drop you and your babysitter off on the way back." He glanced sideways at her, adding, "How is it you got captured by the Vedas?"

"Well, they didn't capture us, exactly," Gaiomere

said. "I got injured on a landmine. They provided me medical care but then they just—well, they wouldn't let us leave, not even to find Maggi and Rasta."

"We'll put some Ricin in their water," Raider said with a straight face, and Gaiomere laughed, before she seemed to remember that she was still mad at Raider, and she promptly crossed her arms over her chest and turned to glare out the window once more.

Atlas watched the landscape flash by as Raider sped south. It was clear he was used to traveling the area, for he found the old, worn roads easily, merging on and off any time the bombing damage became too gnarled to drive over.

Thirty minutes later, they slowed to a crawl, and Gaiomere leaned forward, peering over the dash.

"See anyone?" Raider asked her.

"Nope."

"Let's go."

The three of them clambered out of the car, and Raider opened the trunk. Atlas and Gaiomere circled around the car and stared for several moments, bewildered, at the contents of the trunk.

"Are those *drones*?" Gaiomere asked finally.

"They are," Raider said proudly.

"How did you get so many?" Atlas questioned.

Raider leaned against the car, smirking. "Found them holed up in an old military base. They were dead, but Koda figured out how to recharge the batteries. The system is unique, though—he couldn't figure out how to override the previous programmer codes."

"There's no telling I could then," Gaiomere pointed out, though she had already picked up one of the drones and was studying it carefully, separating several of the wires that ran across the top. Peeking out from beneath the drones in the trunk, Atlas thought he saw the hint of a gun barrel, and he felt his stomach clench as he wondered what Raider intended to do with that. Did the gang members always carry guns, or was he planning something?

"I have faith in you." Raider assured her. "Me and Asshat will keep watch."

Gaiomere threw Atlas an apologetic look as he followed the taller boy to a ridge overlooking the valley beneath. The ravine, perhaps a hundred feet below the cliff, stretched as far as his eyes could see. It resembled the South more closely than anything he had come across during his time in the North so far. The ground was dry and cracked and there were hardly any trees or shrubbery, save for a few saplings here and there.

Behind them, the tall evergreens stretched almost all the way to the cliff's edge, but the forest remained silent. Atlas wondered if the Vedas did not patrol the Pass this far from their base.

"When she's done, we're going to drop them on the landmines," Raider told him. He plopped down onto a rock near the ridge, leaning back against his arms. Atlas could have slammed the quarterstaff into Raider's head and he wouldn't even have time to prepare.

But then the blond boy's words actually registered.

"Why?" Atlas asked bewilderedly.

Raider looked at him like he was stupid. "You set off the landmines now, they're dead. Totally useless," he pointed out. He tossed a pebble down the slope, and they listened to it clatter against rock after rock until the sound was swallowed by the canyon. "You don't have to have the biggest army to win a war. You just have to tire the other side out enough."

Atlas sat down too, his mind racing. The landmines being deactivated could be a huge boon for the Obarion—especially if Raider deactivated the landmines further south, closer to their end of the Pass. Though Raider's gang was just trying to exhaust resources on every side, they could actually end up aiding Talikoth's agenda, however unwittingly.

The two of them sat in silence. Atlas watched curiously as Gaiomere sat cross-legged on the ground. She had opened up the back of the drone and fed a green wire into the open compartment. Her curly hair frizzed all around her, and the sun glinted off of her dark skin.

He looked away and saw Raider watching him, his eyebrows raised. After a moment, the taller boy snorted and looked away from him, shaking his head.

"I thought Gaiomere at least had *some* standards," he said wryly.

Atlas' patience suddenly evaporated. "Like what, being a douchebag?"

Raider's eyes flashed, but before he could respond, Gaiomere called, "I think I've got it!"

She had reassembled the drone and detached the remote. For a moment, she fiddled with the buttons, and it looked as though nothing were going to happen, but then the drone began to whir quietly. It lifted into the air and hovered beside Gaiomere.

"Atta girl, Mere-Kat," Raider crooned, clapping her on the back so hard that she stumbled forward a few steps.

"I didn't think that'd actually work," she said, looking rather pleased with herself. She handed the remote to Raider.

"I'm going to go check the coordinates—keep working on the others."

"Yes, Your Majesty," Gaiomere remarked sardonically, her voice low enough that Raider, who had crossed to the opposite side of the ridge, did not hear.

Atlas realized this was the first time they'd had a moment of privacy since they had encountered the gangs.

"He's uh—he seems nice," Atlas observed offhandedly.

Gaiomere looked at him sharply, and before he knew it, they were both laughing. She pulled off the back of this new drone, remarking, "He's more useful than he is pleasant, I'll give you that."

Atlas picked disinterestedly at his nails as he mused, "Seems a bit old for you, though."

She rolled her eyes, her cheeks coloring. "Great gooseberries, you sound like my brother. He's just an ally, for the record, so his age is irrelevant, but...I think he's a little older than Whitsom, twenty-one or so—"

Atlas let out a low whistle, and Gaiomere shot him a glare.

"*Just* an ally," she reminded him scathingly, and he chuckled. "And even if he wasn't, I'm almost seventeen!"

"When's your birthday?" Atlas asked curiously.

Gaiomere was fiddling with what looked like a tiny control panel in her lap, but he could still see the color in her cheeks deepen as she mumbled, "Fifteen days into the second autumn moon cycle."

He let out a bark of laughter. "You *just* turned sixteen—"

"Almost is a relative term—compared to my entire life span, eleven moons is nothing."

Atlas shook his head, still chuckling.

She maneuvered the control panel back into the drone and asked, "When's yours?"

He looked blankly at her.

"When's your birthday?" she clarified.

"Oh—um..." He frowned, wracking his brain as he tried to recall the date upon which he'd arrived at the Vedas' base, and how much time had passed.

"Day after tomorrow, actually," he realized aloud.

She blinked, giving him a strange look. "Oh. How old will you be?"

"Eighteen."

Gaiomere hummed, screwing the back panel into place before handing it to Atlas.

"Want to give it a whirl?" she asked.

He took the remote from her, trying to repress a rather giddy grin as he navigated the drone off the ground. It was sort of...fun. He wasn't sure he'd used such an adjective to describe anything outside of bruiseball in ages.

Gaiomere had begun to work on the next drone. Atlas grinned wickedly as he sent his drone careening towards her, bumping lightly into her back. She was so focused that, at first, she didn't notice, but after a few collisions, she turned and glared at him.

"*Atlas...*"

He snickered, directing the drone away from her. "Sorry."

It took Gaiomere another hour to reprogram the rest of the drones. The sun was beginning to creep its way back down towards the crests of the distant mountain range. When Raider finally made his way back over to them, Gaiomere and Atlas were making their drones battle midair, crashing recklessly into one another.

"When you children are done, we've got a job to do," Raider snapped.

Atlas let out a shout of victory, for Gaiomere had gotten distracted and he had knocked her drone from the air.

Together, the three of them were able to carry all of the drones across the ridge in two trips. When they returned with the second batch, Raider lined up the remotes side by side in rows.

"We'll have to be quick," he told them. "In case there are Vedas nearby that realize what's going on."

"How do we know where they are?" Gaiomere asked. "The land mines, I mean."

He pointed to the ground beneath their feet—he had scratched out long lines in the rock at intervals of about fifteen feet. "Slade and I came down here last week to get an idea of where they are—these aren't perfectly accurate, of course, but close enough that it won't take us hours to find them. The first one is *there* —" He pointed to a spot down in the ravine, about twenty feet from a cluster of feeble trees. "Just stick to the distance intervals and you should be good."

Gaiomere looked apprehensive, and Atlas immediately knew why. She had no loyalty to the Vedas, but to openly make a strike against them...

"We need those capacitors," Atlas reminded her quietly.

She nodded, taking a steadying breath and moving to stand beside Raider in front of the line of remotes. Atlas took his place at the end, and Raider called, "Alright. Let's do it."

A thrill of fear and excitement shot through Atlas as their drones lifted off into the air. He eyeballed the space between his drone and Gaiomere's—comparing it to the markers Raider had drawn on the ground—and sent his drone further east.

"It's a bummer—such awesome technology," Gaiomere muttered regretfully. "Couldn't we just keep *one*—"

"Focus, Mere-kat. Let's begin our descent."

Atlas sent his drone on a steady descent towards the ground, and he watched from his peripherals as Gaiomere and Raider did the same. He thought that he was on the right course...

But no, the drone touched down and nothing happened. Gaiomere, too, missed, but Raider's drone hit spot-on—there was an explosion of smoke and fire that blared across the barren chasm.

"*Boo yah!*" Raider shouted. Gaiomere had already adjusted her drone's landing, and within seconds, there was a second explosion, fumes encompassing her drone. She let out a shriek of surprise and delight. Atlas directed his drone up and west—based on where he'd seen Gaiomere's go off, and—

BOOM. Like gunfire, the blast tore through the air. Atlas' heart pounded, and he quickly moved to the next remote. Raider, who clearly seemed to have a knack for this sort of thing, jumped from remote to remote with such rapidity that he moved far ahead of either of them.

Gaiomere's face was bright, and as she set off the next explosion she gave a whimsical laugh, like a child playing a game, and Atlas cast her an amused glance.

"'Bout halfway!" Raider called as he detonated another landmine.

Atlas was just launching his tenth or eleventh drone when Gaiomere suddenly cried, "Stop! Raider, *stop!*"

Atlas lowered his remote, his drone hovering in the air, as he followed Gaiomere's gaze.

A couple of figures peeled across the ravine. It looked as though one of them limped, and from what Atlas could tell from so far away, they looked small. As though they might have even been children.

Raider, however, had only continued deploying drones. He set off another landmine, drawing closer and closer to where the two figures ran. If Raider kept going —especially at the pace they were moving—they would not get out of the way in time.

"Raider, *stop!*" Gaiomere said again.

"Could be Vedas," Raider said indifferently as he snatched up another remote and sent the drone hurtling into the air. Atlas froze.

At the base of the cliff, the limping figure had fallen, and their companion was attempting to pull them to their feet.

Raider's drone closed in on the next landmine, not a hundred yards away from the pair scrambling across the ravine.

"Raider, *stop*, please!" Gaiomere stormed towards him and grasped onto his arm. "You don't know that they're Vedas—they look like they're just kids."

"Get. *Off*." Raider snarled, flinging her aside like a ragdoll.

Atlas didn't even think. He strode towards Raider, who had turned back to his task, and slammed his fist into the side of Raider's jaw. The blond swore, dropping the remote and stumbling sideways. Atlas snatched the remote off of the ground and tossed it off of the cliff. The drone veered sideways, coasting before it slammed into the cliffside with a *crunch*.

Raider stood stock-still, his hands curled into fists at his side.

"Atlas..." Gaiomere said, her voice anxious. She pulled herself to her feet, looking at Raider with undisguised fear. A bruise was forming where her chin had collided with the ground.

The taller boy turned back to him slowly, his teeth bared in a wild grin.

"You're going to die for that, Peewee," he said quietly.

Raider lunged, and Atlas jerked out of the way, his hands instinctively coming up to protect his face. Adrenaline coursed through him unlike he'd ever felt, except perhaps during his fight with Talikoth—but no, he shouldn't think about that. It wouldn't do to ruminate on the only fight he'd ever lost.

Raider circled him like a predator, his blue eyes glinting with malice.

"You know how many scrubs I've killed, Peewee? Bigger and stronger than you." He kicked towards Atlas' stomach, and Atlas pulled his hips back, dodging the blow by inches. "You dance like Whitsom. Whitsom teach you how to dance?"

"Raider, stop!" Gaiomere pleaded. "I did what you wanted, please—we can—"

"You should know better than anyone, Mere-kat, what I do to people who interfere with my plans," Raider interrupted. He delivered several jabs in quick succession. The first two missed, but the third caught Atlas beneath the chin, and he stumbled backwards.

Raider took his opportunity and delivered a kick to Atlas' stomach so hard that he fell to the ground. The air was knocked from his lungs, and Atlas sucked in a breath, trying to get back to his feet—

But Raider was already there. His foot slammed into Atlas' knees as he got up, and he let out a groan of pain, crumpling back to the ground. And then Raider was on top of him, fists slamming into Atlas' face so hard that his head whipped from side to side. His nose broke. The taste of iron filled his mouth and blood poured down his face.

Spots danced in front of his eyes, but the punches kept coming, and Atlas started to drift in and out of consciousness.

Vaguely, like a half-asleep dream, he heard the trunk slam, pounding footsteps, and then, the cocking of a gun.

"Raider," came Gaiomere's voice. "*Stop*."

The assault on his face ceased, and the weight on top of him lifted. Atlas lifted his head and blinked. The blurriness in his eyes began to dissipate, and he saw Gaiomere holding the rifle he had seen shoved away in the trunk, her finger taut over the trigger, the barrel aimed directly over Raider's heart.

"You're not gonna shoot me, Mere-kat," the blond drawled, but Atlas did not miss the way he moved further away, nor the way his eyes flickered between Gaiomere's face and the barrel of the gun.

"Try me," she muttered through gritted teeth. She looked around, and then jerked her head towards the side of the cliff. "Go stand over there. And keep your hands in the air, too. If I see you move, I'll shoot you." He must have hesitated, because she snapped, "*Now,*

Raider."

He edged towards the cliff face, letting out a bark of laughter, though Atlas could hear the tremor of uncertainty in his voice.

"I can't believe you, Mere-kat. You're gonna shoot me, after all the help we've given your tribe, to help some loser—"

Gaiomere ignored his taunts, kneeling beside Atlas, though she kept the rifle and her eyes trained on the taller boy.

"Can you stand?" she asked quietly.

He nodded, pushing himself to his feet, but he swayed when he straightened, and staggered into Gaiomere.

"I just need you to make it to the car. Do you think you can do that, Atlas?" Her voice was gentle, but burning hot shame coursed through him as he nodded and lurched towards the vehicle.

You don't lose fights, boy. I'm not going to have some loser for a son.

Atlas climbed into the passenger seat, his chest burning as he sucked in lungfuls of air. Raider shifted towards the car, his eyes wide as he realized what they were about to do, but Gaiomere had the rifle trained on him still. Her hands trembled, but her gaze was unwavering. She backed towards the car slowly, and Atlas leaned over and pushed open the door.

Without taking her eyes off Raider, she said, "Do you think you can keep this aimed at him while I figure out how to drive this thing?"

Atlas nodded, rolling down his window and taking the rifle from her, swinging the barrel around and tightening his finger over the trigger. Raider was still about twenty feet from the car, but if he started sprinting...

"Gaiomere, *come on!*" the blond shouted petulantly. He suddenly sounded much younger, and certainly less intimidating, but Atlas could not find it in himself to be smug.

The engine roared to life and Raider became hysteric. His hands tugged at his hair, and his eyes were wild and manic.

"The 'R' is for reverse, and the 'D' is for forward," Atlas muttered from the corner of his mouth. His friends had always teased him for the amount of outdated, seemingly pointless knowledge he had retained from his many hours in the library, but in this moment, he was immensely grateful for it.

Gaiomere kicked the car into reverse and hesitantly pushed on the gas. Raider seemed to decide that he didn't care about the gun aiming at him, for he began to sprint towards the car, his expression deranged. Gaiomere was fumbling with the gear shift, so Atlas made a split second decision. He swiveled the barrel low and pulled the trigger.

The rifle kicked back into Atlas' shoulder and he winced, but his shot was true. Raider let out a roar of pain, his hands grasping at his leg as he fell to the ground.

"Nice shot," Gaiomere praised. She let out a breath of relief as she finally got the car into drive, slamming on the gas and taking off. In the mirror, he could see Raider roaring expletives as they sped away, blood seeping through his fingers where he gripped his shin.

"Holy hazelnut, that was close," Gaiomere breathed. Her hands clutched the steering wheel in a vice grip. The bruise on her chin was purple now, and Atlas felt another surge of anger at the sight of it.

"I can't *believe* you hung around with that guy," he snapped before he could stop himself. His head throbbed, and his nose was painful to the touch, but he ignored it. Now that they were safe, all he could feel was cold fury. "What he did to you—that was—I mean, I just —" He broke off, letting out a strangled sound of rage.

"Atlas, I'm so sorry," she said quietly.

He looked sharply over at her, bewildered.

"Why are you sorry?" he asked, his voice coming out harsher than he'd meant it to, but Gaiomere looked unfazed. In fact, her expression was remarkably calm, save for the tremble of her bottom lip.

"I should have known—should have expected— Raider is so—he can be so temperamental—"

"You didn't know he'd be there," Atlas reasoned, scowling. He leaned his head back against the seat and let his eyes fall closed.

"Why didn't you kill him?" Gaiomere asked timidly.

Atlas jerked his head up, turning to look at her again. Defensiveness welled up in his chest, but he pushed it down. Despite the fact that he was fairly certain she and Raider had been...involved, at the very least—regardless of her denials—it was a sensible question.

"I..." He frowned, staring out at the trees flying by them. Why *hadn't* Atlas killed him? He had spent the whole day carefully restraining his violent impulses to hurt Raider any time the brute opened his stupid mouth —so *why*, when the opportunity had arisen, and Atlas would have been perfectly justified in doing so, didn't he kill him?

"I guess I just—I figured you wouldn't have wanted me to," Atlas settled on finally. It wasn't exactly dishonest. He would not have liked it if Gaiomere had been upset with him for taking the idiot's life—no matter how satisfying it might have been.

"I'm not sure what I would have felt," she admitted.

They had been driving about twenty minutes when Atlas muttered, "Do you think you could pull over?"

She obliged, bringing the car to a halt in a stretch of open field. The sun was setting in earnest now, and the air was cool when he opened the door. He pulled himself out of the car and immediately vomited. The breeze dancing across the field eased some of the pain radiating across his face.

"Here," Gaiomere said quietly, passing him a water bottle. He took only a small sip, before he splashed some of the water on his hands, attempting to clear off some of the dried blood which had caked around his mouth, and cringing as his movements jostled his nose about.

"Wait, Atlas, don't mess with it," Gaiomere said, coming around to the other side of the car and gingerly stepping over his pile of sick. "Just wait—we're only twenty minutes from the Under. The medic there can have a look at it."

He ignored her though, sitting back down in the car and pulling the mirror sideways so that he could look at himself properly. Gritting his teeth, he grasped the bridge of his nose, and attempted to wrench his nose back into place.

"Atlas, no!" Gaiomere protested, yanking his

hands away from his face. "You could make it worse. Listen, you have to wait until we get back to the Under. I promise, the doctor there will fix it—"

"I'm not waiting," he told her, trying to grasp the bridge of his nose again, but she held fast to his wrists. He could have pulled them out of her grip, could have pushed her away with as little effort as it took to lift Whitsom's staff—but the image of Raider tossing her like a ragdoll flashed across his mind like lightning, and he took a deep breath, muttering through gritted teeth, "Gaiomere, let me go. I can fix it—"

"Maybe you'd fix it, or maybe you'd make it worse," she snapped. "Atlas, why can't you just wait twenty minutes—"

"Because they're not going to see me like this!" he burst out, glaring at her. "I'm not going to let Maggi, or Rasta, or Whitsom—especially not Whitsom —see me all battered up like some—some—" He let out a heavy breath, looking down at his bruised knuckles, swallowing thickly as his nostrils burned. "It's bad enough that you saw it. I don't need them to, as well. I don't lose fights. I'm not—it's not allowed. Period."

Atlas' face burned with humiliation. He felt her eyes on him, but he couldn't meet her gaze. All he could see was Talikoth's disappointed glare, his lips turning down in that familiar, disgusted scowl.

Too much like your mother. She was weak, too.

Gaiomere seemed to read his mind.

"Atlas," she said quietly. "We're not—we're not Talikoth." Her hand slid down from his wrist to cover his hand, clenched into a fist atop his thigh, and gave it a squeeze. "Whitsom, and Maggi, and Rasta—they all know what Raider's like. He runs on bloodlust. They wouldn't think any less of you for what happened today. And I don't either, for that matter. I think you were—*are* —the bravest person I've ever met."

His breath slowly evened, and his hands unclenched.

"Let's get back—I'm sure the others are worried," she said softly, releasing his hand and moving back to the driver's side.

They began driving again, and Atlas tried very hard to ignore the tingling he felt where her hand had held his.

"Say, Gaiomere?"

"Hmm?"

"Do you think we'll be putting the Under in danger of exposure, bringing a big, noisy vehicle so close to its entrance?"

Gaiomere nodded. "That's why we'll ditch the car a couple miles out and walk. I've already got a spot in mind."

Atlas smiled a little. "You think of everything."

Her cheeks darkened with color, and his smile broadened. They rode in silence the rest of the way back. Gaiomere parked the car in a thicket of foliage, stuffed the rifle back into the trunk, and started to tuck the leafy branches of several nearby trees over the car top like some strange parody of a blanket. By the end of it, the two of them had hidden it so well that, when Atlas glanced over his shoulder as they walked away, he could not make it out beneath the thick covering of leaves.

Gaiomere slung her backpack over her shoulders, and Atlas elected to use Whitsom's quarterstaff as a walking stick. Most of his dizziness had gone, but every now and again, he felt a surge of vertigo, and had to take a second to steady himself.

It was so dark when they arrived at the cluster of old, dilapidated buildings that they wandered around for nearly ten minutes before they finally found the entrance to the old storm cellar.

The guards greeted them stoically, taking their weapons, and the two of them began the steep descent down the treacherous stairway.

He broke the silence a few minutes into their descent. "Hey uh—Gaiomere?"

She glanced over at him, and he rubbed the back of his neck awkwardly.

"Thanks for uh—well, you know, with Raider..." He broke off, frowning as he added, "Well, actually, and with Jereis, for that matter. I don't think I ever said—well, thanks."

They had just reached the bottom of the stairs, but she stopped in front of the large double doors. Her hickory brown eyes blinked up at him, and then her lips split into a smile. Before he registered what was happening, she stood on her tiptoes and kissed his cheek.

"Don't mention it," she said, before pulling open the door and disappearing into the main hall. Atlas stilled, staring after her for a full five seconds, before he shook himself and followed her, a rather dopey grin on his lips.

CHAPTER TWELVE

"**W**hat happened to your *face*?"

Atlas rolled his eyes. He contemplated giving Maggi a rather rude finger, before he remembered that she was twelve, and thought better of it.

"We um...we sort of ran into Raider," Gaiomere said, pulling a face. Maggi's jaw dropped, and Rasta's eyes widened. Whitsom sat up very quickly in his bed and gawked at Atlas and Gaiomere.

"I thought they went north?" Whitsom demanded.

"They did," Gaiomere said, sighing as she plopped down into a chair and pulled her backpack onto her lap. "Then they came back and took over this Ramshackle again."

"He didn't give you any trouble, did he?" Whitsom asked, his eyes flickering over Atlas' bruised and bloody face.

"We got what we needed," Gaiomere said shortly.

"Wait, that still doesn't explain all *that*," Maggi said, jerking her head towards Atlas and waving her hand in front of her face.

Gaiomere and Atlas looked at each other for a moment.

"Well, I don't know," Atlas drawled finally. "I can't imagine anyone who would want to fight such a well-mannered, charming fellow like Raider." Gaiomere's lips pulled up reluctantly, and Whitsom let out a bark of laughter.

"Same old Raider, huh?" Whitsom said. "So, did you guys—"

But the doctor came in at that moment, took one look at Atlas, and shook his head, striding back out of the room. He returned seconds later with a supply sack and gestured towards the empty bed beside Whitsom's.

"Friendly sparring, right?" the doctor quipped, and Atlas snorted. The doctor gently wiped away the blood surrounding his nose, before he pressed a couple of fingers against the bone and peered up Atlas' nostrils.

"Caught it early," he declared after a few moments. "Looks like I'll just need to realign it and splint it."

Atlas nodded, his eyes wandering to the ceiling as the doctor worked. He gave him a nasal spray, and Atlas immediately felt a numbing sensation spreading across the center of his face.

"So, Raider did that?" he heard Maggi ask Gaiomere quietly.

"He wanted a favor in exchange for the capacitors. He had me reprogram some drones to take out the landmines at the northern edge of the Pass—"

"Gaiomere!" Whitsom interrupted, his tone indignant.

"Whit, we *had* to," Gaiomere said impatiently. "It was the only way he was going to give us those capacitors—you know how Raider is. Besides, they were northern mines—the Obarion would have to make it through hundreds of miles of landmines before they hit that part of the Pass."

Whitsom grumbled quietly under his breath, but did not argue further, and Gaiomere continued.

"Anyway, there were a couple of kids passing by within range of the landmines, and Raider wasn't going to stop detonating them, so Atlas tried to—well, he did stop him. But then Raider got angry, and he tried to kill Atlas, and we had to make a dash for it, so we—" Here Gaiomere broke off. Atlas glanced over, and her face was a mixture of embarrassment and sheer exhilaration. "So we stole his car and Atlas shot him in the leg."

"WHAT?" Whitsom, Maggi, and Rasta exclaimed simultaneously.

A surge of pride swelled in Atlas' chest at the Renegades' admiration, a pride that could not be dampened even as the doctor pushed his nose back into place, though he did flinch.

"Oh, what I would give to have seen the look on Raider's face!" Whitsom chortled, bouncing up and down in his seat. "*Man*, he must have been angry."

"I think he would have killed us both if he could have," Gaiomere murmured. Atlas wondered if he was the only one that picked up the note of sadness in her voice.

The doctor finished up with Atlas and disappeared from the room once more. Gaiomere withdrew some of the food they had brought on their journey, which had been completely forgotten in all of the commotion. She passed Atlas a couple of oranges and a handful of walnuts as he sat down beside her, giving him a small smile.

"Thank you," he said quietly. It felt as though something had shifted between the two of them in the last six hours—like they had reached a mutual understanding.

"You're welcome," she replied, uncharacteristically

shy.

Maggi caught Atlas' eye, waggling her brows, and Atlas chucked a walnut at her head.

"How long do you think it will take you to make the booster?" Whitsom asked, ever oblivious, as he reached over and snatched an orange from Gaiomere's lap.

"At least half a day." She sighed, glancing longingly towards the door of their room. "I should probably get started now, and work through the night. Every minute that passes is another minute that the base could be discovered."

Atlas wanted to argue with her—his own body was heavy with exhaustion, so he was sure hers was too —but he knew she was probably right.

"You can use the Quiet Room," Maggi suggested. "I found it today while I was exploring. It's got some books and ancient newspaper clippings, but hardly anyone's ever in there."

Gaiomere nodded, climbing to her feet. "I've gotta go get the other stuff from the room." She glanced at Maggi and Rasta, adding, "You guys should go to bed soon. Atlas is in charge while I'm working, got it?"

Maggi arched a brow, looking over at Atlas with a sneer. "*Sure* he is, Gai-Gai."

Back in their room, Atlas sprawled out on his bed while he waited for Maggi and Rasta to each take a shower. The two of them squabbled for a while over pillows, before Atlas finally snapped, "If you two don't cut it out, I'll take all of the pillows and hog them to myself."

When the pair had finally quieted down, Atlas sat up, intent on getting a shower himself before he slept for twelve hours straight, but stopped short when he saw Maggi and Rasta sitting up in bed, staring at him expectantly.

"Um—what?"

Maggi grinned mischievously. "You have to sing to us."

Atlas snorted. "Uh, no. I don't sing."

Rasta's big hazel eyes blinked up at him sadly, and his stomach twinged with guilt.

"Gai-Gai *always* sings to us," Rasta told him.

Atlas ran a hand through his hair, muttering under his breath, "Oh, for the love of—"

"We can always go get Gaiomere and tell her you aren't taking your responsibility seriously," Maggi said innocently, starting to climb out of bed. "But she'll be *awfully* upset with being interrupted—"

"No!" Atlas said hastily. Maggi plopped back down beside Rasta, and Atlas scowled, sitting down on the edge of their bed.

"I don't do the whole cuddling thing," he warned them.

Maggi wrinkled her nose. "Good, you probably smell like boy."

She and Rasta tucked themselves in under the quilt, and Atlas stared blankly at them for several moments. He couldn't remember the lyrics to any of the lullabies he had heard Gaiomere sing to them, and it wasn't as though Talikoth had ever put him to bed with a song.

"Uh—okay, I'll just, um..." He sighed, clearing his throat, and sang:

"Hail to the people of enduring strength

Our flag waves from east to west
No enemy shall stand against
Our strength endures times' test
Fate bends to the will of our people—"

"Wait, wait, *what* is *that?*" Maggi interjected. "Were you singing us an Obarion *war* song?"

She mimed gagging and retching into her hand, and Rasta anxiously mumbled, "It was sorta spooky..."

"Well, I don't know what else to sing to you!" Atlas spluttered, his face flushing.

Maggi tilted her head to the side as she peered at him, frowning. "Nobody ever sang to you when you were younger?"

He looked away, the muscles in his face unconsciously tightening.

"No."

She shrugged, lying back down beside Rasta. "Just make something up."

He scowled, leaning back against his arms as he glared at the opposite wall. "Fine, fine, um..."

"Little Renegades, go to sleep
Or Atlas will make you weep
Close your mouths and shut your eyes
Or you're in for a violent surprise
Lay down on that pillow there
Or I will pull out your hair
Seriously just go to sleep, I'm getting bored
Or I'll knock you out with a....board."

Rasta and Maggi had descended into giggles, and Atlas' lips pulled up reluctantly.

"That's the best you're going to get out of me, you rascals." He ruffled Rasta's hair, and the little boy beamed. "Get some sleep."

"Goodnight, Atlas!"

"Night, Atlas!"

By the time he was out of the shower they were already fast asleep. He laid down and wondered briefly if he should check on Gaiomere, or ask if she needed any help, but almost the moment his head hit the pillow, he fell asleep.

When he woke, Maggi and Rasta were still asleep. He blinked into the darkness, glancing at his wrist, before remembering that he didn't have his watch anymore. It must have been early, for it seemed like the Renegades always awoke with the sun—even if, like here in the underground, they couldn't technically see it. He sighed, collapsing back against his pillow and staring blankly at the ceiling.

Atlas lay there for five minutes before deciding that he wasn't going to be able to fall back asleep, so he pulled himself out of bed and tugged on his shoes. He started towards the door, but stopped short, turning back and slipping into the bathroom. He hastily flattened down his hair, eyeing the bruises along his jaw and cheekbones with irritation. Before he left, he grabbed the bag of walnuts from the nightstand and slipped them into his pocket.

The infirmary was empty, save for Whitsom. His arms lay slung over his eyes, and his mouth hung wide open, filling the empty room with heavy snores. Atlas sniggered, pulling open the door to the main hall.

No one else was up, except for a few people here and there. The smell of coffee wafted over him, and his mouth watered. He wandered around the hall for about five minutes before he finally found the door with a plaque above it that read 'Quiet Room.' He pushed the door open gently and peaked inside.

He had half expected Gaiomere to be asleep, or at the very least slouching over her workstation. What he had not expected was to find her standing in front of the table, bouncing excitedly on the balls of her feet as she screwed on the front of a black, metal box.

"Hi, Atlas!" she exclaimed, her voice uncharacteristically chipper.

"Uh...hi. Sorry if I'm interrupting—"

"Not in the slightest. You're right on time!" She stepped back, gesturing towards the box with flourish. "*And*...tada!"

He looked between her and the black box with befuddlement. "You're—you're finished with it?"

"I'm finished!" she gushed, waving him over. Atlas moved across the room and stopped at her side, studying her profile suspiciously. She *looked* as though she had been up all night: heavy bags hung beneath her eyes, and her eyes themselves were red and bloodshot. Did she just get more cheerful as she grew more tired?

"Here's where the input goes—which is where we connect the transmitter—and *this* is what increases the voltage—that's what boosts our signal so that our message can travel such a long distance—and *here*—" She continued to ramble on, but Atlas was only half-listening, still bewildered at her energy.

"Gaiomere," he interrupted finally. "Weren't you just—you were awake *all* night, weren't you?" He looked around for a clock. Perhaps it had only been a few hours since he had fallen asleep?

But no, he located one above a bookcase across the room. It was a little after five in the morning.

"Oh, I was!" she said. She lifted a little bag sitting on the table beside where she'd been working. "This guy traded me some coffee beans—he said if you eat them straight, they're much more concentrated, and I figured I needed it! Well, he didn't tell me how many to eat, or what effect they would have, but I think I must've eaten at least fifty of them, and I've been at it all night just fine! I think I worked even faster because of it actually —these things are like magic! I haven't slept in over twenty-four hours and I feel great, just swell, honestly! Wanna try one?"

She held the baggy out to him, and he blinked, looking between her and the coffee beans clutched in her hand, before he burst out laughing.

"You've never had coffee before, have you?" he asked her, smirking wryly.

"Uh...no. Unless you count accidentally drinking some of Dad's when I was seven, but that was gross." She wrinkled her nose, glancing down at the coffee beans. "To be honest, these are gross too, but it doesn't matter, because they give me *superpowers*."

Atlas laughed again, pulling up a stool beside the table and lifting up the box. "I'm impressed."

Gaiomere shook her head, saying, "Don't be impressed until we're sure that it works."

He pulled the walnuts from his pocket and slid them across the table towards her. "I brought these for you, if you're hungry."

"Hungry? I'm starved." She yanked the walnuts

towards her as Atlas fiddled with the box, observing all of the dials and buttons with curiosity.

"Why're you up so early?" she asked him.

"Couldn't sleep," he said, shrugging, before he added, "Whitsom snores like a whale."

"Whitsom snores like an entire pod of whales," Gaiomere corrected, snickering. "Sweet sesame, when he and my dad both got to snoring—"

Atlas started to chuckle, but stopped when her expression turned sad.

He hesitated for a moment.

"Can I ask you how your parents died?"

She let out a long, slow breath, leaning against the back of her chair, her head tilting back to look at the ceiling.

"My mom and dad got the valiant and heroic deaths that they both deserved." Atlas thought he could hear bitterness coloring her tone, but her expression was impassive. "My father—he died when I was almost eleven. A group of Obarion soldiers were about to slaughter a whole bunch of civilians—mostly children —and my dad tried to stop them." Her voice trembled, but she pressed on. "I watched them cleave his head from his shoulders with my own eyes."

Atlas swallowed thickly, looking away from her. He tried to push his thoughts in a different direction, but he saw the scene play out before his eyes— a young Gaiomere, the same age as Rasta was now, standing wide-eyed as she watched her father die before her, unable to do anything. He imagined the Obarion soldiers cold, taunting even—for that was how Talikoth trained them to be—as they slaughtered an innocent man in front of his family. Had Talikoth been there?

What were the circumstances that had necessitated killing innocent people—children—like pigs in a slaughterhouse? Had they been Renegades? Traitors within the Obarion clan?

Gaiomere cleared her throat. "My mom died when I was fourteen. It was just us left at that point. Maggi's parents died before my dad, and Rasta's, about three years after that—"

"Maggi and Rasta aren't siblings?" Atlas interrupted, his brow furrowing.

Gaiomere gave him a perplexed look. "No, of course not. Do they *look* like siblings?"

Atlas' cheeks prickled with heat. "Well hey, I don't know! Not all siblings look alike..."

"I suppose that's fair," Gaiomere said. "Anyhow, we were traveling through landmine territory—northeast, close to the mountains—and we crossed paths with a group of soldiers."

Atlas wanted her to stop talking. He wanted her to get distracted, to change the subject, anything to keep her from finishing her sentence. But even as she spoke, he already knew what she was going to say.

"Obarion. They caught sight of her, but they hadn't seen us yet, so she told us to run and hide in the forest. They chased her down towards the landmines —there were only two of them, otherwise they might have caught her before—" Her brows knitted together, and she blinked quickly, clearing away the tears from her eyes. "Anyway, Maggi screamed—to warn her, you know, about the landmines—and one of the soldiers heard and started back towards us. So, my mother, she —" Her voice cracked, and she hastily swiped at her eyes. "My mother stepped on the landmine, and it took both of the soldiers out—and—and her with them."

The caffeine seemed to have run its course, for she looked sobered.

"I just—I'll never forget the look on her face—right before she stepped on the landmine. It was like—it was like she was *so afraid*, but not—not for herself. She was afraid for us. And that was what gave her the courage to do it." She lifted her head, almost defiantly, and though she was crying, her eyes were bright and fierce, her tear-streaked face broken and wounded and strikingly beautiful, all at once.

"Gaiomere," Atlas began. "How can you—how can you *not* want to fight in this war—with everything you —I mean, with all that it's—"

She shook her head, biting her lip as she looked down at her hands.

"The Obarion took everything from me. I can't— I can't let them take any more than they already have. Not Maggi or Rasta, not Whitsom. And they need me. I can't let the Obarion kill me, either."

Atlas looked away from her, guilt bubbling thick and hot in his stomach. Had she forgotten he was Obarion? Or was it just that she didn't blame *him* anymore?

A yawn tore from her lips, cutting some of the tension of the moment, and Atlas looked at her concernedly, asking, "Do you want to get some sleep?"

She shook her head, pulling the box towards her.

"We've got to do this as soon as possible." She fiddled with the dials for a moment, and said, "I'm going to show you how to do it, just so you've got an idea. *This* controls the voltage, and *this* is how we adjust the frequency. I've got a few guesses on the frequency of the

Vedas' transmitters, but we'll have to play around with it for a little while until we tap in."

"What's that?" he asked, pointing at a blocky slab of metal clamped down atop several wires.

"That keeps our signal from being traced," she said, grinning rather proudly. "Radio signals give off a frequency that can be tracked, if you have the right technology. I didn't want to accidentally expose the Under to any nearby soldiers patrolling the area."

His amazement must have shown on his face, for she flushed, insisting, "Oh, it's nothing, honestly. Everything I know I learned from someone else. Dad taught me a ton about chemical reactions and computer programming, Raider taught me how to make ethanol —"

"Do me a favor," Atlas interrupted.

She turned to look at him, eyebrows raised, and he continued, "Don't mention him for—oh, let's see—a good seventy-two hours. My ego is still recovering."

She laughed, nudging his shoulder. "Good. Your ego could use a little battering."

He shot her a disparaging look, but he could not maintain his stern expression long before his mouth curled into a smile. He watched her in silence as she turned the dials infinitesimally. Beside her, the receiver emitted a constant static crackle. After about thirty minutes of observing how she shifted the frequency dials in time with the voltage, he got a good idea of what he was looking and listening for.

Atlas nudged her. "I'll take over for a bit. Get some sleep." She had been nodding off in her seat, her head slumping towards the table and then jerking upwards, her hickory brown eyes hooded.

"No, 'm fine," she mumbled, but she did not stop Atlas from sliding the box to his side of the table. He plucked up the receiver, setting it in front of him, and wiggled the frequency dial marginally to the left. Gaiomere's head fell against the table, her curls splaying around her face and across the tabletop, a few of them brushing the skin of his arm. Atlas wondered briefly if he should wake her up so that she could at least move to the couch on the other side of the room. But her breath was coming slow through her lips, and she looked atypically serene, so he decided to leave her where she was.

Minutes turned into hours while he sat there, his eyes narrowed on the tiny black dial. Every now and again, he caught bits and pieces of conversation, but then he would barely twist the dial to home in on the signal and the voices would be lost to the static once more.

The rest of the Under began to wake. Outside of the Quiet Room came muffled greetings, laughter, and the strumming of an instrument—perhaps one of the musicians preparing to perform for the day.

Maggi wandered in around eight, and he gratefully took a couple of slices of bread from her, his eyes still glued to the reader.

"Did she stay up all night?" the little girl asked. Atlas nodded distractedly. There was a sudden surge of static on the receiver, and all at once the voices on the other end became astoundingly clear.

"—sure to notify General Moonstone of the updates to the schedule. Over."

"There!" Atlas burst out, his heart leaping in his chest. Gaiomere sat up very quickly, her eyes foggy and unfocused.

"Wha' happened?" she mumbled.

Atlas jerked his head towards the booster. "Listen! And Maggi, don't you dare leave—"

"I didn't know the Obarion were superstitious," Maggi muttered wryly, but Gaiomere and Atlas both shushed her.

"—also let the General know that we haven't seen any movement on the northern border since Thursday. I have fifteen guys posted there every hour of the day. Over."

"Yes! We did it!" Gaiomere exclaimed, squeezing Atlas' shoulder. He grinned, reaching for the receiver, but then he hesitated, his brow furrowing.

What would he say? What if it *had* been Moonstone who killed his mother? Would he storm into the Vedas' base and kill her? And whatever she told him, how would he know if she was telling the truth?

He cleared his throat, picking up the receiver and pushing down the button. Gaiomere and Maggi were both watching him with bated breath.

"Um...Moonstone? Do you copy? This is Atlas. Over."

He released the button. Blood rushed past his ears as he waited, hardly breathing.

They waited...and waited...and still, there was nothing.

Atlas frowned, a stab of frustration pulsing through his chest. They could not have done all of this for nothing. He wouldn't allow it. He pushed the button again, and said, more firmly, "Moonstone, this is Atlas. Do you copy? I—I have some information that I believe would be beneficial to you. Over."

"*Atlas?*"

He stared down at the receiver. It was not Moonstone's voice, but the voice did sound vaguely familiar.

"Wait a minute!" Gaiomere said suddenly. She snatched the receiver from his hands and pushed the button. "Jacoby?"

Silence, and then, "*Gaiomere? Is that you?*"

"It's me. Whitsom and I are with Atlas. Is—is Moonstone available? Uh...over?"

"*Hey, Gaiomere! Wow, it's great to hear from you—*" Atlas rolled his eyes, and Maggi snickered. "*Moonstone is here, but we send all unfamiliar transmissions through the engineering department. They can't go directly to our base radios. Over.*"

Atlas took the receiver back from her. "Jacoby, you need to go get Moonstone, it's urgent. Over."

The silence was longer this time, and Atlas and Gaiomere exchanged a nervous glance. "*Yeah, see, I'm not technically supposed to do that. You see, unfamiliar transmissions are supposed to go through a thorough analyzation to ensure that the individuals communicating with us aren't a danger to the base—*"

Gaiomere rolled her eyes, ripping the receiver from Atlas' hand. He started to protest, but she gave him a stern look.

"I'll handle this." She pressed the receiver, her face set with determination. "Jacoby, listen very carefully. We have information that could literally mean the life or death of the Vedas' clan. You could save the lives of *hundreds* of people, Jacoby, but only if you have the courage to act. It's all counting on you." She started to set the receiver down, but then hastily added, "Over."

The silence was thick, and Atlas briefly wondered if Jacoby had rejected their transmission, but then he said, "*I'll be back in five minutes with Moonstone.*"

Atlas let out a heavy breath, and Maggi and Gaiomere high-fived each other. "Laid it on a bit thick there, didn't you?" Atlas said, smirking at Gaiomere. She glared at him.

"I'm sorry, shouldn't you be groveling at my feet?"

"See I would, but you aren't wearing your flower crown—"

He broke off. The receiver had kicked on. There was a pause, and then: "*Atlas?*"

His throat suddenly felt incredibly dry. "Hello, Moonstone."

The quiet suddenly felt heavy.

"*You have a lot of explaining to do, Atlas. Over.*"

His face flushed. He felt rather like a child being admonished by a disappointed parent. "I—we were—"

Gaiomere leaned forward. "Um...hi, Moonstone. This is Gaiomere. It's our fault Atlas left. We—Whitsom and I, that is—got tired of waiting for your troops to find Maggi and Rasta, so we—we went to find them ourselves. Atlas took it upon himself to help us, and he —more than once he saved our lives, so—so he's really not to blame. Over."

A rush of gratitude flooded through him. Gaiomere wasn't looking at him, but her cheeks darkened with color, and once she'd released the receiver, she slid her hand over to clasp his hand, just as she had on the drive back from the border of the Pass.

"*I take it that you found your tribe members. Where are you now? Over.*"

"We found them," Atlas told her. "And we—we

can't tell you where we are now. But um...we...we saw something, about thirty miles northwest of the Vedas' base. Something I think you'd want to know about. Over."

The silence seemed to carry on longer this time, and Atlas wondered for a moment if she'd gone. But then she said, "*And what reason would the son of the Obarion General have to provide the Vedas with any information that would be helpful? Over.*"

He took a deep breath. He had expected something like this.

"Just one reason. Over."

There was amusement in Moonstone's voice when she spoke again. "*Atlas, if you think you have to blackmail me into giving you the truth, I am afraid you are mistaken. Over.*"

"I just want to know." His voice was raw, and he kept his eyes carefully trained away from the two girls.

"Maggi, why don't we go see how Whitsom's doing?" Gaiomere said suddenly.

"What? But this is just getting good—"

"Come *on*," Gaiomere grabbed the girl by her shirt and tugged her out of the room. A heavy weight settled on his chest as he was left alone. The receiver blinked bright red, and the idle static blared in the empty room.

"*Your mother came to us almost sixteen years ago with a terrible warning,*" Moonstone began slowly. "*She told us that she had come ahead to give us time to prepare —to give us a chance to survive.*" He heard Moonstone let out a slow exhale. A tension built in his chest, a bubble of apprehension that seemed to grow larger with every breath he took.

"Why did she come to you? Why would she turn

against the Obarion people to give you a *warning*?"

Atlas wished more than anything that he was there with Moonstone. He could watch her face, watch to see if her eyes flickered around the room, observe the stiffness in her shoulders, examine every inflection, every twitch of the face, because he was sure then, at least, he would know whether or not she was lying.

"Caterra said at first, upon assuming power, General Talikoth only wanted to find a way to restore the Fallen Land to its former glory. He saw a problem and he believed that he was well-equipped to fix it..."

Atlas leaned back, his fingers gripping the arms of his chair tightly. That sounded like Talikoth. Atlas had always gotten the impression that Talikoth believed he had some divine right to take the helm of the world—like he had been born to do it. And it wasn't difficult to see how he had come to that conclusion. Atlas hadn't met many people who thought the way Talikoth did—his mind was like a machine, and he fought like one, too. His will was indomitable—this was the genesis of the Obarion code.

"But Caterra told me General Talikoth became drunk with power. She watched him tear across the Southwest with a bloodlust that could not be quenched. Anyone that defied him—even peacefully—was killed. He lied to his people. He hid the horrors he commanded his troops to commit." Moonstone's voice caught in her throat, as she pressed on. *"He killed hundreds of children within the tribes across the Southwest—to kill their hope, she said. When she started to protest, when she begged him to stop, he held her hostage under heavy guard."*

Atlas tried to stop himself from imagining it, but he couldn't. He pictured his mother, the bright-eyed, smiling woman he'd seen in the photograph, terror-stricken and trapped, kept a prisoner by her own husband.

"They reached the coast in the spring, and that was when she managed to escape, by poisoning her guards and slipping off in the dead of night. She found a couple of Renegades traveling east and warned them of the approaching danger in exchange for information. She wanted to know who the largest and strongest tribe was in the West.

"Back then the Vedas were smaller; we were dispersed out across the Westland—a tribe in the South, one in the mountains, one in the North, and a tribe near the middle of the Pass, on the coast—long before the landmines had been planted. I was the leader of the Southern tribe, so it was I who Caterra found first. When she came to me, I did not want to believe her. I thought maybe she was merely a spy sent to cause disorder. But then I reached out to some allies that I had further east. Most of them did not respond. I presume they had been killed. One however, did, and he...he told me that the rumors were true. The Obarion clan had decimated the Southwest, and, as far as he knew, they had no intention of stopping at the coast."

Atlas felt like he was going to throw up. His heart pounded, like it would beat right through his ribcage. He knew that the Obarion had conquered the Southwest —reveled in the fact, even. But he hadn't realized what that meant. He hadn't known that innocent people —civilians, *children,* even—had been slaughtered. It couldn't be true. How could it possibly be true? How could the Obarion people have stood for it? Even if Talikoth lied to them, how could he have covered up the hundreds of deaths across a thousand miles?

"Your mother brought you with her, when she came to warn me of the coming storm. She had no intention of returning to the Obarion clan—not after everything she had seen. She wanted to help in whatever way she could. She trained some of our soldiers to cut off supply chains to the Obarion troops, she showed us where to plant the landmines. She even helped us scout a new location for the Vedas' base, where all four tribes would convene, and unite under one flag. She knew her role was dangerous, so she asked me to promise that I would do whatever I could to protect you, in the event that the Obarion captured her. But then—"

She broke off, and the line went quiet for so long that Atlas frantically checked the frequency reader to ensure he had not lost his connection.

Moonstone cleared her throat, and then she pressed on.

"But then General Talikoth launched an attack on our Southern base. There were troops everywhere. Many of our soldiers perished. After, I searched the base to make sure everyone left alive managed to escape when I found—I found her body. They had killed her on sight. And you—you were nowhere to be found. They had taken you."

The line went silent, and the harsh, static buzz filled the air around him once more. The noises from the main hall faded away, and all he could seem to hear was the static. It filled his ears, his head, all around him.

Atlas' entire body felt numb. He didn't feel sad, he didn't feel angry. He didn't feel...anything. He sat there, watching the receiver blink red, then go black, and then blink red again.

"Atlas?" he heard Moonstone call. *"Are you alright?"*

He swallowed thickly around the cotton in his

mouth, pushed the receiver, and intoned, "We saw Obarion troops about thirty miles northwest of the Vedas' base. They were looking for it. If they haven't found it already, your troops may be able to intercept them before they take any information south back to Talikoth. Over."

Moonstone was silent for a beat, and then, *"Thank you, Atlas. We are indebted to you for this information. I will deploy a squadron immediately. But Atlas, are—are you alright? Over."*

He inhaled sharply, pushing himself to his feet. "Fine. I'm fine. I've got to go, I just wanted to make sure you had that information. Over."

"Atlas, why not—"

He switched the receiver off, and Moonstone's voice, and the static, vanished. He stared at it for several minutes. His mind was strangely silent.

But then the emotions came rushing in, like a flood, and before he knew what he was doing, he pushed the booster off the table. It fell to the ground with a *crash*, and he slammed his foot into it, over, and over, and *over*, until it was just a pile of metal scraps on the ground, and his foot was throbbing, but the physical pain was a welcome distraction.

Atlas let out a harsh breath, running a hand through his hair, and without conscious thought, stalked towards the door, wrenching it open.

The commotion in the main hall was in full swing. Music blared across the room, and the sounds of happy cheers and yells accosted his ears. His feet carried him towards the large double doors that led upstairs, and he pounded up the steps, taking them two at a time. He ignored the guards at the entrance when they offered him the quarterstaff, throwing open the cellar doors and plunging himself into the bright sunlight and fresh air. He sucked in several deep breaths, and the smothering feeling crushing his lungs diminished, though only slightly.

Atlas let out a shout of fury as he paced beneath the clear blue sky. It was almost as though the weather mocked him—the chirping of distant birds, the cloudless stretch of blue above him, all of it *so* idyllic, and he wanted nothing more than to bury himself in six feet of dirt because inside he just felt dark and heavy and dead all at once.

He sat down on a rock, his elbows resting on his knees as he buried his face in his hands. His nostrils pulled in the stench of putrid gas that lingered in the air surrounding the cellar, and he remembered Gaiomere's warning—but what did it matter? He didn't care if the air poisoned him—not when it felt as though the blood in his veins was flooded with toxins already.

Then came the burning—in his nostrils, behind his eyes, and then in his cheeks. He could not, *would* not cry. Not over this.

But he did. The tears came tumbling down his face before he could stop them, as though they had a mind of their own, and then his rage turned back on himself.

Talikoth would sneer, he would shake his head and curl his lip and look at Atlas in disgust.

He pressed the palms of his hands into his eyes, as though he could stop the tears by sheer force, but they kept coming. Even as he slammed his fist into the side of his own head. Even as he pulled his hair so hard that it felt as though it would tear from his scalp. Even as he clenched his arms so tightly his nails drew blood.

He cried. He cried until his body ran out of water to expel, and then he just hunched there on the rock, dry heaving, disgusted and disgraced as tears and mucus ran down his face.

And then finally, *finally* the thoughts came. They erupted like a dam that broke open, and he exploded to his feet and paced again, unknowing and uncaring if anyone would see him. He welcomed a Flesh Flayers attack. It would give his anger a release.

He wanted so badly to believe that Moonstone had been lying. He wanted to trust Talikoth's version of history—but so much in her story added up. He didn't want to believe that Talikoth would have his own wife killed, but he knew how the Obarion treated treason. And if Atlas knew Talikoth would make no exception for his own son, why would his wife be any different?

Atlas sank down heavily on the rock once more, his head pounding. A group of Renegades tentatively approached the entrance to the Under, eyeing him warily, but he paid them no mind. The cold of the morning began to melt away, and the noon rays beat down unrelentingly, but still he did not move. Even as his stomach turned from the toxins, he did not move. He didn't want to.

No, that wasn't quite right. It was that he couldn't find the will to. The world would keep spinning without him, wouldn't it? Just as it had kept on spinning when his mother had been slain. Slain by her own people. Slain on her husband's orders.

Had Talikoth loved his mother? Atlas had never really thought about love, or what it meant. The word brought to mind memories of curling up on Delurah's lap when he was a child while she read to him, or the scent of her strawberry cookies. He could not remember loving his mother, or if she had loved him, but the sight of her smiling face in Moonstone's photograph inspired a feeling of comfort—safety, even.

But Talikoth...

Talikoth and love were two words that didn't seem to belong together. He knew of friends who adored their parents, and whose parents, in turn, seemed to adore them, but Atlas had only ever respected Talikoth, as well as feared him. The thought of hugging Talikoth, or confiding in him, was laughable.

Talikoth had never loved him—but had he, at the very least, loved Atlas' mother? Atlas didn't see how he could have, when he ordered her killed—but then, maybe he had loved her before. Before the siege west, before all of the power, before he had grown so obsessed with reshaping the world to his liking. Perhaps he had loved her then.

Atlas shook his head, scowling. He didn't know why he was thinking about it. It didn't matter—it hadn't changed her fate, in the end.

So why couldn't he *stop* thinking about it? What *wouldn't* Talikoth be willing to sacrifice, when it came to the greater-good? Did he justify all of it—the filicide, the endless destruction, the death of Atlas' mother on his orders—as means to an end?

Atlas got back to his feet, wandering idly over to the tree line, his eyes roving over the ground unseeing. As he moved further away from the reeking bubble of stale, poisonous air, the ache between his temples began to ease, and his stomach settled.

Maybe that was what made Talikoth a great General. Would the descendants of the Obarion clan sit around the dinner table in two hundred years, giving thanks to the Great Obarion War General for all he was willing to do? Would they rest in prosperity and splendor for everything the generations before them had sacrificed?

He leaned against a tree, unthinkingly picking at the bark. Perhaps he was being selfish. Was his mother's death necessary for the good of the people?

He killed hundreds of children...to kill their hope.

Atlas kicked a loose rock angrily, striding deeper into the thicket of trees. Why should the children of today have to die for the prosperity of the children of the future? What made *those* children any more valuable than these? How could Talikoth justify *that*?

Atlas wandered deeper and deeper into the forest, his mind still racing. His anger had diminished to a simmer, but it remained just below the surface, eating away at his insides.

The sun crept lower, and suddenly Atlas found himself having to squint at the dim forest floor to see. He doubled back, pushing through the foliage, until he returned to the storm cellar. By the time he had reached it, night had fallen around him, and the only light was the glow of the vivid full moon.

He stood for several minutes in front of the blank stretch of wall inside the cellar doors before he finally remembered the knocking pattern. *One, two, silence, one, two, three, silence, one, silence, one, two, three, four, five.*

The walls split apart and he trudged down the stairs, a heavy tiredness washing over him. He wanted nothing more than to crawl into his bed and sleep indefinitely. At least until he could make up his mind about what he was going to do.

"Hey!"

He half-turned. Gaiomere stood next to a vendor's booth situated by the entrance and must have seen him come back into the main hall. Her gaze swept over his face, which he hastily schooled into an impassive expression—though he doubted that would do much to hide the puffiness of his eyes—and she stopped in front of him, saying, "We've been looking for you all day."

"Well, you've found me," he said dryly, turning away from her and starting towards the infirmary.

"What happened to the booster?" she asked, hastening after him. "It was completely destroyed."

He pushed open the door to the infirmary, quickening his pace as he crossed the room. He did not look at Whitsom, even as the older boy called, "Hey, Atlas!" but continued to the guest suite, pulling open the door and slamming it shut behind him.

Gaiomere came in after him though. "Atlas, I worked *all* night on that, I hardly got any sleep—" she began.

"And you got what you wanted," he interrupted, flinging himself back on his bed. He gazed up at the ceiling. The anger crawled beneath his skin again, the simmer gradually boiling hotter. "I sent the message to the Vedas—your precious North will be Obarion-free."

She stopped beside his bed, but he did not look at her.

"Atlas, what—what happened in there? Why are you—"

He sprang to his feet, and suddenly, it was as though he was fighting Raider again. The adrenaline coursed through him, and his heart hammered.

"Gaiomere, I don't understand what you want! I *did* what you wanted—I warned the Vedas, what else is there to do?"

She narrowed her eyes, pushing a wayward curl from her face.

"What did Moonstone say to you?"

A bitter laugh slipped from his lips before he could stop it.

"Oh, give it a rest, will you? *'We can help each other, Atlas.'* We've helped each other, haven't we? Your North is safe, I got what I needed out of Moonstone. Done deal, it's over—you can stop pretending to give a shit now—"

"Atlas—"

"What happened to shooting straight with one another? That was what you wanted, wasn't it?" He was shouting now, and he was certain he could be heard outside of their room, but he didn't care. She stared up at him with wide eyes, her hands cradled against her chest. "Wasn't it?"

"I—yes, Atlas, of course, I just—"

"You just *what*? You're off the hook, Gaiomere! You don't have some moral obligation to help anymore, congratulations!"

"Atlas, it wasn't a moral obligation!" she insisted, her face flushed with anger. "I mean, yes, I felt indebted to you, but I *wanted* to help you—"

"Why though?" he sneered, stepping so close that she had to tilt her head to look up at him. Her brown eyes glittered with tears, but he didn't care. "After all, I took everything from you, remember?"

Her eyes widened even further. "Atlas, that wasn't what I meant! I meant the Obarion clan—"

"I *am* from the Obarion clan—"

"But that doesn't mean that—"

"That's who I am. Whatever pretty stories you told yourself while you danced around in your flower crowns—about how we aren't that different, about living in harmony—they were wrong." Hurt flashed across her face, and it filled him with a vindictive sort of pleasure. "Obarion is in my blood. It's who I am. Nothing changes that. Ever."

She looked up at him strangely then, her expression a mixture between sadness and exasperation.

"The blood in your veins doesn't direct your path," she said. "Your choices do."

Her calm demeanor sent a surge of anger through him more intense than anything he had felt yet.

"I—I'm going to—I need to go." He let out a slow breath between his teeth. "I'm leaving. You got your message out. There's no reason for me to stay any longer. I'm going."

She ducked her head, brushing the tears from her eyes, and when she looked back up at him, her expression was determinedly impassive. "Back to the South?"

He ran a hand through his hair, moving around her and pulling open the door. "I don't—I'm not— I'm just going." He stormed across the infirmary and out the door before either she or Whitsom could say anything to try to convince him to stay.

CHAPTER THIRTEEN

A tlas awoke to find a spider crawling across his face, and hastily batted it off, though he promptly regretted it when he jostled his broken nose. He sat up quickly and looked around, for he had momentarily forgotten where he was.

But then he remembered. He had stormed out of the Under and stood, for several minutes, beside the storm cellar as he peered around apprehensively at the black of the night surrounding him. The moon's glow still left much of the area beneath the canopy of trees hidden from view, and the foliage obscured anything—or anyone—that might be watching him.

Finally, he swallowed his fear, clutching his knife between white knuckles, and plunged into the foliage, until he found a spot so thickly concealed that he was sure no human or animal would notice him. He thought it would take him hours to even fall asleep—if he slept at all—that every snapped twig, every rustled leaf would have him leaping from his skin. But in a matter of minutes he dozed off, too exhausted to fight off his tiredness any longer.

Or perhaps it was just the fact that now that he had gotten the information he needed from Moonstone, he could not see anything in his future but a dense, black cloud, so the prospect of being eaten by a mountain lion was not nearly so daunting as it once might have been.

The sun had already long-since risen. He must have gotten at least twelve hours of sleep. The muscles of his back ached from sleeping on the ground, and his neck had a crick in it, but he felt significantly calmer than the day before.

He wandered the forest awhile. The morning was quiet, and it settled over him like a salve. After about a half an hour, he came across some wild berries, and began to gather them. He would have to take some back to Gaiomere. He knew they were her favorite—

Atlas stopped, his stomach plummeting. The previous evening flashed across his mind, and a wave of guilt washed over him as he recalled the hurt on her face and the tears in her eyes. It wasn't as though he had never seen her cry before—no, it was just that *he* had never been the cause. Shame settled in his stomach as though he were going to be sick, and quite suddenly he no longer felt hungry. He tossed the wild berries to the ground.

Should he go back? No, he couldn't. Even though he had been harsh, he hadn't been wrong when he'd told her that they'd done what they'd meant to. Now the Renegades were just waiting for Whitsom to recover, and then they'd be back on their way, and Atlas would go...

Where? Where would he go? He had been so caught up in delivering the message to the Vedas, so determined that Moonstone spilled the truth, that he had forgotten—forgotten that he was an outcast, a traitor, and that he had no place in the Obarion clan any longer.

Unless...

He walked slowly through the forest. What if

Moonstone *did* manage to detain the Obarion soldiers? He had been so sure that even if he arrived at Obarion headquarters before them, once Talikoth heard of his treason, he would be doomed, but...what if Talikoth never heard of it at all? What if they never made it back south?

His steps quickened. Moonstone had said that they didn't kill children, but Jereis and Bettoni were both a few months older than Atlas, and Crowley certainly wouldn't be mistaken for a child...

Four Obarion soldiers attempting to scout the location of the Vedas' base for an ambush attack— surely that would be a transgression warranting death? Vailhelm wouldn't settle for less.

Atlas' feet came to a halt.

He could take the car. He had forgotten, in his exhaustion the night before, how close they had left it. He could take the car and be back to the Obarion headquarters by nightfall.

Turning back in the direction he'd come, his feet carried him briskly over roots and boulders, his excitement spurring him on with each step. He would not have to lose *anything* for his blunders. He could continue on, as though he'd never left. Captain, and then Major, and eventually Lieutenant General...

Atlas was nearly jogging as he continued down the dusty dirt path towards the spot where they had abandoned the car. He would have to recruit a new squad member to replace Bettoni, but he felt confident. The two Academy years beneath his own held promising recruits, though most had been hardly more than children at the time he'd graduated.

Atlas' feet stuttered, and his pace slowed to a walk.

He killed hundreds of children...to kill their hope.

The faces of some of the boys he had known in Academy swam before his eyes. Demarki, who was thirteen. Wendillan, who was twelve. Coral's little brother.

Rasta's face floated across his mind.

Then he felt sick with himself. Could he really just go back to the South and leave Bettoni to die at the hands of the Vedas?

How could he go back? How could he look Talikoth in the face, knowing what he knew now?

Atlas shook his head, quickening his steps once more. He would just ask him about it—and the other soldiers, too. Maybe even Coral or Maddex's parents. He was sure they would have an explanation.

Atlas frowned, staring at the ground beneath his feet as he walked. What would they say, though— what could any of them say that would explain? That would justify such senseless murder? Death in war was inevitable, but what Talikoth was waging did not seem to be war—it was genocide.

His indecision grew with every step he took towards the car. Should he go south? See what he could find out? Was it even safe to do so, or would asking questions mark him a traitor, like his mother?

Gunfire split through the air, and Atlas instinctively dropped to the ground. The bullet whizzed over his head and his eyes darted to the source of the sound.

Raider leaned against the car. Atlas hadn't seen him, partially obscured by a tree, but now he moved out from behind it, a cocky smirk on his lips.

"You should have taken more care to hide your

tracks," he drawled, pointing the barrel towards Atlas for a second time. "There aren't many cars out here—easy to follow, if you know what to look for."

Atlas got slowly to his feet, his gaze flickering between the rifle and Raider's face. There were perhaps forty feet between them, but he knew Raider would have little trouble hitting a target at triple that distance.

"I don't want any trouble," he said slowly.

Raider let out a bark of laughter.

"You should have thought about that before you shot me in the leg, Peewee."

Atlas rolled to the side, just as a second bullet pelted towards him. This one missed him by half an inch. He could feel the heat of the metal against the skin of his cheek.

The hulking blond went to take aim for a third time, and it was then that Atlas noticed he was moving strangely. His motion was slow, lagging almost, and his movements clumsy. Atlas looked closer and realized that the boy's face was flushed so red that it looked as though it had been burned, and his eyes were dull and flat. Atlas glanced down at Raider's leg and his stomach turned. The spot where the bullet had entered was swollen, the skin around it yellow and oozing.

Atlas made a split-second decision. He sprinted towards Raider, zigzagging back and forth, keeping his upper body hunched towards the ground. As Atlas suspected, Raider could not keep the barrel trained on him.

He took the last few steps at a dive, knocking the rifle from Raider's hands before he could aim it. He swung a fist towards Atlas, but his movements were slow, and his delivery weak—Atlas only had to step back to avoid the blow. He grabbed the rifle from the ground where it had fallen, aiming it between Raider's eyes. The small struggle seemed to have sapped whatever energy Raider had left, for he slumped against the car, sliding to the ground. He stared up at Atlas, his head lolling to the side.

"You gonna kill me, Peewee?"

It wasn't like two days ago, when he and Gaiomere had stolen Raider's car, and Atlas had not even thought about killing him. No, staring down the gun's barrel at Raider's collapsed figure, his finger clasped loosely over the trigger, and the anger of the last twenty-four hours rushing through him like a current, he wanted nothing more to take it out on this scumbag of a human being who belittled him, who beat him senseless, who flirted with the girl that Atlas wanted all to himself. But something stopped him.

She trained some of our soldiers to cut off supply chains to the Obarion troops.

The thought struck against every corner of his brain like a mantra. His mother had trained *Vedas* troops to cut off supply chains to the Obarion. But now, the only tribes that interfered with supply chains... were the gangs. Which meant that either the soldiers who had facilitated the supply disruptions had parted ways with the Vedas clan and become Renegades, or it meant that the Vedas and Renegades had been working together. Gaiomere had said that Raider and his gang planted gangs in the Ramshackles of the South before moving north, but what if that hadn't been their idea? What if they were only carrying on a tradition?

Atlas stared down at Raider soberly. The older boy, for his part, seemed off-put by the silence. He looked up at Atlas with a mixture of annoyance and fear.

"Look, if you don't have the guts—" Raider began, but Atlas interrupted him.

"Shut up, I'm thinking."

Was it possible that the Vedas and Renegades *had* been working together? Even if it had been soldiers who had separated themselves from the Vedas—how many more Renegades were former Vedas clansmen, who might have more sympathy for their cause then the typical Renegade? Who might more readily take up the fight, if the need arose?

He glared down at the Raider caustically. Atlas wanted to leave him out here to rot. He wanted to turn his back and walk away, to ensure that he'd never have to see that smug, taunting face again.

But he couldn't. Not when here, in front of his very eyes, was proof that his mother's legacy lived on. That even in death, she played her part in the Long War.

"Can you walk?" he asked Raider finally, lowering the rifle.

Raider stared at him for several moments, dumbfounded.

"Well, can you?" Atlas repeated.

"I'd rather you kill me than help me, Peewee," Raider spat.

Atlas rolled his eyes, slinging the rifle onto his back. "I'm guessing you haven't eaten anything since we left you. Or had any water? Three days without it will kill you, you know."

"I came straight here. I knew you'd come back to the car eventually, I just had to—*don't you dare touch me!*"

Atlas had knelt beside him and started to sling the

larger boy's arm over his shoulder, but hastily hopped back to avoid the fist that came swinging—albeit rather slowly—towards him.

"Raider, you're severely dehydrated, and I'm pretty sure that gunshot wound is infected. If you don't—"

"I'd rather *die*," he ground out through gritted teeth. "I'd rather die than—"

"Don't be stupid, your gang needs you," Atlas snapped impatiently. Raider stopped struggling away from him, his icy blue eyes narrowed as he looked sharply at Atlas. "You can't die. Who else is going to lead them?"

"Koda's my second—" Raider started in a grumble.

"They won't listen to him," Atlas said, scoffing. "Don't be an idiot. Get up."

Raider looked at him thoughtfully.

"This doesn't change anything," he mumbled.

Atlas snorted. "Damn. And here I was hoping you'd let me join your gang."

Raider's lips twitched. He hesitated, and then took Atlas' offered hand, grunting as he was pulled to his feet. He took a few steps, but his legs started to give. Atlas pulled Raider's arm over his shoulder, grimacing as the larger boy's body weight bore down on him.

"Where are we going?" Raider asked. His eyes were screwed up tight, and with every step he seemed to wince. It was a wonder he had made it even this far.

"We're a couple of miles from the Under. You been there?"

Raider nodded. "It's where I met Whitsom and Mere-kat."

Atlas pulled a face, but said nothing.

They moved at turtle pace. Raider's arm kept

slipping off of his shoulders and Atlas had to hike it back up, the muscles of his back protesting under the weight.

It took them almost an hour to finally get back to the cellar. As Atlas handed the rifle to the guard, he stared down the long staircase apprehensively. They had made it this far, but the stairs were steep, and Raider was unusually weak. If he stumbled, the fall could be fatal.

"Forgot how much I...hated this part," Raider muttered, his jaw taut. "I uh...I'm not crazy about heights."

Atlas looked at him sharply and felt the bizarre urge to laugh. He wasn't sure why the idea of Raider being afraid of heights was so amusing.

When they reached the bottom, Atlas let out a breath of relief, pushing open the doors to the main hall and leading Raider towards the infirmary. His stomach fluttered as he wondered if Gaiomere would be in there with Whitsom. He didn't think he could look her in the eye—not after the things he'd said to her.

But as it turned out, Whitsom was the only one in the infirmary. Upon seeing the pair of them his eyes widened so dramatically that it looked as though they'd bugged out of his head.

"Is that you, Raider?"

"Hey, Wolfman," Raider called weakly, raising a hand in greeting. Atlas helped the taller boy lower himself on the bed beside Whitsom, just as the doctor came out. He cast the newcomer an exasperated glance —Atlas vaguely wondered if he'd seen nearly half so much action, before their arrival—and hurried over to look at Raider's infected leg , calling for one of the nurses to bring water.

Whitsom glanced between the two of them incredulously, and Atlas sighed, pulling up a chair and taking a seat beside the Ren boy's bed. He knew he'd have to face the questions eventually. Only just now, he was ever so tired, and severely regretted having thrown out those wild berries hours before.

"I thought you'd left," Whitsom demanded, the moment he'd sat down. "Gaiomere said you had, and well, I *heard* you—nice one, by the way—"

"I'm sorry," Atlas said immediately.

"Oh, it's not me you should be apologizing to," Whitsom said, scowling. "You should have seen her— she was crying on and off all night. And look, I get it— Moonstone clearly said something that messed you up, but don't take that out on my baby sister. Got it?"

Atlas swallowed. It was the first time that Whitsom had been upset with him, and it made his stomach churn guiltily. "Yeah. Absolutely."

"Good. Now, do you want to tell me what that was all about? Or are you just going to go back to sulking and breaking things?"

Atlas' face flushed. He stared at his lap for a few moments, absently picking at a loose thread on his pants as he battled with himself. A part of him wanted to keep it to himself, to hide the truth that he'd discovered. He didn't want to see their pity, for them to look at him like a sad little sufferer with nowhere to go. But on the other hand, he didn't think he could keep it to himself. He had too many different emotions blazing through him, and he didn't know what else he could do but talk. Otherwise, he felt like he might burst.

"It wasn't the Vedas that killed my mother," Atlas

said finally, his voice quiet. "It was the Obarion."

Whitsom swore, shaking his head.

"You're kidding! How could he—I mean—" He glanced around, lowering his voice. "How could your pops do that?"

Atlas' gaze stayed fixed on his lap, his throat bobbing as he swallowed.

"The penalty for treason is death. No matter who commits the treason." He glanced up at the shorter boy, his lips pulling into a grimace as he admitted, "You were right. About everything. The Obarion, they—they did some horrible things, all across the Southwest. My mother abandoned the clan to warn the Vedas, and he—he had her killed for it."

Whitsom's eyebrows lifted, and he let out a low whistle.

"Your mother was a hero," Whitsom said. He shot a wary glance towards the figure occupying the bed beside his. "Uh...but why is *he* here?"

"He was waiting by the car when I went back to it," Atlas told him. He decided not to mention why he had been going back to the car in the first place. "He was dehydrated, and his wound was infected, so I brought him back here."

Whitsom gave him a disbelieving look. He glanced over once more at Raider, before leaning over and whispering, "And he *let* you? Raider is stubborn as hell. He doesn't take help from anybody."

Atlas shrugged. "I don't know. I just managed to convince him, I guess."

The infirmary door swung open, and Maggi's aggravated voice came flooding into the room.

"—do something adorable Rasta, maybe that will

stop her from snapping at everyone that so much as breathes wrong—"

"I can sing her the song I made up!" Rasta chirped at her side. They both stopped when they saw Atlas.

"You're back!" Rasta exclaimed. He ran across the room and threw his arms around Atlas' middle.

Atlas blinked, staring down at the boy for several moments before he hesitantly patted him on the back. "Hey, little guy."

"Why'd you come back?" Maggi asked, her voice uncharacteristically cold.

Atlas glanced up. She still stood near the door, her arms crossed over her chest and eyes narrowed to slits.

"I just..." How could he explain? He hardly understood it himself. All he knew was that he couldn't go back to Headquarters. "Raider needed help," he said finally.

"And Peewee has deluded himself into thinking that I *won't* kill him as soon as I'm back to full strength."

Maggi and Rasta's heads swiveled towards the second bed, where Raider—his eyes half-lidded and face sweating profusely now that he'd gotten some water into his system—grinned, waving at the two of them.

"Okay, now I'm *really* confused," Maggi said, plopping into a chair across from Atlas.

Whitsom quickly filled her in on everything, but every few minutes, Atlas found himself glancing towards the door. After the fifth or sixth time, Whitsom leaned over and muttered, "She's been holed up in the Quiet Room all morning."

"Yelling at anyone who interrupts her," Maggi added, rolling her eyes.

Atlas felt his cheeks burning, and he shifted in his

seat.

The doctor wandered over at that moment and informed them he'd be taking Raider into surgery to remove the bullet, which had lodged into his calf. The four of them silently watched as Raider was carted away, and Rasta asked nervously, "Do you really think he'll try to kill Atlas once he's better?"

"He can't do anything while we're in the Under," Whitsom assured him. "And after that, he'll have to go through all of us. We take care of our own."

Atlas' chest swelled with an outpouring of warmth towards Whitsom, but the moment was quickly shattered when Maggi muttered, "He could probably kill all five of us at once...it *is* Raider we're talking about."

After about a half an hour of snarky insults, Maggi must have decided that Atlas had been adequately punished, for she passed him over a few slices of cinnamon bread. He spent most of the day playing cards with Whitsom and wandering around the main hall with Maggi and Rasta. A few times, he started towards the Quiet Room door, but stopped himself. What would he even say? She clearly didn't want to see him—after all, he had seen Maggi leaving the room a number of times. Surely she had told Gaiomere of his return.

They were eating dinner around Whitsom's bed when Raider was carted out from the operation room. He looked semi-conscious, but his lips still curled into a sneer when he saw Atlas.

"How you feelin', Raider?" Whitsom called.

"Like I could take on the entire Obarion army," the tall boy quipped, grinning crookedly. Atlas snorted.

The infirmary door banged open, and Gaiomere

came stalking into the room. Atlas half-raised his arm to wave at her, but then thought better of it, and awkwardly scratched his head instead. Maggi sniggered at him.

Gaiomere didn't even look in their direction, but instead stopped by Raider's bedside.

"Hey, Mere-kat," the blond boy said.

She held out a handful of bright green leaves to him.

"I found these about a mile from here. They'll kill the infection better than anything the doctors could give you—Dad used to use them all the time."

"The infection *your* little boyfriend caused in the first place," Raider snarked.

"Don't act like you were innocent," Gaiomere snapped, unconsciously scratching her chin, where the bruise still lingered.

Raider's face softened, ever so slightly.

"I lost my temper," he muttered.

"Funny, that doesn't sound like an apology," said Gaiomere coolly.

"I'm *sorry*," Raider spat, scowling as he tossed the leaves into his mouth, grimacing at the taste. But Gaiomere wasn't finished.

"To him too." She jerked her head in Atlas' direction.

Raider gave her an incredulous look. "To Peewee? Are you *joking*? Absolutely not. I won't."

"You *will*, or your left leg is going to match your right." His face whitened at that. "The only reason you're alive is because Atlas gave you mercy that you didn't deserve."

Atlas suddenly found himself very fascinated by

the pattern on the quilt atop Whitsom's bed. Gaiomere's praise might have felt gratifying, if it weren't for the fact that Atlas had mostly spared Raider's life for his mother's sake—and the fact that he would likely need the gang leader's help.

Raider glared at a spot on the opposite wall. Finally, he mumbled, "I'm...sorry."

Atlas nodded, but before he could reply, Raider's lips lifted in a sardonic smirk, and he added, "That your daddy didn't teach you to fight better."

"*Raider!*" Gaiomere chided, her face darkening furiously. Whitsom and Maggi both burst into laughter, and even Atlas felt his lips twitch. The wild-haired girl threw Raider one last deprecating glare before she disappeared into their room.

Atlas didn't get a chance to speak to her for the rest of the evening. It seemed like every time he was going to, Gaiomere seemed busy with something else, or was in deep conversation with one of the other Renegades. By the third or fourth time this happened, Atlas began to suspect it was intentional.

He laid down that night, his hands folded behind his head as he listened placidly to Gaiomere sing Maggi and Rasta to sleep. It was only when their breathing was soft and even that he whispered into the black, "Gaiomere?"

She didn't answer. He sighed, settling back against his pillow, staring up at the ceiling as he watched the shadows shift above him.

Atlas' eyes flickered open. He wasn't sure when he'd fallen asleep, but he was certain it had only been a couple hours ago, for his eyes still felt heavy. Like the very first night they stayed in the Under, the bathroom door was cracked, and the light on.

The muscles in his back and arms protested as he pulled himself out of bed and trudged to the bathroom. He stood in the doorway for several moments, just watching her as she dragged her pencil along the paper, her curls piled on top of her head like a leaning tower.

Gaiomere did not even look up as she spoke, "Do you need to use the bathroom?"

"No."

"Then you don't have much of a reason for hovering there, do you?"

Atlas sighed, running a hand through his hair as he slipped inside the tiny room and pushed the door closed behind him. "Gai, I'm s—"

"*Don't* call me that," she snapped.

"Oh, what should I call you? *Mere-kat?*" he retorted without thinking. Her head shot up, and he immediately looked away, his cheeks reddening.

"Atlas, why—why did you save him?" Gaiomere asked, her brows knitted together.

Atlas glared at a spot on the wall above her head, muttering, "You already said it, didn't you? Out of the goodness of my heart—I guess I'm just that charitable —"

"Holy honeysuckle, what is *wrong* with you?" she demanded, and he sucked in a sharp breath, realizing only belatedly that his anger had begun to bubble over again, before he had even realized it. "I know you're upset but you can't just take it out on everyone else! You're not the only one who's lost a parent to the Obarion, okay?"

Atlas looked up at her sharply, and her eyes went wide as she registered what she had said.

"Sorry," she said hastily. "Sorry, I don't think Whitsom was supposed to have told me that."

He let out a heavy exhale, leaning back against the door. "No, it's—it's fine. I probably would have told you too eventually."

She peered at him with more curiosity than pity, and that, at least, settled some of his anger. His brow furrowed as he said slowly, "My mother—my mother was the one that started the gang planting. At least—at least, I think she was."

Gaiomere's brows shot up. "Are you—that's—that's, I mean—"

"It's insane," Atlas finished for her.

"Yeah. So that's why you saved Raider," she concluded.

He nodded, his eyes roving contemplatively up towards the ceiling. "I just want to know—I mean, I want to know why. Was she just trying to cause chaos for Talikoth and my clan? Or was it an effort to actually —I mean, to actually—"

"Win the war," Gaiomere said grimly.

"Yeah."

She leaned back against the mirror and pulled her legs against her chest.

"Talking to Raider would be helpful," she told him. "He's—he's a bit of a jerk, but he knows his stuff. He'll be able to tell you what their real aims are. He might even be able to remember before—when it first started, I mean. He told me he learned from his father."

Atlas nodded again, his mind still racing. "I just— I can't help but think that—that him being back in the

Ramshackle—him following the car all the way here—I can't help but think none of it's a coincidence."

A crease appeared between her brows and she smiled wryly, letting out an uncomfortable laugh.

"What, like fate?"

He arched a brow, shrugging.

"You don't actually believe in all that, do you?"

"Well, I have to, don't I?" Atlas said with a straight face, adding, in a mocking tone, *"Fate bends to the will of the Obarion people—"*

She snorted, swatting him on the shoulder. "Oh, please."

"I just think it's an awful lot of coincidences, that's all," Atlas said quietly, absently scratching his chin.

"And *I* think it's two in the morning and all of that sleep deprivation is going to your head," she teased.

He chuckled, pushing away from the door and pulling it open.

"You're probably right." He started back towards his bed, but stopped, realizing that he hadn't actually done what he'd come for in the first place. "Hey, Gaiomere?"

She had already returned to her drawing, but she glanced up at him questioningly.

"I really am sorry. I didn't—I didn't mean the things I said."

"I know," she said softly.

"And I'm sorry about the booster. I shouldn't have —that was completely stupid—"

She shrugged. "I was pretty mad, but I cheered up when I realized how many flower crowns you'll have to get me to make up for it." A mischievous grin suddenly stole across her face, and she said, "By the way...Maggi told me about you singing to her and Rasta."

Atlas' face burned. "No she didn't."

Gaiomere laughed quietly, nodding, and he cursed, running a hand through his hair as he attempted to will down the color in his cheeks.

"I was just messing around—"

"Oh shut up, she said it was their favorite lullaby yet."

A reluctant smile tugged at his lips. He started to turn away a second time, but then she called, "Oh, and Atlas? Happy Birthday."

His stomach flipped. With all of the commotion, he had completely forgotten.

It was the first birthday in many years he had not spent celebrating with his friends, the first birthday he hadn't had Delurah to make him a cake.

He glanced back at Gaiomere, her hickory brown eyes glittering as she peered back at him, a small smile still playing around her lips.

"Thank you," he said quietly. His eyes affixed on her face for a moment longer than was probably necessary, before he padded across the room and slipped into his bed to drift back off to sleep.

All things considered it was not, by any means, his worst birthday.

CHAPTER FOURTEEN

T he days quickly blended together into weeks, and for the first time in his life, Atlas felt like a normal eighteen-year-old boy. A weight seemed to have lifted from his shoulders, and he felt more relaxed than he had in a very long time.

Whitsom was finally allowed to get out of bed and move around the Under, provided he used his walking stick. He was decidedly more sociable than Atlas, so he often perched on a stool near one of the vendors, where they regaled him with their travels across the Westland.

The five of them had long since run out of items to barter, so they'd had to get resourceful. The doctor said that if they helped him out in the infirmary, he'd give them barter chips to use with the vendors, so they switched off each evening, turning down the sheets in the infirmary, sweeping the floor, or sometimes, if they were particularly unlucky, washing out the sick pan.

Some evenings Gaiomere got up on the makeshift stage the musicians performed on and strummed a tune with an instrument she'd told him was called a guitar. She'd sing songs about the Westland, songs about freedom, or hope, or sometimes love. One night she sang a song making fun of Whitsom's snoring that had most of the audience in tears from laughing so hard. On a good night, they could collect enough barter chips to last them a few days. Her voice was resonant, rich and sweet all at once, and she seemed to have a knack with the crowd.

But then, that made sense, Atlas supposed. He knew how easily she had charmed Kendo, how she had convinced Jacoby to do exactly what they needed. Even Raider, who acted so tough, clearly had a soft spot for her.

He had decided to wait until Raider's wound had completely healed before he approached him. Atlas hoped his regained mobility would put him in a better mood—even if the only reason he had lost it in the first place was technically because of Atlas.

Two weeks into their stay, the day finally arrived. Atlas came out of their room to find Raider's infirmary bed empty. He found the blond boy in the Quiet Room, sitting at a table with Gaiomere, a game of chess spread out between them. She had evidently just beaten him, for when Atlas walked in he had grasped his bishop and flung it at the nearest wall.

Gaiomere caught Atlas' eye and smirked. "He's not a very graceful loser."

Raider shot her a dirty look and disappeared between the bookshelves.

Atlas walked over to retrieve the bishop from where it lay behind an end table, and then returned to the table and took Raider's vacated seat. He got the sense that now would not be the best time to talk to the older boy, so instead he challenged Gaiomere to a game of chess.

"Did you find anything helpful in those old papers?" she asked him as the two of them set up the board.

Atlas had been scouring what few newspaper

clippings he could find in the Under for any information on the supply chain interference. The problem was, after the First War, print became entirely localized with the fall of civilization's structures. The press became a means to relay information across large clans.

But *because* the print was so localized, most of the newspaper clippings here were virtually useless. Many were decades old, and most pertained to tribes he had never even heard of.

"I don't think there's anything in there that will help me," Atlas said. His brow furrowed when Gaiomere spun the board around, so that the white pieces were in front of him, rather than her.

"I just figured you could use the advantage of going first," she explained with an impish smile.

"Oh, I'm so excited to beat you," Atlas drawled, smirking.

Gaiomere's face was very serious as they played. Her brows were furrowed, and she was chewing on the inside of her cheek with particular intensity. Atlas found himself watching her when it was not his turn to move, but then she would glance up at him and he would hastily look away.

Raider must have gotten bored of his sulking, for he wandered out from between the bookshelves and came back over to the table.

"Move your rook there," he told Gaiomere, his hands on either side of her chair as he peered over her head. The blond sent Atlas a smug smirk, and irritation stabbed at the pit of his stomach.

"I'm not going to move it there, that gives him a perfect opportunity to set up to take my queen next turn," Gaiomere argued, shooting Raider a disparaging glare. "You're just trying to help Atlas win."

"Oh yeah, cause he's just my *favorite* person," the blond said with a snort. He leaned against the back of her chair, absently twisting one of her curls around his finger.

Atlas' eye twitched.

"*Ooh*, no way, don't move your bishop there, Mere-kat—"

"Raider, go away!" Gaiomere spun around to smack him, but he dodged her, sniggering as he crossed the room and plopped down on the couch.

Atlas rolled his eyes, trying very hard to focus back in on the game, but his vexation was distracting. He knew Raider's information was essential, but Atlas suddenly rather wished that he was still confined to a hospital bed, preferably floundering around in an exorbitant amount of pain.

"He doesn't actually like me like that, you know," Gaiomere said, quietly enough that Raider wouldn't hear her, and Atlas looked up at her abruptly. "He sees me like a little sister. He only does that because he knows it gets to you."

"It doesn't get to me," Atlas said immediately. Which of course, was not true, but at this point deflection was almost an instinct. And besides, it wasn't as though he even had a right to be jealous. Gaiomere wasn't *his* girl, and after all, Raider had known her longer...

When he glanced up, her eyes were narrowed, and her mouth was set into a straight line.

"So much for shooting straight with each other, hmm?" Gaiomere said coolly. She slammed her queen down on the board, effectively checkmating his king, and disappeared out of the room before he could say another word.

Atlas ran a hand through his hair, staring blindly at the chess board. He knew she had wanted him to be honest with her in regard to his intentions with the Renegades, and with thwarting the Obarion scouts, but even the thought of being honest with her about his feelings for her made his stomach writhe with nerves.

It was several moments before he remembered he wasn't alone. He glanced up and saw that Raider was already watching him.

"You're pretty gutsy to be in here without your bodyguard," the blond boy muttered. "I could have killed you that day, you know. I would have, if she hadn't stopped me."

"I believe you," Atlas said quietly. Raider tilted his head sideways, peering at him.

"And yet, here you are. I don't even think you're afraid of me."

Atlas met his gaze unflinchingly. He decided honesty was probably his best chance of earning Raider's trust, even if it could end up backfiring on him.

"I'm not very easily intimidated. Byproduct of having Talikoth for a father, I suppose."

He watched Raider's face carefully. It was a moment before he processed what Atlas said. Confusion flashed across his expression, then comprehension, then finally, rage. He sprang to his feet, letting out a string of expletives and running a hand through his hair agitatedly. "You—you're—"

"Obarion, yeah," Atlas said calmly.

Raider let out a harsh breath. "You—you have *some*

nerve. Do you have any idea what I do to guys like you
—"

"I'm not really interested in a play-by-play narration," Atlas said in a bored voice. "I told you this because I have a favor to ask of you."

The blond boy's eyes narrowed, and he let out a bark of laughter.

"A favor? If you think I would trust you enough to ever—"

"Let me ask you something," Atlas interrupted. The taller boy's mouth snapped shut, his glower so venomous that Atlas briefly wondered if he were going to attack. "Do you think for a second that Gaiomere and Whitsom would have brought me here if I was a danger to any of you? Do you think they would have exposed the Renegade underground if they didn't absolutely trust me?"

"Whitsom is too trusting, I've always told him that," Raider spat. He began to pace in front of the table, and Atlas wondered if the older boy was expelling pent-up energy to keep from punching him in the face.

"But Gaiomere isn't," Atlas said reasonably. "You know that."

Raider stopped, whirling around to look at him, piercing blue eyes fixed on Atlas with such intensity that he might have shifted, if he weren't working so hard to keep his composure.

"I don't work with clansmen. I work against them. That's my whole life. I will spend the rest of my life fighting against this war—against people like you."

Atlas leaned forward. "You can spend the rest of your life fighting against it—but all your work will mean nothing. It will have been a lifetime of wasted effort, because at the end of the day, it won't be enough. The only way we survive is together. Talikoth figured that out a long time ago, that's why he's got the numbers —"

"So, you're saying he can never be beaten," Raider growled, shaking his head. "He's got thousands of men. We'll never have those numbers—"

"It's not just about numbers. It's about the collective—it's about the people uniting against one common enemy. About coordinating efforts rather than running ourselves ragged and treating everyone we cross as an adversary." Raider started to speak, but Atlas pressed on, "You can't fight the Vedas *and* the Obarion forever. It won't work. You're trying to deplete their resources, but you're really only depleting your own. If all your efforts were concentrated on one or the other you could have broken them by now."

Raider's expression remained suspicious, but Atlas could see the cogs turning in his head, and knew he needed to seal the deal.

"The reason the Under is here—the reason the Ren exist in the first place —is because a portion of the population decided they didn't want to fight this war. But even though you all have opted out of the war, it's still taken its toll on each and every person across the Westland. Rebels are still slaughtered by the Obarion. Renegades are still forced to work on the Rigs. Nomads still die passing through landmine territory. As long as this war continues, every single one of us will be a part of it—until it's finished. So you can choose to opt out and act as a bystander while the wrong side takes command of the Westland—or you can use all that energy and brilliance that you're already expending chasing your own tail to actually do something useful."

Raider stared at him impassively, his shoulders taut and hands clenched in fists at his sides. Atlas held his breath, for if ever he was going to strike, now was probably the moment.

The blond boy sank slowly back into his chair, his eyes never leaving Atlas'. After a moment, he cautiously asked:

"So what's the favor?"

Gaiomere was waiting up for him when Atlas returned late that evening from working in the infirmary. His fingers had pruned, and his forearms ached from all of the scrubbing. She sat on the end of his bed with a pair of knitting needles, deftly winding them through yarn as she wove together what looked like a pair of socks.

She had been decidedly cool towards him since the chess incident, ignoring him most of the afternoon, but her curiosity must have won out, for as soon as the door closed behind him, she immediately asked in a low voice, "Did you get anything out of Raider earlier?"

Maggi and Rasta were fast asleep in their bed, so Atlas replied in a whisper. "Surprisingly, yes." He sat down next to her, pulling off his boots and peeling the sweater from his already-overheated torso. "Once he started talking, I couldn't get him to stop."

She quirked a brow. "How'd you manage that?"

Atlas shrugged. "He's unexpectedly receptive of criticism." He told her about their conversation, and by the end, her brows had lifted to her hairline.

"I'm impressed," Gaiomere said, smirking wryly. "I

half-expected you to come out of there with another black eye."

Atlas smiled a little, leaning back on his arms as his eyes roved up to the ceiling thoughtfully. "My mother trained his father."

Gaiomere nearly dropped her knitting needles. "You're kidding. Small world." Atlas gave her a look. "What?"

"Gaiomere, that's not a coincidence. There's something bigger at play here. It's like—it's like I was supposed to get captured by the Vedas."

The wild-haired girl gnawed at her lip anxiously. "I just think—I think that—well, that sort of thinking can be dangerous."

"What do you mean?" he demanded.

"I just think it's dangerous when people get these big, grand ideas about their place, or feel like they have this massive responsibility to—I don't know, save the world, or something. All that happens is they end up getting hurt. And hurting the people that care about them."

There was something in her voice that roused his interest, and his gaze flickered over her face.

"That's why my dad died," she said bitterly. "Because he felt he had a responsibility to save the world —he would have rather died to try to save a bunch of other kids than stay alive to protect his own."

His chest gave a pang at the utter despondency on her face. Suddenly all of her incongruity made sense. Why she was so moralizing in some regards but struggled so deeply with finding the courage to fight— except when it came to life or death. Their father had shown them, all of their lives, that they must stand up for what was right, but she had watched him die by that creed, and had grown to resent it.

"Gaiomere, you can't tell me that if a bunch of kids were about to be murdered in front of you, you wouldn't do exactly what he did."

She frowned, looking down at her half-finished sock. "I—I don't know. Maybe I would, but—but Maggi and Rasta need me, and—"

"I know that you would," Atlas said firmly. "Because I know that I would, and you're better than I am." Her brow furrowed, but she said nothing. After a few moments, he continued, "Raider remembered her. My mother, I mean."

"Really?" Gaiomere had set down her knitting needles altogether and leaned back on her arms as well. Their shoulders pressed together, and her hand rested atop the quilt, so close to his that he could reach out and grasp it, if he wanted.

He shook his head, redirecting his thoughts.

"He said he was about six when she came to train his father, so he doesn't remember much, but he does remember her." Atlas thought it rather unfair, that this numskull Renegade remembered more about Atlas' own mother than he himself.

Gaiomere's voice was tentative as she asked, "Did you find out why she—why she—why she did all of that?"

Atlas sighed, lying down onto his back and lacing his fingers behind his head.

"Raider's father told him that the gangs were started so that the Obarion troops would surrender. *Just* the Obarion troops. It was only when Raider took over that he started attacking the Vedas whenever the opportunity arose. But as far as he knows, my mother didn't do all that. She worked with the Vedas, to defeat the Obarion. For good."

Gaiomere had turned to face him. "Why do you sound so unhappy about that?"

He massaged his temples with the pads of his thumbs, frowning up at the ceiling..

"I just—I wish I knew for sure, you know? What she was fighting against. Because I don't want to—"

"Atlas?" Gaiomere interrupted, and he broke off, lifting his head up to look at her. She was toying nervously with a thread that had come loose from the quilt, her forehead creased. "It seems like you're afraid to pick a side."

"Why do you say that?" he challenged, scowling. "I'm here, aren't I? I helped you guys fight off Bettoni, and Jereis, and Macky. I didn't—"

"I'm not calling your loyalty to *us* into question," she said patiently. "You're as good as part of our tribe. I just meant..." She let out a heavy breath, her eyes flickering over his face. "It just seems like you won't stand against your dad until you know you have your mom's blessing."

He opened his mouth, but then closed it again, his mind working to make sense of what she had just said. Gaiomere continued.

"You spent your whole life under your dad's influence, I get it. But now that you're out from under it, it seems like you're not willing to take a step in any direction until you know beyond a doubt what your mom fought for. And yeah, it might be...encouraging, I suppose, to know that she was brave enough to stand up to him too, but Atlas—you have to be willing to walk down a path because *you* know it's right, not because it's what either of them would want for you.

Atlas blinked. The anger swelled up again in his chest, but it felt significantly more muted this time. He wanted to yell at her, to tell her that she was wrong, that he was an adult and was perfectly capable of making his own decision without his parents' input—and what did she know? She was two years younger than him anyway.

But then he stopped, his mind filling with a strange quiet. Because she was right. He didn't want to —couldn't afford to misstep. And his entire life, he'd never even had to take the risk. His path had always been carved out for him, but that meant that he'd never had the pressure to choose. He'd never sat down and thought about what was important to *him*, or what *his* values were, what *he* was willing to fight for, or to die for —rather than just what Talikoth prescribed.

That same anxiety from the night of their arrival to the Under swelled in his chest like a tidal wave. Who was he, when he stripped everything else away? Atlas, son of Talikoth, the Obarion General. Atlas, Captain of the 632nd squadron. Atlas, top of his year at Academy, who had only ever lost one—now, two—fights. Atlas, who studied late into the night and trained until his knuckles bled, who outworked anyone and everyone else in competition, because he'd always thought that maybe then, if he was the best of the best, he would feel good enough. But it never seemed to be enough. Because then Talikoth would look at him with *that* look—and it always made him feel small.

Until he had come here. Here, Whitsom and Jacoby praised his fighting, and Maggi and Rasta had been sad when he'd left, and Gaiomere...

Gaiomere trusted him, and laughed at his stupid jokes. Gaiomere had defended him to Moonstone, and saved his life on multiple occasions, and she trusted him. She and Whitsom *both* trusted him, in a way Talikoth never had. They had said he was as good as a part of their tribe, and Talikoth had never even treated him like family, let alone like his only son.

"Atlas?" Gaiomere said tentatively. "I'm sorry, it wasn't my place to—"

"You're right," he broke in, glancing up at her. "You're completely right." His eyebrows lifted and his lips pulled up into a smirk. "Although you know it goes both ways, right?"

She gave him a quizzical look.

"Are you never going to stand up for anything that's important to you just because something horrible happened to your dad?"

She blew a curl from her face, leaning down next to him, her arm bent to pillow her head and her legs stretching across the top of the quilt.

"It's different. I'm not a fighter. That's what you were born to be, I think."

He snorted. "Tell that to that Flesh Flayer. Or Jereis. They'll have a real laugh—"

"That's *totally* different!" she burst out. Rasta shifted in his sleep, and Gaiomere lowered her voice. "It's different when it's for the people that mean something to me." Atlas' eyes had roved up to the ceiling, but he looked at her sharply then. Her face colored as she belatedly realized what she said, and she hastily made to clarify, "I'm not willing to fight for just —just strangers, people that I don't even know—"

Atlas knew he was probably already on thin ice, but he couldn't help himself. "So much for shooting straight with each other, huh?" he drawled.

Gaiomere's eyes narrowed, and she let out an affronted little huff. "You're—you're annoying," she muttered. Atlas bit back a smile, but only continued to watch her. A few moments passed, during which she looked as though she were warring with herself, before she finally admitted, "I suppose you'd fall into the category of people that mean something to me."

"I'm flattered to have made the cut," Atlas said dryly. Gaiomere rolled her eyes. He hesitated, his face prickling with heat, and then said, in as casual a tone as he could muster, "You would too. For—for me, I mean." There. That hadn't been so bad. Like ripping off a band aid.

Gaiomere smiled, and the last remnants of coolness seemed to fade from her gaze. She settled down next to him, a little closer this time, and asked, "Why are you working so hard to convince me to fight?"

He chuckled a little. "Gee, I don't know, maybe because you're the smartest person I've ever met?"

"Yeah, but why are you—" She broke off, understanding dawning on her face. "That's what you and Raider are planning, aren't you? You're going to try to take down the Obarion."

Atlas nodded slowly.

"We went and talked to Whitsom already," he admitted. "Once he's released, the three of us are going to go back to the Vedas base—and you with us, if you'd like."

"What about Maggi and Rasta?"

Atlas picked absently at the quilt. "Of course, they

could come too...but Whitsom and I were thinking: he gets a small stipend for serving as a guard—clothing and antibiotics and the likes—well, most of it he won't use, so every so often we can use Raider's car and bring Maggi and Rasta barter chips—enough that would last them a week or two—so that they could stay here. They'd be safer here, if the base was attacked."

"No," Gaiomere said firmly. "We're not going to be separated again. You and Whitsom aren't going without me either. We'll keep them safe if the base is attacked."

Atlas inclined his head. He had expected this response from her, and he couldn't say he blamed her. Not with how close Maggi and Rasta had come to dying, the last time they had been separated.

She still had not moved from the spot where she lay next to him, so close that he could see the flecks of bronze and amber in her eyes, and Atlas wondered what she might do if he kissed her.

"We should probably get some sleep," Gaiomere said suddenly, though she made no move to get up.

"I'm not really tired," Atlas said, too quickly. The hint of a smile wriggled at the corner of her lips, and his cheeks flushed. A thought that had been swimming at the back of his mind for the last few hours flashed through his head, and he said, "Gaiomere?"

She arched a brow, and he continued

"That—that day, with—with bobby-pin girl...I don't usually—I mean, I didn't—I don't normally do that sort of thing, or—or treat girls like that. I'm not some sort of..."

"Philanderer?" she supplied, her eyes twinkling with amusement.

"Um, yeah." His cheeks, which had already felt

warm, suddenly were ablaze.

Gaiomere's lips split into that familiar, impish smile. "I didn't think you were."

"Oh, okay," he said, relieved. "Good."

"I have been curious though," she continued, her fingers tracing patterns atop the quilt, "how you got the nickname 'Attie the Baddie'."

Atlas groaned, slapping a hand over his face in embarrassment, and she laughed.

"I was sort of hoping you'd forgotten about that," he muttered, and she laughed again.

"You know I don't forget things."

He rolled onto his side, leaning his head against the palm of his hand. "It's a long story," he told her. "Incidentally involving my training squad, a military demonstration rally, and seventeen roosters."

He launched into the story, and Gaiomere listened raptly. He talked to her for far longer, he was sure, than he'd ever talked to anyone in his entire life—at one time, anyway. She told him about all of the places she'd traveled with her tribe, and he told her about all of the pranks he, Coral, and Bettoni had played on Crowley and Caddo. They argued about which was better—the North or the South—and Gaiomere gave him an impassioned lecture about why his clan's practice of regulating trade between individuals was a form of dictatorship.

Atlas lost track of how long they had been talking before his eyes had begun to grow heavy. Gaiomere's head lolled sideways against his shoulder, and he blearily thought perhaps he should move her to her own bed. No sooner, however, had the thought crossed his mind, before he too drifted off to sleep.

It was the last week of Whitsom's recovery, and Atlas had felt a strange sort of dejection lingering in the back of his mind. Their time spent in the Under seemed something like a recess from the real world, like he had seamlessly slipped into a chapter out of someone else's life. The worst thing he had to worry about here was whether or not the sick pan would need to be cleaned out during his shift in the infirmary.

It wouldn't be the same at the Vedas' base. Still, he was glad that he hadn't left that night, after he and Gaiomere's fight—not only because of what he'd discovered from Raider, but because he actually liked having...well, friends. Not that Coral and Bettoni *hadn't* been his friends—just that there was an underlying awkwardness with him being the General's son. Like he could never really escape from beneath the shadow of who his father was.

Not that he ever really forgot, even being here. It was just that the weight felt lighter somehow.

He, Whitsom, and Raider spent many hours holed up in the Quiet Room, formulating their plan, although Whitsom seemed to disappear into the main hall at least three times an hour to retrieve food.

"Question," Whitsom said, as he plopped down in the chair between Atlas and Raider with two handfuls of sticky, powdered donuts. "Assuming that we do convince Moonstone to ally with the gangs, aren't we going to also need to convince all of *these* folks in the Under to fight too?" He wrinkled his nose, leaning back in his chair. "I've spoken to a lot of them—most of them think the war is none of their business. A whole bunch of them are so afraid of the Obarion that even if they wanted to fight back, they don't believe they could."

"Thanks, Asshat," Raider muttered, as though the entire Obarion influence over the past sixteen years was his fault. "So it's just us and the Vedas then? Sounds promising."

"Not...necessarily," Atlas said slowly, drumming his fingers against the table. "These people—they're only willing to live like this because they believe there's no other choice. Nobody wants to constantly live in fear and hiding, or to have to move all over the place to avoid being killed. The only thing that needs to happen in order to convince them that they can't afford *not* to fight, is to show them how much they have to lose."

Raider scowled. "How do we do that?"

Atlas didn't answer. The truth was, the most effective way to show the Renegades that fighting was in their best interest was to force change through unbearable discomfort. After all, that was how Talikoth had trained him to discipline his mind and body so effectively.

But *how* was the question. The Northerners were shielded by their distance from the Obarion, but he was sure that those in closer proximity to Headquarters felt the weight of their occupation more heavily.

"What do you know about the Renegades in the South?" he asked Raider.

"Well, that's where the gangs started," Raider explained, folding his hands behind his head. "The tribes are larger, too—"

"Larger?" Atlas said, surprised. "But wouldn't that make it harder for them to—"

"Well, they've got weapons, see. And they know the land better than the Obarion, too. They know they're coming miles in advance and can send tribe soldiers to the high ground to pick them off."

Atlas sat back, his mind whirring. So, there *were* other Renegades with weapons—and what was more, Talikoth had known. He must have, if they were going head-to-head with his own soldiers. So why had he hidden it? Why had he told all of his people that the Renegades were only cowardly savages fleeing the fight?

"You didn't know we had weapons, did you?" Raider asked, smirking wryly.

"Talikoth told us the Renegades were primitive," Atlas said.

Raider let out a bark of laughter. "Your daddy's a smart man, that's for sure."

Whitsom, who had been occupied with a donut, asked, "Why do you say that?"

"It's pretty typical fear-mongering. You convince your people that the opposing population is inferior, dangerous, threatening to the common good of the people. It keeps civilians from recognizing the humanity in their adversaries—they're more easily able to justify wrongdoing against the enemy."

"Like trying to kill a couple of children with a landmine just because they might be Vedas," Atlas deliberated, arching a brow. "Something like that?" Raider's mouth twisted, and Atlas held his hands up in front of his chest. "Just making sure I'm understanding correctly."

Whitsom hastily turned his laugh into a hacking cough.

"It's *different*, Asshat," Raider snapped. "These goons have all been causing chaos for too long —"

"So the corrective action, then, is to contribute to the chaos—"

"What are we doing going to the Vedas base then, huh, Peewee?" The blond boy was visibly angry now. His hands were braced on the table as though he intended to stand, and his jaw was taut. "What the *hell* have we been doing wasting our time the last few weeks, trying to come up with a plan to integrate the gangs with the Vedas—"

"What we've been doing is organizing a resistance —a coordinated, systematized resistance that's only chance of success relies *solely* on cohesive cooperation. Everything falls to shambles if any one person goes rogue or tries to do things their own way." His voice was cold, and Raider's eyes flashed dangerously, but he didn't care, not one bit. "You may have tangoed with soldiers in the South, but the only person here who has any real idea of what the Obarion army is capable of is me. So I know what I'm saying when I tell you: pull anything like you did at the border with Gaiomere and I, and I promise, I'll make you regret it."

Whitsom was twiddling his fingers in front of him, his eyes affixed on the ceiling in obvious discomfort, but Atlas ignored him.

He had expected Raider to sneer, to make a clever remark reminding him of the pummeling he'd been delivered. He expected Raider to lunge across the table and attempt to kill him right there, in the middle of the Quiet Room.

But what he had not expected was for Raider to stiffen in his chair. Nor had he expected the measured, calculating look that the gang leader gave him.

"It's funny," Raider muttered, lugging himself to

his feet. "You almost sound like him." He stormed away from the table and yanked the door open, slamming it shut behind him.

Atlas swallowed thickly, pushing away from the table as well. Whitsom gave him a confused look, but he only muttered, "I'll be back in a bit," and strode from the room.

His feet carried him to the guest suite, which, thankfully, was empty. He sank down onto his bed slowly, his eyes roving unseeingly up to the ceiling. *You almost sound like him.*

He was used to being told that he looked like his father—even used to being compared to him. And his entire life, the praise made his chest puff up and filled him with a sense of pride.

But that was before he had discovered that Talikoth had ordered his mother killed. That was before he had found out about the senseless slaughtering, before he had learned how unrepentantly Talikoth lied —about their clan's history, about the Renegades, about everything. He used the truth to control his people, to shape the world the way he wanted it.

Atlas did not particularly care for Raider's good opinion. He was an excellent fighter, certainly, but Atlas also didn't think he'd ever disliked anyone so much. Still, the fact that Raider had told him he sounded like Talikoth didn't sit well with him. He certainly didn't *want* to be like Talikoth. Perhaps maybe to fight as well as he could, or to be able to ignore basic human needs in favor of strategy sessions—but to sacrifice so many lives for the sake of accumulating more power? No, he would never stoop that low. Never.

And yet, a niggling sense of doubt pervaded in the

back of his mind.

...at first, General Talikoth only wanted to find a way to restore the Fallen Land to its former glory. He saw a problem and he believed that he knew how to fix it.

According to his mother, Talikoth, too, had started with good intentions. He had only begun with the desire to correct the path of annihilation that the inhabitants of the Fallen Land had continued so determinedly on for hundreds of years.

Was he *really* that different from Talikoth? Or had he already developed an insatiable hunger for power, in the same way Talikoth had? He thought of how eager he had been, when he had at first been captured by the Vedas, to supply Talikoth with information—not for the sake of his clan, but for glory.

He shook his head, pushing to his feet and pacing in front of the bed. No, he would never, *could* never be like Talikoth. He wouldn't let himself.

But then something else crossed his mind. *You almost sound like him.* Raider had met Talikoth, Atlas was certain of it, and even seemed familiar enough with him that he could recognize him in Atlas. It felt strange, knowing that. Like a fusing of two worlds that, in his life previous to this point, had remained completely separate.

As though he had been summoned by Atlas' thoughts, Raider strode into the room, his shoulders stiff, and face red in the way that it got when he was angry. He must have been looking for Atlas, because the moment he saw him, his hands curled into fists. They stared at one another for several seconds, as though waiting for the other to make the first advance.

Finally, Raider moved towards him, and Atlas

tensed, his heart rate speeding up, only slightly disconcerted by the couple-inch height advantage that the blond boy had over him.

"If you *ever*," Raider hissed, "speak to me like that in front of anyone else again, I will *kill you*."

"You should know better than anyone that a unit can't operate effectively if its soldiers don't act like a team," Atlas countered.

"And what the *hell* gave you the impression that you're in charge of this one?" Raider stepped closer and his eyes narrowed to slits. "Just because your daddy is a General doesn't make you one. I don't take orders from anyone."

Atlas held his ground, his hands twitching at his sides. "Neither do I."

They were at an impasse, and they both knew it. Raider's eyes twitched towards the door, and Atlas suspected he would have already initiated his attack if it weren't for the fact that the Under had a strict policy against violence, and a brawl might attract the guards, and with them, their firearms.

"Look, we can steer clear of each other for the most part," Atlas said quietly. "Just so long as you aren't being stupid, and putting the rest of our lives in danger, I really couldn't care less what you do. But I meant what I said. If you really want the Obarion to lose, you're going to have to learn to work with other people, clansmen or not."

Raider scowled, jerking his head in what might have been a semblance of agreement, before he started towards the door. Atlas hesitated, and then called, "How did you meet Talikoth?"

The blond boy looked like he was battling with

himself for several moments, before he let out a harsh breath.

"We had a hunting party about fifty miles south of the Pass, and on our way back, we spotted a group of soldiers," Raider began. "Obarion, obviously. There were only about ten of them. Must have just been recon or something—a few of them didn't even have guns."

He leaned heavily against the wall beside the door, continuing, "It was just me and two of our other boys —Rilee and Kremble—so we decided to move to higher ground to pick them off. We found a good ledge, close enough to get off a few shots—they didn't suspect a thing, we listened to them talking and ripping around for at least ten minutes—before we struck. We managed to kill four of them before they rounded on us. I only knew it was him because one of them—some old man, looked too weak to fight—shouted his name just as I shot at him. I got him right in the shoulder—"

Raider broke off, swearing violently and slamming his hand down against the chair that sat near the door.

"I was *so close*—*so close* to shooting him dead. He would have been—it would have—" He snarled, shaking his head. "Well, I told Gaiomere her mom might not be dead if I had done what I needed to."

Atlas could see the scene play out so vividly in his mind. See the soldiers scrambling for cover, watching them round their weapons on the Renegades and firing towards the cliff. He could see Raider's focused glare, see his finger tighten around the trigger. But most lucidly, he could see Talikoth's face, hear his roar of fury as the bullet lodged into his shoulder, see his dark, glittering eyes—so dark that they sometimes looked black—swivel up towards Raider with a death stare so poisonous that even the fearless gang leader might have quivered, might have scrambled back from the edge of the cliff to shield himself from view.

"How did you get away?" Atlas asked.

"We ran for it. We were high enough up that they were never going to catch us, especially not with most of their party injured or dead."

Atlas remembered the exact night that Raider spoke of—he had been fifteen, and Talikoth had come home with a wounded shoulder. He had shrugged it off, acted like it was nothing, had insisted that it was merely a scuffle with the Vedas. Atlas had thought little of it—he certainly had no understanding of how close to death Talikoth had been that day.

"I wish I had killed him," Raider told him unflinchingly.

Atlas wanted to say, *I wish you had, too.* He wanted to push the words casually out of his mouth with as much conviction as his body could muster, and he wanted to mean them. With everything that Talikoth had done, all of the devastation he had caused and lives he had destroyed, Atlas knew those were the only words appropriate to pass from his lips.

"I believe you," he said instead, because he couldn't. He couldn't say what he was supposed to.

Atlas sunk back onto his bed as Raider left him alone to his thoughts. What was wrong with him, that despite everything Talikoth had done, everything he knew, he still could not wish his father dead? What kind of son was he, knowing that his mother's vengeance lay in the grave of that monster, and yet...and yet he could not say the words. And if Atlas could not even speak against Talikoth...how on *earth* was he to fight against him?

CHAPTER FIFTEEN

B efore Atlas knew it, the day arrived that they were packing up as much food as they could carry and retrieving their weapons from the entrance guards. Raider had taken off with the car early that morning, but thankfully, he'd left his rifle for them to use, since his journey was much shorter.

"You're gonna have to teach me how to use that, man," Whitsom said, gazing admiringly at the rifle as Atlas slung it over his back.

They elected to leave early Tuesday morning. The sun was only just beginning to creep up over the tops of the distant mountains, and the morning air was icy.

It felt strange to be on the move again, after so much time in one place. Atlas was atypically jumpy—probably because the last month they had been protected in a heavily-guarded underground lair whose location was completely hidden from Vedas and Obarion alike.

Still, the fresh air was satisfying, and he was grateful to be back beneath the sun, rather than the harsh, artificial lighting in the Under.

The first few hours of their journey passed quietly. The five of them all exhausted—Maggi had convinced the group to stay up late playing cards—and they had a long, grueling journey ahead of them.

The sun rose higher and higher. They finally stopped for food and water about four hours in.

Whitsom followed the slope of the mountain until he found a small pond, little more than a puddle, where rainwater had collected in the aperture. He and Gaiomere refilled the water bottles, while Atlas kept watch. Rasta passed around handfuls of nuts and divvied out slices of cinnamon bread that they had brought from the Under.

"Do you think Moonstone is going to give us a hard time?" Whitsom asked quietly.

Atlas frowned. "I'm not sure." He thought of how much Moonstone had trusted him, even from the beginning, even when many of her council members had advised against it. But then he thought of the vehement hatred Vailhelm had treated him with, the fear that Augusto had displayed. He had already snuck out of his room once before the three of them had left the base—perhaps a second transgression was enough to shatter his chances.

Still, he thought, as they got back on their way, he *had* warned the Vedas about the Obarion soldiers —when he had no real obligation to do so. Sure, Moonstone had told him the truth about his mother, but she had admitted herself that he hadn't needed to blackmail her into doing that. She would have told him eventually, regardless. So his contribution, the information that he'd given them—surely that would be enough to convince them...

When they hit the halfway point, the five of them were all sweaty and irritable—save for perhaps Rasta, who was trotting along beside Gaiomere, his hand clutched in hers, his expression decidedly chipper.

"Are there kids my age there, Gai-Gai?" he asked.

"There are kids you and Maggi's age."

"Woah," the little boy beamed. "I've never met another ten-year-old before."

"I'll be needing to keep this knife on me, Gai," Maggi said, stroking the blade affectionately. "New turf —gotta make sure they understand who the new Alpha is—"

"You are not going to threaten the other kids, Maggi," Gaiomere said exasperatedly. Whitsom snickered. "You're going to keep your head down while the boys do—whatever they're going to do—and then we leave."

Atlas glanced over at the curly-haired girl. He knew eventually he would have to admit to her that their plans involved her more than she had any idea of. After all, Atlas could give them every scrap of information they could possibly need about Obarion headquarters, and Raider could organize attacks so debilitating that the troops wouldn't know what had hit them—but without Gaiomere's input, their efforts would be little more than minor inconveniences.

With the sun bearing down on them from its highest point in the sky, sweat drenched Atlas' clothes, even with the coolness of the northern air. His hair stuck to his forehead, and his shoulders ached where the strap of the gun dug into them.

Whitsom found them a river, and it looked so familiar that Atlas was sure they must be near where he and the siblings had stopped on their journey out. They had finished the food from the Under, so Whitsom and Rasta disappeared into the foliage to forage, while Gaiomere refilled the waters. Maggi sat on the ground, sharpening her knife on a rock.

Atlas ambled over to the water's edge, plopping

down beside Gaiomere as she dropped a couple of detoxifiers into each of the bottles.

"What happens when you run out of those?" he asked her curiously.

She arched a brow, casting him an amused glance. "Then I make more, of course."

Atlas gazed thoughtfully at the tiny black crystals. "I wonder if those would work in the South. The water's said to be worse down there."

Gaiomere shook her head. "I don't think they do. But my dad—" She reached for her bag and withdrew her notebook, flipping through the pages until she came to the one she was looking for. "My dad was working on a modification—a strengthener, so to speak, for these little guys." He glanced down at the notebook and saw a series of equations in unfamiliar handwriting.

"These are his? You've kept them, all this time?"

She smiled. "A lot in here was his. Ideas he shared with me, things we worked on together. It's my most prized possession...which probably sounds stupid—"

"It doesn't sound stupid," he said immediately. "So, this strengthener—that's his equation for it?"

She frowned down at the notebook. "That's the start of it. He never finished it—never got the opportunity to."

He tilted his head as he studied her. "Why haven't you finished it?"

Her teeth gnawed at her lip. "I—I don't know. Just haven't gotten around to it, I suppose."

"Oh, great grizzly!"

They both whipped around, Atlas' hand flying to the rifle—but Whitsom was only walking through the clearing, his shirt folded to carry his berry haul.

"What is it?" Gaiomere demanded furiously. "I thought we were being attacked—"

"I just remembered it's Tuesday!" Whitsom exclaimed, grinning. "Which means there will be chicken tonight!"

Gaiomere rolled her eyes, and Atlas snorted.

Perhaps it was simply that they were all tired, but the last two hours of their journey seemed to pass at a sluggish pace. This final stretch was unfamiliar to Atlas —for he had been unconscious upon being brought to the base, and they had escaped deep in the forest, far from the main entrance—but Gaiomere said she had a rough idea of where the gate was located, based on the glimpses of the perimeter fence she'd gotten.

Atlas passed the rifle to Whitsom and offered to carry Rasta the last stretch. The boy was tiny, even for his age, but still, the extra sixty pounds on his back made the uphill stretches brutalizing.

"You sure we're going the right way?" Whitsom asked Gaiomere, his tone uncharacteristically sullen.

"For the fifth time, *yes*," she retorted, taking a long sip of water and passing it to Maggi, whose face was bright red.

"It just seems like we should have hit it by now, if your map was right—"

"My map *was* right, Whit, we just aren't there yet —"

"Will you two cut it out?" Atlas snapped. "Gate's right there."

Both their heads snapped forward. The barbed wire-topped fence loomed about a quarter mile in front of them. Two watchtowers, each at least fifty feet tall, stood on either side of the massive gate. As they drew nearer, Atlas could see figures moving around the watchtowers, as well as a line of about fifteen soldiers stationed just inside the gate.

"Do you think they'll try to shoot us if we get too close?" Maggi murmured. Gaiomere and Atlas exchanged a nervous glance.

"Here, let me handle this," Whitsom said. He lengthened his stride, moving ahead of them, only the faintest trace of a limp still distinguishable in his gait, and Atlas watched as the soldiers straightened, several of them clenching their fingers around the triggers of their guns.

"Mabes, is that you, man?" Whitsom called.

One of the guards shifted, his shotgun lowering half an inch. "Whitsom? Thought you were dead."

"Can't kill me so easy," Whitsom replied, grinning. He reached the bars of the gate. Several of the other guards eyed him uneasily, but the soldier Whitsom was familiar with—Mabes—had already withdrawn his receiver.

"—to Moonstone, come in, Moonstone."

Atlas hesitated a moment, then moved closer, Maggi and Rasta clustered nervously behind him.

"—the two Renegades. And they've got that Obarion boy with them—oh, and it looks like two other little kids, I've never seen them before."

Whitsom chatted with another guard, completely at ease, despite the fact that several of the other soldiers still had their guns aimed loosely in his direction.

"Trust Whitsom's extroversion to save the day," Maggi muttered, rolling her eyes.

"Yes, General, we'll bring them straight away."

The Mabes fellow tucked his receiver away and

signaled up to the watchtower guards. The gate split open, and the guards fell to either side, save for Mabes and another guard.

"We're to take you straight to Moonstone," he told them. He and the other guard fell into step on either side of their group.

"We don't normally have so many soldiers posted at the gate," Mabes told Whitsom. "There's been a lot of Obarion activity around the Pass. They've clearly had some success in finding pockets where small squads can make it between the mountains and the land mines—"

"Any of them make it near the base?" Whitsom asked.

Mabes shrugged. "Not that I know of. But Moonstone has been very hush-hush lately. Think she doesn't want to scare us—'course, if it was me, I'd rather know if a 3,000-man army was headed my way, wouldn't you?"

The soldiers led them not to Moonstone's office, but all the way down the stairwell, into the basement, and stopped in front of the heavy metal door that guarded the meeting room.

Moonstone waited inside, along with at least half of the Council. Her expression remained impassive as the group filed in, but her dark eyes glinted shrewdly.

"Thank you, Kusuke. Mabury."

The five of them stood in the doorway, shifting awkwardly. Vailhelm's cold glare pinned Atlas to the spot.

"I am glad to see you found your companions," Moonstone said. "Perhaps Mabury, if you would be so kind, you could take—Maggi and Rasta, was it not? Take them to the dining hall. I am sure you all are quite hungry."

Mabury started to put a hand on Maggi's shoulder, but Gaiomere grasped her arm and pulled her away from him, her other arm coming around Rasta's shoulder. Her gaze fixed on Moonstone, her eyes narrowed to slits.

"It's okay, Gai," Whitsom assured her. "They won't hurt them."

Gaiomere gradually loosened her grip, but Maggi looked between Moonstone and the guards with a frown.

"We're obviously being ousted from an 'adults only' conversation—so I'll only go if there's hot chocolate."

Moonstone's lips twitched. "I am sure that could be arranged."

Rasta's eyes lit up, but Maggi merely arched an eyebrow, looking unimpressed. "*With* marshmallows?"

There was scattered laughter across the long table, and Moonstone smiled, giving Maggi a nod. The little girl seemed satisfied, for she allowed the two soldiers to lead her and Rasta from the room, the door falling shut behind them with a resounding *clang*.

"Did you manage to intercept them?" Atlas asked immediately, his eyes fixed on Moonstone.

Vailhelm made a noise, presumably to protest Atlas' impertinence, but Moonstone held up a hand to silence him.

"We managed to intercept three of them, but...one of them got away."

Whitsom cursed, running a hand over his short curls and plopping down into a chair at the end of the table.

"When?" Atlas demanded.

"A little over two weeks ago. We have been interrogating the three we managed to capture every day, but have gotten very little out of them."

Atlas had to repress a snort. Somehow, he doubted that whatever "interrogation" methods the Vedas employed were terribly effective.

"General," Vailhelm began, leaning forward, "our agreement was clear. This boy was not to put another toe out of line, and he snuck off of base—could have exposed our location—"

"Atlas is the one that warned us of the Obarion soldiers' reconnaissance, Vailhelm," Moonstone interrupted impatiently. Murmurs broke out along the table, but she ignored them. "We owe him a great deal —"

"But one of them still got away—" Vailhelm protested.

"But he tried," Moonstone said firmly, "when he had no obligation to." Vailhelm looked as though he wanted to argue further, but she turned back to Atlas. "How long would you suspect we have?"

Atlas looked down at the table, drumming his fingers against the wood pensively. "Maybe a month? Possibly longer, but..."

Chaos erupted in the meeting room. "General, we've got to abandon the base—"

"We can't possibly counter an attack of this magnitude—"

"If they breach the Pass, they will take the North —"

"Unless—" Atlas said, speaking over the hubbub. "Unless you go to them first, instead of the other way around."

His words were met with silence, and the Council gaped at him.

"Go to *them*?" the blonde woman—Jaina, he thought—said. "It would be a suicide mission."

"He's trying to get us killed," Vailhelm agreed in his gruff voice.

"What reason do we have to trust him?" Augusto squeaked.

Atlas' eyes met Moonstone's. His face prickled with heat; he had no real desire to share with the room full of strangers that the only reason he was helping them—the only reason he cared at *all* was because of his mother. The Vedas, as a clan, meant very little to him. But they were the last force that stood between Talikoth and unimpeded control.

"I will never put our soldiers into harm's way unnecessarily," Moonstone said finally, breaking his gaze. "But I have reason to trust Atlas, and there could be no harm in having an insider's perspective." She nodded for him to continue.

"Uh—okay, so—" He gestured towards the chalkboard as he made his way to the front of the room. "Do you—do you mind if I—"

"Not at all," Moonstone allowed.

He wiped the board clean and began hastily sketching a map of the Westland.

"The Obarion headquarters are *here*," Atlas told them, and he saw a few faces flicker with surprise. He had never even thought about the fact that the location of the Headquarters was considered a secret. The base was massive, so it was not exactly easy to hide, and it wasn't as though anyone in their right mind would ever be caught trying to sneak *on* to the Obarion base.

"About thirty miles northwest of where we are now—here—there's a band of Renegades—a gang, really—who have been orchestrating attacks on—well, on both of the clans for almost six years."

"We have crossed paths with them, yes," Moonstone confirmed, nodding.

"Right, well they have allies all over the place—down south, too—and they've been coordinating interference with the Obarion supply chain—"

"As well as ours," Vailhelm grumbled.

"Just as the Vedas once did," Atlas pressed on firmly. "We met their leader. And he's agreed that they'll stop initiating attacks on the Vedas, as long as it proves to be mutually beneficial. They want to ally with us against the Obarion."

Us, he realized belatedly. He hadn't meant to say us, but there it was. The last shred of his denial that he was working against Talikoth ripped away like flimsy paper.

"How are a couple of gangs going to do us any good against an army of 3,000 men, boy?" Vailhelm said.

Across the room, Whitsom piped up, "Raider has been planting gangs since he was sixteen, and his father before him. They occupy Ramshackles all across the Westland—"

"Ramshackles?" Jaina asked, her brow furrowing in confusion.

"Former cities," Atlas explained. "Raider's gang has got to have at least sixty guys, but that's only *one* gang. He's planted fifteen that we know of—some of them larger than his own—"

"Almost a thousand soldiers," Moonstone noted.

She leaned back in her seat, gazing contemplatively at the chalkboard. "And they are good at what they do—we know this from experience…"

"But General," Vailhelm interjected, "these are *Renegades*—they aren't soldiers, they aren't warriors, they aren't anything but mercenaries that seek to cause chaos. And how can we even trust that they wouldn't turn against us, if the opportunity arose?"

Atlas met the bearded man's glower unflinchingly. "We can trust them because if the Obarion take the North, it isn't just the Vedas that lose everything."

Gaiomere, who had been mostly quiet, said, "That's why we stay in the North—it's why the only Renegades in the South are the ones with weapons or massive tribes—the Vedas, for the most part, let us live in peace. We left the South because there's nothing like peace down there."

Atlas turned back to the chalkboard, marking off several spots on the map.

"Raider's gangs in the South are strategically positioned at five points that loosely surround Obarion headquarters. They've been largely focused on cutting off their meat supply—Talikoth told us that he'd cut it from the budget to expand our military, because he didn't want to admit how much damage they were doing—but that only takes a few of them. Raider said if they concentrate their efforts, the destruction could be more effective. Burning crops, damaging raid vehicles— we could possibly even strike the Rigs."

He saw scattered nods on either side of the table. Gaiomere glanced up at him, a crease between her brows.

"Atlas—what about—" The eyes of the Council

turned on her, and her face flushed, but she continued determinedly, "What about the civilians? That food goes to them, too, doesn't it?"

Vailhelm made a frustrated noise. "That hardly matters—"

"No, she's right," Atlas interjected, frowning thoughtfully.

"What about the Hole?" Whitsom suggested, and they all stared at him blankly. "It's like the South's version of the Under—oh, sorry, that's like our secret underground where we trade food and goods and stuff, y'all aren't supposed to know about it—and it's right on the Fringe. We could open it up to civilians who need food—"

"Without Obarion soldiers following them?" Gaiomere pointed out. "Whit, that would be putting our people in danger—"

"There's a pass," Atlas remembered suddenly. "The cliffside. It's the only part of the entire base that isn't secured behind the wall."

Several pairs of eyes gawked at him. Atlas turned back to the chalkboard, depicting what he meant. "The perimeter of the Obarion headquarters is encased by a thirty-foot shockshield with an amperage of around two hundred."

"Holy hedgehogs," Gaiomere whispered, her eyes wide.

Atlas nodded. "Yeah, it'll kill you instantly. The shockshield spans the entire three-hundred acres *except* the cliffside. The wall meets either side of the cliff, which overlooks the ocean. The cliff is so treacherous and the waves so brutal they figured it was a defense in itself."

"So…why is this a viable option?" Vailhelm grunted.

"Because you can climb down it," Atlas said. "I've done it." It had been on a dare, and he had nearly died doing it, but it was still feasible. "We can enlist a soldier to sneak food onto base for the civilians. That'll be our path to strike the Rigs, too. The access bridge is located on the western border of Headquarters."

"If that's the only gap in the shockshield," Gaiomere said slowly, "then that's our only way in."

He smirked. "Exactly."

"Wait, wait, wait!" The sallow-faced man leaned forward, scowling. "This is all fine and dandy—we cut off their supplies, drain them out, sneak their civilians food—but from what you've told us we've got a thousand extra soldiers at our disposal, plus the thousand that our clan already has—there is no possible way that we can sneak two thousand soldiers up a treacherous cliff and through a *tiny gap* in an electrified wall without the Obarion noticing!"

Atlas smiled, absently fiddling with the chalk in his hands.

"We don't need to sneak two thousand soldiers up the cliff and onto the base. We just need one soldier—to climb the cliff, sneak into the control room, and disable the shockshield to let the rest of us in." His eyes found Whitsom, who wore a grin so devilish that Atlas was certain the older boy was reading his mind. "And I know just the fellow to do it."

CHAPTER SIXTEEN

T he Ramshackle gang arrived around ten in the morning. As Atlas suspected, they did no favors for themselves in earning the Vedas confidence. They climbed out of their cars with guns slung over their shoulders, sneering at the entrance guards, who suddenly looked rather small and feeble, compared to Raider, or Grit, who wore a necklace that looked to be made from bones.

Atlas and Whitsom waited on the front lawn with Moonstone to greet them.

"Asshat!" Raider called, grinning crookedly. "Did you get shorter?" Atlas rolled his eyes, his gaze roving over the rest of the gang as Raider greeted Whitsom. It looked, as far as he could tell, like Raider had kept his promise—fifty or sixty young men swarmed out around them on the grounds, peering curiously at the tall watchtowers, or glaring frostily at the guards.

Moonstone stepped forward, stretching out a hand. "Thank you for coming, Raider. Your assistance means a great deal to us. I am General Moonstone."

Atlas thought for a moment that Raider would not take her offered hand. His eyes flashed with a malice that Atlas had become very familiar with—but then he grasped her hand, shaking it quickly, and muttering, "Happy to help."

Atlas' brows flitted up in surprise. Perhaps Raider was actually taking his responsibility seriously—or maybe it was just the fact that Moonstone's no-nonsense energy told him that she was not someone to be trifled with.

Moonstone continued, "Our soldiers' quarters have been prepared to accommodate you and your tribe during your stay. Bowduck and Mit would be happy to show your soldiers to their quarters, if you would not mind joining me for a briefing." Bowduck and another guard that Atlas didn't recognize immediately stepped forward.

Raider glanced over his shoulder. "Alright, runts, listen up!" The chatter immediately died, and the group of young men looked at him attentively. Atlas glanced around with reluctant admiration. "Follow these two gents to your rooms and stay put till you hear otherwise. Anyone causes any trouble, you deal with me, got it?"

The horde scrambled to form a line behind Bowduck and Mit, and Moonstone led Atlas, Raider, and Whitsom not towards the meeting room, but rather around the building and down a long, sloping hill, towards the eastern perimeter of the Vedas' base, where Atlas had never ventured.

"I think we can all agree that we are taking a lot of chances with this plan, so it is essential that every person is pulling their weight," Moonstone said, glancing sideways at Raider as they walked. "My biggest concern is communication. Without the assistance of all of the tri—um...gangs...you have planted, our forces will not stand a chance. How are we going to get the message out to each of them?"

Raider arched an eyebrow. "We got twelve cars. We send a couple of boys to each Ramshackle to deliver the message—word will be out by tomorrow at the latest. Furthest Ramshackle is the Gamp—that's about a ten-hour drive."

They approached a massive metal structure, perhaps a hundred feet tall, and four times as wide. A gargantuan steel door spanned almost the entirety of its western face.

Gaiomere leaned against one of the tall metal walls, scrawling away in her notebook, but she looked up at the sound of their approach.

"Won't the Obarion see or hear you if you're roaring up and down the Westland?" Atlas asked Raider, frowning.

"Why don't you leave that to us, pretty boy, I think we can handle ourselves—"

"If they suspect that something is going on, they'll double their soldier count—"

"At which point, we'll already be out of there," the blond boy said, crossing his arms over his chest as he came to a halt next to the metal building.

Atlas shook his head, scowling. "Don't make the mistake of getting too arrogant—"

Gaiomere must have picked up on what they were talking about, for she hastily cut in, "I can install a deadener on each of the cars." She was looking between the two of them nervously, as though she were afraid they would start brawling again. "It won't stop the Obarion from seeing them if they cross their paths, but it will at least stop them from being heard."

"I would like you to get that done as soon as possible if you can, Gaiomere," Moonstone said. "The quicker we can get the message out, the better. As for the rest of the Renegades?"

"I'll have one of my cars drop by the Hole to see who we can wrangle up there," Raider supplied. "Whitsom, you should go with whatever car is going closest to the Under. They're familiar with you there. They'll listen to you over any bonehead I could send."

Moonstone nodded. "Now, about the aviation—"

"Aviation?" Raider interrupted, his eyes narrowing. "What, like planes?"

Whitsom's brow furrowed. "What's a plane?"

Gaiomere sprang forward, practically bouncing on the balls of her feet. "Can I show them?" she asked Moonstone imploringly. "Oh, *please* let me show them!"

Moonstone's mouth twitched into a smile. "Very well, you may—"

She had not even finished her sentence before Gaiomere bounded over to a small entryway on the side of the building and disappeared inside.

Seconds later, the colossal steel door began to retract upward, and then inward, sliding along several rows of heavy tracks grafted into the high ceiling, until it creaked to a stop.

Atlas' jaw inadvertently slackened.

The building was not a warehouse, as he had assumed, but a plane hangar. And inside, parked not fifty feet away from the gaping doorway, were four massive planes.

Gaiomere stood just inside the doorway, her face split into a broad smile and her arms spread out on either side of her. "Tada! They're giant metal birds!"

Whitsom was looking between she and the planes in bewilderment.

"I thought it was insane, too, but Atlas showed me pictures of them, and then Moonstone brought me down to the hangar to see them in person yesterday. They're incredible—apparently they used to carry tons of people, *tens* of thousands of feet above the ground—"

"Wait, wait, let me get this straight," Whitsom interrupted, pointing a finger towards the planes. "People used to go inside of those things, to fly *tens of thousands of feet* above the ground... on purpose?" He looked between Moonstone and Gaiomere as though waiting for one of them to burst out laughing. "Y'all playing a prank?"

"I thought they were all out of operation?" Raider said, ignoring Whitsom.

"These planes were downed on the base when we took it over," Moonstone told him. "According to what we know, this used to be a military base, but the other planes were all in use throughout the First War. These four were the only ones left behind, because they were outdated models."

"Okay, so let's say hypothetically we were able to make them operable again," Raider mused, frowning. "It wouldn't matter. We can't fly them without fuel, they'd be useless—"

"Unless..." Atlas piped up, turning to look at Gaiomere. "We could produce a fuel source." He held his breath, watching her face carefully.

Her brows knitted together, and her lips curved into a frown. "To transport soldiers?"

Atlas didn't answer, but she interpreted his silence.

"No, to drop bombs," she concluded, her frown deepening. "Atlas, there are—there are civilians on their base—children—"

"Our stealth strike is integral to the success of the

attack, Gaiomere," Moonstone said quietly.

Gaiomere shook her head. "I'm not going to participate in something like that—"

"What if we just bomb the artillery warehouse?" Atlas said suddenly.

She broke off, her teeth tugging at her lip. "That's just where their weapons are stored?"

Atlas nodded. "It's all the way across base from the civilians' quarters, and at the time of our strike the only people near it will be soldiers." He would not admit to any of them that the idea of dropping bombs on his own people made his stomach turn. Fighting against Talikoth was one thing, even the nameless, faceless soldiers that Atlas had never encountered—but he wasn't sure how he would feel if the barrel of his gun was aimed at Coral, or Maddex, and he certainly couldn't imagine turning their weapons on any of the civilians.

Raider's brows were furrowed with evident annoyance, and he opened his mouth, presumably to argue, but Gaiomere did not give him the chance.

"That—that could work," she said slowly, nodding. "I couldn't use ethanol—I'm not familiar enough with plane engines and we don't have time to test it, but..." She began to speak more quickly, in the excitable way she did when she got a new idea, as though her brain was moving so quickly that her mouth couldn't keep up. "If I can set up a controlled environment in the lab to magnify thermal energy and create a peak-heat environment...that could yield us a fuel source—I'd need cerium, and I'll need to monitor CO_2 levels..."

Moonstone's iron grey brows flitted up in surprise. "You are willing to share your solar conversion with us," she confirmed.

"As long as you swear the bombs only fall on the artillery warehouse," Gaiomere amended.

Before the older woman could reply, Raider broke in. "That's not how war is waged, Mere-Kat—"

"Well, waging war the 'normal' way is what got us into this mess, so perhaps it's time for something different," Atlas snapped.

Moonstone nodded slowly, her dark, shrewd eyes flitting between the four of them. Finally, she said, "I agree to your stipulations, Gaiomere. We will only strike the artillery warehouse. Atlas is quite right—it is time for a change."

Atlas' days quickly became a blur of lengthy tactics meetings, training sessions, and spending hours in the engineering lab, giving Jacoby as much direction as he could possibly provide about how to navigate Obarion headquarters without drawing any suspicion.

Moonstone had given Atlas' garb he had arrived in to a seamstress so that she could replicate the Obarion uniform, and Jacoby's had been fitted with a camera and a receiver so that Atlas could guide him across Headquarters.

The Ramshackle gangs had already begun their phase of the operations. They struck the Obarion paddy field, their plantation, and two of their three crop fields. Some of the gangs hunted the animals in the area and delivered them to the Hole. Another one destroyed a tank that had been on its way to defend the third crop field.

Atlas was in the engineering lab with Gaiomere and Jacoby when Raider found him one afternoon to recount a new batch of information.

"There weren't any Renegades on the Rigs," Raider announced, plopping down in the chair next to Atlas.

"What do you mean?" Atlas demanded, frowning. "Talikoth has captured hundreds of Renegades, the place should be swarming with them—"

"Well, it wasn't," Raider insisted. "Unless Talikoth has them in Obarion garb—"

Atlas shook his head. "No, he'd never risk it. It would be too easy for them to sneak off and escape, if they were dressed like us."

He looked sideways at Gaiomere, and she seemed to guess what he was thinking. "Maybe Talikoth has just moved them somewhere else, with all the attacks going on?" she suggested tentatively. She drummed her fingers pensively on the desktop. "Whatever you do, don't mention anything to Whitsom. It'll only worry him, and there's no sense in making him wonder until we know for sure what Talikoth has done with them..." She cast Atlas a worried glance. "Unless he's moved them somewhere on base. They could end up getting caught in the cross-fire, if Moonstone's dropping bombs every which way—"

"Moonstone *won't* be dropping bombs every which way," Atlas said firmly, giving her shoulder a comforting squeeze. "She won't go back on her word."

Over her head, Atlas caught Raider's eye, and he knew they were wondering the same thing.

Gaiomere could not take back her contribution now, even if Moonstone *did* renege on her word. Two of the planes had already undergone successful launches with the fuel she had developed. Atlas could only hope that Moonstone would keep her word—he didn't want to think about how Gaiomere would feel, if her planes were used to bomb civilians.

Despite the rapidity of their progress, an inescapable tension descended on the Vedas' base over the coming days. Many of the soldiers were young, younger than Raider, or even Whitsom, and had not seen the early days of the war—back before the Vedas retreated to the North, when open conflict with the Obarion was a fact of daily life. Many of them grew more anxious the closer they drew to the upcoming siege.

One day Atlas found Kendo vomiting in the men's bathroom. "Should I avoid the fish for lunch?" he asked jokingly.

Kendo grimaced as he swished a mouthful of water. "Something like that."

Atlas leaned against the sink, his brow furrowing as he gazed unseeingly at the chipped black and white tile of the bathroom floor.

"It's just like training," he said quietly.

"Except you can die," Kendo muttered.

"Except you can die," Atlas agreed.

"A lot of the guys think we're going to, you know," Kendo told him. His face was impassive, but the trepidation was evident in his eyes. "They think we're all going to be slaughtered."

"What do you think?" Atlas asked curiously

Kendo shrugged. "I think—I think sometimes crazy things happen. But...I don't know. I think it would take a miracle to defeat the Obarion, and I don't believe much in miracles."

Atlas mulled over that conversation the rest of the

day. He knew, of course, that if certain strategies didn't play out, they would lose. But if they went into the conflict already believing that they would...

These sentiments, it quickly became obvious, were not exclusive to Kendo. The tension on base had permeated their training sessions, for in the days following, many of the soldiers were noticeably dejected throughout their morning drills and their sparring matches. Kendo lost a fight with Liv, who was half his size and whose biceps were the breadth of Atlas' wrist, and even Whitsom was not his normally chipper self. The Ramshackle boys, who could always be counted on for heckling if nothing else, stood brooding in the corner of the training yard.

"Alright, let's have a huddle," Atlas called after fifteen minutes of unproductive rubbish. The boys amassed in a corner, plopping themselves down on the floor or clambering up on top of the lockers. Whitsom leaned against the fence, wiping his forehead with his shirt.

"What's the deal?" Atlas looked around at the group of them, arching a brow. "Seriously, you guys look like crap."

None of them seemed to be willing to meet his eyes, until one of the Ramshacklers piped up, "Maybe it's the instructor?" A few of his comrades sniggered, and he continued, "What would we expect though? Raider said he made you cry so loud your daddy heard you down south."

Adrenaline surged through Atlas' body, as though it had been waiting for a fight. He caught Whitsom's eye, and the older boy wordlessly tossed him a pair of sparring gloves.

He walked towards the Ramshackler who had spoken—the pallid-skinned boy who had been briefing Raider in the warehouse. Now that Atlas looked more closely, he was sure that the boy could not be older than fifteen. "What's your name?" Atlas asked him quietly.

The boy gazed up at him in an unbothered sort of way. "Zarr."

"Zarr," he repeated, nodding slowly. "Care to?" He tilted his head toward the sparring circle.

The black-haired boy arched a brow, glancing back at his companions, who were goading him on. "Only if you promise not to cry." The boys snickered again.

"I'll try to refrain," Atlas murmured, stepping into the sparring circle. Zarr followed him, pulling on his gloves and leering at Atlas.

The two of them danced around one another for a few moments. Zarr was only a few inches shorter than Atlas, and it quickly became clear that he used his stringiness to his advantage. He could slip easily around Atlas' jabs with very little exertion. But he was gangly, and didn't yet understand his center of gravity—rather like Bettoni when he had sprouted up a foot in the span of a few months.

Atlas saw his opportunity when Zarr came in with a wild overhand. He spun quickly, grasping the boy's arm and pulling him over his shoulder, "So *this*—" He slammed Zarr into the ground, and the boy let out a groan, "is what happens when you're off balance."

"*Ooh*," he heard Whitsom and Kendo call, snickering.

"Get up, man!" one of the Ramshackle boys shouted.

Zarr scrambled to his feet, his pale cheeks bright

pink, and came at Atlas again, throwing several jabs in quick succession. Atlas leaned out of his range, continuing, "And *this*—" Zarr's fourth punch came, and Atlas used his momentum against him, wrapping an arm around his shoulder and twisting his other arm behind his back. He tried to wrench his arm from Atlas' grasp, cringing when Atlas twisted it further, "is what happens when you become too predictable."

Atlas let go of the boy, shoving him forward, and he stumbled a few steps before he caught himself. He whirled back around towards Atlas and snarled, his face contorting as he came forward again. Atlas checked his first two kicks. The third came higher, so he hooked his arm around his foot and stepped between his legs, sweeping his standing foot from beneath him and slamming him to the ground.

Zarr's head collided with the hard concrete beneath them, and he let out a whimper.

Atlas stepped back, arching an eyebrow down at the boy. "Had enough?"

Zarr nodded, his eyes watering, and two of his comrades hustled over and helped him to his feet.

"That's right, Renegade, you don't mess with our Captain!" one of the soldiers called, and they broke into sniggers.

Atlas scowled at the group of them. "Don't look so high-and-mighty, you all would look like Zarr just did, if we were facing off with the Obarion today," he said coldly. The laughter silenced, and the Vedas soldiers looked adequately rebuked. "You're all acting like they've already won."

"Might as well have," one of the boys muttered. A few boys shifted uncomfortably, while others nodded their agreement.

Atlas frowned. "Nobody's going to get better training half-heartedly," he pointed out.

It was Zarr who retorted, "What's it matter? Doesn't matter how hard we train or how much better we get—we're facing an army that's never lost a battle. They tore through half the Fallen Land, and now they're gonna tear through us, too."

"You don't know that, man," Whitsom remarked, but even he did not sound terribly confident.

Atlas arched a brow, lifting a shoulder lazily and asking, "Look, you guys want to go?"

Several pairs of eyes blinked back at him, and both of his brows lifted this time.

"Seriously, there's still time. If you pack up now, take off, head east. You might have *years* before the Obarion Army heads back that way and picks you off. I'm serious, none of you have been forced to stay here. Anyone who wants to leave can go."

Nobody spoke, nor did anyone move. He stared at them, meeting each boy's eye, but still nobody uttered a word, until finally, a Ramshackle boy that Atlas did not know by name intoned, "Easy for you to talk about fighting. What's the worst that happens to you? General's son gets a slap on the wrist."

"Hey, that's too far—"

"No, Whit, it's alright," Atlas interrupted. He glanced at the boy who had spoken. "What's your name?"

"Clancy."

"Clancy," Atlas repeated, nodding. "Truth is, Clancy, much more than a slap on the wrist awaits me, if we lose. Talikoth has no tolerance for treason—not even from his own son. And leading a battalion into a battle where my soldiers could lose their lives, while I would lose nothing—there would be no greater dishonor."

He looked around at each of them once more.

"Talikoth spoke to me often of war—of the Renegades and the Vedas and the strength of the Obarion clan. There's something he said that I remember so vividly—because he said it so often. It's as though it haunted his nightmares, and his waking hours, too." Atlas shook his head, smirking a little.

"He would always stress to me how vulnerable the Renegades were—because they spread themselves out, traveled in small packs, rather than unifying as one clan. He told me that the Renegades were dangerous —because they couldn't be controlled. And once, just once...he told me that if the Renegades ever united with the Vedas—if the people of the Westland ever put aside their differences and merged, as one, consolidated tribe —he told me it could mean the end of the Obarion people."

Whitsom straightened up, his dark eyes narrowing. The furrow in Zarr's brow softened, and his expression turned quizzical.

"He really said that?" Clancy asked.

Atlas nodded. "It's every authoritarian's worst fear —if you can keep the people distracted, keep them fighting against one another over inconsequentials, then they're blinded to the true evil. The cooperation of the people is the death of absolute power."

Kendo still looked unconvinced. "You really think we can overthrow them? They killed off thousands of people, hundreds of tribes—"

"Little tribes, of no more than a hundred," Atlas

reminded him. "Tribes fighting for their own survival, their own individual lives. Don't you see this is bigger than that? I mean, what happens if we go out there and lose?"

No one answered.

"If we lose, we lay the foundation for the next generation—" He glanced at Whitsom. "For Maggi, and Rasta, and the Vedas and Renegades that survive to see what it looks like to stand up against tyranny—this isn't about us. This isn't about *our* lives, and whether we live or die. Don't get me wrong, I believe we can win. I believe it more than I've ever believed in anything, but if all we're protecting is our bones, and lungs, and organs, we might as well just let Talikoth take the North. Let him take the whole world, because that's not what this is about. We survive when the other tribes didn't because our lives are a testament to *hope*—hope that when it matters most, we can stand side by side—next to Vedas and Renegades—hell, next to an Obarion like me—and fight against what we know is wrong."

Clancy and Zarr grinned, and Whitsom's eyes glittered zealously. Many of the soldiers were nodding, and some of the oppressive tension that had appeared so impenetrable the last week seemed to dissipate. Kendo strode over and clapped him on the back, and one of the Ramshackle boys called, "Hell yeah!"

"Now can we actually get to training, instead of that half-assed garbage you guys were giving me earlier?" Atlas said wryly, and the boys sniggered, scrambling to their feet and making their way back to the sparring circles.

He realized, only belatedly, that Moonstone was standing near the corner of the sparring yard. When he looked up, her mouth was curled into a small smile.

"Nice speech," she said quietly when he approached her.

Atlas rubbed the back of his neck, his face prickling with embarrassment. "Well, they were never going to do any damage fighting like that," he muttered.

Moonstone was gazing at him in that penetrating way, her dark eyes narrowed. "Thank you, Atlas," she said after a moment. "You have instilled a sense of hope into our people that I feared we would never recover." The heat in Atlas' cheeks was steadily spreading to the rest of his face, and he had just opened his mouth to remind Moonstone that his motivations hadn't exactly been selfless, when she continued, "The Vedas are indebted to you."

His mouth snapped closed, an idea suddenly striking him. "General? If you are all indebted to me...I do have one request."

PART III:

THE OBARION

CHAPTER SEVENTEEN

"**E**ighteen, man, he's at eighteen!"

"Yo, but Kendo's at nineteen!"

Atlas leaned his elbows against the table, watching with amusement as the two boys across from him shoveled sausage link after sausage link into their mouths. Kendo was currently beating Whitsom by one —now two—but both of their faces looked rather green around the edges.

"You two are going to regret this later today when you have to walk thirty miles," Atlas pointed out, smirking. Unsurprisingly, nobody listened to him. Two of the Ramshackle boys—Neo and Jax—were cheering them on heartily, and the Vedas soldiers were exchanging bets.

Atlas could hardly keep his mind on all the commotion. The planes had gone out last night, around three in the morning, to strike the landmines and clear a direct path south, and some of Raider's gangs were already assembling on the Fringe, just a couple dozen miles from Obarion headquarters.

Atlas glanced at the clock that hung on the wall. "Alright, Whitsom, you had better be in the meeting room in five minutes!" he called over the hubbub. Whitsom grunted a sound that might have indicated consensus, but Atlas couldn't really tell, for his cheeks were puffed out like a chipmunk.

He took the steps two at a time down to the

basement and rounded the corner to make his way to the meeting room, but his feet stuttered to a halt.

Gaiomere stood outside of the meeting room with Moonstone, her cheeks darkened with color and her curls frizzing out around her head as if they had their own electric charge.

"—wasn't part of the plan!" she hissed at the older woman.

Atlas glanced around quickly, his eyes flickering between the supply closet and the engineering room, wondering which would be a better place to hide, and he was just contemplating making his way back up the steps and arriving to the meeting a few minutes late when Gaiomere turned and saw him, and her eyes flashed.

"Atlas!" she growled, her voice low and dangerous. Several passing soldiers glanced up, looking between the two of them nervously.

Throwing one more longing glance at the stairwell, he walked towards her, trying very hard to keep his expression impassive.

"Yes, Gaiomere?"

His blank face didn't seem to fool her for a second.

"This was your doing, wasn't it?" she snarled.

He rubbed the back of his neck, glancing at Moonstone, as though she might suddenly be inclined to help him, but she just arched a dark eyebrow—she even had the audacity to look amused.

"Uh—you'll have to be more specific," Atlas muttered. "I wouldn't want to accidentally take responsibility for the polar melts or the oil spills—"

"*Atlas.*"

"Sorry."

"I am going to prepare for the meeting," Moonstone told them, pulling open the heavy metal door. "I will see you two in there." Atlas gaped at Moonstone's retreating head. He had half a mind to call her back, just to have some kind of barrier between him and Gaiomere's anger.

"Yesterday," Gaiomere began, "which was the last time I had talked to Moonstone, it was agreed that I would drive down south with Koda and Jacoby and meet up with the rest of the Renegades at the Fringe. And yet today Moonstone informed me that there has been a sudden change in plans, and that—oh, how did she put it—*there's no longer room in the car.*"

Atlas blinked, mumbling, "Well, yeah, sometimes that happens I guess—"

"ATLAS!"

"Okay, fine, I convinced Moonstone to make you stay."

"You *what?*"

"Gaiomere, there's no need for you to go," he insisted, taking her by the elbow and pulling her out of the way, for Jaina and Augusto were attempting to squeeze by them into the meeting room, the both of them giving Atlas and Gaiomere strange looks. "You've already helped tremendously—"

"And I can help more going down south with you guys!" she insisted.

"Jacoby can crack anything they have in place in the control room," Atlas said reasonably. "And if not, the other engineers will be there to help—"

"Exactly!" Gaiomere burst out. "Why do they get to go and help but I don't?"

"Because it's too dangerous," Atlas said, anger

brimming up into his tone. "Anything could happen—"

"Anything could happen to any of us!" Gaiomere spluttered furiously, her eyes narrowing. "Same for you, or Whitsom, or Raider—"

"Yes, but we can fight. We can protect ourselves." He cracked a small smile, trying to ease the anger in her expression. "Maybe if you had taken me up on my offer to teach you to fight—"

Her glare intensified, and she spat, "Oh, be honest, Atlas, even if I had, you still wouldn't want me to go."

He stared down at her for several moments, running a hand through his hair.

"No, you're right, I wouldn't," he finally agreed.

She threw her hands up in the air. "This is so unfair. You don't even have a right to—"

"Whitsom agrees with me—"

"Whitsom's not in charge of me—"

"No, he's not, but he's the only one you've got left that cares about you as much as I do," Atlas snapped. She closed her mouth abruptly, her eyes welling with angry tears, and her hands curling into fists, as though she wanted to hit him.

"You two wanna take your lovers' spat somewhere else?" Vailhelm muttered as he pushed past them.

"Oh, shut up!" Atlas and Gaiomere said at the same time.

"*Hmph*," Vailhelm grunted. The door snapped shut behind him, and the two of them stood there, glaring at one another for several moments.

"Look," Atlas said quietly. "Maggi and Rasta will feel better, having you here. They'd be worried sick— you know they would—"

"I am *not* just going to sit here while you and

Whitsom are out there risking your lives!" she shouted. The tears in her eyes had finally welled over, tumbling down her cheeks and leaving bright, glistening tracks across her dark skin.

Atlas wanted very much to pull her against his chest, to tell her that everything would be fine and that she had nothing to fear. But war was not so simple.

"You don't have a choice," he said

"You made sure of that," she bit back scathingly, and he flinched at the ice in her tone.

"Gaiomere—" He reached for her hand, but she ripped it from his grasp and stormed down the corridor, disappearing into the stairwell.

Atlas could not focus the entirety of the meeting. He remembered thinking, when he'd yelled at her, back at the Under, that Gaiomere would never forgive him —but this time, this time he was certain. Especially if something happened to Whitsom...

He shook his head, clearing those thoughts.

As soon as the meeting was dismissed, he and Whitsom, with their heavy packs slung over their backs, made their way out towards the front lawn, where they convened with the rest of the soldiers. The training sessions had always been conducted in smaller groups, and the soldiers were always spread out across the base, so Atlas had never really gotten a grasp on just how many troops the Vedas had at their disposal. But seeing them all lined up impressed upon him the weight of what they were actually doing. Involuntarily, it crossed his mind how much more formidable Talikoth's army of three thousand must look.

Atlas glanced around the grounds in a way that he had thought was inconspicuous, but after a few minutes, Whitsom leaned over and muttered, "She's pretty distraught. I saw her on the way down to the meeting. I doubt she'll come out here. I don't think she can come say goodbye. Just—just in case it's—well, you know."

Atlas swallowed thickly, directing his gaze forward. "I was only trying to keep her safe."

"You did the right thing," Whitsom assured him. "Even if she doesn't see it. I'm glad you did it, anyway." He glanced sideways at Atlas, smirking wryly as he added, "You never asked for my blessing, by the way."

"Your blessing?"

Whitsom's smirk widened, just a fraction of an inch. "I've seen you two making googly eyes at each other."

Atlas' cheeks burned, and he hastily looked away from the older boy, who sniggered. He was saved the embarrassment of replying when Moonstone approached them, her hands folded behind her back.

"We are separating into pods now—Atlas, if you will?"

They had opted to stagger the group's departures. The Ramshacklers would cover their arrival and ensure that no Obarion soldiers wandered close enough to see the Vedas' exiting the Pass, but Moonstone still thought it safest for the Vedas to arrive in smaller, interspersed groups to be less conspicuous. Each captain had been assigned a pod of twenty soldiers, and they would each travel a couple of miles apart.

Whitsom and Kendo were in Atlas' pod, as well as a pair of twins with black hair and an abundance of freckles. A boy named Nachi, who did not look a day over fourteen, but who assured Atlas he would be eighteen in a week. Ten soldiers in their mid-twenties who had been in uniform since before Atlas had even started Academy—he was rather intimidated by them —and a few boys he had gotten glimpses of at training sessions but had never spoken to.

This journey would be the longest Atlas had ever undertaken—consciously, anyway, since he didn't remember being brought to the Vedas' base—and though he knew it would be many days of miles and miles of walking, he could not help but feel a sense of giddy anticipation, for he was going home. Not home to the Obarion headquarters—for that hardly felt like home anymore—but home, with its rugged mountains, and tall palm trees that arched overhead like great vaults. Home, with bristled cacti and the crumbling pier and the cliffs that jutted like blades into the ocean. The North was beautiful with its dense evergreen forests and snow-capped peaks, but nothing was quite so appealing as what was familiar.

He thought quite suddenly of Delurah, and a stab of guilt pierced his stomach. He wondered how she was faring, with him gone. Talikoth had never been particularly kind to her—had Talikoth dismissed her, without Atlas there to care for? Not that, by the time he was captured, he had needed much caring for, but she had still found her ways to look after him where she could.

They were passing through the final stretch of forest before they entered the Pass. According to what Whitsom told them, it would be their last consistent shade for a very long time. At least with the massive backpacks that the Vedas had provided, they could carry more water than when he was traveling with the

Ren. Still, the backpack felt rather like having Rasta draped across his shoulders again, and it made him sluggish.

He chatted with a couple of the older soldiers for a while. One of them, Olli, a stocky cedar-skinned boy with long dreadlocks, had grown up a Renegade his entire life, but when his family was killed when he was twelve, he decided to seek shelter with the Vedas, and they took him in. Another soldier, Cami, a tall girl with ash blonde hair, had a father who had been a Colonel before he'd passed—her mother had made her swear when she was little that she'd never be a soldier, but when he died in combat, she broke her promise.

Atlas had never seen any soldiers that were girls before—there had been his guard, back when the Vedas were keeping him in his cell, but he had just assumed that was because she was only a base guard. It was something that Talikoth hadn't allowed, and Atlas had never really questioned it.

"I suppose because we're smaller, and usually a little less fast and strong," Cami said with a shrug when he told her this. "Moonstone doesn't care as long as we can pass the fitness tests."

"Not many girls do though," said Yacielle. He was olive-skinned and strapping, with hair cut so short he looked bald.

"It's only fair," Cami conceded. "I trained for *years* to get strong enough, and I failed the test three times before I made the cut." She grinned roguishly. "But now it's worth it—I can beat all my brothers in arm wrestling."

On and on they walked, as the sun crept higher. Their late start meant that they were pushing through the hottest part of the day, and that they would most likely not stop until well after nightfall. As they trudged deeper into the Pass, Atlas could not help being wary. Shards of metal littered the ground in every direction, and, when they had first arrived at the mouth of the Pass, a faint layer of smoke still hung in the air, corroborating the success of the thermobaric bombs. But Atlas was still nervous. If the blast wave had missed just one landmine, if there were only one explosive that had not been detonated—it would be enough to take out an entire pod.

When they finally stopped for the night, Atlas' feet were stiff and blistered. The other soldiers gathered around the fire, laughing and talking, but Atlas just pulled off his boots and hastily shoveled down his sandwich. All he could focus on was curling into his sleeping bag and getting some sleep, and as soon as he was finished, that was precisely what he did.

The days blended together as they walked on and on. Atlas had never seen so much of the Westland, but he did not think he could fully appreciate it, what with the fact that his muscles ached and he was always just *slightly* hungry. Halfway through their journey, a couple of Ramshackle cars came through the Pass, distributing food and water to the traveling soldiers.

"What if the Obarion wipe all of the gangs out before we get there?" Kendo asked one afternoon, as he kicked aside a chunk of concrete.

The group was making their way through an abandoned Ramshackle. It was barely distinguishable from the Ramshackle he'd visited with Gaiomere in the North; the streets were covered in debris, great chunks of roadway missing here and there, and the buildings were crumbled and derelict. Atlas wondered if there had been a gang in this Ramshackle, or if it had been completely deserted after the First War.

"I doubt the Obarion soldiers give any of the Ramshackle boys so much as a nosebleed," Whitsom said. "This is their art—hit and run, stealth attacks, snipes and strikes so fast and sly they're hardly even seen. You can't kill what you can't catch."

Guerrilla warfare. Atlas had read the term in a special forces' text several years ago, but had thought little of it, for it was not the way that Talikoth fought. Storm in, show your muscle, and ensure the opponent knows who has the bigger guns. That was Talikoth's way.

"Do you think Moonstone will try to negotiate with him first?" Cami called from the middle of the pack. "The Obarion General, I mean."

Sitch, who had ebony skin and was perhaps only an inch or two taller than Gaiomere, snorted.

"Not if she's smart. I'll bet Talikoth doesn't play." He glanced back at Atlas. "Am I wrong, Tally Jr.?"

Atlas rolled his eyes. "No, you're right. Attempting to negotiate with Talikoth would be foolish."

He wasn't even sure what such negotiations would look like. If Talikoth would agree to stop attacking the Vedas, and to allow the Ren to roam free —but no, that would never suffice. Because the Vedas had access to resources that Talikoth wanted—though how long those resources would last, he wasn't sure— and the Renegades, Talikoth believed, were a liability. No, he would never agree to any level of freedom—for the Vedas, for the Ren, or even, to an extent, for his own people. Because that freedom came with the expense of his ability to control them—all of them.

Days turned into nights, and then nights back into days again. The exhaustion Atlas felt was ever-present, and there was an irrational part of him that feared they would never arrive in the South. That they would continue to roam this barren, ugly wasteland forever.

But on their sixteenth day of walking, early in the morning, about an hour after they had started off, Yacielle called from the front, "Masks on—we're approaching Lunglock."

Atlas hastily pulled his mask over his face. They came over a hill, and his eyes fell on a sprawling, desolate Ramshackle, nearly invisible in the thick smog. The trees and grass were dead, and the air was unnaturally still here, as though there was not so much as a breath of life in the land around them.

"Can't believe Raider had a gang here," Whitsom said, his voice muffled through his thick mask. "What'd they do, sleep in these things?"

"Why is it like this?" Cami asked. She had confessed to them a few days ago that she had never been more than fifty miles away from the Vedas' base her entire life.

"Legend has it that even before the First War, it was bad," Olli told her. "All of the air pollution settles here—not like the cities on the coast, where at least they've got the sea breeze to move the air around a little."

"There was a lot of oil drilling in this area too, so the air was full of all sorts of pollutants," Atlas supplied. "According to—"

"—what I've read," Whitsom and Kendo finished for him simultaneously. The two of them broke into sniggers, and Atlas grabbed a clod of dirt off the ground and chucked it at the back of Whitsom's head.

It took them four full hours to make it through Lunglock. When Yacielle signaled that it was safe, Atlas briskly ripped his mask from his face, sucking in lungfuls of fresh air. The inside of the mask was humid and heavy with moisture and carbon dioxide, and his shirt came away drenched when he pulled it up to wipe his face.

When they set up camp that evening, the anticipation Atlas had felt at the beginning of their venture started to resurface. The landscape was growing more familiar, and he even recognized various landmarks, like the tree that Coral had fallen out of when they were sent to assess damage after an earthquake. The fall had broken two bones in his arm. Even as Atlas had knelt beside him and checked the damage, Coral had been laughing and cracking jokes.

Would he have to face Coral in just a few days' time, gun to gun, acknowledging one another as enemies? His stomach turned at the thought.

All the soldiers are grown men, he reminded himself. *They know what they signed themselves up for.*

And yet, Atlas could not help but think that if Bettoni or Coral knew the truth, if they really knew the horrors that Talikoth had committed, they would not be so inclined to fight for him. They might even turn against him, under the right circumstances.

He thought about it often all throughout the next day. What would it take to convince his friends of the truth? For he knew that *he* certainly would not have had the courage to turn against Talikoth, if he had believed that he was alone. If Moonstone had not told him the truth, and he found out on his own, Atlas did not believe he would have had the courage to stand against Talikoth by himself. To call out an injustice, when it would most certainly guarantee death. And the worst kind of death—solitary, forlorn, without his soldiers by his side or his squad at his back. No, what had solidified his courage was the knowledge that the Vedas had *already* been standing against Talikoth—that he would have reinforcements there, even if his whole clan was against him.

Still, his stomach writhed uncomfortably at the thought of looking at Coral down the barrel of a gun. When he had fought against Bettoni, it was to preserve his own life, and Whitsom's, and Gaiomere's. He had only ever intended to protect them—but to strike against a friend...to attack was so different than to defend.

The eighteenth day of their trek had arrived, and Atlas recognized exactly where they were now. He'd patrolled these hills, rolling and rugged, interspersed with catclaws, ironwoods, and crooked mesquite trees that left scattered yellow pods of beans along their path.

One of Raider's gangs from a place he called Big Red, two hundred miles west of the Vedas' base—met them at the mouth of the Pass.

Their leader was a tall, gangly fellow with a mop of brown curls and a plethora of scars crisscrossing the skin of his face. He had a bow and a quiver of arrows slung across his back.

"I'm Niko," he said, grinning and offering a hand to shake.

"Atlas."

"We'll escort you guys—sorry, uh, and girls—the

last fifteen miles. My boys are spanned out in a ten-mile radius around us to ensure no Obarion soldiers see us crossing to the Fringe."

"Thanks very much."

Niko fell into step with him, glancing sideways at Atlas as they walked, and asking, "Is it uh—is it true that you're really Talikoth's son?"

Atlas felt his cheeks heating, and he kept his gaze trained ahead of him. "Uh, yeah. Guilty as charged, I'm afraid."

Niko swore under his breath, grinning roguishly. "That's kinda badass. What did he do, kick up your curfew? Give you too many chores for the week?"

Atlas raised his eyebrows, a sardonic smirk flitting across his mouth before he could help it. "He had my mother killed."

Niko stared at him for several moments, as though he were waiting for Atlas to say he'd been making a joke. When he didn't, Niko let out a low whistle, shaking his head and clapping Atlas on the back, saying, "Yep, that'll do it."

The last fifteen miles seemed to stretch on longer than the rest of the journey, though the Ramshacklers' company made it a little more bearable. They passed around food and extra water, and entertained the soldiers with stories of attacks they'd afflicted on the Obarion, and even a few pranks they had managed to pull off.

"The guy in the back didn't have a gun, *por lo demás* I wouldn't have risked it," one of the Ramshackle boys—Luca, a boy of fifteen or so—told them around fits of laughter. He had an accent that Atlas recognized from many families in his clan and seemed to switch back and forth between English and his native tongue. "But I was swinging along in the trees—*mira*, I hook the branches with these—" He spun a pair of hooks around his hands, tied to a couple lengths of long twine. "—and swing myself from tree to tree. This *tonto* wasn't paying attention, so I lowered myself over him, and I snatched the dude's hat, *como eso!*" The soldiers were laughing heartily at this point, and Luca was red in the face from trying to repress his own laughter. "Well, he suddenly notices, and he shouts, '*Oye*, where's my hat! And I dropped it back on his head just as the other dudes were turning around, and they're like '*Hombre*, you're off your rocker.'"

Atlas snorted, shaking his head. He valued his own training immensely, but the way that the Ramshackle boys navigated combat was an entirely different beast. He had been doubtful, at first, but it was quickly becoming clear why the Obarion army had such a difficult time catching the boys, let alone putting a stop to their antics.

"We're close. Maybe a half hour or so," Niko called out to them, once they had been traveling together almost five hours. The sun dipped low in the sky, and Atlas surmised they would probably reach camp right around sundown.

Atlas could hear the noise of the Vedas-Renegade base camp as they approached. He wondered, at first, why they weren't quieter, but he quickly realized that there were gunmen everywhere. They lined the perimeter of the camp, their eyes flitting over the arriving soldiers, across the foliage, between the trees, detailing each shift of dirt, each rustling leaf on every side of them.

Atlas spotted a few snipers dotting the tops of old abandoned buildings, the long barrels of their guns poised carefully as they waited for any sign of approaching Obarion soldiers.

"Asshat!" came a familiar voice, and Atlas turned to see Raider swaggering towards him, a bottle of what looked like beer clutched in his hand. "And here I was hoping a stray landmine would have taken you out."

"Well, there's still hope," Atlas said.

Raider grinned, jostling Whitsom around the shoulders when he joined the two of them.

"Moonstone just arrived about an hour ago," Raider told them. "Stayed on to ensure all the kids and everyone were secure up north." Atlas nodded, glancing around the camp.

The site was swarming with Vedas, Ramshacklers, and Renegades alike. Some sat near the fire, sharing food, while others bent over tables, with long maps spread out atop them. A gaggle of Renegade boys that looked a little younger than Atlas tossed a strangely shaped ball encased in leathery-looking material.

Atlas and Whitsom were depositing their packs near a couple of empty tents when Moonstone strode over to them. A tall man with rugged copper skin followed close behind her. "Atlas, Whitsom, this is—"

"*Harcliff!*" Whitsom exclaimed, and the older man's rough face broke into a broad grin. Whitsom strode forward and grasped Harcliff's hand in both of his. "It's so good to see you!"

"You're a man now," Harcliff said. His voice was deep and tranquilizing. "You must have only been fourteen the last time we met. How are your parents?"

"They've actually both passed. Our pops was killed

just a few moons after we saw you, and Ma, a couple of years ago."

Harcliff bowed his head, his face solemn. "I'm sorry to hear that."

Whitsom slapped a hand against the back of Atlas' head. "This is my boy, Atlas. He's our little Obarion mole. He helped Gai and I find Maggi and Rasta—you remember them, right?"

Harcliff nodded, but he was looking at Atlas. His gaze was penetrating.

"You look just like your father," Harcliff said finally.

Atlas met Harcliff's gaze, despite his unease.

"So I'm told," he said quietly. "Though I suppose we can't help what we're born into."

The older man's lips quirked upwards, ever so slightly.

"No," he agreed. "We can't."

"According to Raider's surveillance, the Obarion have been thronging the south border of the Fringe," Moonstone said. "We have had to double our efforts to keep them from penetrating our camp—"

"They must know something isn't right," Atlas said, nodding. "We only need the distraction for a few hours longer. Has Jacoby arrived?"

"He will be here any minute," she told him.

"I'll want to speak with him when he gets here. Security will likely be higher, what with all of the attacks on the crop fields and the hunting range. He'll need to be careful navigating the base."

"Has the Hole been evacuated?" Whitsom asked.

It was Harcliff that responded. "Completely. My tribe has put together makeshift shelters for any who were residing there long term—their doctors have also agreed to set up a temporary field hospital—for any injuries that may transpire during tomorrow's escapades."

Atlas nodded, saying, "That's very kind of them." He glanced at Moonstone. "Any sightings of Bettoni—"

"The Renegades confirmed they saw the Obarion boy pass through one of their eastern stations about eighteen hours ago. They let him pass through unharmed," she added when she saw the look on Atlas' face.

"Talikoth could be sending soldiers any moment now—they could already be there, as a matter of fact—" Atlas began nervously, but the General interrupted him.

"Raider just left with a squad—they are keeping watch."

He nodded, only marginally appeased.

Moonstone and Harcliff were summoned away by a couple of Majors that had just arrived, and Whitsom leaned over and asked, "Wait, what's going on?"

Atlas glanced around, and then said lowly, "The night before we left, I went into Bettoni's room and told him that the Vedas were going to head down south, and that they were meeting at the Hole. I told him I was going to help him escape the Vedas' base, and to head back down to Talikoth as quickly as he could to relay the message."

Whitsom's eyes were wide. "So *that's* why we evacuated the Hole. Damn, so he thought this whole time you were just tricking us all into trusting you. And when he reports all that to Talikoth—"

"Talikoth will think I'm leading the Vedas down here on a suicide mission," Atlas finished, smiling grimly. He glanced back at Moonstone, and added, "The problem is—Talikoth is suspicious of *everyone*. I don't know that he'll actually believe Bettoni."

"What, you think he won't take the bait?"

"Oh, I think he'll send a battalion or two, for sure," Atlas said. "But we're still going to have our work cut out for us at Headquarters, make no mistake. We're just taking a few soldiers out of the equation. Raider and his gang will be waiting at the Hole—when the Obarion soldiers head down—"

"They're going to trap them in," Whitsom nodded eagerly, grinning. "You come up with that yourself?"

Atlas shrugged, and Whitsom chortled, punching him on the shoulder. "You're pretty smart. For an Obarion, anyway." Atlas laughed, shaking his head, and Whitsom wandered off into the throng of soldiers, presumably to get food.

A car tore into the clearing, sending a cloud of dust and dirt into the air. Several of the Ramshackle boys chucked rocks at the side of the car, and one of them shouted, "Koda, you asshole!"

The bearded young man sniggered as he clambered out of the car. Jacoby climbed out of the passenger side, straightening his glasses and lugging a massive backpack behind him.

Atlas started towards him, as Grit was climbing out of the backseat.

"Hey, Atlas," Jacoby said, beaming. "Safe travels?"

"Not too bad," Atlas said easily. He opened his mouth to ask Jacoby if he wanted to go over the layout once more, but he was distracted when he noticed Koda moving around to the trunk.

"Hang on, Grit," Koda was saying. "Let me just free

our little stowaway."

He pulled open the trunk, reaching into it and grasping something—or, as Atlas quickly realized, *someone*—around the middle and pulling them out of the trunk. He set the figure on their feet, and even with her wild curls flattened and her skin glistening with sweat—presumably from lying in a trunk for eight hours—Atlas recognized her immediately.

"Thanks, Koda!" Gaiomere said cheerfully, beaming up at the bearded young man.

"Anything for you, little one," he quipped, patting her on the head. "Alright, Grit. Let's get you dinner." The two of them trudged away. Gaiomere's eyes immediately fell on Atlas and grew so wide that it may have been amusing, if he didn't have the inclination to throttle her.

"Oh," she whispered.

Atlas took a deep breath, trying very hard to steady the sudden throb of anger he felt surging through him like a tidal wave.

"Jacoby," he muttered in a measured voice. "I'll speak to you later."

The red-haired boy seemed to be oblivious to anything passing between Gaiomere and Atlas in that moment.

"Oh, yeah, for sure!" he said agreeably. "I'm going to go get some grub."

Atlas started towards Gaiomere, who let out a squeak and darted into a throng of soldiers. But her wild hair stuck up a few inches from her head, tall enough that he could keep track of her, even as she wound her way between bodies, practically jogging.

She danced around a couple of soldiers toting

machine guns and might have managed to disappear into the crowd of Renegades if she didn't run headlong into Whitsom.

Her brother whirled around, the easy grin sliding off of his face as soon as he saw who had bumped into him.

"What the *hell* are you doing here?"

Atlas caught up seconds later. "She snuck out in Koda's trunk," he growled, before Gaiomere could get in a word.

"Gaiomere, how could you?" Whitsom said harshly, glaring down at her. He looked angrier than Atlas had ever seen him, and it made his own anger feel justified somehow, almost vindicated. "That was stupid, and reckless, and just—you just—"

"You directly disobeyed the General's orders," Atlas pointed out, and Whitsom wagged a finger in his direction.

"Yeah, that's right—"

"You interfered with our plans for the operation—which was negligent—"

"Completely negligent!" Whitsom agreed, cursing as he ran a hand over his short hair. "I mean, what were you thinking?"

"I was thinking I could help!" she finally managed to get out. She crossed her arms over her chest, looking between the two of them with narrowed eyes.

"You left Maggi and Rasta on their own!" Atlas shouted, pacing in front of her.

She rolled her eyes. "They're fine. They're totally safe—that's what's important."

"Yeah, and what about you?" Atlas hurled at her. "Gaiomere, you weren't thinking—"

"I'm not staying in the North while the last family I have left gets killed!" she yelled. She buried her face in her hands, but Atlas could tell that she was crying, the way her shoulders trembled.

He and Whitsom shared a look. Atlas felt squirming guilt in the pit of his stomach.

"Hey," Whitsom said softly. "Come here, Gai." She shook her head, and he clicked his tongue impatiently, tugging on her elbows until he had pulled her into his chest. "Gai, I'm not gonna die," Whitsom told her, stroking her curls. "Nothing's gonna happen to us, we'll be just fine—"

"You can't promise that," she mumbled into his chest, her voice muffled against his shirt.

"No, I can't promise," he agreed patiently. "But I can do my best not to get killed. And besides, Atlas has got my back."

Gaiomere pulled back, her eyes red, and gave her brother a watery smile. Atlas noticed Moonstone moving towards them, and Gaiomere must have too, for she clutched onto Whitsom's shirt, looking up at him pleadingly. "Whit, please don't let her send me back. *Please.*"

Whitsom looked away from her, glancing at Atlas, but before he could say anything, Moonstone joined them.

"Gaiomere," she said impassively. "I am...surprised to see you here."

"I had one request, Moonstone," Atlas snapped, shooting the older woman a glare.

"It's not her fault, Attie," Whitsom reasoned. Atlas rolled his eyes. He felt bad snapping at Gaiomere when she was tearful, but he wanted *someone* to be angry at.

"A couple of the Renegades can take her back now —surely we can spare a few of them—" he started, but Gaiomere interrupted him.

"Atlas, no, I won't!" she said firmly. "I'll sit down right here and I won't move an inch. They'll have to drag me back to the North—"

"Yes, because that'll be so difficult—you're a hundred pounds soaking wet," Atlas snapped. "You're acting like a child—"

"And you're acting like you can control everything and everyone!" she retorted. "But I guess you got that from daddy—"

Atlas jerked back, as though she had slapped him.

"Gaiomere!" Whitsom scolded, shooting his sister a disapproving frown.

But she had already strode away from them, crossing the clearing and plopping down onto a log beside Jacoby, tossing one more glare in Atlas' direction before she pulled a plate of food towards her.

"She can stay in the field hospital during the battle," Moonstone said quietly. Atlas had forgotten, momentarily, that she was there. "She will be safe there."

Whitsom nodded slowly, as though he were actually considering it, and Atlas let out a frustrated noise.

"Moonstone's right, she'll be okay here, Attie." Whitsom reasoned. "I'm sure we were planning on leaving a few soldiers here to guard the field hospital anyway." Moonstone nodded affirmatively, and Whitsom continued, "We'll make sure she doesn't go anywhere near—"

But Atlas wasn't listening anymore. He stormed

away, across the clearing and past the soldiers chattering affably. He climbed over a low stone wall and made his way down the hill that sloped into the ocean.

He let out a heavy breath as he plopped down into the sand, grasping a rock unthinkingly and hurling it as hard as he could into the water.

But I guess you got that from daddy.

His ears rang, loud and resounding, and his heart pounded against his ribcage so fast that it hurt.

Atlas let out a harsh breath, leaning back against his arms and watching the waves gather and break.

The last hint of sun hovered on the crest of the horizon, and the light reflected against the water, orange and luminescent. As he sat there, the anger in his system slowly ebbed away until there was little left in his mind but a muted buzz.

Behind him, the talk and laughter around the fire died down as the soldiers all began to drift off into their tents. But Atlas did not feel tired, and he stayed where he was, silent as the sun disappeared and the moon took its place.

"Hey, Atlas."

He did not turn around, but his jaw tightened unconsciously. Gaiomere sank down in the sand beside him, the light of the moon casting her features into an ethereal glow.

"I brought some food. I figured you'd be hungry."

He was, in fact, quite hungry, but he didn't want to let her know that.

"No, thanks."

"Atlas, I'm so sorry," she said softly. "I didn't mean what I said—"

"Evidently, you did," he said coolly. "Otherwise

you wouldn't have said it—"

She rolled her eyes. "Oh yeah, cause you've never said anything cruel to me when you're upset—"

"Oh, so we're keeping score, are we?"

"Atlas—" She broke off, letting out a heavy exhale. "No, you're right, I'm—I'm sorry. But Atlas, I really— I didn't mean it. I was just trying to hurt you because I was just—I was just so angry—and I know that's no excuse."

He shook his head, glowering at her. "Can't you understand that I'm just trying to keep you safe?"

"I know that," she said quietly. "I know you are, I just—I can't be five hundred miles away from you and Whitsom while you're both fighting for your lives. You have to understand that."

His eyes raked over her face, and after a moment, he gave a reluctant huff of concession

Gaiomere smiled, and then nudged the plate towards him.

"Will you stop pretending you're not hungry and eat now?" He snorted and took the plate from her.

She sat in silence beside him while he ate for several moments, before she tentatively mumbled, "I uh —I made you something, by the way." Her fingers ran absentmindedly through the sand shifting beneath her knees. "I was working on it over the last few weeks, while I was waiting to leave with Koda and Jacoby."

She lifted something—she must have set it in the sand beside her without him noticing—and held it out.

"I melted the metal down, and Grit showed me how to weld it together." He set his plate down, and she passed him a strange metal vest, the fibers welded together so close that the gaps between them were less than a quarter inch—when he lifted it, he found that the metal was fluid, and melded to the shape of his hands.

"Because of its composition, it can absorb energy better than practical any metal on earth. It *should* —hypothetically, of course—be fireproof, as well as bulletproof." His jaw slackened, his eyes widening as his gaze met hers, and she quickly interjected, "This is the first I've made, though, so don't go jumping in front of any bullets or anything."

"Gaiomere, this is—you really—well, thank you. Really."

She smiled in a pleased sort of way. "I made one for Whitsom, too. But I just—I didn't have time to make more—otherwise I would have made them for all of the soldiers."

"I know you would have," Atlas said.

She was gazing up at him with an imperceptible expression, but after a moment, she said quietly, "You should get some sleep. Early morning and all."

Atlas rubbed the back of his neck nervously. "I— yeah, probably right."

He started to get to his feet, but stopped, glancing back over at her. She was gazing out over the tumultuous waves.

"Gaiomere?"

She looked up at him, her brows knitting together.

"Can I—can I kiss you?" His cheeks lit aflame the moment the words left his mouth, but once they were gone, he could not take them back. He cursed internally, wondering if maybe it would be too late for him to take off east and go into hiding—he doubted anyone besides Whitsom or Moonstone would notice he had gone—

But she interrupted his panicking by leaning

forward and pressing her lips against his. When she pulled away again, Atlas grinned rather stupidly, and she gave a breathless laugh. Before he could stop himself, he kissed her again. Her hand had just come to his cheek when—

"Bleh! You know, I could have gone my whole life not seeing that and been just fine."

They broke apart, and Atlas called Raider a rather rude name under his breath, though the older boy must have heard, for he chuckled.

"Right back at you, Asshat. I was just coming to tell you that the Hole has been secured, but if you've got more important things to do than the rebellion we're executing—"

"How did you secure it?" Gaiomere asked, pushing herself to her feet.

"Put a couple of cars on top of the hideyhole," Raider said, smirking devilishly. "Even Grit couldn't lift that sucker."

Gaiomere nodded, glancing sideways at Atlas.

"I'm going to get some sleep. You guys—stay safe tomorrow." She leaned over to kiss Atlas once more, and then made her way across the beach and up the slope to the campsite.

"Oh, c'mon, I don't get a kiss too, Mere-kat?" Raider called. She sent him the finger over her shoulder, and he sniggered.

Atlas stood there for a few moments longer, staring out towards the sea, and heard Raider step up beside him.

"I meant to tell you," Atlas began, clearing his throat. "Thank you—for everything you and your gangs have done, I mean."

"Not for you, pretty boy."

"I can still say thank you," Atlas said firmly, turning to look at him. "You can pretend all day long like you don't give a shit, but I know better."

Raider arched a condescending brow, but Atlas did not miss the way he shifted his weight uncomfortably from one foot to the other. "I can still kick your ass, you know," he muttered.

"I know," Atlas said shortly, looking away from the blond boy and back towards the sea. "I guess I just don't mind losing a fight if the opponent's worthy."

Raider stared at him, his face impassive. After a few moments, he held out a hand.

"Don't die tomorrow," Raider said quietly. Atlas took his hand and shook it, just as the blond added, "It'd be a shame if I couldn't kill you myself." Atlas snorted, rolling his eyes. The taller boy turned and strode back towards the camp, calling, "See you bright and early...Atlas."

Atlas grinned, feeling another surge of respect for the gang leader, stronger than ever before. A surge that was promptly squashed when Raider added, "That's a stupid name, by the way."

He shook his head, smiling as he followed Raider up the slope and made his way across the clearing towards he and Whitsom's tent to get whatever sleep he could manage with the adrenaline already coursing through him like ichor in his bloodstream.

CHAPTER EIGHTEEN

A tlas awoke at three in the morning with his heartbeat already racing. He and Whitsom dressed in silence, neither of them willing to break the still hush that had descended upon the camp. It was strange, when he had officially been a soldier for over two years now, that the hush felt foreign to him. It was the weighty acknowledgement, between each of them, that this might be the last sunrise some of them saw. An acknowledgement that by the end of the day, one way or another, their world would look vastly different.

He realized, as he pulled his rifle over his shoulder and followed Whitsom out into the clearing, that the hush was not familiar to him because he had never left Headquarters, with his boots strapped up and gun loaded, *truly* fearing that he was going to die. He had never worried that any foe would ever be strong enough or clever enough to overpower or outwit the Obarion forces.

The group of them moved silently through the run-down streets. The palm trees drooped wearily overhead, the wind rustling their massive fronds. The tall buildings on either side obstructed them from view to the north and south, and ahead of them, the Ramshackle boys crept quietly, moving through alleyways and along rooftops.

The moon was still high and bright in the sky, but the shadows shifted in such a way that had Atlas' fingers jumping frequently to the trigger of his rifle.

They had been walking over an hour before the terrain gradually grew steeper, and the concrete was replaced with dirt the color of sandstone, and barbed foliage. When Atlas glanced back, he could see the jagged angle of the Fringe against the broad stretch of ocean, blending into the dark skyline.

They reached their post, just a mile away from the perimeter of Headquarters. Atlas spotted two of the engineers crouched over a small screen towards the front of the group, so he made his way over to them. The screen sat atop a stump, which they had propped a couple of fold up chairs in front of.

"How's he doing?" Atlas asked them.

"He's almost up," one of them—Elian, Atlas thought—told him. "He's had a bit of a rough time—"

"It's a brutal climb," Atlas said, his eyes zeroing in on the screen. The tiny camera had been mounted just below Jacoby's collar, so all Atlas could see at the moment was a slab of serrated rock, and all he could hear was Jacoby's laborious grunts and heavy breathing.

"How does this work?" Atlas asked them.

"It's similar to the transmitter," the other engineer, Xenarius, explained. "In the same way the frequency sends a signal from one device to the other, Jacoby's camera and our reader communicate with one another. The difference is, the camera has a tiny little chip in it—identical to the chip in our reader. It's cloning technology—the two chips are inscribed with the same coding, same accessories, *everything*. In essence, they're confused into thinking they have the same identity, even though they're more...twins, than anything. So whatever one sees—"

"The other sees." Atlas nodded. "Brilliant. Who came up with that?"

"Jacoby worked on it for weeks," Xenarius said. "But that little Ren girl helped him tons."

"Oh, almost there!" Elian exclaimed in an excited whisper. The three of them leaned towards the screen and watched as Jacoby pulled himself over the top of the cliff. The angle of the camera allowed for a view of the woods, stretching around him in every direction, a sea of catclaws, acacias, and oak trees.

"Alright, you're up, Obarion," Xenarius said, handing him the receiver and moving from his seat in front of the reader. Atlas sat down, watching as Jacoby clambered to his feet, taking a moment to catch his breath.

"How are you doing, Cobes?" Atlas muttered.

"*Not too...bad...all things...considered,*" the ginger said breathlessly. "*Pretty cool view—*"

Atlas rolled his eyes. "You can get the scenic tour another time. Do you see that tall, crooked tree in front of you? Head that way. Keep heading east."

Jacoby moved through the forest quickly, his breath coming in short pants as he walked. "You'll reach the edge of the woods in about a quarter mile," Atlas told him quietly.

Behind him, he heard one of the Majors announce, "Planes are preparing for liftoff, soldiers. Get your bearings."

Atlas' stomach clenched with anticipation. The soldiers around him shifted anxiously, none of them speaking.

"*Just reached the edge, Atlas,*" Jacoby said in a low

voice. Atlas glanced at the screen, and there it was, not four hundred yards away—the massive, boxy buildings, separated by long, narrow hallways. The structures were so familiar, and yet, it felt like something from a different life.

"Wait for my cue, Jacoby," Atlas murmured, and even as he spoke, he heard a colossal rush of wind above them, and then another. His gaze shot towards the sky, and saw the planes hurtle over their heads, low—lower than he had expected.

"They're too far down!" one of the soldiers behind him cried.

"Precision," Atlas muttered, his eyes darting back to the screen as the other two planes came speeding over them.

And indeed, he had been correct—the first plane came whizzing into the frame, no more than a hundred feet above the artillery warehouse—but the pilot's timing was flawless. There was a beat of silence, and then—

BOOM!

A cloud of smoke and fire enveloped the artillery warehouse. Only a moment passed before the second bomb dropped, and then the third. Yes, every margin of the warehouse was aflame, smoke filling the air so thick that for a moment it obscured Atlas' view. But where was the fourth...

There was another eruption of smoke and fire, and Atlas' eyes narrowed as he peered through the smoldering wreckage on the camera screen.

The central pass was engulfed in flame. Moonstone had not only ordered the artillery warehouse to be destroyed, but she had directed the fourth pilot to drop a bomb on the main channel between the soldiers' quarters and the communication hub.

Which meant...

She had just made Jacoby's job appreciably easier. The communication hub and soldiers' quarters were directly connected by the channel—with the passage demolished, they would have to exit their quarters and go all the way around. It wouldn't stop them completely, of course, but it would buy Jacoby time.

The soldiers behind him broke out in cheers. They did not have a front-row seat, as Atlas had, but the explosions had echoed across the mountainside, and even in the dim early-morning light, the smoke spiraled above the treetops.

On the screen figures sprinted towards the artillery warehouse. "Jacoby, *now*," Atlas commanded urgently. The bespectacled boy stumbled forward, walking swiftly across the grounds. "And *blend*. They're panicking, so you act like you're panicking too."

It was not, unsurprisingly, difficult for Jacoby to pretend to be panicking. As he drew level with the buildings, a group of Obarion soldiers came running out of the Main, which housed the dining hall and the rec room.

"*What happened?*" one of the soldiers asked him, his gravelly voice carrying through the receiver.

"*I—I don't know!*" Jacoby stuttered out timidly. "*Everything was quiet, and all of a sudden—the planes —they just—*" He shuddered, and the soldier rolled his eyes, shoving past him.

"*Get your wits about you, newb,*" the soldier snapped, and he and the other troops sprinted towards the warehouse.

"Directly forward. The code is 2745," Atlas told him. Jacoby darted towards the communication hub, clumsily punching in the code. He sounded like he might have been hyperventilating. "Jacoby, listen to me. You know what you need to do, okay? Focus."

Atlas heard him take several deep breaths. *"Okay. Straight forward and left down the fourth hall, right?"*

"You got it, man," Atlas confirmed.

Jacoby moved silently along the dark halls. He only passed a couple of soldiers, but all were rushing in the opposite direction, pulling on their gear as they went, shouting frantically to one another. Atlas realized with a jolt that he would be in their exact position, if he was still with the Obarion. It would be he who shouted directives at his squad, gathering whatever weapons they could get their hands on and commanding his soldiers to spread so that they could determine the damage.

"Sixth door?" came Jacoby's nervous voice through the crackle of static.

"Sixth door," Atlas verified.

All too quickly, Jacoby had arrived at the control room. He gazed through the window in the metal door, and Atlas could see four soldiers perched in front of several massive monitors. They spoke loudly to one another and gestured wildly to the screens, arguing over something that Atlas couldn't make out.

"There's four of them, Atlas!"

"I can see that, Jacoby," he muttered, pushing to his feet and pacing reflectively in front of the screen. Xenarius and Elian were watching him silently.

"Doesn't he have a gun? Can't he just bust in there

and blow a hole in their heads?" Elian asked.

"Yes, he does have a gun, but he can't just *bust* in there—" Atlas took a deep breath, leaning against the stump the screen rested upon. "Okay, listen to me, Jacoby. I need you to go in there, and say exactly what I tell you, understood?"

"*Considering the alternative is imminent death,*" Jacoby said jokingly, though his voice was rather weak, "*I'd say I'm inclined to listen to you.*"

Atlas nodded, his fingertips gripping the edges of the stump so tightly that his knuckles turned white. "Alright. Punch the code."

As soon as Jacoby pulled open the door, the four seated in front of the screens turned to face him. Atlas recognized Jamiah, who had been a year ahead of him in Academy, as well as Reed, who was one of Macky's good friends, but the other two soldiers were unfamiliar.

"*What are you doing in here, private?*" one of the unfamiliar soldiers said gruffly.

Atlas whispered so quickly that he feared Jacoby wouldn't be able to hear him, but the boy threw his arms up and repeated Atlas' words, exclaiming, "*What do you mean what am I doing here? Do you not realize the base is being attacked? Isn't that your* job?"

"*We're monitoring the borders*—that's *our job, private,*" Reed sneered. "*The four planes released bombs on our artillery—*"

"*And they landed their planes near the south border and are unloading soldiers onto our grounds as we speak!*" Jacoby's voice took on a hysterical note that had not been present when Atlas spoke, but he was not going to complain. The soldiers looked alarmed, and sprang to their feet.

"*Sound an alarm, if they haven't already,*" one of the older soldiers commanded Reed and Jamiah. The two boys moved past Jacoby wordlessly. "*Takan, you stay to ensure that the other borders remain secured— we don't want them inviting in any friends.*" He gave Jacoby a patronizing look. "*You'd best run along and join the other privates, soldier.*" He walked briskly past and disappeared down the hall.

"You can handle this guy, right Jacoby?" Atlas asked.

The remaining soldier, Takan, had sunk back into his chair. His gaze was laser-focused on the screens. Jacoby shuffled the rifle around his body, and slammed the butt of the gun into the soldier's head. Takan let out a low groan and slid to the floor.

Atlas grinned. "Nice blow."

"*Sorry, I just couldn't shoot him,*" Jacoby said, striding across the room to lock the door. "*How long do you think I have?*"

"Minutes, maybe. I'm sure that old pompous poodle will be back to check on things."

Jacoby rolled up his sleeves, plopping himself down on the chair in front of the screens.

"*Perfect. That's all I need.*"

Atlas set down the reader.

"Let's move!" he called. He heard the directive echo across the horde of soldiers, and pulled the rifle onto his back once more. "Do you mind if I take these?" he asked Elian, holding up the receiver and reader. "I just want to make sure he gets out okay."

Elian nodded. "Good luck, Obarion."

Atlas fell into step with the soldiers, his eyes occasionally flickering back to the reader. There had been no sound on Jacoby's end, but at any point, another soldier could burst into the room, could shoot him dead —and if he failed, everything, all of their efforts, the bombs, trapping the soldiers in the Hole—all of it would be for nothing.

They drew nearer to the perimeter and shouts echoed across the night. As they emerged from the trees, the smoke from the explosions could be seen more clearly, billowing magnificently against the dark sky.

"Oi!" said one of the watchtower guards as the front line pushed through the foliage. "Stop right there! This is Obarion territory—"

Almost quicker than Atlas' eyes could follow, Luca swung himself across a tree bordering the wall, hitched his shotgun onto his shoulder, and pulled the trigger. The watchtower guard yelled as the bullet struck its target, and he fell out of sight.

The other Obarion guards leapt into action, and within seconds, bullets rained down on the soldiers. They fell back behind the tree line. Atlas took cover behind a thick hedge, whipping his rifle around and yanking it up onto his shoulder. He narrowed his eyes, pulling the trigger, and one of the tower guards toppled over the rail and plunged fifty feet to the ground.

However much damage the Vedas' soldiers inflicted on the Obarion troops, the Ramshacklers doubled it. Now that they no longer had to be silent, they emerged from the greenery to fight in earnest. Cars roared into the glade, their passengers firing bullets up at the watchtower guards so fast that they dropped like flies.

"*Atlas!*" Jacoby cried through the receiver. "*I think*

we're in!"

"What do you mean you *think* we're in?" Atlas shouted, sinking to the ground as a bullet jetted past his head. "Two hundred amps isn't something that I really want to take a risk on, Jacoby—"

"*I'm ninety percent sure.*"

"*Ninety* percent...Jacoby, I swear on all things—"

"*No—no, I've got it—I'm sure! All of the sensors are down—the reader isn't picking up anything. I've got it, Atlas. We're in!*"

Atlas swallowed thickly, glancing out across the clearing. There were only a few watchtower guards left now, but the other soldiers had noticed the commotion at the entrance and sprinted towards the gate. Atlas made a split second decision and sprang to his feet, bolting across the clearing as fast as his feet could carry him.

He found the guard that had fallen from the watchtower in a crumpled heap. Miraculously, he was still breathing, though his legs were bent at an awkward angle. Atlas was glad he did not recognize him.

"Sorry about this," he muttered, grabbing the man under the arms and dragging him towards the barrier.

The watchtower guards had noticed him, but Atlas was directly beneath them, so their angle of fire was distorted. The other soldiers surged forward, storming towards the gate.

Taking a deep breath, Atlas lifted the man and pressed him against the metal of the barrier, bracing for the horrible screams, and the revolting smell of melting flesh—

But it never came. Nothing happened.

There was a beat of astounded silence, in which no

one moved—not Renegade or Ramshackler, nor Vedas or Obarion.

But then one of the Ramshacklers pelted something at the gate, and there was a great blast of smoke. Atlas threw his hands up to shield his eyes, just as bits of metal and rubble collided with the skin of his arms.

When the smoke cleared, it revealed a wide, gaping hole in the gate, and the soldiers surged forward, pouring through the gap like a wave of rushing water carving the path of a canyon.

They were in.

◆ ◆ ◆

Whitsom materialized at Atlas' shoulder in seconds.

"Send half our pod to the warehouse to head off the Obarion soldiers," Atlas commanded. "They're going to try to salvage what they can, but not if we get there first." He hitched his rifle onto his shoulder, lifting the receiver to his mouth. "Jacoby, what's your twenty?"

No answer came, and Atlas cursed, his eyes flickering around the grounds. Chaos had erupted in every direction. The Obarion soldiers were trying to fall into formation, but without access to the majority of their weapons, they were scrambling. The Vedas and Renegades had managed to push halfway across the curtilage already.

"Fall in with Dante's pod—they're pushing through towards the soldiers' quarters," Atlas said to Whitsom. "I'm going to make a break for the communication hub—I think Jacoby might be in danger."

Whitsom nodded, shouting out commands to the other soldiers, and started across the lawn, but turned back briefly, giving Atlas a meaningful look.

"Stay safe, Attie."

Atlas nodded. "You too, Whit."

He slung his rifle over his back and sprinted up the slope towards the four looming buildings. Obarion soldiers ran in every direction, but most of them seemed to be focusing on the mass of attackers advancing from the gate, so they hardly noticed Atlas—though it helped that he'd donned his Obarion uniform.

As he approached the hub, he slowed to a walk, glancing in either direction as he punched in the code.

He was halfway down the hall when a voice called, "Private! Where's your squad?"

Atlas froze. He recognized that voice. He glanced over his shoulder, careful to keep his face from view—but yes, it was Colonel Caddo.

"I asked where your squad was, private—"

"I was asked to check the progress on reestablishing the border," Atlas said smoothly, keeping his back to the older man. He did not dare to reach for the rifle on his back—not when the Colonel had not yet recognized him.

Caddo approached him, and Atlas could hear the sneer in his voice as he said, "We didn't assign any privates to..." He paused, stepping closer, and Atlas' hands unconsciously clenched into fists. "*Atlas?*"

Atlas didn't even think. He spun around, swinging his leg into Caddo and sending him careening into the wall. The Colonel had reached for his handgun, but Atlas grasped it with both hands, sending a foot into his stomach as he ripped it from Caddo's grip. Atlas took a few steps backwards, keeping the handgun trained carefully between the Colonel's eyes.

"Sorry," he muttered, dropping his aim to Caddo's stomach and pulling the trigger. The man crumpled to the ground, but Atlas wasted no time. He took off, darting down the fourth corridor.

He stopped just a few steps down the hall. Three soldiers clustered outside of the control room door. One of them was fiercely punching the code into the keypad over and over, shouting frustratedly, "It's not *working*, why isn't it *working*—"

Another soldier tugged uselessly at the handle, and a third aimed his rifle at the small glass window of the control room, inside which, Atlas presumed, Jacoby was crouching.

"I wouldn't do that if I were you," Atlas drawled. "It's bulletproof."

The three of them whirled around to look at him, and Atlas immediately recognized Squid and Orion, who were in Academy with him, and a blond boy who he did not remember.

"Atlas," Squid said, his eyes narrowing. "Thought you were dead—"

"Thought you were traitor scum," Orion said, grinning nastily, and the two of them advanced. Atlas' eyes were on the blond boy, who tentatively lifted his rifle, but Atlas swung the handgun's barrel and fired three shots into his arm. He let out a cry of pain, staggering sideways. Squid and Orion charged.

Atlas swung the handgun into the side of Squid's face, ducking under Orion's fist. They must not have been on duty when the bombs dropped, for neither had any kind of weapon. Atlas sent a knee into Orion's stomach, slamming the gun down atop his head, and Orion collapsed to the floor. He rounded the barrel on Squid, who stumbled back into the wall, his hands held up against his chest.

"Please—please don't, I'm not any trouble, honest..."

Atlas rolled his eyes, letting out an undignified snort.

"Have some class, Squid," he muttered, striking the dense metal against the boy's temple and knocking him unconscious.

Atlas hurried towards the door. Jacoby peered back from the other side of the glass, his eyes wide behind his glasses. When he saw Atlas, he hastily pushed the door open.

"I reprogrammed the code when I heard them coming," Jacoby gasped out. "I didn't think I could take so many of them."

"Good thinking," Atlas said. "Come on, we've got to get out to the others."

By the time they emerged from the hub, the Obarion soldiers had begun to organize. The ones who had been patrolling off-base must have been called back, because a horde came rushing through the hole in the gate. Even as Atlas watched, they fired towards the Vedas and Renegades, and soldiers dropped left and right, not expecting the assault from behind.

"Make a dash for the main gate," Atlas told Jacoby. "I'm going to go meet up with the others—"

"What, no way!" the redhead burst out. "I'm not just *leaving*—"

Atlas made an impatient noise, but did not have

time to argue.

"Fine, stay close." The two of them sprinted towards the artillery warehouse. The smoke hung thick in the air, and flames licked up the side of the building. The Obarion who did have weapons had attempted to advance towards the artillery, but the Vedas formed a thick wall between them and the building.

"*Atlas—Koda to Atlas, do you copy?*"

Atlas' hand plunged into his pocket for the receiver.

"What do you need, Koda?"

"*Talikoth sent a battalion down to the Hole—my boys are holding them off for now, but they're drawing closer—*"

"I've got an idea," Atlas said, glancing towards the artillery warehouse. "Can you hold them off for ten or so minutes?"

"*We'll do our best. Over.*"

Atlas shoved through the crowd of soldiers. "Move it, move it!" He spotted Whitsom near the door. "I'm going in," he told him.

Whitsom's eyes widened. "Atlas, it's cooking in there—" he started, but Atlas interrupted.

"The Hole's under attack—I've got an idea. Move."

Whitsom's brow furrowed, but he nodded, making to follow Atlas.

"No, you stay here," Atlas said, shaking his head. "You too, Jacoby." The redhead looked put out, but thankfully did not argue.

The moment the warehouse door closed behind him, Atlas had to dive out of the way as a wooden beam came plummeting down from the ceiling. A thick layer of sweat formed on his forehead, and he pulled his shirt up over his nose and mouth as the smoke began to fill his lungs.

He stumbled over shattered boxes of ammunition, crawled under still smoldering beams, and jumped out of the way as another chunk of the ceiling crashed to the ground. The deeper he traveled into the warehouse, the thicker the smoke grew. He spotted a few un-detonated grenades and hastily gathered them into his free arm, his eyes watering as he squinted across the warehouse.

But yes, there it was. Sitting in the corner, completely undamaged, was the tank. Atlas started towards it, but stopped, a surge of fear coursing through him. Here sat one of the tanks, and the Ramshacklers, he knew, had destroyed another. But where was the third?

He shook his head and started forward again. He couldn't worry about that now. Atlas clambered up the tank, wincing as he pulled himself across scalding metal to lower himself in.

The hatch slammed closed above him, and he stared around for a few moments, bewildered. He had never, strictly speaking, driven a tank before, but with all the books he had read, he was confident he could figure it out.

The tank's gas wasn't full, but it would be enough to get him to the Hole. Atlas plopped down into the seat, laying back and studying the levers and buttons on the U-shaped dash that encircled him. He glanced into the periscope. The artillery warehouse continued to collapse around him, but inside of the tank, he felt invincible.

"Alright, Atlas," he muttered to himself. "Easy does

it..."

He yanked the acceleration handle and pressed tentatively on the pedal at his feet. The tank lurched forward.

"Left and right tracks," he murmured to himself, grasping the levers on either side of him. The tank inched across the warehouse at a sluggish pace, running over boxes and weapons indiscriminately.

"*Left...*" He tugged the lever back, and the tank shifted, veering towards the rear wall. "And...*right*, ha!"

He let out a huff of disbelieving laughter, a grin creeping onto his face.

"Not so hard—okay, *now*—" He jerked the right lever back once more, toeing the foot pedal and shifting the tank into the next gear. It surged forward, and Atlas panicked for a moment as he sped towards the warehouse wall. He winced instinctively, bracing himself...

But the tank plowed through the wall easily, pieces of wood and metal raining down, bouncing off of the metal roof of the tank.

"Holy shit, this is *awesome!*" Atlas shouted.

The soldiers outside the warehouse stumbled away from the sudden commotion. The Vedas' soldiers eyed the tank warily—a few began to back away.

Atlas reached for his receiver. "Atlas to Whitsom?"

"*Uh, Attie—where'd you go, man? There's a massive tank—*"

Atlas grinned. "Whitsom, half of you need to split off and guard this big hole I've created—most of the guns are destroyed, but there are still some grenades. See if some of you can't slip in and get to them first."

"*Atlas, are you in that tank?*"

"On my cue, Whit."

"*Wait, wait, what's your cue? Atlas, tell me what you're—*"

Atlas reached across the hull and engaged the auto-loader.

"Here goes nothing," he said to himself. He pulled the lever above him, swiveling the turret towards the Obarion soldiers, and fired.

They had only begun to scramble out of the way when the shell tore through the group. It must have been loud, for many of the Vedas threw their hands over their ears, but inside the tank the blast was muffled.

"I'm going to go help at the Hole, but I'll be back," he told Whitsom, shifting the tracks towards the perimeter of the grounds.

"*Ooh, Atlas, I can't* believe *you didn't let me go with you!*"

Atlas sniggered, skirting the battlefield as best as he could. The periscope gave him nearly a full range of vision, but the tank was massive and hard to maneuver. He didn't want to accidentally run over any Vedas or Renegades.

He shifted into the next gear and surged towards the fence. Vedas and Obarion still fought near the entrance, but as they saw him coming, they scrambled out of the way, and he plowed through the gap, shifting the gears even higher, just as static burst from above his head.

"*Tanker number three, state your business.*"

A smirk twitched at the corner of Atlas' lips as he reached up and clicked the button.

"Hello, yes, this is tanker number three, just going for a joy ride—you don't mind, do you?"

"Tanker number three, please identify yourself immediately—"

"I'm Talikoth, obviously."

"Tanker number three, you are in danger of discharge due to insubordination and unauthorized use of an Obarion vehicle—"

"Oh, go to hell." Atlas slammed his fist into the speaker, and the man's voice petered out. He crashed through the trees, toggling the levers back and forth as he steered the tank down the slope, towards the coast.

"Koda to Atlas."

He held his receiver between his cheek and shoulder. "I'm on my way, Koda. Give me maybe another five minutes."

As Atlas barreled towards the Hole, he began to see signs of the commotion. One of the cars sped by, about fifty feet ahead of him, and a squad of Obarion soldiers ran west, their guns held ready at their sides.

Koda and Raider stood back to back, about a hundred yards from the Hole, shouting directions at a group of Ramshackle boys as they fired shot after shot at the soldiers approaching from the opposite direction. The Ramshacklers had formed a tight circle around the Hole. The innermost ring had their backs pressed against the sides of the cars that lie toppled on the entrance.

About twenty-five feet away from them, Atlas spotted another battalion of Obarion soldiers, firing on the Ramshacklers with disciplined intensity.

Atlas hastily toed the gear shift, reaching up and swiveling the turret once more. He squinted through the periscope, pulling back the left lever as his pace slowed. He pressed the autoloader once more, as the tank pulled forward onto level ground, and fired.

The shell blasted through the Obarion soldiers, and the ones that had managed to get out of the way bolted backwards, sprinting towards higher ground as Atlas rotated the turret to fire again. The battalion fell backwards, disappearing into the foliage.

He turned the turret towards the soldiers advancing on Koda and Raider, blasting a shell into the center of their advancing squad. Three of them were propelled backwards, and the two remaining soldiers jetted back towards Headquarters.

The Ramshacklers eyed the tank warily, and Koda and Raider were pelting across the clearing when Atlas popped his head out of the hatch.

"Hey, guys."

"*Atlas!*" several of the boys exclaimed, and Koda shouted, "You stole a *tank*, man?"

He snatched up the grenades, clambering out of the hatch and jumping down to the ground in front of the Raider. The blond boy rolled his eyes, smacking Atlas across the back of the head.

"Okay, *show-off*. We're all out here slumming it and you gotta go and steal a tank."

"You're just mad you didn't think of it."

Raider grinned, shrugging. "Yeah, pretty much."

"I'm leaving it here," Atlas said. "The soldiers are bound to be back with reinforcements and it's more use to you down here than to us up there—everyone is all clustered together, it's too risky—I could end up hitting our guys."

"Show me how to use it," Koda said.

Atlas quickly ran him through the gears and levers, before telling them, "There's a bigger problem though—they've got another tank, and I've got no idea where it is. For all I know, it could be at headquarters by now—"

Koda frowned, scratching his beard. "If it's already in commission, we won't be able to stop it—we'd need a tank missile, and we don't exactly have any of *those* lying around."

Atlas cursed, running a hand through his hair, but Koda's eyes grew wide.

"Unless..."

"Unless *what*?" Atlas asked impatiently.

Koda glanced over at the tank. "Is it like this? The other one?"

Atlas frowned. "It's bigger. This is a one-man rig—the other needs a crew, I think."

Koda nodded slowly, moving around the tank and inspecting it.

"Typically, large artillery pieces are primed with shock-sensitive chemicals that are released through an electrical impulse—"

"Give us the abridged version, Koda," Raider snapped.

"You could attach a snuffer to the outside of the tank, which would override the electrical signal. The rounds wouldn't fire."

"A snuffer?" Atlas queried, bewildered.

"It's a little device with four prongs that hook onto a host. We've done it before."

Raider nodded. "We used to attach them to cars to override their systems when we were overtaking rival gangs."

Atlas' brow furrowed. "But this is a *tank*—"

"Hypothetically speaking, it shouldn't matter. The

electrical override is conducted by metal just the same as a car—like lightning."

"And do you have these snuffers with you?"

"Got a few in the trunk of my car, but we haven't been able to use them for at least six moons. There was a bad storm a while back and one of our signal poles got struck. The snuffers have been going haywire ever since."

"You don't know how to fix them?" Atlas growled. If they didn't find a way to get that tank off the battlefield, their efforts to protect the warehouse would be for nothing.

"I didn't make them," Koda said, glancing sideways at Raider who paced beside them, his jaw taut and hands clenched into fists. "But Gaiomere could fix them in a heartbeat."

Raider's brows knitted together, his expression uneasy.

"Couldn't we just take them to her? Have her fix them at the campsite?" Atlas reasoned.

Raider shook his head. "She can reconfigure them, but then she would have to reprogram the code to override the electric impulse—"

Atlas stared at him blankly, and Raider gave him an annoyed look.

"The snuffer is programmed based on the system of the vehicle it's being used to override. The programming never changed back when we were using it in the Ramshackles—we were always using it for cars. But in order to override the tank, she'd have to attach the prongs to the back of the tank and analyze the electrical system before she could complete the override."

Atlas stared at him for a full ten seconds, his jaw going slack. "She'd have to climb onto the back of the tank."

"She'd have to climb onto the back of the tank," Raider confirmed grimly.

"Absolutely not."

"How how else are we going to stop that thing? The only reason we've been able to hold off those goons this long is because half of their troops don't have weapons. If they bring a tank in—"

"It's too dangerous," Atlas maintained, shaking his head. "No, I'm sure Jacoby can figure it out..."

The blond boy's expression, however, looked resolute. "Jacoby might be able to figure it out within a few days. We don't have a few days."

"We're not going to ask her to climb onto a *tank* in the middle of the battlefield." Atlas growled out through gritted teeth, his face flushing with anger.

"We don't have a choice," Raider snapped, glaring at him. "I'll cover her."

"No way," Atlas said, but the blond was already jogging towards the car. "Raider, don't even think about it—"

"Koda, you stay here, help the boys hold down the fort," Raider called, pulling open the driver's door.

"Raider, we aren't doing this—"

The taller boy rolled his eyes. "Are you coming or not?"

Atlas let out a string of curses, storming across the clearing and pulling open the passenger's side door. Raider tore off as he was still tugging the door shut behind him.

"She can just explain how to do it to one of us—"

Atlas began, but Raider interrupted with a snort.

"Yeah right, that'll all go right over your head, and even I can't keep up with half the things she says."

"Well, if we're going to climb onto the tank anyway, why don't we just take out the soldiers operating it?" Atlas reasoned.

"Yeah, and then we'll have to guard that too, in addition to the Hole, and the artillery warehouse, so that none of the other Obarion soldiers put it back in action," Raider said brusquely, shaking his head. "We've got to take it out of commission completely."

"Whitsom will kill us. No way he'd stand for this —"

"Whitsom isn't here, Atlas. And by the time he finds out, we'll be done." Raider took a sharp turn, veering towards the coast. Buildings flashed past so quickly they blurred. "Besides, I told you, I'll protect her." He gave Atlas a sideways look, his eyes flashing as he added, "Don't make the mistake of thinking you're the only one in this car who cares about her."

Atlas looked away, scowling. He wanted to argue further, but within seconds, the car came screeching to a halt, and Raider hopped out.

"Alright, Mere-kat, you're up!" he shouted.

The curly-haired girl poked her head out of the medical tent, her eyes wide as they flickered between Raider and Atlas.

"Where's Whitsom?" she asked immediately.

"He's fine," Atlas assured her. "He's protecting the warehouse. We uh—we came to ask you a favor." Gaiomere approached the car, her brows knitted in confusion.

Raider opened the trunk and circled around the

car carrying a strange grey object with four prongs that resembled insect legs extending from its underbelly.

"Oh, I remember these!" Gaiomere exclaimed, smiling fondly.

"They were fried in a storm a few moons ago—" Raider began, but Gaiomere waved him off. She already opened a compartment in the back of the snuffer and had slid her fingers in between a couple of wires.

"They aren't fried, the system's just confused," she muttered.

"Do you think they'll work on a tank?" the blond boy asked from beside her.

She snorted, giving Raider a smirk.

"Do you think I'm a scrub?" she retorted. He laughed.

Atlas frowned at her. "Raider said you'd have to climb up on the tank to program it."

He hoped, perhaps, that she'd contradict him. But instead she only raised her eyebrows, meeting his gaze evenly as she confirmed, "I will."

Atlas clenched his jaw, looking away from her.

"You don't have to be afraid, Mere-kat," Raider said, nudging her shoulder. "Atlas and I will cover you. All you have to worry about is getting that tank reprogrammed."

"I'm not afraid," Gaiomere said quietly.

She turned to Raider, holding out the snuffer. "All you need to do is unplug the green and yellow wires for thirty seconds, and then plug them back in. Hold the black button, and that will reset the system."

Raider blinked, scowling.

"That's it? Man, I'm gonna kill Koda!" He snatched the snuffer from her, stalking towards the car and hopping up to sit on the trunk while he fiddled with the strange little device.

Gaiomere reached up and brushed a finger across Atlas' cheekbone, where a piece of metal falling from the warehouse ceiling had snagged him.

"You okay?" she asked softly.

"Yeah," he said. "You really don't have to do this, you know—"

"Yes, I do," she said firmly.

He sighed, running a hand through his hair.

"Well, at least—" He remembered the handgun he had taken from the Colonel, and he unhooked it from his belt. "At least take this." She gazed down at the gun suspiciously, and he rolled his eyes, gripping the handle and revolving it towards a nearby tree, clamping his fingers down around the trigger. The bullet tore from the muzzle and buried itself into the bark.

"See," he told her, spinning the gun around so that the grip was facing her. "Easy."

She snorted, grasping the handle and taking the gun from him.

"Yeah, easy for you to say," she muttered. She squared her feet, facing the tree and lifting the gun in front of her.

"Hold it with both hands," Atlas told her. "There's going to be some kickback."

She shot him a dirty look, reluctantly lifting her second hand as she pointed out, "You didn't hold it with both hands."

He smirked, leaning down beside her and murmuring, "Well, that's because I'm stronger than you."

She made a disparaging noise, and he snickered.

"Drop your shoulders a little," he instructed, pressing against the tension between her shoulder blades. "Your grip should be firm, but not a death grip."

Her eyes narrowed, and she wrinkled her nose as she focused on the tree. He heard the breath catch in her throat as she pulled the trigger.

The bullet snagged a branch about ten feet from where his bullet had lodged into the tree, and Atlas glanced sideways at her, his lips twitching. "Wow, that was...pretty much the worst shot I've ever seen—"

Gaiomere's face colored, and she punched him in the shoulder.

"Alright, I got it!" Raider called. "Let's go!"

The two of them hurried towards the car. Atlas climbed into the front, and Gaiomere slipped into the backseat, taking the snuffer from Raider. They took off, zigzagging between buildings and speeding over chunks of missing road, until they rounded a corner and came to the stretch of trees surrounding Headquarters.

"Drop me off at the gate," Atlas said. "I'll help the others until we spot the tank, then I can come help you cover Gaiomere—"

"Uh, guys?" she said quietly from the backseat, but neither of them were listening.

"Gaiomere and I can circle the battlefield and pick guys off," Raider said as he veered around a tree, narrowly missing its wide trunk. "I can have her take the wheel, since I'm a better shot—"

"Guys!" she said louder, and Atlas glanced back at her. Her eyes were wide as she peered through the trees, and she rolled down her window to extend a finger south. "I don't think we're going to need to wait for the tank."

Atlas followed her gaze. There, barreling through the trees, pelting up the slope faster than Atlas had dared to go, was the second tank. Its tracks slid effortlessly over massive roots and felled trees, climbing higher and higher, and though Raider's car moved faster, there was no mistaking which direction it was going.

The tank was headed straight for the battlefield.

CHAPTER NINETEEN

T hey beat the tank to Headquarters by a couple of minutes, and Raider slammed on the brakes to bring the car to a halt just beneath the furthest watchtower. Atlas pulled the receiver from his pocket, hastily jamming the button.

"Whitsom, what's your twenty?"

"Half our troops have got the Obarion soldiers detained in their quarters. We've got five hundred guns on them and doors and windows are secured."

Atlas cast a glance through the fence, towards the opposite end of the base. "Civilians?"

"We sent a battalion to ensure there wouldn't be any militia activity—it's been quiet on that end. But, Atlas, the armed soldiers are pushing back hard to get through to the quarters. We're holding steady, but they've been picking us off little by little—and Koda said more are on their way."

"Whitsom, listen, there's a tank coming. "

There was a beat of silence, and then, *"I'm assuming you aren't driving this one."*

"We're going to try to disable it, but we're going to need time. Can you guys try to keep the Obarion off of us?"

"We'll do our best, Attie."

He looked back at Gaiomere, sliding the receiver into his pocket once more. A part of him felt like he needed to tell Whitsom that his sister would be helping them, that she could be in danger, just in case.

Atlas shook his head, pushing his thoughts in a different direction. He couldn't think like that—not now, when they were so close.

"Here it comes," Raider muttered. He jerked the gearshift into reverse and steered the car backwards, into the foliage. "We'll flank them soon as they make it through the fence."

Seconds later, the tank came climbing over the hill, its turret spinning towards the battlefield. It bulldozed past the spot where they were hidden in the foliage, and Raider stomped on the gas.

"We're not gonna be able to climb on from the ground while it's moving!" the blond called over the roar of the engine, as they drew nearer to the tank. "We'll have to jump from the roof of the car!"

Atlas did not give his fear even a second to set in. He rolled down the window, grasped the edge of the car, and lugged himself up onto the roof.

"This is insane," Gaiomere muttered, as she clambered up after him. The roof bent under their weight as they both pushed to their feet, and she grasped onto his arm to keep her balance. She was eying the distance between the car and the tank anxiously. "I can't make that jump, Atlas."

Atlas held out a hand, and she took it unhesitatingly. Before she could question him, he yanked her towards him and pulled her onto his back, edging towards the far side of the roof to get a running start. Her lips were at his ear, and he heard her breath catch.

"I won't let you fall," he said quietly. He took two bounding steps and leapt from the roof, landing on the back of the tank with a grunt.

Gaiomere slid off of his back, and the two of them glanced back towards the car. Raider had pulled himself onto the roof now, and with no one steering, the car had started to veer sideways, towards the forest. Raider cleared the gap in one large leap—and not a second too soon. The car careened in the opposite direction, slamming into an oak tree with a *crunch*.

Atlas unslung his rifle from his back—just in time, for the noise they had made must have alerted the crew. The hatch popped open, perhaps twenty feet from where they stood, and Atlas fired off a shot just as a figure popped their head out. His shot struck the soldier's throat, and blood gurgled from his mouth as he slid back down into the hole.

"Nice one," Raider muttered, crossing to the other side of the tank, his feet treading nimbly over where the metal sloped downward towards the tracks. He trained his rifle on the Obarion clansmen dispersed across the grounds. Talikoth's soldiers would be hard-pressed to hit them while they were moving, but they could not be too careful.

Gaiomere sank down into a crouch and attached the snuffer to the tank.

"Incoming!" Raider shouted, and Atlas ducked in the nick of time. The turret swiveled around, swinging the tank barrel through the air where their heads had been moments before.

The remaining members of the tank crew took advantage of the distraction. One popped their head out and blasted off a shot towards Atlas. The bullet tore through his shoulder, but strangely, he didn't feel any pain—just a sudden burst of adrenaline. He swung his rifle around and sent a bullet through the soldier's head.

The hatch slammed shut once again.

He groaned, dropping to his knees. The pain had been nonexistent, and then suddenly it was all-pervading, a throbbing, pulsating sting radiating from the point where the bullet had entered his flesh.

"Are you okay?" Gaiomere asked frantically, her eyes wide as they raked over him, and zeroed in on his injured shoulder.

"I'm—*fine*—" he ground out through gritted teeth. "Just—*focus*."

She nodded, turning back to the snuffer.

Raider knelt down next to him, pulling back the fabric of his jacket.

"You're losing a lot of blood," Raider muttered, almost to himself.

"I'm fine," Atlas repeated, trying to push himself up to his feet, but the older boy shoved him back down with scarcely any effort.

"Press your hand against the front," he directed. "The entry wound is bigger."

Atlas begrudgingly complied, and Raider glanced over at Gaiomere, who sat back on her haunches.

"It just needs to calibrate now," she said quietly, shooting Atlas another worried look as she continued, "I'm not sure how long that will take."

Raider nodded his head towards the handgun that Gaiomere had latched to her pants.

"Mere-kat, keep that on the ground soldiers. I'm gonna go finish off the crew—before they get another shot at any of us."

Gaiomere gave him a timid nod, pressing unsteadily to her feet and grasping the gun in trembling hands.

Raider climbed up to the tank's upper level, ducking under the turret, and moved towards the hatch.

"Atlas," Gaiomere said quietly, and he looked at her. "Can you hold this, do you think?"

He glanced down at the gun. He couldn't maneuver his arms to hold his rifle, but he could lift a handgun. He took it from her, and she moved around him, pulling off her sweater and wrapping it around his injured shoulder, so tightly that it ached.

There was a sudden ear-splitting blast from in front of them, and the tank shuddered.

"Oh no," Gaiomere murmured, leaning over and peering at the snuffer. "Please hurry, please hurry." She tied her sweater off in a knot. "That should help with the blood flow," she said, moving back over to the snuffer.

There was a shout above them. Raider had opened the hatch, and the Obarion soldier nearest the door fired off a shot. He clearly hadn't expected Raider to be so close, for he missed wildly, and Raider lunged at him, attempting to rip the rifle from his hand.

"Got it—it's calibrated!" Gaiomere cried. Atlas wasn't paying attention though. A second figure peeked their head from the hatch. Atlas tried to aim at him, but the soldier let the hatch drop closed, leaving his companion alone atop the tank, still attempting to wrestle his rifle out of Raider's hands.

A second roaring eruption sounded from the front of the tank, and Gaiomere let out a small groan.

"*Whitsom*," she whispered like a prayer. She adjusted the prongs on the snuffer. "Hang on just a little longer."

Atop the tank, Raider managed to wrench the rifle from the soldier. He clubbed him over the head with it, grasped his shirt, and flung him from the top of the tank.

A great shudder ripped through the heavy metal machine, but no shell was fired. Atlas glanced over at Gaiomere.

"Was that—"

She was breathless in her excitement. "It worked."

But the tank still barreled towards the Vedas. "Stay here," Atlas told Gaiomere, before he clambered up the side of the tank, his boots sliding against the slick metal.

"The controls to stop it are in the front hatch," he said as soon as he reached Raider. "If we don't shut it off, they'll just run over all our soldiers."

The two hastened across the top of the tank and climbed clumsily down from the turret. Raider reached the front hatch first. He yanked it open, and Atlas heard someone shout, "What the—"

The blond grasped the soldier by the scruff of his neck and yanked him upwards.

"You've been demoted, pipsqueak," he said loudly, shoving the boy off of the tank and swinging himself down into the hatch.

"Red lever, Raider, red lever!" Atlas called, wobbling a little as the tank tread over an abandoned Ramshackler car.

Raider must have heard him, because they lurched to a halt. Atlas jumped down from the tank, and circled around to the back—but Gaiomere was nowhere to be found.

Atlas cursed. She'd left him with the handgun,

which meant she was completely unarmed. His eyes skirted across the grounds, and saw Zarr and Luca sprinting towards him. "Have you seen Gaiomere?" he asked, as soon as they reached his side.

"She was heading that way," Zarr said, extending a finger in the direction they'd come.

"It looked like she was going towards the campsite," Luca added.

Atlas attempted to steady his breath, though he was only marginally reassured. Zarr must have noticed, for he said, "I'll find her." Atlas gave him a grateful nod, and the two of them disappeared once more.

A sudden clang sounded overhead. The last of the Obarion crew members scrambled from the top hatch and aimed his rifle towards Raider, who was just climbing from the front, and had his back turned. The soldier's fingers were tightening around the trigger when Atlas lifted his gun and sent a bullet through the side of the soldier's head.

Raider looked over at him, his mouth pinched with annoyance. "Thank...you," he managed to force out, though it looked as though it caused him physical pain.

"Don't mention it," Atlas muttered.

Shouting suddenly echoed across the grounds. A group of soldiers came pouring out from the sloping wooden bridge that led to the Stadium. Atlas recognized the bright red insignia of the Inner Ring. And surrounded by soldiers, his dark eyes glinting and face set into a hard, cold glare, was Talikoth.

Raider jumped down from the tank next to Atlas. "Where'd they come from?"

Atlas shook his head, frowning. It was bizarre

that Talikoth's best soldiers would join the fray so late —where had they been? Had they managed to defeat the Ramshacklers at the Hole and released the soldiers trapped there?

Atlas took half a step towards Talikoth, nerves writhing in the pit of his stomach.

"Stanton to Atlas."

He ripped the receiver from his pocket, pulling his gaze away from his father, who was surveying the battlefield impassively.

"Stanton, where's Koda?" Atlas demanded

"Atlas, we couldn't—we couldn't stop them. Talikoth came in with a bunch of soldiers, and they had an anti-tank missile—Koda—Koda didn't make it. Talikoth and his soldiers took back off for the battlefield as soon as they destroyed the cars on top of the Hole and we—we tried to hold the rest of his soldiers in there as long as we could, Atlas—we really did, but—they're on their way."

A lump formed in Atlas' throat, and he glanced towards Raider, who had certainly been standing close enough to hear Stanton's message.

A strange look passed over the blond boy's face, his brows furrowing, "It's fine," he mumbled, shaking his head, as though flicking off an irksome fly. "It's—he—he knew what he was signing up for."

An idea flashed through Atlas' mind. "It won't have been for nothing," he promised. "Help me move the tank back in front of that hole in the fence." Before the older boy could reply, Atlas pressed the button on his receiver and said, "Atlas to Jacoby. Cobes, are you near the control room?"

The redhead was short of breath when he replied, *"Near enough."*

"Head in that direction. I've got a job for you."

Atlas hastily recounted his plan to Jacoby as Raider steered the tank back across the grounds. By the time the two of them parked it in front of the gaping hole in the fence, Yacielle and a couple dozen other soldiers had sprinted down from the warehouse and were waiting for instruction next to the watchtower.

"Keep your guns trained over the tank, they've got reinforcements coming," Atlas instructed. The soldiers immediately made to comply, lining themselves up along the side of the tank, and beside the fence. Raider had climbed a quarter of the way up the watchtower ladder, his piercing blue eyes trained over the tank for any sign of movement.

"Should be any minute—" Atlas said to himself, but he broke off, a sudden movement to his right distracting him.

A figure was streaking towards the tank, his black hair glinting in the light of the rising sun, his hands already nocking an arrow to his bow. Atlas didn't even think—his legs carried him forward, charging towards the figure and tackling him to the ground.

Jereis sprang back to his feet, grinning wildly.

"Hey, Attie. I was hoping we'd run into each other." His bow had fallen to the ground at his feet, but he made no move to reach for it.

"Oh, I'm sure," Atlas said, his eyes fastened on the black-haired boy, who was circling him rather like a predator might stalk their prey. "You didn't get to finish your artwork."

Jereis laughed coldly. "I'll be finishing more than just artwork, Atlas. I doubt General Talikoth will even mourn your death."

He lunged and Atlas ducked beneath his fist, swiftly slamming a punch into his stomach, and then another to his chest. The pale boy's foot swung towards him, but Atlas checked his kick, catching him with a hook in the side of the face. Jereis stumbled backwards, but within seconds he came at Atlas again, his face contorted with fury.

Back and forth they went, blow after blow. Atlas heard one of the soldiers—Yacielle, he thought—shout, "Atlas, you need help?"

"Focus on the tank!" he yelled back without taking his eyes off Jereis. And even now he thought he could hear yells through the foliage on the other side of the fence, hear the pounding of footsteps drawing nearer.

"Jacoby to Atlas."

Atlas couldn't respond. Jereis had swung a kick towards him once more, and Atlas attempted to check it, but Jereis dove forward, his arm wrapping around Atlas' thigh as he drove him backwards towards the tank, slamming his head into the metal frame. Dots danced in front of his eyes.

"Jacoby to Atlas. Atlas, we're up."

Atlas hooked an arm around Jereis' throat, tightening it around his trachea. The boy gagged, panicking as he attempted to wrench his head from Atlas' grip, but Atlas held on tighter. Jereis' fists slammed into Atlas' leg, his feet pushing upwards against the ground beneath him, trying to throw Atlas off him...

But Atlas had always been stronger. Had always been faster, smarter. Had always been a better fighter. He'd made sure of it.

And for what? To be maneuvered by Talikoth like

a marionette. Just like the rest of the soldiers. Just like Jereis.

Atlas unhooked his arm, pushing Jereis away and straightening up. Jereis' face was red as he gasped for air.

"Don't stand against me again, Jereis," Atlas said coldly. "Next time you'll receive no mercy."

Something wild and deranged flashed through Jereis' eyes, and he ripped one of the arrows from the holster on his back.

"*Mercy?*" he shrieked, spit flying from his mouth. "I'll show you mercy, you traitorous scum!" He lunged at Atlas once more, his arrow raised to pierce him, and Atlas swung his body low, swiveling a foot around and planting it into Jereis' ribcage.

It happened in slow motion. The boy flew backwards, stumbling and trying to catch himself—but his body slammed into the fence. He let out a scream so horrible that Atlas was sure it would haunt him for the rest of his life. His body writhed against the fence for several moments, and even as Atlas watched, the skin on his face and his arms split open, reddening and blistering with massive burns. He seized for a few moments longer, and then there was a repulsive snap, and he crumpled to the ground.

Atlas stared at the body at his feet, nausea rolling in his stomach. He did not have time to dwell on what he'd just seen—what he'd just *done*— for Raider shouted, "They're coming!"

He stepped over Jereis' body, peering through the fence into the foliage. The shouts, indeed, were growing louder, but through the clamor of noise, it almost sounded like engines...

One of the Ramshackler cars flew over the hill, screeching to a stop in front of the tank.

"Don't shoot!" Atlas shouted immediately. The Ramshacklers came pouring from the vehicle—they must have squeezed at least fifteen boys into the car, all seated atop one another and cramped into the trunk—and Atlas could hear another car coming.

"We beat 'em here, boys!" called a familiar voice. Niko clambered over the tank, grinning at the waiting Vedas. "What a welcoming party!"

He hopped down, and the other Ramshacklers followed after him.

"Sorry we couldn't hold them off," he said to Atlas. "But we came to join the fun at least."

"We'll take all the help we can get," Atlas said. "Jacoby got the fence back up, so if we can keep this hole covered, they shouldn't be able to breach the base." It crossed his mind that this *also* meant the Vedas and Renegades would be trapped inside, should things go awry, but he thought it better not to voice this sentiment.

A third car arrived, and a freckle-faced young man sprang out of it, declaring: "They're right behind us!"

Two boys lugged what looked like a missile launcher out of the backseat, and Atlas climbed up onto the tank to help them haul it over.

Raider jumped down off of the ladder. "Those new soldiers that came with Talikoth are doing some serious damage," he observed, nodding his head towards the warehouse. Atlas turned. Moonstone's soldiers had perhaps half of the Inner Ring backed up on the bridge that led to the Stadium, unable to advance, but they were still firing shots into the crowd with frightening accuracy, and the soldiers that had made it across the bridge and onto the battlefield with Talikoth were mowing through the Vedas as though it were child's play.

Atlas hitched his gun up onto his shoulder. "Come on, let's see if we can take a few of them out of the equation."

The two of them took off towards the warehouse, and behind them, Atlas heard a clamor of footsteps and voices—the Obarion reinforcements had arrived.

At the dead center of the battlefield, Talikoth was shouting orders to his soldiers, the barrel of his gun aimed at the Vedas near the bridge, as he picked them off one-by-one. Atlas caught Raider's eye, and the two of them veered towards him. The apprehension in Atlas' stomach grew heavier with every step he took nearer to his father.

"Oh, no," Raider murmured, his steps stuttering to a halt, and Atlas immediately saw what had distracted him: a tiny figure sprinting across the grounds towards the bridge. The Inner Ring soldiers had started to make a push onto the battlefield, and the Vedas soldiers were falling back under the barrage of gunfire.

"Go," Raider said immediately. He jerked his head towards Talikoth, adding, "I'll handle him. If he's anything like you, I'll have him crying 'uncle' in no time."

Without another word, Atlas took off. His legs were much longer than hers, but Gaiomere had a considerable lead on him. She was only fifty feet away from the bridge when she stopped and fiddled with something in her hands, before she hurled it with all of her might.

It landed right at the end of the bridge that was closest to her, and the explosion was immediate. The Inner Ring soldiers were blasted backwards, fragments of metal flying in every direction, but Gaiomere was already launching another grenade, her face set with determination. The second grenade landed further up the bridge, and the wood planks splintered apart.

Atlas reached her side, and she immediately thrust a couple of the grenades into his hands.

"I saw you leave them in the car—I went over to where it crashed," she said. "Here, you probably have a better arm."

Even with his injured shoulder, her assumption proved true. His throw landed a quarter of the way up the bridge, and the explosion shattered the supports. The bridge began to crack, and several of the soldiers slid into the gap, plummeting into the ravine below.

As soon as they had released the last grenade, he turned to Gaiomere and thrust the handgun into her arms. "Get to the gate," he said. "I don't think you'll be able to get out, but you can at least climb into the tank, where you'll be safe—"

Gaiomere did not seem to be listening to him. Her gaze had fixed on something over his shoulder, her eyes widening in alarm.

He glanced over his shoulder. Across the battlefield, Talikoth and Raider exchanged blows so quickly that Atlas could scarcely tell whose limbs were whose, brawling with such intensity that several of the Inner Ring soldiers near them were looking over nervously—though none of them made any move to interfere.

Gaiomere shot Atlas a sideways glance, tentatively

asking, "Is that—"

"Yeah," Atlas said, before she could finish. He did not need to ask how she knew, nor was he keen on hearing, at that moment, how much he looked like his father.

He swallowed, forcing his eyes away from the pair. "Go, Gaiomere."

She looked as though she wanted to argue, but Atlas cut her off before she could. "I'll make sure Whitsom's safe," he assured her. After another second of hesitation, she nodded, pressing a fleeting kiss to his cheek and taking off in a sprint across the clearing.

Atlas glanced towards Raider and Talikoth. The blond boy looked, at the very least, as though he were holding his own—and if anyone had a chance in beating Talikoth, it was Raider. Atlas would only get in the way.

He turned his attention to the Inner Ring soldiers who seemed to be causing the most strife—-three dozen of them were pushing towards the soldiers' quarters, and through the crowd of Vedas and Renegades, Atlas could not get a clear shot on any of them.

He darted into the fray, shoving his way through soldiers, many of whom had resorted to fists, without weapons at their disposal, and posted up behind a stone pillar near the entrance of the Main. Here, he had enough of a vantage point to land a couple of shots on the Inner Ring soldiers, who had not been expecting an attack from his direction.

Atlas dove behind the pillar as a handful of them swiveled their guns towards him, and hastily yanked his receiver from his pocket. "Atlas to Niko."

"*Shoot, Atlas.*"

"Do you guys still have that missile launcher on

you?"

"*We've got it,*" came Niko's uncertain reply. "*But there's no way we'll be able to get a clear shot—*"

"I might have a workaround," Atlas muttered, flinching as a bullet shattered a chunk of stone three inches from his head. He leaned around the pillar and fired off a series of rounds towards the Obarion soldiers nearest him.

It was Gaiomere's voice that came through his receiver next. "*I'm closest to the watchtower—I'll take the missile launcher up there for higher ground.*"

"No!" Atlas said quickly. "Someone else—anybody else—"

"*Uh...Paleem sort of already gave it to her, At,*" Nico said apologetically. Atlas squinted towards the fence; even from here, he could see Gaiomere scrambling up the ladder. "*She's the fastest climber, anyway—except maybe Luca, but I've got no idea where he is—*"

"Fine," Atlas snapped. "Just—somebody cover her."

"*On it.*"

Twenty feet from where he stood, Atlas spotted Whitsom, his rifle nowhere to be found, fighting hand-to-hand with a soldier who had dirty blond hair and plump cheeks. Coral...

"*I'm up, Atlas,*" came Gaiomere's breathless voice.

He shook his head, refocusing. "Can you hit the warehouse from there?"

"*I think so, but—again?*"

"Just trust me. On my cue." He pressed the button again. "Atlas to Moonstone?"

Her reply was instant. "*Atlas. What do you need?*"

He wondered if she was perched atop a building

nearby, or if she was stationed further away, watching from one of the mountaintops. He had not seen her since they had left the campsite.

"Can you order our troops to fall back towards the Main—away from the warehouse?" he asked her.

Five seconds passed, and then she said, "*Atlas, if we abandon the warehouse, whatever weapons that can be salvaged will be available for the Obarion's taking.*"

"I know. Can you trust me?"

Atlas could picture her face in that moment, her shrewd eyes boring through him like she could see through him.

"*Very well,*" Moonstone agreed, before she added, "*Vedas. Fall back to the Main. Station reinforcements at the soldiers' quarters. I repeat, Vedas, fall back.*"

Atlas heard the echo across the receivers around him, and Olli, who had just taken out a soldier near the alcove where Atlas stood, whipped around to look at him.

"The Obarion can take those weapons," he said nervously.

Atlas' gaze roved towards the artillery warehouse, some four hundred feet away. The Vedas and Renegades had already begun to peel away from the door, and the wide gaping hole where Atlas had driven the tank through the wall. "They can try," he murmured.

He trusted his knowledge of how Talikoth trained his soldiers. Even if Talikoth himself kept his cards close to his chest, his soldiers were trained, tried and true, to respond by the book. The Vedas were wasting their time, battling senselessly with the Obarion when Atlas knew Talikoth was just biding his time, letting his Inner Ring pick off Moonstone's soldiers while they waited for their reinforcements to break through the gate.

A surge of satisfaction swelled in Atlas' chest, for Talikoth's soldiers behaved just as he'd expected them to. The Obarion soldiers surged towards the warehouse. Leading the charge was a sea of red-embroidered uniforms—the half of Talikoth's Inner Ring that had arrived unarmed. It was they that would reach the warehouse first.

The soldiers that fought closer to the Main had hardly even noticed the commotion taking place near the warehouse. Whitsom and Coral were still fighting ruthlessly, and it crossed Atlas' mind that Coral would not hesitate to kill him, if the opportunity arose.

Halfway between the watchtower and the warehouse, he could see Talikoth and Raider. The blond boy stumbled backwards as Talikoth delivered a brutal punch, and Atlas didn't think he had ever seen Raider look so broken—not even when he was severely dehydrated with an infected leg. Molten guilt bubbled in the pit of Atlas' stomach, and his hands clenched and unclenched at his sides.

"Ready, Gaiomere," he said quietly.

The Obarion soldiers drew closer to the warehouse. He waited until the lead soldier was within ten feet, before he lifted the receiver to his mouth, and murmured, "Fire."

An explosion like a cannon erupted from the watchtower, and Gaiomere was flung back against the barricade—but still, her aim was true. Atlas watched as the missile spiraled towards the warehouse, colliding with the door just as the lead soldier reached it.

BOOM!

This blast of smoke and fire was the largest yet,

and the Inner Ring soldiers were launched in every direction, flung across the grass, slamming into the walls of the Main, thrown between the crumbling beams of the warehouse.

The remaining soldiers turned at the noise, and Talikoth did as well.

"*Vedas*," came Moonstone's voice over the receiver, "*Attack.*"

Renegades, Vedas, and Ramshacklers surged towards the remaining Obarion soldiers, who all collectively seemed to have frozen on the spot.

Atlas' eyes, though, were on Talikoth, who had Raider by the scruff of his shirt, a fist reared back. The explosion had distracted him, but his eyes were not on the Inner Ring, most of whom lie perished on the ground, or else so monumentally injured that they could scarcely move. Nor were his eyes on his soldiers, who were quickly being overwhelmed by the advancing Vedas.

No, his gaze was cast in the direction from which the missile had fired. His dark eyes were locked on Gaiomere.

He released Raider, stalking towards the girl, who had just gotten both feet back on solid ground. Atlas made a split-second decision, shoving his way through the throng of soldiers on every side of him.

But a familiar silhouette shifted in his peripherals. Whitsom had been distracted by the explosion, just as the other soldiers had, and Coral had taken advantage of it. Atlas turned his head just in time to see the blond boy withdraw a knife from his pocket, and plunge it into Whitsom's stomach.

"WHIT!" Atlas yelled. Whitsom crumpled to the

ground, and Atlas' stomach plummeted with him.

Coral advanced on Whitsom again, so focused that he did not notice Atlas approaching. Atlas forgot all about the rifle slung across his back. The sight of Whitsom lying on the ground sent adrenaline coursing through him anew, and he reared back his arm, smashing his fist into Coral's face.

The plump boy stumbled backwards, crying out in shock. But then he seemed to register who punched him, and his eyes blew wide, his mouth gaping open rather like a fish.

"Atlas?"

Atlas could not be bothered to waste a second. He kicked the side of Coral's knees, and the blond collapsed to the ground, the knife knocked loose from his hands; his blue eyes flickered over Atlas' face as though he was looking at a ghost.

Atlas turned away from him, dropping to his knees beside Whitsom. Blood pooled on his stomach, and his fingers grasped helplessly at the wound.

"Where's your vest?" Atlas demanded.

"I gave it—to Zarr—" Whitsom gasped out. "He's just a—just a kid, At—"

Atlas let out a growl of frustration, shoving the loosed knife into his pocket and grabbing Whitsom under the arms, dragging him away from the throng. He spared a brief glance back towards Coral, but the blond boy had made no move to stop them. He was still staring at Atlas as though he couldn't comprehend what he was seeing.

"You—are such—an idiot!" Atlas grunted to Whitsom.

He looked up and saw Olli and Jacoby running

towards him, but his eyes roved past them.

Gaiomere had knelt at the foot of the ladder. It looked as though she were trying to reload the missile launcher—she didn't even notice Talikoth until his shadow loomed over her.

"Take him," Atlas said, thrusting Whitsom's upper half towards Olli. His rifle slipped from his shoulders in the process, but he didn't even bother reaching for it.

"Atlas, what—" Olli started to protest.

"Take him!" he repeated urgently. "Get him to the camp hospital safely. *Now!*"

Atlas took off, sprinting across the clearing. Raider knelt in the middle of the battlefield, and was attempting to push himself to his feet. His face and his shirt were drenched in blood, but Atlas could not stop to help him, not now, not when it would take Talikoth only seconds to kill Gaiomere—

She'd tried to scramble away, but he'd caught her by her hair, and Atlas saw her wince. Talikoth wrapped his fingers around her neck, which suddenly looked so thin and delicate enveloped in his father's large hand that Atlas feared for a moment that it would simply snap on contact. Talikoth lifted her off the ground, and Gaiomere's eyes went wide, her fingers clutching desperately at the hand around her throat. And Atlas was still, *still* too far—

He reached around his back, pulling the knife he had taken from Coral out of his pocket, gripping the handle between his fingers, and hurling it towards Talikoth.

It plunged into the dead center of his father's back, and he roared in pain, dropping Gaiomere. She coughed, taking great heaving breaths of air as she scrambled away from him.

Talikoth turned, his piercing dark eyes meeting Atlas' for the first time since he had been captured by the Vedas all those months ago. His father straightened, his face impassive, save for the ever so familiar smirk tugging at the corner of his mouth.

"Nice throw."

Atlas thought it was ironic that the fourth time in his entire life—and he was quite certain of the fact that it was the fourth, for he had filed each occasion away like a prized treasure—that Talikoth had ever praised him, was when Atlas had, quite literally, stabbed him in the back.

Atlas shrugged, feigning nonchalance as he said, "Well, I had a good teacher."

Talikoth chuckled darkly. Atlas noticed him subtly reaching for the knife, attempting to grasp the grip and pull it from his flesh, but he could not reach. He made it look as though he weren't trying to, though—as though it didn't bother him. As though pain and discomfort were beneath him.

Gaiomere had gotten to her feet and edged along the fence behind Talikoth's back, her eyes intent on Raider, who was prone on the ground, retching.

Talikoth followed Atlas' gaze.

"Your friend's a good fighter," he remarked conversationally, waving a hand lazily in Raider's direction. "He might even be better than you, Atlas."

It was the first time he had heard his name from Talikoth's mouth in so long that Atlas flinched. Even before he had been captured, it was so often "private," or "soldier," or most commonly, "boy."

"It's a shame he isn't one of ours," Talikoth

continued. "But he'll do well on the Rigs—did I say you could move, princess?" His head tilted towards Gaiomere, who had started to shuffle out from behind him to cross the clearing, and she promptly froze.

"You won't be sending any more Renegades to the Rigs," Atlas said quickly, distracting Talikoth from the curly-haired girl.

Talikoth smiled, but his eyes remained cold. "Is that so?" he mused, his voice dangerously quiet.

Atlas' receiver was going berserk. "*Moonstone, they're dropping their weapons—*"

"*We've got them surrounded, General—*"

Atlas took a step towards his father, the resonating shouts from the battlefield in the distance fading to nothingness. The startings of adrenaline burst in his veins, and his heart raced against his ribcage.

"No more enslaving Renegades," Atlas said coldly. "Or silencing your own clanspeople that speak against you. No more attacking the Vedas. And no more slaughtering children."

And finally, *finally* the smile slid from Talikoth's face. He watched Atlas calculatedly, his nostrils flaring, but Atlas didn't feel so much as a trace of fear. His voice had raised, and he took another step closer to his father. "Do you even see what you've done? Our clan was supposed to restore the Westland, not destroy it! How could you act against everything you've ever proclaimed?"

Atlas could see the receiver hooked on Talikoth's belt, and even in the space between them, he heard, "*General—they've got us surrounded—there are too many of them. We must surrender. General, do you—*" Talikoth's hand snapped against the receiver, silencing the voice on the other end.

"I have only ever ensured the well-being of the Obarion people—" Talikoth said loudly.

"Unless they spoke against you," Atlas interjected, moving even closer. "Unless they disagreed with your strategies, or contradicted your methods, unless they didn't bend to your every whim—"

Talikoth's face flashed with unbridled rage, and his hand twitched, but anger raced through Atlas like a wildfire now, and he stepped closer, a mere yard separating the two of them.

"And what is the well-being of the Obarion people at the expense of the rest of the world?" he asked quietly. "We can slaughter *their* children to preserve the lives of our own?" His heart hammered near his throat as he searched Talikoth's face, searched it for *something*. Some indication that he had ever simply been Atlas' father, that he had ever looked at his son with fondness or pride, that he had ever seen him as anything more than a tool to be used and then discarded. "Because we *do* slaughter them, don't we?"

Talikoth watched him silently but said nothing.

"Oil rigs don't take more than twenty workers to operate, and yours are only operated by Obarion soldiers—Raider's boys saw it with their own eyes." Atlas' stomach was in knots, but he pressed on, "The Rigs were never where you sent the Renegades. Your Inner Ring would cart them off and slaughter them. Deny it!"

Talikoth arched a brow. There was not so much as a flicker of shame on his face as he said, "How many times have I told you that the Renegades are a liability,

Atlas? They cannot be controlled—"

"You sent *hundreds of children to their death*!" Atlas shouted.

"So *emotional*—just like your mother—"

Before he could stop himself, Atlas slammed his hands into Talikoth's chest, shoving him backwards. He was eye-to-eye with his father now. In all of these years, Atlas had never realized that they were the same height. Talikoth always seemed to tower over everyone and everything.

"Look me in the eyes—" Atlas said lowly, "and deny that you had my mother ordered killed that day." His hands trembled, and he balled them into fists. "Look me in the eyes and deny it."

Talikoth's gaze raked over his face, and for a moment, just a moment, Atlas thought he would see something behind the cold hard mask that had been his companion for eighteen years. But then Talikoth's lips lifted into that smirk once again.

"I will deny it," he said softly, and Atlas' stomach filled with dread, for he knew—before the words had even left Talikoth's mouth. He leaned towards Atlas. "I'll deny it a million times over, because I didn't order her killed. I killed her myself."

Atlas saw red, and he only realized he had swung his fist after it impacted Talikoth's face. But Talikoth hardly flinched. He grinned, wild and manic, and lunged towards Atlas.

Atlas' mind buzzed with a strange white noise. He couldn't think, he couldn't even feel it as Talikoth's fist made contact with his nose—his body's instincts seemed to take over, and adrenaline raced through him like fire.

He had no perception of time or space; all he could feel was a burning hunger. Never had he wanted to hurt anyone so badly.

I killed her myself.

I killed her myself.

I killed her myself.

Talikoth dove at him, wrapping both of his thighs and driving him backwards, and Atlas instinctively reached for his neck, cranking his head sideways and driving his weight to the ground. Talikoth managed to grasp onto one of his legs as he went down, and Atlas slammed his thigh into Talikoth's backside, knocking him forward. Atlas pummeled his fists into the side of his father's face, the back of his neck, wherever he could reach, and Talikoth groaned.

Through the haze of wrath and adrenaline, he could hear Gaiomere, not ten feet from them, coaxing Raider to his feet.

"Come on, Raider, you've got to get up. Come on, that's it."

The Vedas' soldiers still stood with their guns aimed loosely over the tank, but most of their eyes were affixed on Talikoth and Atlas. The Obarion soldiers peered through the other side of the fence.

"*General!*" came the emission from Talikoth's receiver. "*General, Moonstone is arriving in a plane—we cannot continue—*"

The dispatch seemed to send a new wave of energy through Talikoth, for he reached between his legs and grabbed Atlas' other foot, yanking his feet from under him and pulling him to the ground. Talikoth spun around and reared back to hit him, but Atlas locked his legs around his father's waist.

"Look—around you—Talikoth," Atlas grunted, sweat dripping into his eyes and down his face as his legs tightened further around his father, and he raised his arms to block the man's blows. "Your soldiers—are surrendering. Continuing to—fight—will only—get more of them—killed—"

Talikoth let out a furious noise. He relaxed his legs, his upper body becoming deadweight, and he slammed his elbows down into Atlas' stomach. All the breath launched from his lungs, and Talikoth's fists were suddenly pummeling his face.

Atlas gasped for air, struggling to get an arm up front of him, but Talikoth was moving too fast. Stars danced in his vision—

Quite suddenly, Talikoth let out a roar of pain and arched his back, falling off of Atlas, who scrambled to his feet. Raider was behind him, the bloody knife that had been lodged in Talikoth's back gripped tightly in his hand. When Talikoth turned, there was a terrible gash down his spine, from which blood was flowing profusely.

Behind Raider, Obarion and Vedas soldiers clambered to move out of the way as a plane came skidding to a halt on a long stretch of grass, landing at the forest's edge. Moonstone climbed off of the plane, with a pair of large, bulky soldiers, one of whom held a pair of handcuffs.

"General Talikoth, we—"

Talikoth pushed himself to his feet, ripping the receiver from his belt and flinging it sideways, into the fence, where it sizzled and fell to the ground in a smoking pile of useless metal scraps.

Atlas and Raider stood on either side of him, and

Talikoth looked between them, a smirk flickering across his face even as blood saturated his shirt. Raider looked as though he could barely stand, but his teeth were gritted in determination. Atlas lunged at Talikoth first, making to kick in his knee, but Talikoth lifted his leg out of the way to plant a foot in Raider's stomach, who had moved simultaneously to attack. Atlas slammed his fist into Talikoth's back, and the man bellowed, bucking his head back and ramming it into Atlas' face.

Atlas stumbled back a few feet. Raider wrapped Talikoth around the thigh, and tried to drive the knife towards his femoral artery, but Talikoth had his wrist in a vice grip, and slammed his fist into the side of Raider's face.

Atlas wrapped an arm around Talikoth's throat, tightening his hold and leaning back as Talikoth tried to headbutt him again.

"Atlas!"

He glanced up and saw Gaiomere holding his handgun. She tossed it to him, and it landed with a *clunk* in the grass, three feet away. Atlas tried to reach for it, but Talikoth jerked in his grasp, and he quickly clutched his other hand, yanking it upwards and back. Talikoth's throat contracted, searching for oxygen that was not there.

All at once, Talikoth kneed Raider's face, and the blond let out a grunt of pain, his grip slackening as he stumbled. With full use of his legs, Talikoth grasped onto Atlas' arm, throwing him over his shoulder and slamming him into the ground. Atlas groaned, his vision going blurry for a moment as he rolled over onto his hands and knees, trying to push to his feet, but his muscles would not cooperate with him. Through cloudy eyes, he watched Raider charge Talikoth, and then it happened in the blink of an eye. Talikoth stepped to the side, using Raider's own momentum against him to swing him around and bring his knees to the ground. He brought an elbow to the pressure point in Raider's shoulder, and his grip on the knife loosened as he let out a cry of pain. Talikoth ripped the knife from Raider's hand, brought it to his neck, and slit his throat.

"*NO!*" Atlas shouted. Gaiomere screamed behind him, and the Ramshacklers cried out in the distance, but Atlas' eyes were affixed on Raider's face, and the glassy, lifeless stare of his normally-piercing blue eyes.

Talikoth was still kneeling behind Raider, even as his stiff body slumped to the ground, and Atlas dove sideways to grab the handgun, rolling to his feet and aiming the barrel directly at Talikoth's head.

Those cold, dark eyes blinked up at him, looking first at the muzzle aimed directly between his eyes, and then at Atlas, that provoking smirk curling around his mouth.

"Are you going to kill me, Atlas?" Talikoth asked quietly.

Time slowed, and Atlas' breath caught in his throat as he stared at his father. Talikoth's eyes glittered with mirth.

"You can't do it, can you?" he taunted. "You don't have the guts."

Atlas continued to stare at him, his fingers trembling as they tightened around the trigger. His mother's face floated in front of his mind's eyes. *Only one choice would avenge his mother in the way she deserved.*

"Do it," Talikoth goaded, his smirk widening into a derisive leer. "Prove you're not the spineless disappointment that I've always believed you to be. Do it."

Atlas didn't respond, and annoyance flashed across Talikoth's face.

"*Do it,* boy! You trained for years, you won the fight, and now you're going to be a *coward*? *DO IT!*" His roar echoed across the grounds, resonating between the buildings and reverberating through the trees of the forest on every side of them.

Atlas swallowed, his fingers releasing the trigger, and Talikoth shook his head.

"I knew it," he spat disgustedly. "You've never been your father's son."

"You're right," Atlas agreed quietly. "I've always been my mother's."

White hot anger incomparable to anything Atlas had seen from him yet flashed across Talikoth's face, and quicker than lightning he dropped the knife, bringing both of his hands down on the barrel of the gun as he sent a kick towards Atlas' stomach. Atlas jerked his hips back, but Talikoth wrenched the gun from his hands, spinning it around and grasping the grip between his fingers. He pointed the muzzle directly at Atlas' heart and pulled the trigger.

The bang that signaled the release of the bullet, to Atlas, sounded louder than all of the bombs, the grenades, the missile, even the tank's explosions, and he grasped at his chest, which seared with pain, but not nearly so intense as he would have expected, expecting blood, expecting hot, gaping flesh...

But instead his fingers met the fabric of his shirt,

and beneath it, the cool threads of metal, within which the bullet had embedded itself. Talikoth stared at him, and Atlas saw surprise on his father's face for perhaps the first time in his entire life.

Talikoth pulled the trigger again, and Atlas felt the pressure of the second bullet against his sternum, but nothing more. He fired another shot, his expression growing increasingly manic.

Atlas felt the bizarre urge to laugh, even as his nose burned and his eyes prickled, even as he watched, from his peripherals, as Moonstone approached with her soldiers. There had been a part of him, desperately hopeful, that clung to the idea that Talikoth might not have it in him—that despite Atlas' treason, the man would not be able to bring himself to kill his own son.

But that hope had been dashed.

Atlas moved so fast that Talikoth didn't even have time to react. He shoved the handgun's barrel towards the ground, hooking a leg around his father and kicking his knees inward. Talikoth dropped to the ground, and Moonstone's soldiers moved in, one of them holding Talikoth's arms while the other hooked the handcuffs around his wrists.

Talikoth glared up at Atlas, who shrugged, lifting his shirt and showing Talikoth the threaded metal vest that had saved his life. He jerked his head towards Gaiomere, and Talikoth followed his gaze.

"A gift from the Renegades," Atlas told him, his lips curling into a smirk as he added wryly, "You know, since they're so primitive."

Talikoth's nostrils flared. "Congratulations. You're a traitor, just like your mother."

Atlas schooled his features into a blank

expression, even as a stab of pain shot through his chest so forceful that it threatened to overwhelm him, far worse than the impact of Talikoth's bullets. He felt the most peculiar urge to reach for his father, to embrace him, as though that might fill the hole inside of him that felt like it was being ripped open and sewn together again, over and over.

But no, that wasn't quite right. For he had done the right thing, hadn't he? His mother had been a hero—so why did he feel so frail? Why did Talikoth's words feel as though they had run him through?

He watched as the soldiers pulled his father across the grounds, past the Obarion and the Vedas clustered next to the warehouse, up the ramp and onto the plane. The Vedas and Renegades broke into cheers, but Atlas couldn't bring himself to join them.

Moonstone's eyes met his. Raider's body lay at their feet, but Atlas couldn't seem to look at him. He suddenly felt like a child again, disoriented and helpless.

"What do we do now?" he asked her, a hint of desperation creeping into his voice, despite his best efforts to force it back.

Her dark eyes flickered over his face, over the blood still leaking from his nose, and the bruises he could feel forming under his eyes.

"We won, didn't we?" he added, when she said nothing.

She smiled a little then, her gaze roving over to where the Vedas were still celebrating as they guided the remaining Obarion—who had surrendered their guns on the ground in a pile—into the soldiers' quarters.

"Yes, Atlas. We won," Moonstone said quietly. "But

now comes the hard part."

CHAPTER TWENTY

When he arrived back at the campsite, Whitsom was sitting up in his cot in the medical tent.

"Where's Gaiomere?" he asked immediately.

"She's fine," Atlas said, sinking down onto the end of Whitsom's cot. "She—she was taking care of—" His voice broke, and he looked away from Whitsom, swallowing thickly as he forced out, "Raider's dead."

Whitsom's dark eyes widened to saucers.

"You're joking," he muttered. Atlas shook his head, and Whitsom swore, flinging himself back against his pillow. "I just—I can't believe it. He was the best fighter we had—"

"I know," Atlas said, running a hand through his hair. "Talikoth killed him personally."

Whitsom glanced sideways at Atlas, his face schooled carefully into an impassive mask. "Is he—is Talikoth—"

"Moonstone took him into custody," Atlas told him, and Whitsom nodded.

"So, we—we won?"

"The Obarion surrendered, yeah," Atlas confirmed. "Talikoth wouldn't, but the Lieutenant Colonel declared his refusal to surrender unlawful, and an endangerment to the Obarion people, so he overrode him." His voice was strangely flat as he spoke.

This wasn't, he thought, how he was supposed to feel, after they had won. He should be out celebrating with the rest of the soldiers arriving at the campsite. Even as he and Whitsom spoke, he could hear their *whoops* and cheers of exultation. So why did Atlas feel as though something inside of him were dying?

Whitsom asked for details of the parts of the battle that he'd missed and Atlas filled him in on what he could. As one of the doctors cleaned Atlas' bullet wound, he recounted Gaiomere taking out a quarter of the Inner Ring with the grenades, told him about the Vedas blocking the gate with the tank and about Jacoby turning the fence back on and barring the Obarion from their own Headquarters. He told him about Jereis' gruesome death, and about Gaiomere climbing the watchtower to fire off the missile.

But he hesitated when he reached the part where Talikoth had been choking Gaiomere. Whitsom, though, seemed to interpret his silence. "You fought him, didn't you?" the older boy asked. He nodded his head towards Atlas' shirt, which was shredded with bullet holes. "And you were—I mean...I'm guessing he's the one that did all that, too."

Atlas swallowed thickly, and the question that had been burning in the back of his mind for hours came tumbling from his lips. "He could have killed me. I don't know why—I mean—all he had to do was lift the gun to my head, and he—I don't understand why he didn't."

Whitsom gave him an uncharacteristically penetrating look that reminded him of Gaiomere. "Maybe...he was angry at first—I'll bet he was pissed as hell that his only son betrayed him, but then—maybe once the initial anger simmered down, he couldn't do it. Maybe he didn't really want you dead."

Atlas scoffed, shooting Whitsom a perturbed

glare. "You didn't see the way he looked at me."

Whitsom shrugged. He was picking absently at the bandage wound around his stomach, and when he spoke next, his voice was determinedly nonchalant. "Is it uh—is it true that they couldn't find anybody at the Rigs?"

"It was just Obarion soldiers," Atlas confirmed, frowning. Whitsom nodded slowly, but his brows furrowed as though he were in pain.

"There's a chance she escaped before they ever even made it south, though...you never know," Atlas added hastily.

Whitsom straightened up, brightening. "I'll bet she did," he said earnestly. "Gwen was more of a survivor than all of us combined. We'll find her, I'm sure of it."

Atlas tried to smile, but it felt like more of a grimace on his lips. It crossed his mind that Whitsom, who tried so hard to maintain a constant guise of enthusiasm—to keep his loved ones from succumbing to hopelessness, Atlas had always assumed—was protecting himself from the harsh realities of life in the Westland, just as much as he was the people around him.

Moonstone arrived at the campsite around noon to call a meeting for all of the remaining soldiers. Five hundred troops had stayed on base to guard the Obarion.

They gathered around the firepit, soldiers slung across on logs, stumps, and broken concrete blocks. Many of the Vedas had already carted in gallons and gallons of booze—Atlas suspected the Ramshacklers had a large role in this—and it took several minutes for them to settle down so that the General could speak.

Moonstone got straight to the point. "The Obarion are currently detained, but their technical surrender does not mean that we will face no resistance efforts, from both soldiers and civilians. They need to be convinced that we are trustworthy—that we did not defeat them just so they could be under the rule of new tyranny, but rather, for the collective freedom of the Westland." Across the clearing, Atlas saw Gaiomere rolling her eyes.

His mind, however, was preoccupied with the first part of Moonstone's statement. Delurah, then, would have been confined in her quarters with the rest of the civilians. Her husband and son, who would now be around Talikoth's age, had both died before Atlas was born, so she would have been sentenced to her confinement alone—terrified out of her mind, he was sure, with no solace to find in family, and no idea what was to become of she and the rest of her clan.

Moonstone cleared her throat, and Atlas was jerked from his thoughts as she continued, "Which is why tomorrow, we shall hold a public trial for Talikoth in the Stadium, in which all interested parties will come forth with their testaments to the devastation that he has caused in the Westland, and beyond. The Obarion people will be required to attend this trial—it is imperative that they understand much of what they have been told has been a lie."

Chatter broke out among the soldiers, and Atlas' stomach plummeted as Moonstone's eyes landed on him. He knew exactly where this was going, and what she would expect of him.

He stood up, stalking away until several buildings

stood between him and the rest of the soldiers. The noise around the firepit died away, until all he could hear was the distant roar of engines, and the waves crashing into the shore.

What was wrong with him? He had realized that Talikoth needed to be stopped, had even been willing to fight against him—but the idea of standing in front of a crowd of thousands of people and testifying of the horrors that his father had committed—the thought made him sick.

Atlas wandered through the Ramshackle rubble along the Fringe for hours, his mind racing and emotions fluctuating. Waves of sadness undulated beneath his anger, swelling up so large that, in moments, he felt as though they would overwhelm him, but he pushed them down, letting the pulsing thrum of hot fury take their place.

He didn't return to the campsite until dinnertime, so he was irritated to see that Moonstone was still there. She got to her feet as soon as she saw him and strode over.

"Atlas, can I have a word?"

He silently followed her outside of the throng of soldiers, his hands clenched into fists at his sides. He prepared to yell at her, to give her all the reasons why he didn't need to testify at the trial, to scream until he was red in the face about how much he had already done for the resistance.

But then she turned to face him and said, "I think that you should stay at the campsite during the trial."

"*Do you have any idea—*" Atlas burst out loudly, before he broke off, only belatedly registering what she had said. He stared blankly at her for several moments.

"What?"

Moonstone raised a brow.

"I think it would be a good idea if you did not attend the trial," she repeated. He continued to stare at her, and she frowned, saying, "Atlas, you have been through an unbelievable amount of stress these last few months. I cannot even begin to imagine the range of feelings you have experienced. Attending the trial tomorrow—hearing firsthand accounts of all of the crimes that General Talikoth committed—I do not think you need to take that on, on top of everything else."

Atlas' mouth snapped shut, and he stared unseeingly at the ground beneath his feet.

"Of course, if you really want to come, I will not stop you," Moonstone conceded. "I only hope that you will consider what is best for you at this time."

Atlas nodded stiffly, running a hand through his hair. "I—yeah. Yeah, I will."

Moonstone returned to the fireside, but Atlas stood there a few moments longer, gazing at the dancing flames across the clearing. After a while, he wound through the celebrating soldiers and Renegades, making his way down the slope, towards the water's edge. He pulled off his boots as he walked, and the texture of the sand against the soles of his feet kept him firmly in his body and prevented him from drowning in his thoughts, though all he wanted most was to float away. To feel nothing.

He didn't notice Gaiomere until he was a few feet away from where she sat cross-legged in the sand. The sunset reflected off the water and glinted in her dark curls. When she turned to look at him, her eyes were red and puffy. There was a scratch across her cheek that he hadn't noticed before and fingerprint-shaped bruises decorated her skin, where Talikoth's hand had wrapped around her throat.

"Hey," she murmured in a watery voice. "The Ramshackle boys are taking Raider to the Gamp, to be buried beside his father."

Atlas nodded, as he vaguely recalled Raider telling him about the Ramshackle he hailed from, at the southernmost edge of the Westland, which had once been known as San Diego.

He sat down beside her, and she looked over at him, her hickory brown eyes raking over his face. Before he even realized what was happening, before he could even stop himself, fat, hot tears streamed down his cheeks, and a wretched sound ripped itself from his throat.

She pulled him against her, and Atlas buried his face into the crook of her neck, his arms clutching her like she was the only thing tethering him to earth. He wasn't sure how long they stayed like that—Atlas crying into her shoulder, and her arms wrapped around his neck, her fingers running through his hair.

When he finally pulled back, he started to mutter, "Sorry—"

"Atlas, don't," she said immediately. "You don't have to act so tough all of the time."

He pulled his knees against his chest, resting his arms against them as he said, "I just don't—I just get why I feel so—so—"

"He was still your dad," Gaiomere said reasonably. "Even if he's—well, even if he's Talikoth. He was still your dad."

Atlas nodded slowly. He wasn't sure that helped him to understand it any better, but he didn't have the energy to argue. He gazed out over the ocean, his mind wandering back to tomorrow's trial, and to what it would mean. For the Vedas. For the Obarion. For everyone in the Westland.

Gaiomere seemed to be thinking along the same lines.

"What happens now?" she asked. "Are the Vedas just going to take over the Obarion clan? The Headquarters get a flag change and they declare everything settled?"

A particularly large wave crested and broke in the distance, and Atlas watched it ripple towards the shoreline.

"The only way Moonstone is going to keep the peace is by abandoning the status quo," he said hoarsely. "Talikoth represented the last of the ideology that the world is won with division and gunfire—well, perhaps not the last, but certainly the largest. If Moonstone isn't careful, though, someone will just rise up in his stead."

Gaiomere watched the sand sift through the cracks in her fingers, but he could tell the cogs in her mind were turning. "But...she's still going to be the one calling the shots now," she said slowly.

"Well, someone has to," Atlas reasoned.

"I don't think that's true. We took out the impending threat, now can't we all just go on with our lives?"

"There needs to be *some* kind of regulation," Atlas maintained, frowning.

"Regulation?" she spluttered. "What, are we all going to be issued name tags—"

"Not like that," Atlas said impatiently, rolling his eyes. He marveled briefly at how he and Gaiomere could go from crying together one second to arguing the next. It was patently absurd. He sort of liked it. "I just mean that there has to be *some* kind of edict to prevent some people from infringing upon the freedoms of others."

Gaiomere was gazing at him with that penetrating look. "Institutional freedom. That's what you're talking about."

Atlas shrugged. "Yeah, I suppose that's what I mean."

She looked out towards the ocean once more, her dark brows knitted together. When she spoke, her tone was somber. "My dad told Whit and I that over a thousand years ago, our ancestors were brought to this land in shackles."

Atlas' mind flashed back to the books he'd read of chattel slavery—when the people in power used the color of skin to perpetuate oppression, rather than wealth or intelligence, or access to resources.

Gaiomere's lips twisted wryly as she continued, "Institutional freedom is the world's biggest lie."

"It doesn't have to be that way," Atlas said firmly. "Moonstone will call the shots, but if she's trustworthy —and believe or not, I actually sort of think she might be—she'll place people around her to keep her focused on what's best for the people at large—an equipoise to keep any one party from getting too influential. One colossal institution holding all of the power is a recipe for corruption."

A small smile tugged at the corner of her lips. "Hmm, that sounds familiar..."

Atlas snorted, winding an arm around her waist.

"I think we've already established that you're the brains of this operation."

Gaiomere let out a peal of laughter, and he leaned down to kiss her—this time, unlike their first kiss, without so much as a trace of hesitation. She must have been waiting for him to do just that, for her arms immediately looped around his neck, and he grinned against her lips; the notion that he could just kiss her whenever he wanted made him strangely giddy.

He pulled her into his lap, carding his fingers into her wild hair—surprisingly soft against the pads of his fingers—and the two of them stayed in that spot in the sand until the moon replaced the sun.

Atlas aimlessly wandered the grounds the morning of the trial. He had tossed and turned the entire night before, and still had not made up his mind about whether or not he would attend. A very big part of him wanted to skip the trial—perhaps to skip out altogether. To head east, or south, to get away from the weighty stares of the Vedas and the Obarion alike, to escape the oppressive umbrella of Talikoth's influence, to find a place where nobody knew his name or recognized his face.

He had almost done it, that morning when he had awoken. He had almost slipped some food from breakfast into his bag, refilled his water, and taken off. But something had kept him, though he wasn't sure what.

Atlas came to the edge of the woods and gazed towards the cluster of buildings that formed

Headquarters. Though the flames had long since been extinguished, the warehouse still sat in charred ruins.

He glanced in the direction of the detached building near the soldiers' quarters, which housed the officers. Atlas deliberated with himself for a moment, before circling around the building, and coming to a stop face-to-face with two Vedas soldiers who he did not recognize.

"Oh—hey," Atlas said, surprised, though he realized he shouldn't have been. If the soldiers' quarters were being guarded, of course the officers' quarters would be as well. "Can I um—can I go in?"

The two young men glanced at one another. "The residents are being escorted to the trial by our soldiers," the taller of the two explained. "And we're not *technically* supposed to allow anyone in that doesn't live here."

"Well...*technically*, I do," Atlas pointed out, raising his eyebrows.

The two of them looked at each other once more.

"Don't have any weapons on you, do you?" the shorter one asked.

Atlas glanced down at himself. "Uh...just my socks. I suppose I could strangle someone with those if I really put my mind to it." They stared, and he rubbed the back of his neck awkwardly. "That was a joke. So, can I...?"

The taller soldier sighed, stepping out of the way. "Alright, make it quick."

Atlas pushed open the door and strode down the hall, winding around a corner and making his way to the door at the very end of the corridor.

The door was unlocked, and when Atlas pushed it

open, he half expected Talikoth to be standing at the table with one of his massive maps spread out in front of him, or to see him pacing beside the bookshelf, deep in thought.

Atlas stopped in the doorway, a strange lump in his throat. Dirty dishes sat in the sink, presumably from the evening before the battle. Atlas' sweater hung over the armchair where he'd left it, months and months ago, the night before his squad had departed for the Pass. He had been reading *War and Peace*, and had grown too warm. It simultaneously felt like only hours had passed, and yet, like several lifetimes.

He shook his head, turning back towards the door —he shouldn't have come at all—when a voice said, "Atlas?"

He whirled around. Delurah stood in the doorway of the bathroom, her grey-streaked brunette hair pulled into a bun, and her seaweed green eyes so wide that they looked as though they might roll right out of her head.

Atlas stumbled towards her, wrapping his arms tight around her, and she burst into tears against his chest.

"I thought y-you were d-dead, my sweet boy!" she wailed in her lilting accent, and he chuckled a little, though his own eyes burned. "I heard s-so many d-different rumors—that the V-Vedas had killed you, that y-you were being t-tortured for information, oh, I just c-couldn't bear it!"

"I'm *fine*," Atlas insisted.

She clucked her tongue disapprovingly, tilting her head back to gaze up at him, her eyes flickering over the bruises decorating his face.

"You don't *look* fine..." She held him at an arms'

length, looking up and down his frame. "You're too *skinny*, sweet boy—" Her eyes narrowed, and she added, "And your hair's too long!"

He laughed, a retort on the tip of his tongue, but she had already shuffled around him into the kitchen and had begun pulling food from the pantry.

Atlas rolled his eyes.

"Delurah, honestly, I'm *fine*." He peered over her shoulder, asking, with a weak attempt at nonchalance, "Are you making strawberry cookies?"

She gave him a knowing smile.

"Say, how come you aren't being escorted to the trial?" Atlas asked, as he ran his fingers absentmindedly over the checkered quilt that hung over the back of the sofa. Delurah had made it for his tenth birthday, and though he hadn't thought much of it at the time—he was peeved at not getting a weapon—a sudden wave of gratitude overwhelmed him at the sight of the frayed fabric.

Delurah smirked, quipping, "Oh, all I had to do is tell them they didn't need to waste any time convincing *me* what Talikoth was like."

Atlas snorted. "So, what are you still doing here, then?" he asked her. "You know you don't have to stay anymore."

She wasn't looking at him, but he could see her disconsolate expression all the same.

"I didn't want to give up hope that you'd come back," she said softly. She turned to look at him, frowning. "But you're alright now, aren't you?"

Atlas sank down onto the sofa, his brows furrowing as he met her gaze.

"Did you—did you know?" he began, in a measured

voice, "About my mother?"

Delurah's fingers tensed around the stirring spoon, and that gave Atlas all the answer he needed. He swore, springing back to his feet and running a hand through his hair as he paced in front of the sofa.

"I can't *believe* you!" Atlas snapped. "All this time, and you *knew*—"

"Atlas, I wasn't supposed to find out!" Delurah told him insistently. There were tears in her eyes as she spoke. "He made me swear that I would never tell you."

Atlas let out a harsh breath, sinking back down onto the sofa. Delurah left her baking and came to sit beside him. He glared at his hands clenched in fists atop his thighs and flinched when she reached over and brushed his hair from his face.

"Will you ever forgive me, sweet boy?"

"Of course I will," he muttered. "I just—I feel sucker-punched, is all." Atlas felt stupid, voicing the thoughts that had been running through his mind, but once he started speaking, he felt as though he couldn't stop. "It just feels like nothing was real."

"Oh no, Atlas—if you start thinking like that, Talikoth might as well have won," Delurah said, her voice suddenly stern. "He wanted you to feel alone. Like all you were—all you did, it meant nothing."

"All I *was*, was Obarion," Atlas maintained, frustration seeping into his tone. "And that's what Talikoth made me—"

"No, no, Talikoth didn't make you Obarion—" she interrupted, but Atlas cut her off.

"Talikoth was the one that made the Obarion so powerful!" he burst out. "He was the only reason our clan survived—"

"We survived because of our *resilience*." Delurah's voice was so firm that his mouth instinctively snapped shut. "Generations before Talikoth, our clan survived—without the senseless slaughter. A few black marks on our clan's history doesn't define us as a people." He wanted to keep arguing, and she seemed to have read his mind, for she reached over and poked him in the chest, hard.

"Talikoth is *not* the Obarion clan. This is your clan, whether you like it or not, and you can decide that the last eighteen years of your life have meant nothing because some very unfair things happened to you, or you can buck up and help to rebuild a new legacy for your people."

Atlas leaned against the back of the sofa, gazing at the ceiling. "I just—I just don't want people thinking that I'm like him."

Delurah snorted, pushing herself to her feet and ambling back into the kitchen. "And I don't want all these cookies to go to my middle—but there you have it. You can't just want people to think you're not like him—you have to show them."

The Stadium was crowded as Atlas made his way down the long tunnel leading into the pit. Moonstone was already there, along with Vailhelm and the rest of the Council. Atlas spotted Harcliff, and Niko, who was representing the Ramshacklers in Raider's place.

"Atlas!" Moonstone said, surprise evident in her expression. "I did not expect you to come."

"There's something I'd like to say." He said simply. She stared at him for a few moments longer, before she nodded, turning away to speak to Vailhelm.

Atlas glanced around at the thousands of faces in the stands, his stomach writhing, but as his mind turned over his conversations with Gaiomere and Delurah, his resolve strengthened—stronger than his fear, than his hurt, than his confusion. Stronger than the part of him, deep down, that still wanted to make Talikoth proud, even now.

Atlas took a seat towards the front of the Stadium, beside the Renegades and Vedas who would be testifying. It was a massive group—they took up several rows— and Atlas could not begin to identify all the faces before him.

After a few minutes, a couple of soldiers came in with Talikoth, their hands gripping his arms on either side, his wrists cuffed behind his back. Atlas looked away, flexing his jaw.

As the last Obarion civilians trailed in, Moonstone stood, a microphone in her hands.

"Good morning. This commences the trial of General Talikoth, of the Obarion. We will now hear testimonies from the witnesses."

Atlas only half-listened as one by one, the individuals in the rows beside and in front of him climbed up onto the dais, and recounted tale after tale of atrocities. Some were Renegades, whose family and friends had been captured and killed under the guise of being sent to work on the Rigs. Some were Ramshacklers who saw their parents, brothers and sisters slaughtered.

A jolt of surprise shot through Atlas when Vailhelm rose from the Council seat and made his way onto the dais, taking the microphone from Moonstone.

"State your name," she said in a clear voice.

"Vailhelm, of the Vedas."

"Please proceed. What is your connection to General Talikoth?"

"Sixteen years ago, my wife and daughter were traveling from the South, protected, as civilians," Vailhelm said in his gruff voice. "A band of his soldiers captured them, and ordered my wife and daughter murdered." His voice broke, as his head lowered, as he added, "My daughter was six years old."

"Thank you, Vailhelm."

A numb sensation spread from Atlas' chest to the tips of his fingers. He had always assumed Vailhelm had hated him on principle—because he was Obarion. He had never considered that Vailhelm had suffered such a poignant loss at the hands of his clansmen.

The rows around him continued to empty, slowly but surely, until it was only Atlas left.

Moonstone waved him onto the stage. He made his way across the Stadium floor and climbed up onto the dais, worried, for half a second, that he would trip, in front of all these people...

But he reached the podium that stood in front of the Council's table without any falter in his step, and Moonstone said, "State your name."

He cleared his throat, bending closer to the microphone, and said, "Atlas, of the Obarion."

"What is your connection to General Talikoth?"

Atlas felt a smirk tug at his lips. "Um—are you serious?"

Quiet laughter rang across the Stadium, and Moonstone looked as though she was repressing her own smile.

"For the sake of the integrity of this trial, Atlas," she implored him.

He nodded, swallowing around the knot in his throat. "He's my father. I'm his son. I can give you a biology rundown, if they don't teach that up north." The laughter rang out again, louder this time, and it seemed to pacify his nerves.

Moonstone chuckled. "That will do. Please proceed."

"Talikoth killed my mother," Atlas said unhesitatingly.

The silence that followed his words was deafening, and then, all at once, whispers broke out among the Obarion citizens. Moonstone tapped her hand against the microphone.

"Silence. Please, Atlas, proceed."

"My mother did betray information from the Obarion clan to the Vedas," Atlas admitted, "but only as a warning to protect their people."

"Are you aware that treason, under our laws of war, as well as the laws of the Obarion clan, is an offense punishable by death?" Moonstone asked, her expression impassive.

Atlas was aware, but he had not come unprepared. He had spent the hour before the trial picking Delurah's brain, and he would not let that time go to waste now. The whispers had grown louder, and Atlas raised his voice to be heard over them.

"I'm aware that under our laws treason committed by a *soldier* is punishable by death. But my mother wasn't a soldier, or an officer. She was an apothecary." Up to this point, he had been avoiding looking at his father, but he turned to face him now, and found

Talikoth's dark eyes already affixed on him. "Therefore, he had no legal justification for killing her."

Instantaneously, the whispers erupted into a thunderous outpouring of unrestrained disorder, but this time, Moonstone did nothing to stop it.

"Thank you, Atlas," she said quietly, and he nodded, climbing down from the dais. He did not turn to go sit beside the other witnesses that had testified, but instead made his way down the long corridor leading out of the Stadium. He had no desire to watch the rest of the trial unfold, nor did he have any real inclination to be surrounded by the Obarion, or the Vedas, or the Renegades, who all ogled him every direction he looked.

No, Atlas had endured quite enough excitement over the past few months. And Moonstone was right —the most difficult part was yet to come. They had a population of at least five thousand Obarion civilians— angry, betrayed, and scared—to earn the trust of, and the entire Westland to rebuild, from the ground up.

But for now, Atlas thought that could wait. Now, he wanted some rest. Maybe he would show Gaiomere the library.

And he most certainly could not play his part in uniting the Westland without first having some of Delurah's strawberry cookies.

Made in the USA
Middletown, DE
05 November 2022

14129862R00255